"*Synthesis* is a great story with a real message!"
Congressman Jack Metcalf

◆ ◆ ◆

"*Synthesis* is a spellbinding novel paralleling current events. C.A. Curtis has captured the essence of the New Age movement, as it is gaining control of society through the education system."
Senator Val Stevens

◆ ◆ ◆

"A stimulating and thought-provoking novel which focuses on the natural consequences of a misguided educational philosophy."
M. Burke, M.Ed., Literacy Coordinator

◆ ◆ ◆

"This novel is an eye-opener. After reading this book, working in higher education I see the subtle things I never saw before — like how students are taught to think in medical ethics. This is an excellent book for your student to read before going to college."
Jean Lytle, University Medical School,
Program Coordinator

◆ ◆ ◆

"It made me humble in appreciation for my faith. How terrifying it is to think of not having the freedom to believe and worship. This book will change lives and free souls."
Judith Hendrix, Research Writer

◆ ◆ ◆

"I appreciated this novel's truthful diversion from the hyped New Age rheteric taught in some of my classes."
Amy Codispoti, University Student

Computer Parented...With Rights and Equality for All

SYNTHESIS

C. A. CURTIS

To Frank & Ramona,
Enjoy the adventure!
C. A. Curtis
6-5-2001

Computer Parented...With Rights and Equality for All

SYNTHESIS

C. A. CURTIS

REALITY Publishing
Mill Creek, Washington 98082-1576

This is a work of fiction. Apart from obvious historical references to public
figures and events, all characters and events are a creation of the author's
imagination. Any similarities to any person living or dead are purely
coincidental.

Scripture quotations are taken from the King James Version of the Bible.

Synthesis is book one in the *Synthesis Trilogy*

Requests for information should be addressed to:
REALITY   Publishing
PO Box 13576
Mill Creek, Washington 98082-1576

http://www.regeneration-ink.com

Publisher's Cataloging-in-Publication
(Provided by Quality Books, Inc.)

Curtis, C. A. (Carolyn A.)
    Synthesis : computer parented-- with rights and
equality for all / C.A. Curtis. -- 1st ed.
    p. cm. -- (Synthesis trilogy ; book 1)
    LCCN: 99-96093
    ISBN: 0-9674461-0-4

    1. Education--Philosophy--Fiction.   2. Social
engineering--Fiction.   3. Computers and
civilization--Fiction.   4. Millennium--Fiction.
I. Title.

PS3553.U689S96 2000   813'.54
                    QB199-1252

Printed in the United States of America

DEDICATION

To my children and grandchildren,
may you reclaim, preserve and enjoy
liberty and justice for all.

CONTENTS

PROLOGUE

Puzzle pieces were sorted by color; Batman and Robin had taken shape and he searched for the missing piece of their batmobile. Finding it, he locked it into place. His desk was cluttered with favorite plastic characters and he picked the largest Batman to stand guard over his project. Each piece was placed and the picture sprung to life in his mind. His heros again conquered the evil Joker! "Mommy. Come see Batman," he called. Silence.

He ran to the door. It was his door with his own drawings taped in a colorful display, but it opened to emptiness, a long barren hallway. Slamming it in terror, he turned. His bed was in the corner piled high with familiar stuffed teddy bears. Everything was in place: posters of zoo babies stared back at him— Robotman sat in the corner by his train set—Mother's rocking chair was by the window. The window wasn't his. It was narrow and solid. Looking out, with his hands and face pressed to the glass, he saw them.

"Mommy," he whimpered. "Daddy." When they didn't stop, he cried and pounded the window, "Wait, wait for me."

"Everything is all right, honey," she said softly, closing the door behind her. "There, there now, we'll wave goodbye together. They will come visit, lots, and we'll have so much fun together with the other children. Didn't you have fun with your new friends?"

"Yes," he mumbled, waved and watched his parents fade into the distance. They had said the same thing when they hugged him and kissed him and left him to play in his room. But it wasn't his room. And the nice lady, who gathered him onto her lap, sang and rocked him to sleep, wasn't his mother.

I GRADUATION

MAY 1, 2000 Millennial Synthesis

SAN JUAN Academy graduates stood in cap and gown, arms extended in salute, paying homage to their mentor, giving voice to their oneness. David Winston stared at the illusive symbol of Synthesis. His long awaited job assignment had failed to materialize. He had studied while other students slept, worked while others played—all that, for a low-level maintenance job. Meditation failed to dissolve his fear, failed to extinguish his anger. His smoldering anger masked with serenity, David parroted the words:

> *We pledge our allegiance to the symbol of Synthesis*
> *And to the unity for which it stands,*
> *Oneness with earth, our Body,*
> *Oneness with creatures, our Soul,*
> *Oneness with cosmos, our Spirit,*
> *Indivisible,*
> *With rights and equality for all.*

Even the symbol reflected failure. It was a prototype, a last minute computer etching, enlarged, displayed on a screen. The long awaited hologram symbol hadn't materialized, but that would be remedied and the faded flags replaced. There was no remedy for him.

Earlier that morning, the message glared from David's IBM monitor. No explanations. No instructions. Nothing. All departments were closed and his questions went unanswered.

David had finished dressing and left his room. Carefully guarded, his emotions went undetected as he moved mechanically through the baccalaureate. He made the right moves: listened to speeches, accepted his doctorate, attended the reception, then flowed with the crowd back to hear the final speech. When his friends bragged about their new jobs, he laughed, congratulated and distracted them, never mentioning his own job.

Humiliation was a foreign, demeaning announcement of his value—worthless—not acceptable among his peers. Yet not totally foreign, unlocked from his memory an event clouded his mind. The same humiliation—he was a gangly twelve-year-old racing for the finish line. Classmates cheered as he sprinted ahead in the final lap. He was focused on winning with only four yards to go; the trophy was within his reach. Instead, he hit the ground hard; it knocked the breath out of him. Spit or sweat, something slimy on the track had robbed him of victory. Recovering, he limped across the finish line. Hegelthor had told him it was a good try. Good try? Trying wasn't winning, then or now. He determined to shake the feeling. Cancel the thought.

Yet, above the din of celebration, the message hammered, demanding his attention.

DAVID ALAN WINSTON — MAINTENANCE

Hegelthor hadn't prepared him. Synthesis hadn't prepared him. Reality mocked unity. The hollow symbol still flickered overhead. "With rights and equality for all," David repeated.

"Graduates, be seated promptly. Cancel!"

Silence engulfed the auditorium as all students obeyed Facilitator Hegelthor's command, with one exception.

At Hegie's words, David's mind snapped to attention, then wandered back to his dilemma. Seated next to him was Greg Foster, his attention fixed on Hegie. The red-haired, sinewy young man was more than David's roommate. Foster was his confidante and close friend, yet they had no chance to talk, not today. He didn't dare nudge him. Again, David willed himself to focus his intense, dark eyes on Hegie. Stubbornly, his mind resisted. Mind and will wrestled. Hope flickered.

Maintenance! No real job—no future. No! This is crazy. Every grad gets assigned, he corrected himself. With practiced determination, he relaxed his six-foot-one frame, muscles between his shoulder blades softened. Still, the message hammered. He focused, breathing deeply. David knew he was breaking the rules. Hegie would know.

From the podium, Facilitator Thomas Evan Hegelthor savored the moment, absorbing the energy. His students' immediate response pleased him, especially today. Seated before him was the fruition of his lifelong dream, holding the seeds of a much larger dream. He labored thirty of his forty-nine years to lay the groundwork for the millennium and these one-hundred and ninety-nine graduates immortalized his efforts. Only one detail languished unfulfilled; his first born had wasted a year battling mononucleosis and failed to graduate. Initially, the disappointment drained Hegelthor. Dinner-table debates with his wife, Athelia, centered on whether or not to bend the rules for their son. Hegie refused and paid the price. He pondered the irony. He ran the Academy yet could not have everything he wanted. Agitated, he canceled the thought.

At the auditorium entrance, massive double doors closed. For an instant, Hegelthor caught the sunlight reflecting off the marble Apex, highlighting the deserted commons. He had transversed the earth searching for the ideal location for his school. Each place had some annoying drawback, too hot, too humid, too crowded, always falling short of this, his own Washington State home. Here, Mother Earth was adorned with her finest. In the Pacific Northwest's San Juan Islands, she was crowned with spiraling emerald evergreens, gowned with shimmering teal waters. Destined, his Academy nestled in an Orcas Island meadow at the foot of Mount Constitution.

Under the hot spotlights human frailty again mocked godhood, and beads of sweat collected on Facilitator Hegelthor's forehead. A heavy purple robe draped his corpulent, dignified frame, and he struggled for air.

Hurriedly, he introduced fourteen honor students who paraded across the stage, accepting their awards and his praises, then returned to their seats. "First," he announced. "Because of you, our Academy was selected as the model for Impartation International. You achieved excellence and earned your doctoral degrees by persistence, cooperation, and hard work. Other experimental programs produced graduates contaminated by inferior philosophies, unable to attain your level of harmony, unable to achieve godhood as the Synthesis Species. Those people will, however, be useful to you as you effect change in your communities.

"This morning, you received assignments as area leaders. Your challenge now? Share what you learned here with those less fortunate. United in Synthesis, we will . . ."

David shifted. Hegie's words empowered his peers, but accused him without mercy. *Some assignment*, he moaned inwardly. Pacing his breathing, he stared at Hegie. Stage spotlights beamed, creating a bright aura around the Facilitator's silvering hair. The middle-aged, round, smiling face of the academic, strong yet approachable, grandfatherly, strengthened his trust. David relaxed and again concentrated on his caregiver's words.

". . . Academy has received international recognition and acclaim. Therefore, Malchor requested we choose a Youth Facilitator from this graduating class. The Youth Facilitator will report directly to Malchor at Impartation International Headquarters in Fairfax, Virginia, and will insure the implementation of our program in all learning centers. Of course, I will assist as needed."

Reminiscent, Hegie sought out the most familiar faces, recalling their names, struck with the knowledge that this was their last assembly together. The memory of their arrival intermixed with the finality of the moment. All of them, even those with muddled names and faces, were his children year round. Indeed, except during begrudged holidays and the token two-week annual visits with birth parents, they had been his since

6

entering the Academy at age five. Fully satiated with his feeling of parentage, he called Chairman Hodges forward to announce the new Youth Facilitator.

With the pomp of a courting peacock, Chairman Frederick Hodges ascended the stairs leading to the podium. His oversized gown billowed around him, a hollow extension of his moment of glory. It struck Hegelthor that Hodges had the demeanor of a plucked turkey and was clueless about the humbling reality. The chairman leaned forward, his angular jaw jutted proudly toward the microphone. Time was suspended.

"Dearly beloved graduates," Hodges finally said, grasping the microphone head, his flesh grating the metal. "I'm pleased to have been a part of this selection process. It was difficult, yet rewarding, to sift through the transcripts and the dissertations of so many deserving finalists."

Minutes stretched ahead with boring phrases. Hodges had exceeded his level of competence. Contempt built in Hegelthor. He didn't like the term *finalist* and he didn't like self-promotion. He searched the restless audience for his prodigy.

Meanwhile, Hodges droned on, building expectation like a beauty pageant host, pausing between each phrase. "Based upon his excellence in all nine study areas . . . and his record of unsurpassed Synthesis . . . we've chosen our own . . ."

Impatient, Hegelthor stepped toward Hodges, towering behind him.

"Yes!" Hodges shouted. "We've chosen our own—David Alan Winston!"

Excitement vibrated through the crowd; yet Hodges plodded on, accenting each syllable, "We salute the . . ."

"Graduates!" thundered Facilitator Hegelthor, with a brush of his hand dismissing the chairman, sparing the class and himself more bloated dialogue.

"What is harmonious?" he asked, sighting David and noting the youth's poorly veiled confusion.

"All is harmonious in the Synthesis of life!" The other graduates responded, voices ringing throughout the hall with spontaneous cheers and applause.

"David, for Trib's sake, that's you!" Greg shouted above the din. Reaching over, he prodded his stunned friend to his feet.

"Hegie wants you up there. Go on!" he urged as the entire assembly stood. "He's motioning for you to . . ."

"But I wasn't assigned that," muttered David, groping past Greg. He moved toward the middle aisle, struggling for balance and composure, hesitating next to Kendra Addington. "I want to take you with me," he whispered, surprised that the prospect of not seeing her was suddenly an urgent matter. Blushing, she pushed him past her. He looked back, spun honey highlights shown from her brown hair, doe brown eyes questioned him. Her touch lingered.

Chairman Hodges intercepted David, enveloped him in an awkward hug and the governing board, known as the Committee of Ten, gave their regards and shook his hand as he moved past. Straining against excitement, unsure what was expected, he joined Facilitator Hegelthor at the podium.

"Congratulations, David!" boomed Hegelthor, silencing the exuberant graduates. "The nations' leaders are looking to us, their model for Impartation. Test results of pilot-restructuring programs prove the Academy has a superior method of instilling the principles of universal peace."

David was motionless, face-to-face, somber, weighing Hegie's words. The reality of his assignment quickly routed the fear, relieving his unspent anger. He had studied since primary class, these past nineteen years, for top honors. This reward and the right to pride were his, earned and deserved.

"Under your direction," Hegelthor commanded, "current school buildings will be adapted and new ones built. Under your direction, young people everywhere will be prepared as unity-minded, cosmic citizens and guided with our Orion computer system. It is toward this purpose that I bestow upon you, David Alan Winston, the honorable title of Youth Facilitator."

Applause again exploded around the room when the two shook hands. It was a foreign, heady event, and the seed of arrogance crept into David's soul. The image clashed with his nature, yet took root even in retreat. Hegelthor's grip tightened, steel-gray eyes testing for loyalty. Submitting, David released his grip. "Thank you, sir," he said, with revived gratitude.

Hegelthor's concluding remarks to the graduates were lost on the new Youth Facilitator. David Winston felt vindicated and reveled in his new identity, until the morning's anxieties resurfaced. This time the Maintenance assignment was viewed as a cruel hoax. He discarded the thought—canceled it from his mind like background noise—then strained unsuccessfully for another glimpse of Kendra. Spotlights faded and solemn music set the tone for the ceremonial dismissal of the committee members and students. Their orderly movement cleansed humanity from the auditorium.

From his vantage point, David saw the full panorama and detailed scenes captured in the stained-glass windows that graced both sides of the main entrance. Radiating the afternoon light, the evolution of humanity unfolded across six glass frames to its final phase, the Being of Synthesis. He embraced the message, cherishing it. *I am the Being of Synthesis*, he thought, *the fulfillment of evolution.* Gothic architecture in the auditorium swept before him, giving him a sense of mastery and ownership—mastery over himself and ownership of the future as well as the present.

Too soon, David was led toward the side exit, Hegie's arm affectionately around his shoulders. "After the visit with your secondary caregivers," he said, "you'll return to the Academy for three weeks of orientation, then prepare for your assignment with Malchor. Your schedule's set."

Malchor! Each time he heard it, the name loomed in David's mind like Vesuvius erupting molten lava, a purging fire, raw power. Building Academies for Malchor was beyond anything he had expected to do in one lifetime.

Opening the door, Hegie added, "Enjoy yourself at Maxi Dome tonight."

During the farewell handshake, David found his voice.

9

"Thank you, sir," he offered. "I'll always appreciate what you've done here at the Academy to prepare me . . ."

"Yes, yes, David," he interrupted. "Now we're peers; in private, call me Hegie."

"Thank you, sir," David gasped. "Thank you!" Reluctant to leave, he found himself prodded outside.

Indulgent, Hegie smiled and waved. David took several steps backward, finally reeled around and headed across campus toward the dormitory.

Automatically, David Winston pulled the black Diversity unit from his shirt pocket and reviewed his orders, scrolled across the micro screen. Then he typed a special, personal request. That finished, he laughed with relief, mentally processing the radical changes in his life. With privileges, Kendra Addington was his at least for the rest of the day.

"Hegie's peer! The Youth Facilitator! Incredible!" he marveled aloud. As far back as David could remember, Hegie had been the central figure, the primary caregiver in his life. During his ninth summer at the Academy, while bragging to a classmate about Hegie's personal message, he realized Hegie was central to all the students. Hegie's disapproval was the only serious negative thing in their world. More important, his approval was their reward for each small accomplishment as well as each major triumph. The small Diversity unit he carried in his pocket had been his personal interactive link with Hegie since puberty. As he evolved toward Synthesis, his reward included a growing list of choices.

It never occurred to David how Hegie could be personally close to each student, yet it was that closeness which formed a basis for David's security and his self-confidence. It was that closeness which inspired him to emulate his mentor. Throughout his education, David's highest goal was to share and fulfill Facilitator Hegelthor's dream.

Deep in thought, he didn't notice his friends, until Greg Foster, Reana Miller, and Kendra surrounded him in jubilation. Shouting and laughing together, typical graduates, they jogged toward the Apex. Kendra outdistanced them, running with the grace of a gazelle.

Nineteen years earlier, while looking out his dorm window, the Apex had reminded David of the front wheel on his treasured, red tricycle. At the center was an open-air dome, held aloft by eight marble pillars. The spoke-like paths leading out to the surrounding campus structures gave him a feeling of unity. Everything was interconnected, yet in its own place. Their lives had been interconnected in much the same way and for almost as long, secure within the Academy fortress.

Best friends, especially during doctoral studies, they melded as a foursome every spare minute. Sundays they attended temple. Week nights they held scheduled times at the Maxi Dome, tennis on Tuesday, swimming on Wednesday, virtual reality ventures on Thursday, dancing on Friday, hiking on Saturday. It was their weekly routine at the Academy. And for the past year, David and Kendra added the role of chaperons to their friendship, while Greg and Reana courted.

"This marble's always cold," Kendra said, staking her favorite spot before the others flopped down on the circular seats.

"And will be as long as rain's wet." Reana laughed.

The Apex dome arched overhead. Kendra shed her graduation cap and ran both hands through her shoulder-length hair, loosening the light brown strands. "Remember when Reana and I first met you, David?"

"You mean," David challenged, "when you crazies attacked me with your lethal weapon?" Grabbing for Kendra's cap, he was intercepted by a push from Reana that almost sent him sprawling backwards over the bench.

"Lethal!" Reana said. "Didn't mean to bowl you over, your honor, Youth Facilitator, sir. Yes, we only sprayed the cute, skinny guys with *Deep Passion*."

"Thank Trib I didn't meet you women before I turned nine. I'd never have survived the trauma. I don't know," he chided in mock fear. "Is it safe to sit next to you now, Kendra?" Waving her arm, grinning, she pretended to spray him. Flailing, he ducked toward Greg. "Those boys in the dorm, including my trusted buddy here, teased me for weeks. Such trauma!"

"Hey, I feel left out. You never thought I was cute, huh?"

"No, Greg, absolutely not," Reana insisted, settling opposite him. "With those blue eyes, you could never have been just cute." She winked, "Besides, they confiscated the stuff before I discovered you."

"Speaking of us," Greg said, "we have an announcement. Our unity plans have changed."

"What? You're not . . ."

"No. We are, David, but next week instead of this fall."

"Next week!"

"Hegie gave his blessings last night," Greg explained. "We didn't want to get settled, then have to move again so soon. We're both assigned to Baltimore."

"I'll send a disk, so you can see the ceremony." Kendra offered.

"I'd rather be there."

"Can't you visualize their progeny?" Kendra offered cheerfully. "A tow-headed son with her freckles and a daughter with his red hair."

"Spoken like a true geneticist," David said, appreciating her effort to cheer him up, tempted to ask her what their children might look like. He studied the arch of her brows, smooth texture of her cheeks, wanting to break the rules.

"I'm sorry you won't be there," Kendra offered, stroking his arm, aware of the taut feel of his skin, but unaware of his intense feelings. She struggled with her own, flustered by her curiosity about his genetic encoding.

One muted chime from the clock tower above the auditorium brought them back to the present. It chimed a second and third time, a reminder that their hours together were closing fast, and the future would end their foursome.

"We're happy for you, David," Kendra said, sliding closer, wanting to stall time. "Remember to share our appreciation for Malchor when you see him. Incredible!" she gushed, squeezing his

12

arm. "Imagine seeing Malchor in person! Imagine talking to him!"

With heightened awareness, David searched Kendra's brown eyes. Innocent exuberance beamed from her sculpted, oval face, tilted toward his, temptingly close. "Imagine seeing you in person. Imagine talking to you," he countered softly.

Reana stood, feigning shock. "Hey, Greg. I think I just heard our caregiver calling. Or was that Cupid plucking his little harp?" Giggling, she drew on an imaginary bow sending an arrow into David's heart. "Am I hallucinating, or did our stoic friend murmur tender words to our Kendra?"

"I suspect we heard caregiver and Cupid harmonizing together. You're definitely not hallucinating," Greg laughed, taking Reana's hand. "All right, you two. We'll see you at eight o'clock at Maxi Dome."

Embarrassed by the unexpected attention and jesting, Kendra fumbled with her small, black Diversity unit noting her schedule change.

"Bye bye, sweeties," chimed Reana and Greg as they left for a game of tennis.

"I'm sorry, Kendra," entreated David, turning toward her. "I didn't mean to put you in an awkward position."

"It's okay. This entire day has been awkward. I have such mixed feelings. There are so many changes; nothing will be the same. I'm happy with my assignment, but I don't like leaving the Academy."

"Why?" he asked, leaning toward her for confidentiality as a group of undergrads hurried past.

"David, you're not making this easier."

"Why don't you want to leave?"

"Because," she admitted hesitantly, "you won't be where I'm going." Turning abruptly she added, over her shoulder, "See you back here in forty-five minutes." Running felt good to her, dispelling the hovering anxiety about her own future, with or without David.

Perplexed, David watched her until she disappeared into her dormitory.

THEY met for an early, quiet dinner at Maxi Dome. Afterwards, they walked along the familiar trails that stretched two miles east of the campus, to the salt-water's edge. To the south, Mount Constitution towered almost a half-mile above sea level. As children, David and Kendra made annual pilgrimages to the 2,409 foot summit with their classmates. On those clear August days they could see a panorama of forested islands below; the horizon stretched from the Olympic Peninsula to the mainland Cascade Mountains, with Mount Baker in the north and Mount Rainier in the south. Here in Moran State Park, they had learned to live in harmony with and to protect the sanctity of Mother Nature. They felt one with her, a part of her, as she was a part of them.

Silent, they scaled the bluff and watched the waves crash against the rocks below. It was a cloudless day; across the Strait of Georgia, the skyline of Bellingham shimmered. David rubbed the dirt off his hands onto his jeans, tense and preoccupied with Kendra.

"You don't have far to go tomorrow, do you?" she asked. "You could almost row home."

"I've made the trip a couple times in a fifteen-footer; it can get really choppy in the middle. I wouldn't want to be on anything smaller. Better go," he added, glancing at his watch. "It's time to head back and meet the lovebirds."

"They belong together, don't they?"

"Greg's been so distracted, wants to be with Reana every minute, but she's good for him. She motivated him to think about his future instead of just basketball. Seems like you've known her forever."

"Just about. We lived on the same block in Spokane. My parents, I mean my secondary caregivers, used to get together with the Millers to play games and go places. We were just toddlers then and our caregivers called themselves the neighborhood *Yuppies*. That made us *Yuppie Puppies*," she said with a strained laugh, turning from him and from the cliff's edge. "Every day we played, unless we were sick or on vacation. It was fun. Of course, when we turned five, we both passed the assessment to come here. So our folks drove us. The Anacortes ferry ride was stormy and sort of scary. We clung to each other at the rail, fearing the rolling waves. When we were docking here at Orcas Island, we expected to crash and drown. We had very vivid imaginations!"

They took the descending trail through the madrona grove. Leathery oval evergreen leaves shifted in the evening breeze, held aloft by smooth red branches. Kendra again took the lead on the narrow part of the trail. "I've only seen your secondary caregivers twice," she offered over her shoulder. "Tell me about them. What was it like before you came here?"

"Last time they visited, I asked my dad, Steve, how they first met. I guess I was hoping to hear something extraordinary, but that wasn't the case. They were born and raised in Everett, Washington," he said, launching into his biographical sketch. "They ended up teaching at different high schools in their hometown, went back and earned their doctorates, then Steve taught Communication and Media for a year at Seattle University. Big city life didn't agree with him, so he sent resumes out to other universities. The next year he was accepted on staff at Western Washington University in Bellingham. At their first staff social, he gravitated toward Jenna, hired just the year before, and found they had a lot in common. They even went to the same elementary school but different classes. That next spring they married and bought a ranch thirty-seven miles southeast of Bellingham."

"Sounds extraordinary to me, David," she added. "They almost missed each other. Where would you be?"

"Who knows? But I'm glad to be me, following you," he declared. "Anyway, when I was born, Jenna quit teaching computer science. She stayed home for five years so she could train me to achieve what she called my *maximum potential.*

"I love the ranch," he continued. "Instead of telling you about it, I'm saving it to show you in person this fall, after we've settled into our jobs."

"David, have you cleared that with Diversity?"

The trail widened, and David moved alongside her. "Of course I have." He grinned and continued, "Hegie gave me that concession."

"Concession?"

"One of the rewards for being a Facilitator."

"Are you saying that my presence is one of your rewards?" Kendra frowned, stopping on the trail. "What am I? A trophy."

Courting rejection, David hoped for acceptance and reached for her hands. "Kendra, you know I want to be with you." He waited vainly for a response, then plunged ahead. "That's why I requested assignment in your area. When nothing came through, it took all my energy to maintain control." He wanted to hear a declaration of love or longing or something; instead a pink hue flushed her cheeks. Taking that as a good sign, he asked, "What would you have done if I hadn't been assigned in our level?"

"I don't know," she answered. "I never thought—I guess I'd miss you, and—and look for you if I could, but you know the rules." An undefined shiver went through her. "It's getting chilly, David."

"Kendra, you admitted you'd miss me. I'm willing to admit it. Being without you is a major challenge. I'll miss you until I'm with you again." Bending closer, he brushed his lips against the soft curve of her cheek and imprinted her fragrance and warmth in his mind.

Unsure, she backed away, her heart pounding. A stern look questioned his forwardness, rules were rules, yet her hands had felt secure in his.

David turned from their encounter, rebuked but victorious. Walking in silence through the dusk-laden madrona trees, they retreated to the Dome.

That evening the food, amusements, camaraderie and even his new title, were all secondary to Kendra's presence.

16

II ROOTS

HEGELTHOR'S Piper Cub approached the Winston runway and David looked out the window. Reclusive, nestled in the center of their four hundred acres of prime Washington land, the spacious ranchhouse welcomed him. He pressed his forehead against the cool glass for a better look. Sloping gently away from the house, the meadow wrapped around a small lake and reached beyond to touch the surrounding forested mountains.

For an instant, the plane reflected from the lake. Then, their shadow crossed the rock-lined stream that snaked along the narrow blacktop driveway. A soft whine purred from the engine and motionless wheels verged on the touch down.

Memories of working with his dad to clear the runway, stirred his mind. It had been an unusually miserable, hot summer. Daily for two weeks his sweat had mingled with dirt and dried weeds. Muscles protested the hard labor that mocked athletic training. It was no contest—the glory of the gym succumbed to the grime of reality. David smiled, visualizing his dad wrestling with a tree stump. Working side by side with him made the ordeal worthwhile. When they finished and tested their runway in the family Aerojet, the surface had been smooth, but not anymore. For this touch down, he sat back and braced himself.

Hegie's pilot, Don Samuels, was checking out the gauges and muttering about the delay in his off duty plans. The rock-solid retired Air Force Colonel, in full uniform, made no pretense at trivia and shrugged off David's questions about the sudden

17

change in plans. David's scheduled San Juan Airline flight to Bellingham had been canceled. "Why" was irrelevant. At the last minute Hegie notified them both to report instead to the Academy runway.

During the short flight, Don controlled their conversation, limiting the subject to aviation. The kid passed inspection, still green, but fair stock. David squirmed awkwardly under the Colonel's amused scrutiny.

Don maneuvered the antique Piper Cub in next to the sleek Aero four-seater. "I'll be back for you on the twenty-sixth, 0900 sharp," he announced sternly.

"Yes sir," David said, attempting military zeal.

Once they stopped, the Colonel turned his hulking frame in the narrow cockpit and watched David struggle to pull his things from the storage area. "Step out of the plane before trying to get your gear."

Embarrassed, David jumped out and loose gravel scattered at his feet. "Looks like we need a couple more truck loads to fill in these ruts," he said, getting no response. Taking his things he tried again. "Thank you, sir, good flight. And thanks for the tips. I get my private license this month, before I leave for D.C. and . . ."

"When you get back to Orcas," Don interrupted, "I'll take you up a few times."

"I would appreciate that, sir."

Without further notice, the Colonel had the engine whining. David slammed the door and scrambled to avoid the wing tip.

When his parents greeted him on the back deck, Steve looked past his son as the plane climbed into the cloudless sky. "I haven't seen a Piper in years. Whose is it?"

"Facilitator Hegelthor's, and what a flight! We took the long way, circled around San Juan and Lopez. Say, I'm glad you got the message and didn't go to the airport."

Steve took David's bag from his hand. "Why the change?"

"I don't know," David shrugged, "something about security."

"Dissidents!" Jenna blurted.

18

"Excuse me?"

"Oh," Jenna explained, "it was probably dissidents. The paranoid ingrates are always protesting something."

"What's to protest?" David asked.

"Synthesis," she said. "They don't know what's good for them."

"What a waste of energy," David surmised. "Well, I'll unpack later. We can put this in my room for now."

A portrait for every year of his life was framed and hanging in the hallway to his room. Home, as always, had brownish-gold flooring and wall covering, colors of earth and accents of sky blue. The original three-bedroom rambler had one addition, built shortly after his birth. It was a second story over the garage that provided separate quarters for the ranch caretakers. Two months after he entered the Academy his parents adapted the middle bedroom as an office-guest room but there had been no changes since then. His room extended past the front of the house, affording him windows on three sides, as well as a private patio. A row of healthy rhododendrons hid his westerly view of the front entrance.

Jenna set David's briefcase on his desk, then gave her son a belated, affectionate hug. "I'm glad you're home again." She kissed him lightly on his cheek. "We watched your graduation on the screen."

David beamed and wrapped his arms around her. "I'm glad to be home."

"Top Honors! You couldn't aim higher." Steve left his son's bag by the bed, then took his turn and gave David a bear hug. "I'm proud of you."

Jenna shook her head and sighed. "You two look more alike all the time—same build, same color hair."

Steve stepped back and looked from Jenna to David. His son was his near genetic replication. They were both just over six feet with the same complexion, but his own dark brown hair was losing its waves, beginning to gray at the temples. It was Jenna who appeared ageless, with high cheekbones and deep-set eyes, exquisite in beauty and motion. "He has your dark eyes, Jenna. Brown's still dominant."

"Yes, he does have my eyes." She paused at the door, studying David's face. "When you picked up your diploma yesterday, you didn't seem like yourself."

"What do you mean, Jenna?" David asked, dismissing a twinge of guilt.

"You were smiling, but your eyes weren't."

"Well," David took a deep breath and paced his words, "it was a long ceremony and my assignment wasn't posted in the morning. I was expecting more exams."

"Exams always made me tense," Jenna agreed, touching his arm in understanding. "Never having another test was the best thing about graduation."

Steve frowned at them both. "Jenna, that was before you knew about meditation. And David, you should have canceled that negative thought immediately."

"I did, several times," David said, looking out his sliding patio door, changing the subject. "Say, where's Max? I miss the mutt."

"He's out with Jake and Fran rounding up the horses."

David grinned at his dad. "Fran?" he asked, remembering the housekeeper, her gentle ways and waist length, black braided hair. "She was terrified of horses. What happened?"

With an eloquent sweep of his hand, Steve pointed to Jenna. "Your mother worked a miracle."

"I convinced her that conquering fear was necessary for spiritual growth. Taught her to ride last fall. Now I have to remind her to keep the house clean." Jenna shook her head.

"Solve one problem and inherit another," David agreed. "As for problems, taxiing in I noticed ruts in the runway. But it looks like Jake's keeping the rest of the place in good condition."

"They're both invaluable around here. Come on you two. Let's get comfortable." Jenna headed toward the kitchen, motioning them along.

Close behind her, David inhaled. "Smells like Nirvana.

20

What's cooking?"

"Muffins. They're ready now." Jenna turned off the buzzer, grabbed the potholders and opened the oven door. She lifted two tins of steaming hot muffins out of the oven. "I experimented. There's a surprise in the middle."

"Mmmm. Smells like banana nut."

Jenna beamed, dumping them into a wooden bowl. "You always had a nose for muffins, David. The table's all set. Sit down. We might as well have lunch while they're hot. Steve, would you get the salad?"

They were all together again. Steve set the mixed fruit and the milk on the oak table and joined his family. Lately, this had become the most important time of the year. "Looks good," he said directly to his wife.

"I'll get the butter," David said, starting to stand up.

Jenna stopped him. "No, you won't need it. Try one."

David eyed his muffin, then sank his teeth into the moist texture. "Mmmm. Peanut Butter! Banana nut and peanut butter, it's fantastic." He reached for his glass of milk. "Especially with a chaser."

"I dropped a teaspoon full in the center of each one."

Steve reached for seconds. "Good thing you made two dozen."

"It beats peanut butter sandwiches. Anyway, for David's homecoming, I love to cook."

Jenna had emphasized his name. David glanced up from serving himself fruit salad.

Steve's jaw was set, an uncharacteristic frown on his brow, his eyes on Jenna's profile. David squelched his question, dismissed the uncomfortable feeling. "How's your job?" he asked.

"It's great," she said, "now that the Rapid Rail's back on track." Jenna wiped a smear of peanut butter from her fingers. "If they had started building it earlier, my job would be easier. We have continual traffic tie-ups along the I-5 corridor. No wonder Dr. Jessup had a coronary."

Steve raised his head, "Won't he be returning to his job?"

"No. Last month he took early retirement. I'm the new regional Director of Transportation."

"Congratulations, Mom!"

"David, thank you," Jenna said, delighted to hear 'Mom' from her grown son.

Abruptly, Steve stood up. "Congratulations, Jenna," he said, a crisp edge to his usually warm voice. "I know you'll do an exceptional job." He reached for the milk carton. "I'll put this away," he added quietly, sensing David's concern.

Jenna nodded and looked briefly into her husband's blue eyes. "Of course, that's not the way *I* prefer my promotions," she said. "And David, I'm sorry I'll need to take a run to Olympia tomorrow. The Governor called a special session of the Legislature for approval of the new Transportation Budget."

"That wasn't settled last April?" David asked.

"This is an election year, remember? The shift in management and progress on rail system means more positive press for the Gov." Jenna laughed, then noticed Steve fingering his muffin, staring at her. "You will give us media time, won't you?"

"Sure, Jenna," Steve replied soberly. "Anything for the Gov."

AFTER midnight, David lay in bed still reflecting on the day's events. Uneasiness crept over him. The unresolved tension between his parents was palpable. It was foreign, threatening. Automatically, he meditated. Closing his eyes, he centered on his forehead and slowly inhaled the refreshing night air. Thoughts drifted from his mind into nothingness and a gentle northern breeze ruffled the curtains, lulling him into a deep sleep.

EARLY the next morning, David ducked to avoid a low-hanging cedar branch. It brushed along his shoulders and down his back. With his face pressed against Carmel's tan mane he stroked the horse. "Good boy, thanks for slowing down. You remember this trail better than I do." Steve's chuckle caught his attention and he looked back over his shoulder.

"That one almost gets you every year."

"So, why don't you cut it?" David said, as Steve on his black mare, Lanny, came alongside. The horses kept a steady gait on the mountain trail, headed toward a bluff on the east side of the mountain.

"Don't want to spoil the challenge."

"Thanks!" David said, grinning.

It was a ritual; their ritual, every year since David could remember. At the bluff, they sat astride their horses in silence, with evergreens towering above them like church spires. Reverent, the Winston men welcomed the sunrise as the mantle of darkness faded.

"Dad?"

"Yes, David."

"What happened in the sixties?"

"What do you want to know? A lot of things happened." Steve turned, headed down the trail, his reins wrapped around the saddle horn, trusting Lanny to keep up the steady, slow walk.

David rode alongside. "I watched a civilian orientation film the other day. It showed old news clips about the Hippie movement," he said, fidgeting with his reins. "You know, the riots and the sexual revolution. Were you in any of that?"

"No, thank Trib! I was too young. Why did they bother you with that junk?"

"Just the graduates see it. So we can deal with any throwbacks still loose in society. But, I was wondering what you experienced."

"Hmm, they don't want you to suffer culture shock. I guess that's good." Steve surveyed David with a sense of pride. "It's hard to believe you're a man already." It was equally hard to believe that twenty-four years had passed since his son's birth. Years had been swallowed by the mundane and incessant push toward success, with too few special times together.

His son's interest in his life and opinion made Steve feel better than any promotion ever had. The push for success had

23

proven hollow and pointless. A vague, nagging suspicion charged that his whole value system had jumped track, but he couldn't pinpoint how or when it had happened.

David's question pulled the past into the present and Steve visualized his childhood home, a small, comfortable, wood-frame two-story. He had shared an attic room with his older brother, until the Vietnam war erupted and sucked Adam into the maelstrom. Years passed before he accepted that his brother would never return home. It was a painful loss that the family held inside, covered with busyness. For him it proved the need for Synthesis: mankind united and at peace with no more brother-killing wars. "The sixties were a turning point," he said, dispelling the gloom, "away from the old way of thinking, toward a better way. The transition, however, was rough and mistakes were made. Transitions are always hard."

"What kind of mistakes?"

"It's best not to dwell on them."

"Sometimes you need to know the negatives so you can avoid them," David offered.

"True enough," Steve agreed, planning to avoid details. "For example, social disruptions were planned to facilitate change and a break with the old paradigm dogma. It was excessive. With more skill and patience on the part of leaders, things could have gone smoother." Steve was interrupted when the trail narrowed and they wound their way between boulders and blackberry bushes, his mare in the lead.

Planned. David rolled the thought over in his mind, curious. There hadn't been a clue about that in his social science classes. Or had there been? Oblivious to the scenery he replayed the possibility, reluctant to accept the news that his leaders would purposely create disruptions. The millennial computer crises was a study in excess, with fortunes made and lost. It did give new meaning to the science of conflict resolution. Given a good reason, with high stakes or for the sake of peace, it made sense.

"But," Steve continued, once the trail widened, "getting back to my personal experiences, I was a lucky kid. Arlington was a small town and I was insulated from the hippie thing. When I turned sixteen, in sixty-eight, I started getting curious about the free love idea. My dad must have known because he bought me a camera and put me to work taking shots for his newspaper. That kept me busy and out of trouble. Before I knew it I had graduated, earned my degree and married your mother. But too many kids got out of control."

When they rode into the meadow, resident ducks paddled to shore and waddled toward them expectantly. David pulled a small bag of smashed bread slices out of his jacket pocket and scattered the pieces. "Why did the authorities let that happen?"

"That wasn't explained in the film?"

"No."

"Well, even in those days some authorities lacked self control. To them sexual control was old-fashioned. Reigning sex experts recommended free love and the public bought it. And for two decades it looked like there was no negative consequence other than broken families, and that was even counted as a plus. The free love and open marriage thing never took."

"Dad, excuse me. I'm not sure what you mean by those terms."

"What?"

"Those terms, free love and open marriage. I've never heard them before."

"Sounds like your orientation film left out a few things."

"Four decades in sixty minutes, and half that was spent telling us how to deal with current dissidents."

"Makes sense," Steve said, uncomfortable, searching for words, again planning brevity. "Free love was plain old sexual promiscuity and open marriage meant married couples who were—that is, who included other sexual partners. Jealousy didn't stand by for that one. Marriage takes commitment and trust and hard wor . . ." The word trailed off into an awkward silence. He hadn't worked at it. David didn't take up the slack, just sat staring at him, trying to read him.

"The public message was that promiscuity was expected,"

Steve continued, "even sophisticated. Then the AIDS epidemic hit. Decades earlier, it was the same with smoking. People believed smoking couldn't hurt them. Promiscuous people believed their behavior couldn't hurt them. What they believed was irrelevant when their behavior called its dues and the price had to be paid by their bodies. Only with promiscuity, it didn't take as long to get the message."

"What about the Bureau of Public Health?" David pressed tightening the reins to keep Carmel from bolting across the meadow to the barn.

"Special interest groups took over. Really, the heart of the issue was the proclamation by the population control crowd that the number of births had to be drastically cut and the population reduced," Steve said, shifting into a reporter's mode. "Public Health had to act according to the bigger picture. Overpopulation was seen as an imminent danger that would feed over-consumption of resources and eventually wipe everyone off the face of Mother Earth. The twin goals were depopulation and reduced fertility. At the time, methods included whatever worked most efficiently. So birth control, abortion, homosexuality and euthanasia became the first line of action. In the short term it worked and live births dropped to zero population growth.

"We've maintained replacement level, and stabilized at below six billion. Now, the population control crowd's happy and the Bureau of Public Health can concentrate on reducing disease and those things its name implies. However, their new report's ruffling some feathers. Statistics support heterosexual monogamy. But, the courts still call it discrimination if anyone says promiscuity is unhealthy. Meanwhile, the general public covets their rights more than their health. Health education programs still need improvement. You know what's happening. You'll be able to bring about positive changes there."

"Yes," David agreed, "I've seen the stats. The correlation between disease and promiscuity is hard to ignore. And then there's illiteracy."

"Actually, rampant illiteracy and promiscuity motivated me

to send you to the Academy," Steve admitted. With the barn only yards away, Lanny started into a fast trot and Steve gave her free rein.

David loosened the reins so Carmel could keep pace. "To protect me?" he asked, raising his voice.

Steve deliberated whether or not to go into further detail. "Yes," he said, "from ignorance, disease and superstition."

"Superstition?"

"There was a lot of religious superstition," Steve said, immediately regretting that he had said too much.

"What was it?"

"David, it's not worth knowing about. It's divisive. Forget it." Steve dismounted and led Lanny into the barn to unsaddle her, changing the subject. "Do you want to go to Unity Broadcasting this morning?"

"No thanks. I'll wait till later if you don't mind." David slid from Carmel's back and followed Steve. He wanted to push it, but knew the subject was closed with his dad. He'd save his questions for Hegelthor. "Better study the documents Hegie gave me," he said, hefting his saddle onto the rack in front of Steve's. "But, I'll finish taking care of the horses first."

"Good, I'll go on to town." Steve handed Lanny's reins to his son. "I'll be back this afternoon and we'll go for a swim."

His dad backed the dusty '96 Ford out of the garage and drove off toward Bellingham while Carmel snorted and nudged him, impatient to run free. David took his time, brushing down both horses and then lead them toward the gate. Without warning, Max barreled around the side of the barn, circled David and sniffed curiously.

"Come here boy, don't you remember me? Where have you been?" he asked, scuffing Max around the ears. In recognition, the old German shepherd wagged his back end with excitement and nudged for his quota of head scratches. Impatient, Lanny snorted, pulling against the bit. "Come on Max," David invited. "Help me put the horses to pasture."

Clearing his mind, David locked the gate and watched

Carmel and Lanny gallop toward the west end of the pasture, Max in happy pursuit. Startled ducks took flight and ascended above the mountains, disappearing into the gathering clouds.

DAVID opened his eyes and yawned, restless with anticipation. His bedroom was still shrouded in darkness. "Too early to get up, but maybe my day's been confirmed," he mumbled, retrieving Diversity from the nightstand. On the unit, a small switch yielded with a soft click and the response flashed on screen. David squinted and focused in on the words, then smiled. Satisfied that it would be an exceptionally good day, he settled back on his pillow.

Just as he began to doze, muffled tones exploded in anger, sending an alarm along his spine. Sitting upright and throwing back his covers, David scanned the room trying to identify what had roused him. Moonlight filtered through the leaves of the apple tree forming eerie, shadowed movements on his wall. Heart pounding, he slipped out of bed, edging past his desk. Kneeling in front of his window, he leaned closer to the floor register. The muffled, angry words intensified. David stared at the grating and shuddered. Slowly he pressed his ear against the cold metal.

"Wrong! It's not good enough, Jenna. I won't do it," Steve growled.

"You have to. You started all this. Now it's almost over and I won't discuss it. Just do it! Get out of my . . ." The front door slammed shut behind Steve, cutting off Jenna's angry words and vibrating throughout the house.

David stayed on his knees and placed his hands palm up on the window sill. He closed his eyes and centered on his forehead. Each deep breath helped cancel his painful thoughts. Sweet peace.

IN THE priest's study at the Spokane Freespirit Temple, white satin fabric shimmered, capturing the sunlit glow from the stained glass window. Kendra straightened the heavily beaded train, breathless with the excitement of being Reana's Maid of

28

Honor. "You look perfect," she said surveying the bride. "Greg will be speechless. Well, almost speechless."

Reana giggled, "I never felt so fluttery inside. What if I start to laugh during the ceremony. My family would be mortified."

"Mortified? That's for funerals," Kendra said, joining in with her friend's nervous giggles. They both sobered when the light tap on the door told them it was time to line up for the procession.

Kendra took a quick look at her reflection. Her hair cascaded over the soft blue ruffles that accented her neckline. Blue pumps were barely visible beneath the ruffle of her flowing gathered skirt. A twinge of loneliness touched her heart. Only a week ago David held both her hands in his and lifted them to his lips. She could still feel the tenderness of his kiss. "Oh, Rea, If David was here, he . . ." Kendra caught her wish mid-sentence and knelt down to help Reana on with her satin pumps.

"I wish David was here, too," Reana said, patting Kendra's shoulder in sympathy. The organ music began and a loud knock interrupted their wishful thinking. The wedding was beginning without them.

Permanent decorations were tastefully arranged around the temple. Friends and relatives who responded to the short notice were seated, expectant, straining for a glimpse of the bride.

In time with the prelude, Kendra walked slowly past the white satin bows that clung to the ends of the pews, down the aisle and up three steps to the platform. Greg, in a white tux, waited beside the robed priest. Behind them, the brass candelabra stood as sentinels on each side of the altar.

Greg's mouth almost dropped open, then formed an exultant smile as the *Wedding March* trumpeted the entrance of his bride.

When everyone rose to greet Reana, Kendra surveyed the congregation.

David stood electrified, waiting for her to see him. Her eyes stopped on his and widened in disbelief. She wavered and pulled her bouquet closer to her waist, steadying herself. He wanted to join her on the platform, to touch her, to hold her. Frustration built inside his calm facade. This wasn't how he planned it. He meant to surprise her before the ceremony, then found himself stuck in Spokane's early afternoon traffic. The airport's location on the opposite side of town had proven to be a test of logistics and patience, especially when the relic he rented threatened to die at each traffic stop. Music had already begun when he slipped down the side aisle and into the second row.

Kendra accepted the bridal bouquet from Reana, then returned to her position, left of the couple. David watched every movement she made.

The frail priest stepped behind the altar as Greg and Reana knelt facing him. Raising his arms he gave Malchor's blessing on their union and invoked a blessing from the god of forces. The couple then stood, facing each other and repeated their oaths of allegiance to one another, to Synthesis and to Mother Earth's plan for their lives. Words he longed to share with Kendra echoed in David's mind. Fragrant incense enveloped them and filled the temple as the priest pronounced them united and encouraged their nuptial kiss.

David, disappointed with his own reality, followed the wedding party and the guests into the reception room. He stopped beside the refreshment table and searched the faces in the crowd, looking for Kendra.

A light touch, her hand on his back, almost sent him into an altered state of consciousness. He turned, compelled, enfolding her in his embrace. Burying his face in her soft curls, he whispered, "I love you, Kendra. I had to be here. I had to see you again." He released her slowly, not daring to touch her lips.

"David, when I was standing by the altar, I knew you weren't here, but I was looking for you anyway. When I saw you, I just— I didn't believe you were real." Kendra laughed joyfully. "Or, that you were you. Wait till the newlyweds see you!"

Together they circled around behind Reana and Greg. David stepped in between the couple, placed an arm around each one and announced in a fake Texas drawl, "Howdy, Mista and Missus Fosta. I thought I should mozzy by and give ya'll ma blessin's."

Startled, they stared at David, then stampeded him with

greetings and a smothering foursome hug.

The two couples stood to welcome the rest of the guests. During the sporadic lulls in the crowd, David explained his request, Hegie's approval, and the circumstances of his late arrival at the temple. Whenever possible, David sought out Kendra's hand with his own.

LATER, a moonless night cloaked the ranch. Frustrated, David opened his bedroom window. Only hours ago he had driven Kendra to her parent's suburban home and visited with her family. He was elated to find that her parents and younger brother already knew about him and openly accepted his friendship. The warmth of the family made leaving Kendra even more difficult and his dissatisfaction grew stronger during his flight home.

David stretched out on his bed. For the first time he felt and recognized resistance to Malchor and Hegie. "Why do we have to wait?" His own demand startled him. Obediently, he closed his eyes and canceled the thought.

That morning, breakfast was over when Jenna slipped the laser disk into the DVD player, calling David in to moderate. "That must be Kendra in the blue gown," she said. "Look at her eyes. You certainly did surprise her."

"Did Greg have a best man?" Steve asked.

"No. I wanted to be, but arrived too late." David sat down next to Steve on the couch. "Isn't she beautiful?" he asked, in a hushed voice.

"The bride or Kendra?" inquired Steve with amusement.

"Kendra," he admitted and laughed self-consciously.

"We saw her at the Academy open house this year," Jenna said.

Steve clapped his distracted son on the knee. "What's her assignment?"

"Spokane. She's at the Genetic Selectivity Center."

"You have approval for this relationship?"

"Yes. For now, it's on hold."

31

"It appears to me to be barely on hold. You better watch yourself."

David settled back into the cushions, reaffirmed his commitment to Malchor and agreed, "Yes sir, I will."

III   ORIENTATION

THE massive concrete room felt like the bowels of the Academy, not the brain. Canned background music and full spectrum lights didn't soften the atmosphere or the fact that David had spent three days entombed forty feet below the auditorium. Six Senior Technicians in pale green uniforms blended with the walls, oblivious to his presence. They supervised technicians in the twelve Academy departments and looked like three-dimensional video characters, mere extensions of the ten-foot campus screen they labored over. David rubbed fatigue from his eyes; the system didn't click in his mind. Studying the thick operations manual at the ranch hadn't helped and a vein of frustration threatened to undermine his quiet, methodic observations. Two slow deep breaths cleared his mind and canceled the pointless regret that he wasn't prepared.

David glanced at the clock, pleased it was 12:25 p.m. and time to meet Hegie in the Student Profile Department. The technician job was too lockstep for his interest, too sterile, the repetitious activity of drones. David caught himself relegating the workers to a less than human plane and winced at his attitude. He didn't care to know their names. They didn't know his either. Hegie had purposely been vague, so the technicians wouldn't be distracted from their jobs. It worked; they didn't notice when he left the room.

One floor up, in the Student Profile Department, thirty technicians sat in personalized cubicles working at monitors. David made a feeble attempt to see them as real people, but the drone image persisted. Electronic beeps accented the soft music which accompanied their drone efforts. At the drink dispenser, Facilitator Hegelthor finished off his second cup of cocoa as David approached.

"You'll be in this department for two more days," Hegie directed. "You know from the manual, the operation here is highly structured. You've been studying parts of the system for years so the puzzle pieces should come into focus soon. Do you have any questions?"

"The overall picture's fairly clear from the manual," David offered, stretching truth, "but I wouldn't presume to know the details. For now," he added, eager to dig for detail and to keep Hegie talking. "I have two questions about the Orion system. Who established the criteria for determining each student profile, and how do you make it work?"

"Good, very good. I can see your wheels turning." Hegie put a fatherly hand on David's back and motioned him toward the narrow hardwood table in the lounge corner.

"In 1976, for my doctoral thesis, at Harvard, I developed the profile tracking system and the software program. I was only twenty-four, like you." With the memory, his eyes took on a mystical glow and the lines around his mouth softened. "Old personality profiles didn't address the unified person. They dealt with the mind or the emotions or both and were filled with gaps and meaningless data," he continued and patted David's hand with benevolent affection. "I worked on the problem for ten months before I found the key and recognized the importance of spiritual essence. Yes, spiritual essence," the words vibrated with meaning.

Awed with the unprecedented comradeship, David flushed. "You were the first one to incorporate all four?"

"Yes, Yes. Long before Malchor announced it. Each area is thoroughly covered: genetic determinism, spiritual essence, intellectual capacity and emotional integrity."

"But, Malchor . . ."

"The old saying holds true, 'You get a lot done if you don't care who gets the credit.' Malchor is the means to accomplish these things; therefore, he takes credit."

Anxious for more, David nodded his agreement and asked, "How did you compile the information to put in each profile?" Curiosity etched his face. "In my profile, for example?"

"Ah. Have you ever seen your profile?"

"Of course not."

"Under these circumstances an exception to the rule will be made. Our Youth Facilitator must know everything," he quipped secretively. "Pertaining to the Academy, at least."

Within minutes Hegie returned with a five-page printout and proceeded to explain the categories and the resources he had used to glean the information.

The clinical format reduced David's entire life to flat black and white symbols. He flipped through the pages and laughed to discharge the emotions warring in him. From conception to graduation his profile in the four areas lay before him. "This is incredible. How do you use this information?"

"The profile is the key to the Academy's success." Hegie looked up from the pages to emphasize his point. "You have a personalized program unique to your strengths and your weaknesses."

"My computer and Diversity unit . . ."

"Exactly."

"But, your personal messages to me, how do you do that for everyone?"

"How would you have done it?" Hegie questioned David soberly.

The thought sent shock waves through David. *Nothing personal—just electrical impulses! For Trib's sake!* He held his relaxed state and stifled an accusation. Slowly, a smile spread from the corners of his mouth. Relief soothed his loss of faith and he saw Hegie as a mere mortal. Nothing telepathic between peers. He chose his words prudently, "I would program the computers, Hegie, like you did."

"Certainly you would. Without personalization children grow

up insecure, emotionally distracted and developmentally stunted. Experiments in the old USSR proved that." Hegie stood up, unembarrassed, elated with his own genius. "Computerized Surrogate Parenting: the key to Synthesis!"

Parented by a computer! Now that's personal. The fresh jolt threatened his calm, yet David smiled at his boss. And the smile was real, freedom birthed, sheltered in his mind. "Incredible!" he said.

"Yes, I knew you would appreciate the necessity of all this. For the first time in history, everyone here is equal," Hegie said, patting David on the back. "I'll meet you in the Housing Department in two days at eight a.m. Look over shoulders all you want and shred that profile before you leave here today."

Before Hegie reached the door David turned to study his profile, spread out on the table in numerical order. His genetic factors were encoded on the first page. The format was familiar. He had processed pedigree papers for horses. It appeared the only area horses lacked and he possessed was his evolved spiritual essence. *Man, once an animal, transformed through the evolutionary cycle to spiritual Synthesis. Thank Trib, I'll never be mere animal again.* It wasn't an original thought, but repeated and ingrained words from his first catechism.

Satisfied he had mastered the format of his profile, David dumped the pages into the shredder, then spent the afternoon watching the technicians. There was a human element after all. David watched computer technician number 27 personally handle Diversity requests made by eight fellow graduates. One anomaly showed up. Brad Newton requested approval for uniting in marriage with a girl from his hometown. Number 27 pushed the supervisor code and Brad's denial came from higher up. The girl's genetic code was fifteen points below the minimum standard.

Between the morning and afternoon shift, David slipped into a vacant cubicle, entered his code number in the Quantum computer, retrieved his personal file and quickly backtracked to May 1, 2000. There it was on the screen.

DAVID ALAN WINSTON - NOT ASSIGNED
Stress test * Subject displayed appropriate behavior
DAVID ALAN WINSTON
-ASSIGNED-
YOUTH FACILITATOR

David reread the words, annoyed but accepting the necessity, then continued.

Subject granted Diversity request - sanction relationship
Kendra Marie Addington
genetic code - appropriate for unity

At the sight of her name David tensed. The thought of unity with Kendra blocked his concern about where he was and what he was doing. He scanned the data hoping to find the projected date. There was none.

Padded footsteps, the soft squeak of plastic on tile, alerted him as technicians entered the room for the second eight-hour shift of the day. One walked past the stall where David was sitting. Without flinching, he closed the file. He hadn't reasoned it out; instead, the truth flashed through him again, like an electrical impulse. His thoughts and his emotions were his. Diversity took on a trivial meaning. David exited the program, pushed the chair back in position and casually made his way to the drink dispenser.

He pressed the button for orange juice, the cup rolled out and David peeled the lid from the chilled drink. He purposefully counted the floor tiles which ran from his feet to cubicle 27. No longer numbed by the sterility of the Academy's nerve center, he sipped the tart liquid and observed the drones pushing all the right buttons. "Push the right button and you get what you want," he whispered. David Winston's mind reeled with the sweet rush of freedom and he chuckled quietly, crumpled his empty cup and tossed it into the recycler.

SATURDAY, David banked the Aerojet westward in the misty afternoon sky and climbed above the clouds. "Too bad I didn't file clearance for Canadian airspace," he said; "looks clear to the north."

"You need to practice radar flight," Don said, adding firmly, "Head back into the clouds."

David immediately reduced altitude and reentered the white haze. By their third lesson Don's authoritative manner irritated him, a calculated trade off; lessons for stress.

"Okay kid, let's see what you know." Don reached over and ran his hands over the instrument panel. Instantly the plane twisted away from David's control.

Disoriented by the spinning plane, he held his breath and concentrated on the instrument panel. He searched for clues, a mental check off, stopping at the throttle, glaring, pulled out. "For Trib's sake, you want to see how far we go without gas," he yelled, slammed the throttle to the fire wall and let the Aerojet right itself. Breaking through the cloud cover, Mount Constitution loomed directly ahead. David fought his first impulse to pull up and attempt a climb, instead he banked to the left, circled over the Sound and looked at Don. "Some place to run a test."

"That's right. It's the best place. Green pilots always want to climb what's ahead. If they try it they rarely make it. Too steep. Sometimes, even old aces forget. My uncle tried it in Hawaii; they never found him."

A chill shuddered across David's shoulders. "Thanks for the lesson," he mumbled.

"Hey, Guy, I don't get my kicks running suicide missions. My orders are from the top, to teach you what I know about flying and that's what I'm doing. Circle once more and bring it in. Don't want to keep Hegie waiting." Without idle talk, the lesson proceeded.

DINNER was ready when Facilitator Hegelthor finished going over the details of the Academy with his protégé. "Do you have the protocol down?" he asked, not wanting to belabor the subject.

"Yes," David said. "I finished the videos this morning. There's one thing though; when we stand in receiving lines, will I be directly to Malchor's left?"

"Only when other members of the Tribunal are absent. The general rule is that you'll always stand to the left of the Tribunal. Two honor guards stand directly on Malchor's right and two more will be on your left. Other dignitaries will stand to your left."

"Who belongs to the Tribunal?" David scanned the now familiar office. Displayed on the north wall were the personal pictures, Hegie's hall of fame. The six family shots of Hegie and his wife with their two sons showed the changes which time and habit had brought about. They all looked remarkably alike. Athelia's stocky frame resembled that of her husband and betrayed her love of country cooking. Rumor suggested that the eldest son, Thomas Evan Hegelthor II, with lusterless hazel eyes and bleached out hair, had a health problem. Although David's age he would graduate the following year with his brother. Armond Roth, the youngest, glowed with healthy assurance and had his father's steel-gray eyes. The central, largest portrait showed Malchor and Hegie clasping hands in front of the marble columns of the East Coast Impartation International headquarters.

His question hung in the air as he looked from Malchor's riveting personage to the amused Hegie.

"That is for Malchor to say," Hegelthor said, quietly pronouncing the end of their session, rising, looking down on David. "You're ready for your next step. You'll be leaving early tomorrow."

David stood up, the old awe of Hegie taking hold. "Thank you, sir, for everything." He faced Hegie and groped for the words he had rehearsed.

"What is it?" Hegie demanded. "Get your feelings under control and speak up."

He watched the pupils of Hegie's gray eyes narrow into

small black dots and betray the chuckle that rumbled from his mouth. David checked himself and spoke evenly. "In all deference to the plan, sir, do you know when I'll see Kendra?"

"That also is for Malchor to say."

IV   MALCHOR

THE three-hour flight across the face of America was a welcome break from the hectic pace of orientation. David settled into the plush recliner, grateful that he didn't have to produce idle conversation. A casual sweep of the interior revealed the ever-present video eye with its unblinking surveillance, discretely hidden in the cabin's forward air vent. This was as alone as it would get. David yawned, being a boring specimen had its rewards. The pages of the D.C. tour guide book in his hands were turned absently, as he thought through Hegie's advice on his approach to Malchor Kneal Inyesco.

Hegie's reminder to be loyal to Malchor had an unsettling effect. The idea, once mentioned, played through several scenes, all ending with public humiliation. Disloyalty was unthinkable. Deliberately, he replaced the absurd thought with a rewarding memory of Kendra, her hand secured in his. The Foster wedding replayed in his mind.

Since the announcement of his assignment, his future with Kendra had spun beyond his reach. To stay focused, he exerted double the usual effort meditating. Again, he retreated into his inner world, comforted that obedient service to Malchor meant more because of the cost.

SHROUDED in hand rubbed mahogany, the clock stood out from the ornate wall like a somber monk. Nothing in the reception hall moved, except the gold hands ever circling the grandfather's face. The first half-hour was one of excitement, the

41

next of anticipation; this had given over to weariness while David held his attentive stance. Indignation was taking hold by the end of the second miserable round. If Malchor wasn't going to receive him, he could surely have dismissed him from the marble-floored prison. David no longer felt the pain in his calves and no longer cared that the video eye would reveal his clenched jaw. He glared coldly from the double doors to the clock, rehearsing the crudeness of his welcome to D.C. Another half-hour chimed; instantly, the doors swung open. David flinched.

Malchor towered in the doorway. His eyes bored into David's soul, demanding the miserable truth. Stricken with guilt and grief, David stepped forward at Malchor's nod, knelt and kissed his master's extended hand.

"Come, you must be weary," Malchor said, absolving Winston's weakness, bidding him to rise and enter his office. "Synthesis calls forth continual self-sacrifice from all devotees. You must know, matters of grave importance kept me from seeing you sooner. But I won't trouble you with that. Tell me, how is my dear friend Hegie?"

Relief washed over David and his prepared words poured out, a memorized speech, giving him the chance to regroup, to evaluate the boss. Black as coal, Malchor's irises were indistinguishable from his pupils, unrevealing and foreboding. When he spoke even gentle words, his baritone resonance vibrated with authority and demanded immediate allegiance. He was larger than life and knew it.

The Youth Facilitator's heady elation was accepted as due homage by Tribunalist Malchor Kneal Inyesco, head of the most powerful union in the world, Impartationist International. Malchor broke with the usual formal tradition. Touched by David's sincerity, he invited him to his private suite and questioned him about his schooling for an hour, before turning him over to the office staff.

Silent and efficient, the executive secretary, Ms. Prenz, buzzed the Public Relations Director, then returned to her keyboard. Minutes later, when the director walked in, David stepped forward to introduce himself, eager for conversation. His efforts met with a civil handshake and cold resistance. Frown lines creased the director's face with premature middle age. His once agile but average frame was now sloth-softened, a paunch revealing too many state dinners. With brusk gestures, he escorted David from the second floor offices to the third floor.

"Thanks for the help," David said, again attempting friendship. "What did you say your name is?"

"I didn't. However, I am Franklin Raynaud Higgs IV."

"How long have you worked here?"

"Twelve years and four months."

"What do you do?"

"I'm not at liberty to say, Facilitator. However, I've been assigned to assist you with your project."

"Then you know about the Academy?"

"No, Facilitator. Those details are superfluous to me. What I know is political procedure," Higgs said, not caring to explain. "You will find your personal items in their logical location." Frank swept his hand around the suite, indicating the dressing area, private study and bathroom. "Formal dining clothes have been provided and set out," he continued at a fast clip. "A map of the buildings and grounds is in the study on your desk, along with a schedule. Dinner will be served at 6:00 sharp and I suggest you be five minutes early. Good day sir."

"Please call me David," the Facilitator offered. "And may I call you Frank?"

The frown lines etched deeper in Frank's pallid face. "If you must," he forced. Backing toward the door, he stared at the nation's model of perfection, grated by the muscular leanness and self-assured air.

"Thanks," David muttered to the closed door. "Public Relations, huh?"

THE garage door opened automatically. Activated, the overhead bulb cast light and shadow on the gleaming metallic gray Mercedes.

Reana felt the door open and rolled toward the clock radio, squinting at the numbers, 2:43 a.m. Subconsciously, she had been expecting him, waiting. His footsteps echoing across the entry, brought a smile. Weary, she pulled herself up, changed her mind and sank back onto her down pillow, arranging it under her neck. Being editor of the social science curriculum was demanding enough, but the Baltimore humidity sapped what little energy remained from her long day. It was a minor flaw in their new home. The cooling system was inadequate and their complaints had been ignored. A small circulating fan purred, stirring the air. Silently, she watched him undress in the moonlight.

He settled into the cotton sheets and turned to face his bride. "Trib, I'm glad that's over," he breathed. "I'm sorry, Baby, to be so late. Did you get my message?"

"It's fine, of course I did," she said, snuggling closer. "Your secretary called mine. I stayed late, too, so I could sleep in tomorrow. But, how did the meeting go? Did that new client sign the contract?"

"He signed, but first we had a major protest to deal with. Dissidents accused our law firm of representing corporations that use slave labor. Fereno was accused of running the largest one. They were chanting and waving anti-slavery signs just outside the building. It was ugly, especially when the police dragged them away."

"That's a serious accusation. Is there anything to it?"

"I don't see how there could be. The inspectors gave a thorough report on C.A.M. International last month."

"You don't sound so positive," she pointed out. "So, what does C.A.M. stand for?"

"Chicago Auto Manufacturing, but enough of that," he whispered, fingertips caressing her cheek. "I felt you watching me when I came in." She blushed at being found out and smiled as he continued gently, "I know this has been a difficult adjustment. Let's be good to us. You need a good back rub and I need to cancel that unpleasant event."

ALREADY used to the ritual, the guard opened the back door as David Winston approached. With a courtesy nod, David left the headquarters building, strode briskly down the steps and into the early morning haze. His pattern was the same; he took the outer walk around the circumference of the deserted garden, then looked for a passage to the center of the maze. When the sun's first rays hit the temple spire, David headed up the steps toward the locked doors. Narrow stained glass windows lined the face of the temple, similar to those at the Academy, and it occurred to him they had been crafted by the same hands.

"The human mind, one with nature, interconnected with cosmic reality." David meditated on the precepts from Malchor's daily instruction. Repetitions were necessary. Each morning, immediately following breakfast, Malchor imparted his wisdom, "Evolving through the millennia of time and chance, man has reached the apex. Total unity. Oneness with earth, our Body; Oneness with creatures, our Soul; Oneness with cosmos, our Spirit. Total Synthesis." The words filled David's heart as he studied the dark panels. Humanities evolution to Synthesis was etched in the glass. Without light, the figures showed no life. Without Synthesis, the earth held no hope for life.

"NOW that you've had time to look over the general goals, do you have any suggestions?"

Malchor's question, coming on the second Monday, disarmed David. He wasn't ready to make suggestions. "Sir, I'm only beginning to grow into this job," he said quietly, searching for the right words. "It would be presumptuous of me to . . ."

The deep chuckle broke into laughter that cut David off. "Just don't forget the truth behind that thought. Yes," Malchor said, with a half smile, "Hegelthor was right in sending you."

Thin and bent, the figure moved toward them. David had seen the old man with stark white hair, waiting on his boss, caring for his personal needs. He handed Malchor the folded newspaper, the usual mug of coffee and waited for brief written instructions. As the man leaned over, David stared at his neck;

uneven scar tissue extended above his collar, stretching up from his right shoulder, disappearing under his chin. Openly curious, David watched him leave.

"So, you wonder why I haven't introduced you to Server? There is no need. He already knows you as well as I do. He's seen your file. But then you haven't seen his." Malchor opened the *Wall Street Journal*, spread it on the table and began sipping the steaming brew.

"James Victor Lawrence is, you've surely guessed, my valet, really a personal secretary. He's been with me for about twenty-two years—used to be my security guard. Access his file if you like.

"Oh yes, the scars you noticed," Malchor looked up from the news, his voice growing ominous, "that's from tangling with a letter bomb—meant for me. In '87 he was standing behind my secretary; Ms. Grady took the brunt of it, never knew what hit. It cost James Lawrence, rather Server, his hearing and his voice."

"I'm sorry sir."

"Cancel the thought," he said, returning to the editorial column. "Get on with your job, David. Frank has the files ready. However, do remember the fervor of dissidents—and the price of loyalty."

FLAMES sparked and leapt from bone-dry alder logs, keeping time with Mozart's *Requiem*. Tenderly, Jenna's fingers caressed the pages of the worn family album, the past, held captive with sweet memories. Those moments of joy once held promise for the future. As evening closed in around the ranch, she revisited each page of her life with Steve—their wedding, her eyes kindled with love; their early days, spent building their lives around each other, full of laughter and life.

Jenna slipped from the couch onto the rug, closer to the light and comfort of the fire. A lone tear escaped and trailed down her cheek. The stained photo showed her profile, pregnant, carrying their baby in her womb. Jenna closed her eyes and sighed, remembering the sweetness of life so long ago. Tears stung her eyes; she resisted the ache, struggling back toward the safety of bitterness.

The next page came alive; David was toddling toward his daddy, then chasing butterflies through the garden. By the following year, he proudly rode his first pony. Swimming in their lake was the highlight of his third summer. She stopped at the family portrait, looking closely into Steve's eyes, then into her own. David, at four, stood safe and secure between them.

From the doorway, Steve Winston watched her, hesitating, touched by her private reverie. Clinging to the tender, distant memory of her in his mind, he spoke softly, announcing his presence. "It wouldn't be September without a fire in the fireplace."

Instantly, Jenna was on her feet, livid. "Steve, what are you doing here?" she demanded, glaring.

"We have to talk."

"I don't have to do anything. It's my weekend at the ranch. So get out!"

"Eleven years is too long a time to hide from the truth. Look at the cost. I'm willing to say it, Jenna. For Trib's sake, you were right. For all their lofty plans and projects the state can't . . ."

"You're saying it eleven years too late, Steve."

"Jenna, You owe it to David to . . ."

"Owe it to David!" she challenged. "Owe it! You're one to talk about owing something to your son."

"Listen Jenna, I'm not going to keep this charade going. You're still legally my wife. If you're not going to be a wife to me, I'm going to blow this whole farce. He's old enough to handle seeing us in separate places."

"Oh, wait a minute! So I'm your little wife, and you come here to make your threats and let me guess: I'm supposed to fall all over you with love and adoration?"

A steady burn was building to rage inside of Steve; he gritted his teeth, wanting to shake her to her senses. The couch stood between them, a physical barrier easy to circumvent. His wall of anger mushroomed.

"Oh," she continued, "and what about your own farce, your blessed, all important career. You would risk everything, even your big name with Unity Broadcasting, just for the thrill of telling David the truth. No! You tell my son and I tell the world."

"Come on, Jenna, you have your own job to think about."

"Wrong again, Steve! I don't care anymore. I never did care about my job the way you cared about yours. We were just stepping stones for your career, weren't we."

Steve checked himself; adrenaline pulsated, raging for an outlet. "Stepping stones," he repeated, barely audible. It was only part truth. He had believed it was right, at least most of it, except for the Mother Earth element. But, in truth, he had calculated every step for his own gain. The reality of it hit, felt like a physical blow. "I told you you were right. What more do you want!" he shouted. "We were together in everything until you cut me off eleven years ago. I want to know what happened. You owe me that!"

"I owe you nothing!" Jenna hissed. "You betrayed me and everything I cared about for your self-importance, your greed, your success. You know you haven't made a selfless decision for at least sixteen years."

"Trib, you're stubborn! Sixteen? That's stretching it! What's with you, anyway? I was working for us. Can't you see that?"

"I hate you, Steve. With everything in me, I hate you!" she yelled, stunned by the force of her own anger, furious that she had let him ignite her feelings, stirring her buried pain. "Get out of here!"

He wanted to make her stop, force her. "Jenna, that's not called for," he said evenly. "That's overboard. I want to know why you hate me. I still love you."

"Sixteen years too late," Jenna repeated through clenched teeth. "Malchor can solve your problem, I'm sure."

Steve started toward her.

She turned to pick up the phone. "And do you love Jessica, too?" she added, as she pressed the button for Jake's apartment.

By the first ring, the door slammed behind Steve, rattling the window panes, signaling her victory.

AT HEADQUARTERS, three affiliates vied for position across the street. World Broadcasting arrived earliest and had staked the key location in front of the wrought iron gate. Cameras were ready to roll and newspaper reporters swarmed both lanes by the time David Winston headed back from his morning jog. Unfamiliar Peacekeepers were staked around the grounds, alert, watching. He returned to the office, full of questions. "Are you expecting a demonstration when the regional superintendents arrive?" he asked.

"You are green, aren't you? Frank smirked, shaking his head. "Listen David, we don't just expect it. We count on it. You have to keep track of your enemies. What better way than to draw them out."

"I don't understand. Why draw them out? People get hurt."

"For Trib sake! It's the way it has to be to insure Synthesis. Hey, you take care of training and let me take care of the politics." At that, Frank turned and began directing coded messages for immediate delivery to Diversity units.

"Why coded messages?"

"So our people don't get wasted," Frank muttered. "Mal expects you to have that stuff memorized by 2:00 p.m.," he added, motioning toward the stack on his desk. "There's a file for each of the twelve supers that includes personal data, responsibilities and the Academies in their regions. I pulled the data and printed it; now you learn it," he said, contempt building. "Do your job and let me do mine."

IT WAS 1:00 p.m. and the files lay spread by region across the polished oak desk in his study. David begrudged the idea that Frank knew what he was doing. He rolled his chair away from his work and stared out the window. Peacekeepers were changing their shift. Moving his head from side to side he worked out the stiffness that had settled in his neck and shoulders. Half a dried

49

tuna salad sandwich sat on the lunch tray under the corner of his desk.

He picked up the ten index cards he had prepared. With an hour to go, he already knew more about the superintendents than he knew about his parents. Pacing the office, he reviewed his notes for the third time. They were complete. Confident, he coded notes into his Diversity unit.

V   THE PLAN

"KENDRA, it's David. Did I wake you?"

Her feet recoiled from the cold sheets. "What do you think?" she mumbled, snuggling into her down comforter. "Still dreaming."

"I hope I'm in your dreams," he said, too cheerfully. "Anyway, there's a change of plans. We can't get together in December. But Malchor noticed the number of times I've called you, so he's giving me leave in January."

"January? That's three months away and my leave's in December." Kendra groaned, fumbling for the light switch.

"Your schedules been changed before."

"How could I forget?" she said, squinting to see the clock. "My alarm's set to ring in about thirty minutes." Reaching up, she pressed the off button and shifted toward the edge of her bed. "Please, please, please," she sighed, "remember the three-hour time difference. My eyes aren't ready to see light, and I'm a mess! So, as long as you play wake-up service, don't expect me to turn on the Vis Com."

"That's understandable," he said, still too cheerful.

"Okay David, so January it is. Where? Your state or mine?"

"Yours," he said, finally heeding the edge in her voice. "Sorry to keep waking you up. And sorry we can't get together sooner."

"Cancel the thought," she muttered.

"I'll be touring the Academies from September through December, working my way from the east to the west coast." David waited for an encouraging sound or word, then changed

51

the subject. "Have you heard from Reana or Greg?"

"Yeah. They know you've been too busy calling me to reach them. Just a second, have to find my slippers. I got an e-mail message last night, so I called and brought them up to date with us. They're adjusting to big city life, marriage and their jobs; doing fine. You probably know, Rea's writing social-science curriculum for one of those textbook publishers and Greg's at a law firm." Kendra continued, rummaging through the papers on her desk. "Here it is. Greg had a message for you. He said, 'The best is yet to come, good buddy. Let's get together this month. You can stay at our place and we'll show you the cultural delights of Baltimore.' That's it. He wouldn't say what he meant by the best."

"Probably the part about adjusting to marriage. I'll give him a call after the Superintendent's Conference. I miss you, Kendra."

"Is that today?"

"Yes. Rather, it starts today, but lasts all week. Kendra, I said I miss you."

"I know. I miss you too, but it's better not to dwell on that," she said, retreating to her warm bed. "I'll see you soon."

"See you soon," David said, rebuked. His hand was still on the phone when it rang. Frank called to say the motorcade had arrived.

Pomp and ceremony offered an intoxicating diversion from David's disappointment. It felt good. Limousines dispensed twelve superintendents on the front steps of Impartation International Headquarters. With practiced protocol the men and women filed past Malchor, paying homage, then met Facilitator Winston. Eight senior reporters, allowed inside the gates, shuffled for position with their equipment while their cameras and microphones recorded the event for public consumption. After the formalities, reporters followed Higgs out the gate where he proceeded to read the official press release, headlined, *Academy Consolidation Promotes Unity in Diversity.*

Inside headquarters, the attendees received their conference packets and were shown to their rooms. With thirty minutes to go, David headed up the white marble stairs to the second floor for a final equipment check.

The library, located in the west wing of the mansion, was his retreat. Books lined the mahogany shelves from floor to ceiling. Massive twin leaded-glass windows afforded a southern view of the main garden and temple. On the west wall, David opened the arched double doors leading to the deck and terraced roof garden. He was relieved the landscapers had finished in time for his first meeting. Slate tiles and planters with vigorous golden camellias and colorful rhododendrons had transformed the tar-papered flat roof of the six car garage. In the distance, an autumn-crowned birch grove bordered the airstrip. A twelve-foot privacy wall surrounded headquarters and Malchor's six hundred and sixty-six-acre estate. He surveyed the expansive gardens and noticed the crowd that gathered across the street; pleased, he returned to his preparations.

Large conference tables gave spacious room for the group to work. He switched the overhead on, adjusted it to the retractable screen, then closed the back drapes to reduce light.

Muffled chants erupted into angry shouts. Alarmed, David strode back outside to the deck. Below, the side entrance gate snapped shut and a limo stopped at the garage door. He caught a glimpse of two men greeting Malchor, following him into the building.

The shouting escalated. A group of dissidents waved hand written signs about ten feet from the television cameras. A tall muscular man broke from the rest, lunged toward the Universal Network camera and blocked the lens with his scrawled "Stop Synthesis" sign. With frenzied strength the man struck the camera. Stiff posterboard shredded with his repeated blows, leaving the stake bare. This he wielded on the metal camera frame, wood splintering in all directions. A troubled laugh escaped David, releasing pressure. It was comical from his vantage point, man attacking inanimate object. Undamaged, the camera whirred on, the cameraman untouched. World Broadcasting had the best angle and came in for a close up of the attack, flashing occasionally to the herd of dazed onlookers. Peacekeepers had surrounded the stunned dissidents, gruffly handcuffing and hauling them toward vans. Finally, they subdued the attacker and without further incident shuffled him into an unmarked car.

Rankled by the ignorance of the dissidents, David closed the garden doors, canceled the scene from his mind and reviewed his agenda. Meanwhile, equally disinterested in the abortive protest, the superintendents filed in and took their seats.

David studied their faces and waited for their full attention. They were a diverse group, representing a range of nationalities yet united in their vision, their purpose and their profession.

Without referring to notes, he delivered his opening remarks and was ending the historical overview of the Academy when Malchor showed his companions into the room. They commanded automatic respect, an equal authority with Malchor. David paused, flustered, expecting to be interrupted, but his boss shook his head, motioning him to continue. The twelve regional superintendents remained expressionless.

"It is my responsibility," David asserted, "to help you bring the nation's schools into compliance with Facilitator Hegelthor's Academy." The three observers, standing solemnly within the fringes of his peripheral vision, were not easy to ignore. Slowly in, steadily out, David paced his breathing and focused on his subject. "I know each of you are at different levels of progress with the schools in your area. That is to be expected. During this week, we will review your target dates for completion. Transition workers will travel as needed to locations behind schedule. Each region is unique, so you will not be compared to one another. This is a synergistic effort. We are a team."

Finally, their faces began to soften. A wave of relief followed. David smiled benevolently. Since greeting them on the steps, he was trying to place when he had seen most of them. San Juan was the only logical place—with Hegie. That was it. He remembered Mark Kenner walking through the dorm with Hegie, looking thinner, next to his host. And the rest of them, except for the five women, were sitting in the front row of the visitor's section at his graduation. They were at least one decade older than he, and he was telling them what to do.

It didn't fit—here at the conference they were afraid, but afraid of what? Comparison? Failure? . . . him, the Youth Facilitator?

Power promised the absence of fear. Bolstered by that promise, his own fear dissolved and he continued, "I have the reports from Academy Impartationists already working in your regions. Early Thursday and Friday afternoon, I will meet with each of you to review their recommendations. Remember, I am here to help you meet all the goals of Synthesis. To do that, we must stay focused on those goals. Please open your folder to the fourth page and follow along."

Papers shuffled. When the group was settled, Facilitator Winston began reading.

SYNTHESIS - VISION
Unify all diverse thought systems through Impartation

IMPARTATION - GOALS
Syncretize all doctrines into one reality-defining faith
Incorporate all myths into one cosmic, prophetic history
Codify and enforce uniform ethics for correct behavior
Establish earth-keeping rituals
Build cohesive social and economic institutions
and organizations
Insure seamless human resource career development
and tracking
Generate bonding experiences within Body, Soul and Spirit

The goals weren't anything new to him and appeared to be nothing new to his audience. Each goal was a necessary building block of Systemic Educational Reform. The resulting paradigm shift promised peace.

Methodically, Winston again surveyed the faces before him. There was only one he felt unsure about, Dr. Milton Werling from

Harvard. He realized the feeling was more of an instinctive dislike, but chanted, "All is harmonious in the Synthesis of life," vaguely nagged by his hypocrisy. "What is harmonious?" he challenged, with hollow enthusiasm.

"All is harmonious in the Synthesis of life," they responded. With an approving smile, Malchor turned and escorted his two guests from the room.

Winston switched off the lights and adjusted the overhead, encouraged, feeling like he had passed an exam. A lone fly buzzed toward the glare and he absently brushed it aside. Malchor hadn't said he was expecting friends. *Friends?* It was odd to think of Malchor with friends. Friends were usually peers of some sort. But it was obvious that these men were not the usual awe-filled fare that surrounded his boss. *Tribunal maybe?* With a gulp from his water glass he plunged into his presentation.

"These following charts are detailed in your notebook," he said, straightening the first transparency, backhanding the now irritating fly. "Your system is only as good as your data. Your data must be accurate for your interactions with the pupils to have the proper impact." Recovering in flight, the foul insect lit on Winston's water glass, drinking, cleaning itself, exploring, contaminating its path.

"This flow chart from section one, page eight, shows the skeleton of the Academy's Orion Computer Tracking System," Winston said. "Orion is now available worldwide and will bring us to our unified goal. Student information is collected on disk, cross-referenced for accuracy, then recorded in their profile. We are most concerned about these four areas listed; however, you will enter any factors which could hinder the student's progression toward Sustainable Career Paths and Cosmic Citizenship."

Winston used his pen, pointing to number one on the transparency. Looking up at the screen, he was startled to see the second title, Spiritual Essence, partially covered by a fat body, squat head, magnified bulbous eyes, and frail wings undulating. All eyes were riveted on the infernal insect.

His impulse was to smash the intruder. "Excuse the show," he said. "Speaking of hindering progression toward Cosmic Citizenship . . ." Muffled laughter rippled through the superintendents and Winston took the cue. "This insect is testing our devotion to Mother Earth's smallest wards but at least it is attracted to spiritual essence." Deftly, Facilitator Winston swept his hand from behind, scooping the fly into his fist. Captured, it stormed violently against his palm, seeking an escape through his fingers. "On the other hand," he quipped, walking to the garden door, "This was no doubt left behind by the dissidents. Join your friends!" he exclaimed, flinging the fly outside. By this time, all reserves were down. Unprofessional restrained laughter brought the group to an early break.

Ten minutes later, refreshed and his audience likewise undistracted, Winston continued. "Now, resuming our progress," he said, pointing to number one, "as you can see, each profile area will show what we need to know about the pupil: one, genetic determinism; two, spiritual essence; three, intellectual capacity; and four, emotional integrity." They were with him now, encouraging him with their apparent interest in the topic.

With an aura of sophistication, Dr. Ana Nakashima of Hawaii, nodded an endorsement. Lustrous black hair was wound into a bun and silver abstract stars clung to her ear lobes. Spiritual Essence was her strength. Devotion to Mother Earth had buried her two hundred competitors in region twelve. Nakashima took no notes and barely glanced at her packet.

"Now for an overview of, Orion's *Profiles and Individualized Educational Tracks*, Section two," Winston continued. "The profile data will be used to design Individualized Educational Tracks for students. Under your guidance each track will reflect the goal of Synthesis. Each IET will guide the student to maturity and expertise in the field most appropriate for him or her.

"Within the framework of the four profile areas the pupil's study course will evolve into one of the Seven Rays or intelligence tracks best suited for them. All students will retake the Individual Identity Profile in their ninth year. Results should show that students are in the right track. For example, a level-one pupil gifted in Ray 5 would be engaged in science course work, while a pupil gifted in Ray 4 would be placed in corporate or international law courses, and so on down to level-three training centers.

"You will oversee the work of the supervisors and technicians and any serious diversity messages for honor students." Thoughts of impersonal, green-uniformed technicians bent over his own pre-grad diversity messages grated on Winston, barely condoned.

"Remember, students must identify in an intimate way with one person throughout their early years." *Like I naively identified with Facilitator Hegelthor*, he argued internally, *No, not naive— necessary for the greater good.* "Therefore," he added with forced conviction, "each campus will have a person to supersede the parental role and serve as primary caregiver, a person who will direct the loyalty he fosters to Malchor and Synthesis. Each diversity message will be seen as coming from that person. You are that person at your regional Academy.

"About two hundred Doctors of Impartation will graduate from the San Juan Academy this June," Winston said. "Our goal is to have San Juan graduates placed throughout the system as primary caregivers by the end of this decade. Each level-one school will eventually become an Academy and we will consolidate existing programs into level-two technical schools and level-three training centers.

"Since this program was entered into your computers last spring, we will issue Diversity units to level-one high school students by the winter solstice." He took his unit from his pocket and held up a student unit for comparison. "These aren't as sophisticated as ours. They function as a day planner, notebook and communication link between staff and pupil, but can not be used for peer communication. Further information on Diversity models is in the appendix."

It took him another hour to explain the remaining charts; dry, tedious details of system operations. He tried not to drone, but the information was best tackled head-on and dispensed quickly. He was as relieved as his audience to finish the stack of transparencies.

"Following your return home," he said, "you will receive diversity briefings daily at 11:00 a.m. Eastern Time. Our conference call is scheduled for the first Monday of each month.

"That concludes today's material. You were handpicked by Malchor, based on your strong showing in the four profile areas." As he spoke, the Southwest superintendent kept his folder open and moved ahead to Section Three. Mark Kenner was the most personable of the group and had the highest profile score. Winston had felt a kinship with the lanky Doctor from the time they met and shook hands on the front steps.

"I have your profiles," Winston said, motioning toward the computer. "Just enter your code. For security reasons we're not allowing printouts." He turned on the lights. "Are there any questions?" he asked. His back was toward them and he was opening the drapes when Dr. Lee Thomas hesitated, then addressed him.

"Facilitator Winston, there is something . . ."

"Excuse me, Doctor," Winston said, returning to the table. "Do you have a question?"

"Yes Sir," Thomas answered. "We know that positive genetic determinism, requires stringent behavioral standards. Promiscuous people tend to have unhealthy babies. Would you clarify the purpose behind the lower standards for level-three students? In our region, for the past twenty-five years, we have successfully held all our pupils to high behavioral standards."

"Regarding your first premise," Winston said, "I will remind you, different gene pools have different requirements, of necessity." He brought up Thomas' statistics on the terminal. Those closest strained to see the small print.

"It is noteworthy you have the lowest mortality rate of all the regions. However, you also have the highest birthrate, especially between laborers and certain ethnic populations.

"That, of course, is the problem. We want a contented populace. However, population balance must be maintained.

Unfortunately, when people groups are too fertile, disease becomes a necessary control mechanism. Not to mention its positive effect in weeding out weaker genetic strains. I suggest you read *Eugenics 2000* for further insight into the matter."

Thomas paled at the reprimand. "My apologies, sir; I will correct the problem immediately."

Soberly, Winston eyed Thomas. He didn't like using disease to control population either, and remembered his initial reaction when his Dad pointed out the practice. Who could argue with Mother Earth? Demographic fatigue was her response, not his. It was her way of culling out overpopulation with an increased death rate. It was distasteful, but the need was real enough and he was obliged to comply with the policies of both the Zero Population Committee and World Health, Inc. To salve his conscience, he reasoned that the souls would reincarnate to level-two or even level-one. Of more importance, he didn't want any mavericks in the program. Dr. Lee Thomas had to be watched.

"Seeing there are no more questions," Winston said, surveying the group, "you will have two hours this afternoon to read your packets. Take what time you need throughout the week to commit the contents to memory. The information is confidential, not to be discussed with anyone outside this room."

The session ended with brief comments about universal peace. Winston stayed in the library and prepared for the next day while the men and women dispersed to change for an informal dinner. Holding the conference was his first official duty, and he was relieved the day was over. Later, when Malchor was too preoccupied with his guests to attend further sessions, he was even happier.

BY THURSDAY even the Northeast superintendent was contributing. Winston chided himself for his original dislike of Dr. Milton Werling. Werling proved to be a gifted organizer, finishing his work early, then helping others.

That afternoon, Winston led the group through the reception room to the foyer, anticipating their tour of D.C. Chimes announced the hour and the Facilitator glanced toward the grandfather clock. It was a persistent reminder of his first shameful hours and the dark thoughts that had threatened his future. Guilt shadowed him, echoing the fact that he still didn't deserve Malchor's trust. Shaking the thought, he stepped outside, grateful for a gentle breeze.

Rudely, Frank cut in front of Winston at the portico, his face flushed, eyes glaring. "Malchor would like you to join him for dinner at 7:00 p.m.," he said, with strained civility. "I will be escorting the superintendents on their tour of the capitol." When the others were out of range he hissed, "Aren't you the lucky little prince."

Winston stopped cold. "Check it, Frank. Petty jealousy?"

Abruptly, Franklin Higgs pivoted and stalked to the van. Winston waited at the entrance until the van and security vehicles pulled away from the curb and Higgs was out of sight. With two free hours before his dinner appointment, he headed for his room, sorting out the confrontation. Frank deserved even less of Malchor's trust. The smug politico could be replaced, not easily, but perhaps by spring.

The Youth Facilitator's suite was in the back northwest corner of the brick building. An overstuffed Early American sofa sprawled comfortably between the bookshelf and the oak side table. Lonely, David picked up Greg and Reana's wedding party photo and moved it from the coffee table to his desk. Kendra smiled up from the frame. *Trib*, he thought, *it's not getting easier.*

Taking his phone, David dialed Greg's law office and got stuck on hold. Waiting, he perched on the side of his desk and pulled open the blinds so he could see the gardens below. From his room the towering hedged maze, centered between the house and the temple, looked easy to conquer, but he hadn't made it to the center yet. He studied the intricate curves and blocked passages.

At the yawing doors of the temple, the guard stood rigidly attentive. When Malchor stepped into the sunlight, the man saluted and David backed away from the window. Sunday

61

morning service with staff members wasn't enough. David was severely disappointed over not being invited in with his boss. Malchor attended temple faithfully during the week, but always alone. Today, he wasn't alone.

"David, I've been trying to reach you all week, but you're always in a conference." Greg's voice boomed out, unnerving him.

David rolled his chair around and sat down, yielding to the soft vinyl. "Well, you're not so easy to reach either," he said. "I've been on hold so long I forgot why I called."

"So when are you coming to see us?" Greg asked. "We live close enough, just about two hours away, depending on the traffic."

"This weekend sounds good. I have Saturday afternoon and Sunday morning."

"Great! I'll let Reana know. I think she works on Saturday, but she'll have a little time."

"I'll be there around 4:30 p.m. Why not reserve a racquet ball court so we can work up a good appetite."

"Sounds good! See you."

"Bye, Greg." David hung up the phone absently, staring out the window. Malchor and his guests approached the hedge. The men entered the maze near the temple, wound their way through to the center, then wound their way to the opposite side. Dead ends didn't stop them. They came out facing Malchor's private quarters. If they could do it, David determined, he would.

THAT evening, Server guided him into Malchor's private dining room, then withdrew. David hesitated by the door.

". . . mere pit stops in the march forward." Malchor was saying, "All of those events were predictable. Sloppy leadership!" Noticing his protégé he extended his hand, "Ah, David, come in and join us. Frank was correct in suggesting I introduce my trusted staff member to my guests."

David walked across the room and remained standing, waiting for introductions, amused that Frank had meant the honor for himself.

Malchor motioned to his right. "Cyrus Nascent heads the Cosmic Spirit Council and Arian Tempera, the World Fund. This, of course, is our Youth Facilitator, David Winston."

Cyrus's face was a study of inherited lines and ridges accentuated by slicked, receding, gray-brown hair. His forehead creased with interest when his hazel eyes met David's and his thin, straight lips curved into a friendly smile.

David shook hands across the table and barely sat down between Malchor and Arian, when their debate surged ahead.

"You presume last year's Calgary riot was due to sloppiness," Arian challenged, his Nordic blond hair and blue eyes contrasting with Malchor's dark hair and darker eyes. "Not at all; anarchy was a necessary transition. How else would the untutored masses demand and accept the necessary controls?"

"As usual, my friends," Cyrus observed, "the end vindicates the means."

Throughout dinner, David struggled to follow each detail offered. Cyrus elaborated on his efforts to unify the few remaining cults. The Chosen and the Believers, being the most entrenched in their ways, still balked at the concept of their own godhood. He recognized the subject as the one his Dad had refused to continue and listened, eager for details. Understanding dissident thinking was key in effective deprogramming. He made note of the need for diligence in helping the children of dissidents see their destiny in Synthesis.

"When, along the trail of history, have the people stopped true leaders?" Malchor asked, surprising David.

"Only on rare occasions, Sir."

"Rare indeed! A moment here—a moment there—hardly a pebble on the scene of life; people have no power to stop The Plan. People need leadership! They only manage the simplest things on their own." A deep laugh rumbled from Malchor's throat. "America thought it was honorable to rescue Europe from Hitler's Nazi plan, only to make a pact with his spirit-brother, Marx. They pruned back Hitler and Marx, then eagerly helped

The Plan go worldwide. I love the people!" His laughter rolled out, building in volume. Cyrus and Arian joined and David felt drawn into their felicity. "Remember, David, Marx was a mere piper in The Plan's orchestra and the sound will be carried by the winds of earth into eternity. Where Marx failed, we will prevail!"

"The people are compelled to join in unity and finalize The Plan," Arian agreed. ". . . like children returning from their rebellion, coming home to honor the Tribunal." Cyrus held up his goblet in a toast. "To us. To Synthesis."

"To the success of The Plan," Arian said.

David tasted the sweet wine and drank. The rumors of his childhood were, in truth, sitting around this table. The Body, Mind and Spirit of the incarnate Tribunal were real.

Hours later he lay sleepless, recounting the evening's blessing, astonished by his own fortune.

IN SPITE of his physical exhaustion, the final conference session brought David further satisfaction. Even as they concluded, teams were relocating to carry out his instructions.

Tension registered on the faces of the superintendents seated before him. Perplexed, David followed their corporate stare and turned to face Malchor. The absurdity struck him. These people hadn't feared him. They feared his influence with Malchor. Reverently, he stepped aside.

"You will do. The conversion will proceed as planned," Malchor said, including David with the others. "What you have done here this week will be recorded as key in the reorganization of education, the development of superior human resources and the birthing of universal Synthesis."

He placed his hand on David's shoulder, symbolically transferring authority. The message rang clear. "My Youth Facilitator answers only to me in all matters pertaining to the world's children. He will soon visit each campus."

It was a graduation exercise and David Winston realized it was his, not theirs. He thought he was training them, but they were, in effect, training him, as Mal put it, to be a superior human resource. The superintendents were his mentor class, his final exam and he had passed. He was grateful he hadn't recognized the truth sooner.

"I am sure," Mal concluded, "you will be ready for his arrival and eager to comply with his suggestions. We appreciate your efforts and abilities and know you will fulfill your responsibilities with absolute loyalty. Thank you for accepting your commissions. For your convenience, helicopters will transport you to the D.C. terminal. Your suitcases are already on board."

SATURDAY, Greg Foster wheeled his new Mercedes away from the health club and onto BW Parkway, merging with the traffic flow to Baltimore's Inner Harbor. "Now that we've exhausted ourselves, let's eat!" he said. "This place makes the best pizza on the East Coast. I guarantee it."

"The East Coast has to have some advantages," David complained, "otherwise, who would settle for this humidity? Feels like I'm melting into the seat."

"It's more noticeable in the city, isn't it? You'll feel better down by the waterfront. Here, this will help," Greg said, turning the air conditioner to high. "How long did the commuter train take from Fairfax?"

"I reached Penn Station within thirty minutes. Back home it would take an hour to cover the same distance." David directed the air vents, settled back and glanced over at his friend. Foster was beaming. The fading sun shone on his red hair, giving a ruddy glow to his face. "What's this I heard about the best being yet to come?"

"For me the best is Reana. Although the whole thing is different from what I expected."

"What do you mean?" David could see the Inner Harbor looming ahead, a showcase of splendor built from the demise of unsightly warehouses and docks. His question hung in the air as they drove several blocks past the Pavilion and through the

65

guarded entrance to Harbor Point.

"We were lucky to get one of these townhouses; my law firm connections helped. They're only building fifty more units and there's a waiting list of prospective buyers. It's especially hard to find a place with a garage."

"How are things different?" David persisted.

Greg parked the car at his place. "Come on, it's just a few blocks back to the Pavilion. Aren't they different for you, too?" he asked, setting the pace for the walk around the waterfront park. "You look like you're thirty already—so serious. Relax. So then, is life away from the Academy what you expected?"

"Much better, yes, much better than I ever expected."

"And Kendra?"

"That's the only negative: waiting to have Kendra. I won't see her until January." David didn't want to dwell on that bleak prospect. He shifted back to his original question. "What's different for you?"

"Dealing with traffic, a home and all the associated demands, a law firm where political power commonly overrides justice, and less time to meditate takes its toll. It is more and more difficult to cancel negative thoughts."

"Justice? That's why we're here, to bring justice. Where is justice without Synthesis?" Not needing any answer, he conceded, "I lead a comparatively sheltered life. Missing Kendra is my only negative and it sounds like having Reana is your only positive."

It was true enough. For Greg, life had few positives and they seemed fewer all the time. "David," he said, "I used to believe Hegie could read my mind, but if he could, I would be terminated by now."

"Actually, he never said he could. You must be as relieved as I am that he can't. However, that doesn't diminish the importance of unity. We have a responsibility to keep our thoughts in compliance with . . . Hey, look at that old ship."

The old vessel hovered in its dock, an attraction for tourists, a conversation piece for locals.

66

"That's the Frigate Constellation," Greg explained. "It's the oldest ship of the U.S. Navy, launched sometime in the late seventeen hundreds. She stands as living proof of harder times. Officers' quarters are half the size of my closet. Tour's closed now; we'll board her later."

Greg motioned him on, leading him along the boardwalk toward the building. Once inside, the blended smell of garlic and oregano hit them and they took the stairs to Uno's by two's. It was a rare time for pizza and beer.

FOSTER'S townhouse was larger than it appeared from the outside, snuggled in its orderly row, five units to the east and four to the west. A generous entrance invited them past the laundry and garage up a flight of stairs to the living area. Greg proceeded on to the third-floor bedrooms, describing the work involved in furnishing and decorating, then giving David the pick of the office or den for his stay.

Coming from behind, Reana grabbed his hand and led him to the den couch. "We're still waiting!" she exclaimed.

"Waiting for what?" he asked, expecting her to ask about Kendra and Unity.

"Waiting for you to tell us what Malchor is really like," she answered.

"Oh, is that all," he laughed. "What's the ocean really like or what's a volcano really like?" Reana's blue eyes widened with expectation. "Well," he continued, "it all depends on where you are; what your relationship is."

"That's a help," she said impatiently.

"If you're in a ship riding the waves it's one thing, an extraordinary experience," he added. "But, I wouldn't want to fall overboard in shark infested waters. Likewise, a volcano is awesome to behold, if you're not too close to the molten lava."

"Come on, David. What's he like as a person?" Greg asked.

"He's like Facilitator Hegelthor," David offered. "Only he's more . . ." Somehow it seemed dangerous to compare them, but there was no alternative. ". . . well, more powerful."

"Really?" she asked.

David nodded and said, "Malchor allowed me to meet the Tribunal."

Laughing, Reana clasped her hand to her heart. "They're real! I knew they were," she said. "Who are they?"

"I'm not at liberty to say. Actually, it's the Tribunal concept that's most important, so much more powerful than the members. You know, position above personage. When the time's right, they'll reveal themselves."

"When will that be?"

"When Synthesis is secured."

"Excellent!" she gave David a hug. "Well, the pillow is in the closet with extra blankets; make yourself comfortable. I've got to get some sleep, so I'll see you in the morning." Following her, Greg tossed a hearty good night over his shoulder.

After two fitful hours on the den sofa-bed, David pulled the mattress onto the floor. The day with Greg and then Reana's delight in seeing him made the discomfort worthwhile. Being with them was the closest thing to being with Kendra.

The Sunday temple service sobered the threesome. It was a reminder of the work ahead—the work of bringing unity to every living soul. After brunch, David packed for his return trip, then entered Greg's office to say goodbye. "Do you often bring work home?" he asked, seeing Greg hunched over his computer keyboard.

"No, just finishing up a report for Hegie. We've had some disruptions in industry and I'm requesting an investigation of the complaint. It's probably nothing. Anyway, when does your train leave?"

"Not until 3:00 p.m."

"Good," Greg said. He shut down his PC, flipped on the entertainment channel and turned. "David," he said, his forehead drawn in foreboding. "There's something I've wanted to ask you. But it's not," he shook his head, reconsidering, "it's not something I would mention to anyone else." Greg closed the door and pulled his chair closer.

The room felt oppressive; David shifted awkwardly, wanting to leave, suppressing the urge. "What is it?"

"Do you remember Brockston Andel?"

"Of course. He was student-body President. Everyone knew him."

"Do you know how he died?"

"He accidentally went off the road on the way down Mt. Constitution. Wasn't it something about his steering going out?"

"That's what they said, but that's not what happened. It wasn't a car accident." This time Greg had to say it. The facts hung over him, nagging at his loyalty to David, threatening his loyalty to Malchor. "He killed himself."

"No! That's not possible." David sat back. A nervous laugh escaped.

"Isn't it?" Greg demanded.

"How?" The tiny doubt gnawed at his mind set. "How do you know?"

"Do you remember where he was the week before he died?"

David knew. The words he had canceled, the thoughts he had refused to consider, seeped out. "Brockston was with Malchor, out here. I think they were grooming him to be the Youth Facilitator. Why would he kill himself?"

Civil War erupted from the television screen. Fire engulfed the old southern rail station, distracting them both. Scarlett O'Hara struggled to escape from the carnage. David knew that unlike the screen heroine, Brockston hadn't escaped the carnage of his burning car; he was unrecognizable, his body quickly cremated.

Gone With the Wind played on and David pretended to be absorbed, not wanting to return to the subject. "Greg," he finally asked, "why would he?"

"He was initiated."

"What?"

"Malchor initiated him. He was planning a special temple experience for our class. I was part of the planning team. After Brockston's death, it was canceled. It's the only time I ever saw

Hegie angry. I was in Brockston's room before they sealed it. He left a note." Greg shuddered, his voice low. ". . . something about being chased and suffocated by—by demons. He drew pictures, slimy wart covered creatures. Creepy! He wrote that there was only one way to keep them from getting him. Hegie was furious that it happened and that I knew about it. He ordered me to cancel the thought. I did. It keeps coming back. Just last night . . ."

"Trib! You're saying he was chased to his death by mythical demons. No! He must have been unstable. His mind snapped."

"I'm sure it did snap; being mythical doesn't mean they're nonexistent. I think they're real. I think the initiation opened him to attack."

"Listen, Greg. If Hegie told you to cancel the thought, you had better make it happen."

"Hegie knew we were too young, not strong enough to handle the consequences."

"You'd better cancel!

"Yeah, sure."

VI   EVOLUTION

THE Academies evolved with increasing momentum. Facilitator David Winston's tour began with Northeast Harvard, a pleasant campus protected from city bustle by the surrounding twelve-foot-high brick wall.

Superintendent Werling gave him the grand tour along tree-lined paths. Massive brick and mortar, ivy-covered structures were upgraded to accommodate his students. Classes were small, with room for more pupils. Winston noted the age-appropriate environments and activities, consistent throughout the complex. Sequestered housing offered professors both amenities and aesthetics, while the nursery nurtured their children. From markets to clothing shops, the Academy offered cradle to grave convenience. Werling showed him into the foyer of the palatial temple for a reception. Professors and associates balanced their drinks and plates and showed polite curiosity. In an impromptu speech, Winston commended their membership in Impartation International and their diligent efforts toward Synthesis.

Slower progress at the Southeast, Mideast, and North-central facilities required Winston's full attention until the first weekend in October. He lost count of the times he had criss-crossed the country, supervising personnel changes. Meanwhile, national election campaigns raged with millennial fervor. He mailed his absentee ballot early, having absently checked all of Malchor's recommended issues and candidates. Their names didn't register in his mind, but he had done the important thing and voted.

THE meteorologist's voice crackled from the radio; a frigid storm blanketed the East Coast in snow. Flying solo, Winston banked the Aerojet and circled the stately Notre Dame Academy in Indiana. The runway was clear, no fog, no haze and no snow. Bright splashes of autumn color clung to wind tossed oaks. After touch down, he taxied to a stop several yards from the well-bundled reception committee. Winston pulled on his wool cap and overcoat then opened the door. The wind was biting, whipping at his face. He gripped the rail and hurried down the steps, unaware of trouble until a jostling crowd descended on him.

"Stop the death of our freedoms," a fragile, doe-eyed woman cried. Superintendent Stennem was shoved aside as she threw herself at Winston. Without thinking, he held her to his chest balancing in the shuffle. Desperate, crying above the chaos, she begged him to save her brother. Dissidents surrounded them, arms linked, weaponless, blocking the security guards. Shouting, more guards descended in a blur of billyclubs and subdued them. Two hulking guards then pulled the woman from his arms and shoved her toward the police van.

His hand closed protectively over her folded note. Shaken, he stood silently, straining to hear her above the fray and Stennem's outraged commands. A half-dozen squad cars roared their arrival, sirens screaming and officers scrambling to cordon off the area.

The band started and strains of *America the Beautiful* smoothed the chaos. Stennem apologized and dusted the woman's touch off his guest. Winston endured the attention and ordered a list of the dissidents. With professional detachment, he toured the imposing facility from the safety of a Panther mini van and greeted the resident Impartationists. After lunch he retreated to his suite.

Locked in the security of his room, David dumped the contents of his briefcase on the desk and examined the list. He pulled the wing-backed leather chair around, positioning his back to the ever present camera. Retrieved from his vest pocket the note lay there, begging action, dominating the sterile reports and disks.

Hesitant, as if it were an illicit act, he unfolded the paper and read:

Dear Facilitator Winston,

Please overlook the brash actions that may have accompanied the delivery of this appeal. The pursuit of peace is dear to my heart and to the hearts of my people. We do not wish to clash with your goals for peace nor with your personal belief in Synthesis. We wish only to live quiet lives, earning our own way, caring for our families, worshiping our Maker.

Today, following our traditions is viewed as anathema. Our peaceable matters of conscience are viewed as dangerous. Our tabernacles are closed while our feasts and holy writings are banned.

I implore you to allow us to return to our former Chosen ways with the understanding that we will obey civil law and pursue our common goal of Peace.

My brother, Rabbi Abramson, is consigned to reorientation. His crime was leading our people in Yom Kippur services, our time of penitence for wrongdoing. For the sake of justice, I pray you will arrange his release, while he still has his mind.
Marie Mitchell

It was eerie. The woman's voice haunted the air, repeating her plea. In the past two weeks he had dealt with three dissident disruptions. It was easy, even energizing, to squelch hate crazed radicals. This was different; the poor thing believed her way was harmless to unity. Hoping her children could be spared her confusion, he switched on the Quantum desktop and brought up her file. No children. That made things easier. With no children to remediate there were fewer loose ends, less contamination. He scrolled down to her medical records and frowned. No fertility implant. He saw no reason to allow future risks and coded into the Regional Genetic Selectivity Center. A technician responded to his alert and scheduled an emergency appointment for the woman. Winston scanned her letter and e-mailed it to Malchor.

Tuesday morning he learned the results of his efforts. The Rabbi responded favorably to treatment, renounced his former allegiance, and would be released by the following Saturday. Marie was relieved of her Academy duties as History professor. With her fellow fanatics, she arrived at the Haven for short term reorientation. Her implant was already in place. Winston was confident about complete recovery, convinced that their rescue from delusion would have a positive effect on other dissidents. He had fulfilled justice.

Superintendent Stennem tightened security immediately after the incident. Meanwhile, even though Facilitator Winston had finished inspecting the area and the programs, he was grounded until five bodyguards arrived from Malchor. They checked his plane, checked each room before he entered and smothered him with concern. They rechecked his Aerojet again before departure to the North-Central campus. Winston insisted on taking the pilot's seat, relegating his shadows to the passenger section.

TIME and distance contracted, bringing him closer but not close enough. During the next two Academy tours, superintendents bored him with their excuses, plodding through the remaining structural changes.

Mid-December finally brought Winston some relief from counting the weeks and miles until his time with Kendra. Few places offered more pleasant distractions than the rolling hills of a California resort community. The Santa Barbara Academy ran smoothly under the affable leadership of Dr. Mark Kenner. Winston and Kenner walked the campus together in shirt sleeves, greeting students and checking programs. Security was efficient but well hidden. In the casual warmth, his guards took to rounds

74

of golf, while he caught up on his slipping tennis game. Kenner a formidable player, beat him three to one.

INSIDE the domed temple the next afternoon, Winston gave his speech and a hush settled over the students. While he returned to his seat next to Kenner, the student body president, Bill Grant, took the mike and spoke for his classmates. "Thank you for opening our Winter Solstice Celebration and thank you for the honor and privilege that Diversity brings. We eagerly anticipated the freedom of choice, which we now have with our Diversity units. Thank you, Facilitator Winston. Thank you, Dr.Kenner. Thank Malchor. Thank Synthesis!"

"What is harmonious?" Bill chanted.

The body rose with one exultant voice. "All is harmonious in the Synthesis of life."

Promptly at 3:00 p.m. E.S.T. on December 22, 2000, the hologram symbolizing Synthesis was unveiled above the dais of each Academy across the nation. Silver images of three beings appeared to move forward. The center figure, larger than the rest possessed a third, all-seeing eye in the center of his forehead. Hands linked, their images were transposed over Mother Earth's shimmering blue sphere with the swirling silver-blue galaxy barely visible in the background.

Awed by its beauty, students stood in reverence. Winston walked to the podium and raised his right arm, hand extended, palm down in salute. This was the hope of humanity. This time the words came from his soul. His eyes welled with tears. His words rang clear, joined by all.

We pledge our allegiance to the symbol of Synthesis
And to the Unity for which it stands
Oneness with Earth, our Body
Oneness with Creatures, our Soul
Oneness with Cosmos, our Spirit
Indivisible
With Rights and Equality for All

Silence yielded to symphonic melody and built to a crescendo rendition of *We Are the World*. Students sang as they filed from the temple into the commons. There the celebration continued with food and fun until midnight.

IN DECEMBER, intricate snowflakes dusted the Apex with powdered crystals. David observed from Hegie's office, while students trekked across the whitened landscape. Washington winters were gentle—just enough weather change to invigorate, never enough to deplete energy. Turning away from the window, he noticed a group of framed photographs. There they were, Cyrus, Arion and Malchor bedecked with skis and parkas, years younger, posed in front of a towering Alpine lodge.

"So, you recognize the Tribunal," Facilitator Hegelthor said, closing David's final report. "Those were the days. Time to dream. Time to dance. Even time to ski in Switzerland. I expected you would have met them by now?"

"Yes, they were at the estate with Malchor. We had dinner together."

"And?"

"Why doesn't the world know?"

"It isn't time. Sit here," Hegie motioned toward the sofa. "What's this about Greg in your report? He was your roommate, wasn't he?"

"Yes, sir."

"Well?"

"He failed to cancel as you ordered, sir." David spoke quietly, hesitating to detail the negative report.

"David, bringing this to me is proper. You're in leadership. Anything that threatens unity must be held in thought until the situation is resolved." Hegie's concern softened his face. "Greg can, and will, be helped." He patted David's knee reassuringly.

The weight lifted. Hegie confirmed David's conclusion that Brockston had lost his mind before accidentally careening off the road. "Now, David," he said firmly, "regarding Greg's failure to cancel the note and the suicide. Cancel the thought!"

THAT evening, for another first, David joined the staff with their mates and friends after hours for the New Year's Eve millennial party. His old professors crowded around, respectfully listening to the latest news about worldwide school reformation. Hours passed in lively talk peppered with suggestions, advice and praise. Jubilant, at the stroke of midnight, the comrades ushered in the twenty-first century.

JANUARY 1, 2001, at 10:00 a.m. the plane with Kendra aboard, landed at the Winston ranch. David had the horses saddled and waiting. His guards stood watch protectively. As soon as Kendra's feet touched the ground, he helped her mount with a whispered greeting, leaving her things on the runway for Jake to put away.

Astride Lanny, David led the way up the trail. His father's horse kept shaking her head defiantly, snorting billows of vapor into the crisp afternoon air. To keep her from bolting, David gripped the reins. Following compliantly, Carmel carried Kendra on his groomed back. When the trail widened, David pulled over until Kendra rode alongside.

"I told you I'd show you the ranch. Although at the time, I didn't expect to wait so long. What do you think?"

"I couldn't have pictured it as beautiful as it is. Your vacations must have been . . ."

"Nothing," he interrupted. "They were nothing compared to having you here."

"Is there some place where we can see the valley?"

"In about ten minutes, there's a lookout point. But, from the look of these clouds, you'll see the place covered with snow by tomorrow. You warm enough?"

"Yes, thank you. Although I must look strange wearing your parka."

"On the contrary, you look like the Snow Queen, but with a heart to match your beauty. Trib, Kendra, I missed you! Last night was an eternity. I thought you'd never get here." Her blush was his answer and he took the lead on the narrowing trail.

77

Lookout point was welcome for more than one reason. The guards had retreated out of sight, down the trail. Eagerly, David dismounted, tethered the horses to a tree and helped Kendra. She swung her leg over the saddle horn and slid down into his arms. Her gloved hands rested firmly on his shoulders. He unfastened the parka with one hand, uncovering her moist lips. Slowly, he drew closer until her breath blended with his. Her eyes pulled him closer still. Their lips touched hesitantly, tenderly, passionately.

The view, the ride back, the record snowfall that blocked the road for a week, passed in a blur. Kendra was with him and soon, with Malchor's blessing, would belong with him. He only thought he missed her before, in an expectant but detached sort of way. This was different. This was why Greg was so eager to whisk Reana away from their wedding vows. David revisited the memory of Kendra's lips like a man desperate for air.

OBLIVIOUS to his need, Jenna and Kendra spent long hours looking through family picture albums and examining his carefully wrapped childhood creations. It was best. He couldn't look at her long enough to satisfy himself. He had to get his feelings under control.

Finally, with the roads cleared, Steve joined in their visit. He, too, was delighted with Kendra, eager to hear about her childhood, her parents and how she met his son. It was Kendra who noticed the change in Jenna. Later that night, with only rare moments alone, David wasn't expecting to discuss his parents.

"When he walked toward her, she took a step back. Something's wrong."

"Seriously, I didn't notice. Mom's never been—never shown her affections in front of others."

"Yes, she does. She hugs me every morning, you too. She touches you every time you're within a foot of her. I even saw her hug Fran the other day."

"Kendra, that's different."

"David, no, it isn't," she insisted. "All day, every time Steve

78

walked close to her she averted his look."

"All right then, what do you think?" he asked.

"I don't know. Maybe they had a disagreement."

"Fine, now that's settled. Please, dearest Kendra, don't give it another thought." He traced his finger beneath her lower lip. "You'll see. Everything will be normal in the morning. Besides, I've decided to fly you to Spokane tomorrow afternoon. I want to spend some time on your turf."

"THIS is it," Kendra said. "Now it's my turn to ask. What do you think?"

"I liked your apartment better," he said, "but this is a pleasant office, nice mauve carpet." In truth, he loved any place with her. David picked up the wedding picture from her desk. "The same picture sits on my desk. Next year, we should have our own."

"Our own what?" she asked, glancing up from watering her Boston fern. When he held the picture up for her, she blushed. "Oh," she said, setting the cup on her desk, sorting her memos and mail.

David's nameless ever-present guards were on duty at the parking garage entrance and in the hall outside. Her office was located on the top floor of the Genetic Selectivity Center, the tallest building in Spokane. Behind her desk, two four-by-five-foot abstract oil paintings hung on the pale gray wall, bold mauve and blue strokes splashed across muted shades of gray. To David it appeared that the artist painted one huge picture, then cut the canvas in half. The room was dramatic, but organized for comfort. Her steel-gray molded desk faced matching executive chairs and an expansive view window.

"It's a good thing you face the north—no glare." The comment didn't bring a response. David tried again. "Say. You're not due back to work until Thursday."

Kendra ripped open the personally addressed envelope. "Oh, I'm sorry David. I'll leave the rest of these. I just want to read this one, if you don't mind." She turned to see his nod, then sank onto the cushioned seat, already immersed in the words.

David watched the evening traffic flow away from the city toward the suburbs. Pink and orange traces of the early sunset were stretching across the western horizon.

"Would you like to pay a home visit with me?"

"A what?" he asked.

"A home visit. You know, where I observe a child in the home before making a decision about placement."

"Sure." This was not the candlelight dinner he had planned, yet the concern creasing her brow warned him against pressing for romance. Especially since coming to the office had been his idea.

"You might as well see how the process for genetic selectivity works."

He grabbed their coats, struggled into his and followed her to the parking garage while the guards hurried to their leased station wagon. "Here, you better put this on before you get in the car."

"Thanks, David," she said, barely stopping long enough to let him help her into her winter tweed. "I forget how cold it is."

"Why the rush? Is something wrong?"

"Could be? It's just a feeling. I don't usually get involved like this, but there's something different about this case. We're processing applications as fast as we can. Most of the time it's simple. Either a child qualifies or he doesn't. If they don't, another agency handles their placement.

"I believe this child belongs in the Academy, but someone in data processing entered the data wrong in her file. Anyway, the mother made an appeal, I checked it out and the file was wrong. I ordered a correction, but it looks like someone is trying to cover up their mistake. The file wasn't corrected and this is the mom's second letter. She was notified that Protective Services got an anonymous call charging child abuse. Now the family is under investigation. That alone could disqualify Megan.

"This kind of bureaucracy is . . ." Kendra stopped talking, concentrated on the traffic tangle and passed a slow truck blocking her way.

"I may need your help with this one. If they already have her, it's likely she's traumatized."

"Kendra, it's not going to help if you're pulled over," David said, holding onto his shoulder belt. "Take it easy."

She took her foot off the accelerator, then pressed down to make the light. David, looking for speed cameras, watched the guards make it through on yellow. He was relieved when they pulled into the housing development and slowed to a stop in front of the beige split level. "Luck must be with you, woman. If I drove an officially marked car down the road at half that speed, they would have nailed me."

"Let's hope the luck holds out," she said. "Come on."

The mother intercepted Kendra on the front steps and was pulling her into the house. David hurried to keep up while his guards fanned out, securing the perimeter.

"They just left with her; she doesn't know. I didn't want her to be scared, so I told her they were friends taking her for a visit." The woman stood erect and composed yet the urgency in her steady voice cut into David's complacency. "Please, I know you wouldn't have come if you didn't intend to help."

"What was the charge?" Kendra asked.

"A woman called in, claiming she saw me spank Megan early last week at the park. We haven't had time to go to the park since I filled out her application. And I never spank her!"

"Did they record the voice?" David asked.

Startled the woman swung around. "Oh, I'm so sorry, how rude of me," she said. "I'm Gloria Kassan. And you're . . .?"

"David, David Winston."

"David's the Youth Facilitator. I'm sure he can intervene," Kendra explained.

"Did they record the complaint?" he persisted.

"Oh, yes, they played it for me. I've never heard the voice before." Gloria looked at the time and shuddered. "The office closes in ten minutes. There's no time to drive there."

David strode over to the phone. "Do you have the number?"

81

"Right on that paper."

He dialed, introduced himself and demanded to speak to the director. Finally, the woman answered and when David restated his title her caustic tone faded into compliance. A call from that high up meant trouble and could mean her job. With apologies, she offered to help the Facilitator in any way. He relayed the situation, requested immediate release of the child into his custody and turned the phone over to Kendra.

Once the crisis was over, Gloria Kassan sank onto the sofa and buried her face in her trembling hands.

By the end of the week the energetic five year old was properly placed in the San Juan Academy. Kendra and the mother were elated. David was exhausted and felt it was just as well.

VII   KNOWLEDGE

DAVID managed a semblance of private time with Kendra in spite of the hovering security guards. Being followed took some getting used to. He adjusted by ignoring their existence whenever possible and setting boundaries when it wasn't. While his safety was their business and concern, he was quick to insist that it was their only concern. Captain Stan Jonez complied and was careful to station his men as unobtrusively as possible. By the time they arrived back at headquarters, David appreciated the Captain's efficiency and his congenial nature.

Malchor had spent the week with Cyrus and Arion in Brussels, Belgium, hosting the annual United Governance Conference. On impulse the Tribunal decided to extend their visit an extra two days and ski Glacier des Diableret. Even though David was anxious to report to his boss, he welcomed the weekend to himself. The temple had become his own private place of solitude. In that solitude, he reaffirmed his faith, knelt at the bronze altar and centered on himself. The lone staff priest, moved by the young man's sincerity changed his normal routine and improvised melodies on his wood flute. Kaleidoscopic light filtering through the stained glass panels appeared to sway to the hypnotic music. Obedient to his duty to Synthesis, Facilitator David Winston confessed his passion for Kendra.

Monday, Malchor returned and David left the temple early to keep an appointment with him. He had passed the maze several times a day on his way to and from the temple. It was an obsessive diversion, an unsolved mystery. Back and forth, he walked around the perimeter, then inside from one dead end to another, unable to reach the center. Mal had walked in one side, to the center, then out, apparently unstopped by dead ends. David's efforts had brought nothing. Determined, he reentered the hedged maze and walked to the first turn on the uneven stone pathway.

HEAT soaked into his muscles, dissolving the stress of dreary winter months. *Interludes in Unity* floated from the Barbados Centra Resort sound system and blended pleasantly with the surf. Greg Foster could feel the gentle warmth of Mother Earth's fine sand beneath his beach towel, renewing his energy, stilling his thoughts.

Reana rolled onto her side, resting her head on her arm. He wasn't asleep; she could tell by his uneven breathing. There was a flicker of a smile on his bronzed face. Not a freckle in sight, here he was with red hair and a skin tone to envy, while her own arms were covered with an army of tiny melanin spots. *Who knows what our children will look like. Children.* She closed her eyes and pictured a red-haired infant with her freckles, energetically waving his arms.

It was good to have Greg back to normal. Pressure had been mounting, especially since David's visit. That Sunday afternoon Greg had insisted on playing the T.V. too loudly and had snapped at her when she asked why David left without saying goodbye. Throughout lunch, he had stared glumly from the screen to the untouched place setting. Crabcakes she had labored over stuck in her throat. Upset, she got up, noisily removed the blue china plate and service, left her own food and went for a walk.

For the next few weeks, every time David or Kendra came up in conversation, tension resurfaced until one night in the laundry room when Reana blew up. She dumped the clean laundry basket at his feet and demanded to know what happened. The scene seemed funny now. No wonder Greg had stepped backwards and knocked the detergent over. But she stood her ground like a grizzly bear until he opened up. After all that drama, he just stared at her when she laughed, first at his theory, then at David's overreaction. At least they were talking again. And her husband's refusal to forget the whole thing was easier to live with than silence, so she resigned herself to an extra meditation session whenever he was testy. Life was much more pleasant when he worked with her, and they worked together in unity. And that's what this trip had done. It brought them together again and things were as they should be.

Reana removed her sunglasses, leaned closer and tapped the tip of his chin.

"Ready for more sunscreen?" she whispered.

"Mm huh." Greg sighed, opening one eye, then the other. "Hmm, you rub my back, then I grab you and tickle . . ."

Screeching, she rolled out of reach, onto the sand and scrambled to her feet. Instantly, he took up the chase and they raced barefoot along the beach, veering into the salt spray. He caught her by the bare waist, swung her around and around until she collapsed, laughing, against his chest. Holding her, he stroked her glistening hair, and confided his love. As the first star flickered its light, Greg swung her up into his arms and carried her into the azure-blue Caribbean waters.

From the veranda, two psychiatrists clad in colorful native shorts nodded in satisfaction. This was the best remedy. Hegie was right in sending the couple on a belated honeymoon. Another week of therapy and Foster would be completely healed. Already during morning and afternoon sessions the massage therapist had worked her magic. Skillfully, her hands released the toxic residue, freeing the negative energy from Greg's body while her voice soothed his mental concerns, bringing him back to his center, back to Synthesis. Subtle testing showed he no longer remembered the distasteful Brockston Andel suicide. To guarantee against setbacks, the doctors agreed to recommend a housekeeper for six months. That accomplished, they diverted their attention to other guests.

"NO, CYRUS," Malchor argued, "I saw it, too. He solved

the secret of the maze. So what! He's not ready yet." Shared power was beginning to irritate Malchor. "You remember what happened last time I let you talk me into an initiation. Timing is key," he added, "and I'm sure you'll be rewarded for your patience."

"Just this morning," Cyrus bragged, dropping the subject at the allusion to Andel, "another recalcitrant church joined the Cosmic Spirit Council."

"No doubt they're eager to further the scope of unity," Malchor chided.

"Or desperate to save their tax exempt status," Arion corrected.

"Since when does it really matter?" Cyrus continued, oblivious to the sarcasm. "Most of the heretics have been infiltrated and it's just a matter of time now. Did you hear the morning news about that Faith Fellowship scandal? We got them for practicing medicine. Healings, ha!" Cyrus laughed. "More snake oil, please."

Crass emotionalism, Malchor thought, noticing that Cyrus was showing his age, indulging himself too much. Hours spent in darkened temples had left him with a paleness that didn't compliment his mousy gray hair, and his performance on the Swiss ski slopes had proved embarrassing to all three of them. He couldn't keep up. At least he had the sense to start an exercise program. Malchor nodded absently; he needed this coalition, at least until the consolidation was complete.

"I heard good news this morning, too," Arion announced. "The trial Autonomous voting system is working exceptionally well in Los Angeles, California. We're weeding out the problems. Voters used their system for polling responses during the last elections. When they adopt their new State Constitution they'll be able to vote for or against legislation by pushing the Y or N using the remote control or keyboard. With good press, they will be clamoring for complete Autonomy by September."

Arion was the only man in the world that Malchor considered an equal; even Hegie didn't hold the same place. Most of the minute quota of respect he felt for others was directed toward this man. "How's the Legislature reacting?" he asked.

"It's beautiful, just beautiful. They know what's next. Most of them hate it, but will support the new Constitution in exchange for permanent jobs. The hold outs are thrashing about, mad men drowning in a sea of change. The press is circling, ready for another feeding frenzy. I'll throw in some raw meat." Arion loved the way a well-crafted press release could sway the public. He was already forming the next lead. *No more dirty politics. No more shabby, self-indulging, representative government. Autonomy for a strong America.*

"Don't underestimate your opposition, Arion. What are you going to do with Senator Bradly Newton?" Malchor said, anxious for speedy success. "Things are going too smoothly to let some little detail botch up the works."

Before the World Fund Director could answer, the library doors opened and Server guided David into the room. The Tribunal was seated in front of the fireplace. Four overstuffed reading chairs faced a square coffee table, laden with fruit and pastries.

The men turned, silent and expressionless, observing his approach. David felt naked and cold, a lab specimen being probed with laser scalpels. He focused on Malchor until he was accepted by a wave of his fastidiously manicured hand.

"And here he is, the bearer of my good news, gentlemen." Malchor's mouth spread into a receptive smile. "This morning David reported the success of educational compliance. Consolidation is complete and we are moving into phase three, rapid expansion. This means that Dialectic Materialism has come of age. The thesis has finally merged with the antithesis and is birthing true Synthesis in the dawning of this new century. You know," he bragged, "if I hadn't been willing to study the data and see the truth about the Plan's failings, we would still be using dictatorial methods and inviting defeat. We have just one last hurdle: small town superstition stuck in the throes of illiteracy. But now, with Winston's popularity, those districts still hobbled by the old paradigm will soon be transformed."

David stood at attention between Malchor and Arion, facing the stone fireplace, until Malchor invited him to sit down. Server immediately poured him coffee, poured for the others and began serving sandwiches. David felt dwarfed by the leather chair, swallowed up by the presence of power. He looked up when Cyrus, seated across from him, offered him a pastry from the silver tray. David thanked him and slid a crusty bearclaw onto his plate. He didn't expect to be comfortable around these men. It was a given. He was an outsider, standing with his face against the glass, looking at the inner circle, eager for any crumb of recognition.

"So, David, how long will the process take?" Malchor inquired.

"Your estimate was correct, sir. All Academies, schools and training centers will be in compliance within the year. Then . . ."

"We saw that you mastered the maze," Cyrus interrupted. "I am especially pleased with your interest in the spirit dimension. Tell me David, what pattern did you find?"

Immediately, David's practiced presentation dissolved from his mind and he felt pulled, drawn toward the center of the man's hazel spheres. "Not to be bound by the rock path, sir, or the illusion of solidity. When there was no path, I found one on my knees. Where I could see the absence of root and trunk and then step through the branches, all the way to the center circle."

"What did you see in the center?" Cyrus put his plate down and fingered the ruby grapes in his left hand, jealous of David's flawless skin and clear eyes.

"A red crystal Blazing Star, symbol of Omniscience, was centered on a sundial bordered by astrological engravings." This open approval from Cyrus made David eager to continue. "The Serpent of Knowledge entwined the supporting base. The symbols summarized the past, the present and the future."

"And what did the symbols . . ."

"Very good." Malchor interrupted quietly, touching David's arm, getting his attention. Cyrus' interference was intolerable.

"I am proud of your progress," he said, emphasizing the I. "Now, Facilitator Winston, share briefly with the Tribunal what you told me this morning."

Server cleared the plates and refilled cups while David finished his report. Once out of the limelight, he settled into his chair, waiting to hear Arion elaborate on his plans for Autonomous voting.

"I'll review this for your benefit, David," Arion said. "This is like accounting. To our advantage, it's complex enough for the average citizen's eyes to glaze over during the debates. In California, the first step is winning Initiative 1776 in the general election. There was some flack about the Governor's Executive Order calling for a tax increase. That expected outrage was ridiculed and ignored by our media. Initiative 1776 requires the Secretary of State to provide each voter with an Autonomous voter's code for use in elections. Voters will input their code and vote at home or work or where ever they choose. Autonomy chips are already located in new computers and televisions. The results of their vote will be collected and recorded by the Secretary of State. Basically, this will replace the voting booth and the mail-in ballot.

"Step two calls for the adoption of a constitutional amendment replacing the elected legislature with a Governor appointed ten member Board of Legislation. This will establish Autonomy for all voters, meaning residents with a minimum age of eighteen. Voters will vote directly on the Board's recommendations. The Board will review laws, propose changes and new laws as needed. Residents who wish to propose changes would fax or e-mail their suggestions to the Board. Autonomy offers true democracy with one person one vote.

"California is the beginning. Once Autonomy is established there it will quickly spread to all states. Then the national plan will slide into place. I'll explain that later."

In California, David had experienced the news first hand. Throughout the state, students picketed for the right to Autonomy. The first Monday he was there, Academy classes were canceled for the afternoon so everyone could participate. People marched down the center of Interstate 5 for three hours, carrying banners, passing out flyers and spring flowers. Commuters stopped their cars to join picketers and in every city, from San Diego to Redding, the freeways stood still. Within a week, enough people had signed the Autonomy Initiative to place it on the November ballot.

And here was the man who had planned it telling the details of the campaign, the man who held the monetary power of the world in his hands. David viewed Arion as a true Viking and New Age conqueror who commanded authority without effort. A half century had etched its lines on his face, strengthening his features.

Picturing the California scene added to David's respect for him. Compelling ads, polls, phone banks, television spots and flyers were undeniably effective. The kindling of money and people sparked the spontaneous combustion of an idea that had found its time in history. Arion generously conceded credit to his partners when Malchor reminded him about rally bulletins sent to temples and schools. But David knew it would have happened as easily without the bulletins.

David was struck with the fervor of the people who bought the idea. They clamored for Autonomy, demanding the new Constitution and their right to freedom from representative government. Their faces flashed through his mind. The week's events were carefully planned and carried out on schedule. In Sacramento, he had seen Governor Karn yank a sign from a woman, then run to the front of the people's march, waving the sign with enthusiasm, a new convert. It amazed David that all the people believed it was their idea, their choice. Even those who should have known—Dr. Kenner and the Impartationists—believed it. A sense of raw power gripped David. With the proper conditioning the people would choose what was best for the world. Choice was the key. Played up as individual sovereignty, choice was the real strength of the Tribunal's plan.

FIERY streaks of light silhouetted the temple, sending shadowy fingers across the desk and along the library walls. The striking beauty didn't stir David. He was disappointed. Cyrus had wanted him to attend temple with the Tribunal, yet Malchor had ignored the suggestion and asked him to sort conference reports. Finished, he filed the insignificant job before the men left the building.

The brilliant hues softened and the sun sank lower on the horizon. He pushed away from the desk and went to the window. Outside looking in or inside looking out, it was the same thing. Imagining melodious strains from the wood flute, David stood in the darkening room meditating. He didn't hear anything; instead, he felt a presence. Someone moved toward him. When he turned, Server stood beside him. The scar imprinted hand pointed toward the temple, then to him. A look of intense sadness creased the old man's face and he shook his head somberly. "What?" David shuddered. "Wait." But Server was gone.

"LOOK, Jake, I know it's . . ." Steve reconsidered what he was about to ask, then forged ahead. "You've worked here at the ranch since David was born, so I expect you know more about our situation than anybody else." Jake didn't look up from stirring the paint. His weathered Native-American profile mapped out years of exposure to the whims of nature. Steve picked up two extension rods and screwed them together, then started attaching the roller on the end.

"That's all right, sir. I'll do that." Jake stood and reached toward the roller.

When he finished, Steve Winston handed it over, but held the man's attention. "Jake, I know we've never talked about what's going on here."

"No sir, what's going on in the main house is none of my business." He shifted uncomfortably, stuck the stir stick back in the can and swirled it around.

"I appreciate that. But I know Jenna's fairly close to Fran."

"I wouldn't deny it, sir."

"I expect Fran's talked to you about—about us."

Clearly unnerved, the older man stood up. His dark eyes searched Steve's determined face. "Sir, in my sixty-two years I've never come to understand the talk of women. I understand Mother Nature herself much better."

"Fran has repeated Jenna's words to you, hasn't she?"

"I pay no attention."

"Look Jake, I need you to remember. I want you to remember."

"Sir, I try to do my job. This ranch is my life. I don't pay attention to what's other people's business."

"I respect that, Jake. But I see you with Fran. You've got what Jenna and I used to have. I need to see what I did. I need to know, really know," Steve struggled for the words to continue, "why she hates me. I know that you know."

"Sometimes what a man says he wants isn't what he's ready to hear."

Through clenched teeth, Steve argued, "Try me."

"Please, sir, could I think on it awhile?"

Steve fought the urge to threaten Jake with his job, to force him to talk. Instead, he forced himself to drop it and nodded consent. "I won't be back for several months."

SNOW flurries whipped around David, covered his boot tracks and slowed his progress. He pulled his wool scarf up to cover his chin and trudged along the block wall that surrounded the headquarters. For now, he preferred the four-mile walk and facing the elements to exercising in the gym. The prospect of running into Frank was too great. The public relations king was still trying vainly to arrange a meeting for himself with the Tribunal. He had never gotten over David's meeting with them in his place. Consequently, when he had to work with the Facilitator, the look of petty annoyance on his puffy face was classic. David laughed aloud realizing Higgs wouldn't pass muster in any one of the four profile areas.

Carrying Malchor's briefcase to Brussels had spurred the little bureaucrat to new depths of annoyance. After the trip he tried to entrap David into saying something against the Tribunal. The thought of Frank's flaws germinated as David walked behind the temple building; a profile on Mr. F. R. Higgs would be interesting and entertaining. Energized, he stepped up his pace and jogged between the landing strip and the denuded birch grove. Above the inner wall he could see the tips of more spindly branches that spread for another ten acres. Where he walked the buildings were walled in like a fortress. David hadn't had time to follow the riding trails that laced the rest of the property. He would save that adventure to share with Kendra.

BACK in his office, David adjusted the reception of his office Vis Com. Static threatened, then blurred the screen, evidence of the angry winter storm raging along the eastern coastline. Pushing his keyboard aside, he leaned closer to the screen, wanting to touch her face, relieved when the screen cleared.

"Did you see how Stan looked at you when you hesitated to call Max off?" she said, her laughter joining his with vacation memories shared.

Calling her at a reasonable hour made all the difference. He could see her and hear her laugh, neither of which happened if he woke her. "The guards were laying a wager to see who could hog tie the poor mutt," he added. "I heard them in the barn. They about died when I walked in and acted offended."

"Max flat out hated them. It was a good thing. If he hadn't been so protective of you, they would have followed our every conversation."

"Any fallout from the Kassan affair?" David asked.

"The processor was fired. She wasn't qualified. Now they have to check all her cases. I sent a memo to Personnel to tighten hiring guidelines. What have you been up to?"

"Just doing my job. Except for last night, I met President Chamberlon. Malchor was invited to dinner at the White House and he took me as his guest. They sat at the other end of the table and the President was so intense about whatever Malchor was saying that he barely spoke to anyone else. The place is impressive, filled with history, like a museum with art works and furniture from the past. No wonder it attracts so many tourists. We'll go together sometime."

"I'd like that."

"You'd really like the dining room. I sat on a chair from the late 19th century, ate off President Ford's china and eavesdropped on Ambassador Eckert's conversation. I'm afraid the women I sat between didn't hear anything interesting from me."

"Oh, who were they?"

"I don't even remember. Not very alert, huh."

"I'm sure they adored you. What country is Eckert from?"

"France."

"It's not like you to eavesdrop."

"Oh, he mentioned the Academy. You know, they're replicating our program throughout the European Federation. Malchor would rather I took care of the details. I should be ready to fly over this spring. Meanwhile, my conference presentation's on laser disk for their superintendents. It was interesting to hear about it from an observer, or at least to hear parts of it, the parts that aren't classified. I tried to meet with him, but he left right after dinner."

"Europe in the spring—sounds inviting." Kendra hesitated. "Do you mind if I ask you a technical question? Then I won't have to call Hegie."

"No problem."

"What do you think about the policy of strict genetic selectivity?"

"It's one of the basics. Of course I support it."

"Well, I support it too. The problem is how strict is strict enough."

"That's clearly spelled out in your manual. What are you questioning?"

"No, David, I'm not questioning policy. I just wonder about the judgment calls."

"Example?"

A look at the clock showed her that time was running short; she would be lucky to get a breakfast drink. "You know," she said hurriedly, "the ad campaign for the Academy encouraged people to submit applications for their children. The regs say no child will be admitted whose parent shows any degree of depression. Well, what about drug induced depression, say, resulting from an injury treated with pain killers."

"I see your point. You would have to rule out any possibility of hereditary linkage. Also, you need to look at the injury. Did the person do something to bring on the injury? There are accidents that happen because of carelessness, poor perception or stupidity. Any weakness would affect the fitness of the progeny."

"Speaking of weaknesses, David, we're sending out too many rejection notices and the largest number of rejections have come from the newspaper ads." Kendra knew they would be a problem from the first edition. Special inserts, proclaiming the merits of the Academy system, ran in the Sunday editions for a month. Her office was swamped with applications, some were barely readable. "I haven't had a problem with the subscribers from the professional magazines, but the newspaper ads are creating a bottleneck."

"I've heard similar complaints from other regions. I'm going to pull the ad."

"Good."

"I'll recommend we run inclusive ads, building up the importance of the different levels, tracks and training programs."

"That will help. Back to my original question, would you agree to the admittance of a gifted child if the injured parent's problem resulted from a natural accident?"

"If the interview and tests show the child isn't emotionally affected by the incident, yes."

"I was hoping you'd say that."

"But remember the goal; no inferior species can be allowed to contaminate the Academy's genetic pool. Who's the child?"

"Sorry, David, tell you later. I have to run."

"Bye," David offered, watching her face fade from the screen.

Genetic Inferiority! How could I forget? He could hardly wait to access the little weasel's file. Feverishly, he entered the main program and retrieved the personnel information.

Franklin Raynard Higgs' name was typed in and David clicked on the search space. As he suspected there was no profile. He pulled up the familiar grid and began transferring the raw data. It didn't take long to see the gaps. Higgs was five-feet-eleven inches with brown hair and eyes, but that's where normal stopped. He suffered curvature of the spine, high blood pressure, overweight, capped teeth, IQ of 105, parental maladaptation and genetic inferiority. The man was a reject in all four areas. Inspired, David ran a print-out, exited the system and delivered the copy. Later, when he heard shrill oaths pouring from the other office, he lost five minutes, laughing, imagining the scene.

Frank never mentioned the report that greeted him when he returned from lunch. Livid, he shredded the pages and erased the report from the computer. Higgs knew he would have to be careful, very careful. The games were over.

"SYNTHESIS is greater than the sum of its parts," Malchor said quietly, studying David, weighing the signs: mentally alert, stable, loyal, strong enough. "Just as the Tribunal is greater than its members," he continued. "Be patient David, there are stages for you to grow through. Not all people have reached the place where you stand, as you have not yet reached the place where I stand. Perhaps you're ready for . . . Yes. You would benefit from reading some of the ancient writings."

Malchor pulled the book ladder to the center of the library's north wall. The three volumes he removed from the top shelf left a gaping hole. He climbed down and returned to the fireplace reading area. "I was a bit older than you when I read these. However, I didn't attend or have the benefit of the Academy," he said, placing the embossed leather books on the coffee table and taking his place in the opposite chair. "I'm sure I needn't remind you to never remove any of the volumes from this room."

"Yes, sir," David nodded, not venturing to reach for the books.

"As you finish, return them to the shelf." Mal paused, a flicker of concern registering in his dark eyes. "There is great risk in moving too quickly."

Server attended their needs, as he did each time Malchor called David in for a lesson. Like a master builder, he laid the foundation, explaining the progression of souls and the honor due more evolved beings. Reliving his personal journey, he shared his personal quest from the western halls of learning to the temples of Tibet.

The doorway to master consciousness was opening, welcoming David, and the young pioneer was eager to enter. "Sir, I am willing to do anything I need to do," David vowed, an unfamiliar urgency pressing him onward, "anything you would require, or any higher order being would require. I resolve to know all knowledge and all mystery."

"Then you will." Malchor patted the volumes affectionately and pushed them closer to his spiritual child's extended hand.

THE office reflected its owner, from the ornate, overstated desk and chair to the enlarged photographs of Higgs shaking hands with the nation's most obnoxious politicians. The one with the notoriously arrogant Speaker of the House was classic. Frank was presenting him with a commendation from Malchor; their equally vacuous expressions grinned from the frame.

Winston took a small pleasure in turning his back on Frank during their tedious meetings. He kept his voice evenly moderated, without breaking his thought or his flow of words, while feigning intense interest in Frank's knick-knacks. "Yes, I pulled the ads," he said, "and I didn't expect to have to pull them a second time. They will remain pulled. It is unfortunate you didn't consider the effect they would have on the general population. The Selectivity Centers have been inundated with requests from inferior specimens, all fully expecting their children to be accepted into the Academy. Whatever were you thinking?" Winston turned abruptly, catching the look of abject hatred.

Frank averted the challenge and looked down at the memo on his desk. "I was told to promote the Academy and that's what I did."

"Malchor was not happy to see a copy of the ad in his Sunday morning paper after I had it pulled."

At the mention of his boss, Frank paled.

"Mal's friends in industry want a skilled and compliant workforce. Last Tuesday, I asked for ads promoting level-two. Are they finished?"

"Yes," he muttered, opening the presentation folder.

Winston felt a flicker of pity for the fool. The ads were ready and they were excellent.

BY DAY, he diligently oversaw the progress of the Academies. By night, during every spare moment, Winston studied the intriguing mythologies. Gods of the ancient worlds swirled before him. The exoteric converged with the esoteric. All paths led him to the Vedantic truth of his eternal soul, evolving toward merger with the godhead. He either fasted or took his evening meals in the library, consumed by his search for truth. As he returned the books, he pulled new volumes down, eating fully from the Tree of Knowledge. When Malchor was called to Rome, Winston wandered the grounds, studied and prepared for his spring tour of the Academies.

THE office staff had left two hours earlier. Greg Foster was stuck again, with a contract deadline looming ahead and the rest of the team gone. They would be quick to claim credit when the deal closed. C.A.M. was merging with the European Motor Works under the trade name AMEURO Motor Works. He ran a spell and grammar check of the document a last time. The question of slave labor had been refuted by Fereno, yet there was an aura of musty dankness about the man. An instinctive distrust surfaced in Greg whenever he worked on the contract; Fereno had to be a front man. His talk was as smooth as his tailored silk suits, yet it was obvious he didn't have the smarts to run a company. Greg cleared with Diversity, then dialed the agent.

"Universal Airlines. Jamison speaking. How may I help you?"

"Book me on tomorrow's 9:20 a.m. business flight to Chicago, round trip, return flight around 6:00 p.m." *Why send a law clerk? It wouldn't be unusual for a junior partner to hand carry papers to Chicago.*

"I'm ready for your debit card number, sir."

He pressed nine digits and waited. *A deal this big, joining the two largest auto manufacturers in the world, calls for special treatment.*

"Thank you, Mr. Foster. Your reservations are confirmed. Universal Airlines flight 26 departs BWI gate four at 9:20 a.m. Return flight 79, departs from Chicago International at 6:15 p.m. Please arrive at the gate at least thirty minutes prior to departure."

"Thank you, ma'am," he said, hanging up.

With luck, he could make it home before Reana and have her bath water drawn. He took a single long-stemmed scarlet rose from the reception desk and headed home.

VIII   SPRING TOUR

NO FANFARE, only the cover of night to greet them. As ordered, the tower operator kept radio silence while Facilitator David Winston brought the Aerojet in and headed for the hangar. Guards quietly checked the area. It was his first unannounced arrival and set in motion the new policy to keep dissidents at bay and superintendents in top form. Light was only beginning to touch the South Dakota horizon when Winston and his men made their way from the terminal to the guest rooms.

North-central Academy, just east of Rapid City, was waking up and hummed with the methodic rhythm of a Black Hills prospector searching for gold. No hectic humanity to block out with stone walls. Instead, miles of open rolling hills surrounded the oasis of learning. Six massive domes, concrete and plexiglass, encircled an open space with the temple planted in the middle. A thirty-three foot, quarried marble monolith rose from the peak of the temple pyramid. The domes were joined above ground by arched passageways and underground by a system of tunnels leading to the temple. From the air, Winston noted with approval that the facility envisaged the all-seeing eye, shining its light on the surrounding void. Workers were now in the final phase, completing a series of small dome dwellings on the perimeter of the Academy. The place was self-contained and the low-level classes were filled to capacity. Construction of the facility had proven so cost effective that Winston ordered builders to follow the same model for future open-space sites.

Most residents were still getting dressed when Winston found

Superintendent Norman Lathrup in the library engaged in a mind-bending discussion about Emotional Integrity with a small group of students. Lathrup gave him a hearty welcome and introduced him to the four men and three women seated at the table. It was one of Winston's favorite subjects so he pulled up a chair and joined the debate. "Certainly Freud had his problems, Dr. Lathrup, but for his time in history it was extraordinary how he was able to expand the thinking of his peers, helping free the repressed conscience of the day by the very argument of his First Force Theory. Of course, we are indebted to Jung for bringing in the spiritual dimension that we embrace to this day."

"I was intending no disrespect for either Freud or Jung regarding their foundational accomplishments," Lathrup agreed, with a benevolent nod. "I could only hope to have as much impact on society. However, learning continues to evolve. During my early Harvard days, Skinner's behaviorism had not yet passed from vogue. Some of my professors spent endless hours in the laboratory making dogs salivate on command. We used to pretend we were interested in their latest experiments with mice and mazes so we could avoid the endless animal dissections in the lab."

Superintendent Lathrup was animated and respected for his openness. The review fascinated Winston and he listened intently, hands clasped. Hearing about the old systems from someone who had seen the changes first-hand gave concrete meaning to the textbook version.

"Freud's bleak determinism was totally rejected," Lathrup expounded, "and Skinner's Second Force psychology of behavioral conditioning was being replaced by Humanistic Psychology. That, of course, has evolved into our Fourth Force transpersonal views. Now, we are bringing the world to a state of higher consciousness. As I was a part of the transition from the Second to the Third Force, you are a part of the transition from the Fourth Force to what I have long visualized and planned for—Synthesis."

They nodded in agreement; even Winston had shifted into

the roll of student. Initially, Lathrup had opposed the role of Facilitator going to an inexperienced graduate. Debates with Malchor and later with Hegelthor, had been pointless and endangered his own standing. When he saw the fervor the clear-eyed youth brought to the job and the acceptance of the students, he conceded his error. David embodied Synthesis in a way that none of the old guard did or could.

"Sandre's thesis is titled *Influences of Psychology on Public Education*," Lathrup said. "Her first draft is finished."

Her short-cropped blond hair shone with good health. Smiling broadly, she blinked at the Facilitator seated across the table from her. "Would you like to read it?" she asked. "I would so appreciate your comments, sir." Her blue eyes probed him for a positive response.

It was disconcerting. Winston usually made a point of limiting eye contact with over-eager female students. The younger ones were all right; they were looking forward to years of schooling. But he was fair game for these sweet things. Eligible for unity. The main Mr. Eligible for too many. He caught Lathrup's attention and was relieved when the man sensed his dilemma and intervened.

"Now, now, Sandre, our Youth Facilitator has the responsibility of all academia on his shoulders."

"I'm sure you've done a splendid job; perhaps I could read the review when it's completed," David offered, regretting it when her look again turned into a close encounter. In spite of the rules, he was drawn to her open adoration of him. *Trib*, he thought, knowing life would be easier if he was united with Kendra. *Yes, Kendra*, he reminded himself. The rest of the session he avoided looking at Sandre, even when she spoke.

The incident sparked his memory of something he had brushed aside earlier in the week. At the Harvard Academy, he saw the same adoration in the eyes of a child. The twelve-year-old girl stood near the window in Superintendent Werling's office. When he walked in unannounced, Werling looked at her, then at him, with controlled blankness. What was it he said when he

103

dismissed her? Something about seeing her later. It was her look of longing, her eagerness to please Werling, that nagged him.

Lathrup's students were ready to leave for breakfast. Winston stood, shook hands with the group members and headed toward the exit. "Norm," he said, "How is your lovely wife, Janet? I'm ready for another game of chess."

"She's doing well, thank you," he said, remembering their recent debate. "She's got a sixth sense or something. The board's set up in the living room. I expected you later in the month, but she insisted you were coming out this week. Oh, you may have heard, our daughter Melinda's graduating from the San Juan Academy this year. She'll be assigned here as Social Science Director."

"I understand she's marrying one of your professors. Congratulations." The older man steered the way and Winston could see Hegelthor in the way Lathrup responded to the students, making encouraging comments as they navigated the crowded corridor leading to the administrative offices. "Oh, and thanks for rescuing me. I didn't want to disappoint her."

"You mean Sandre?"

"Yes."

"She's definitely looking for Mr. Right. I think we'll have to arrange some activities with the South-central upperclassmen."

"Sounds good," Winston agreed. "We want well-matched couples."

TRAFFIC snaked along, slowing for toll booths. Greg Foster retrieved seven quarters from his pocket and threw them into the yawning receptacle. Coins clanged while he drove past, wheel in one hand, map in the other, squinting at the fine print. Road construction had cost him an hour already. "What a miserable freeway," he muttered, noting that the next off-ramp would lead him to the main gate of Chicago Auto Manufacturing. His heart continued racing when he slowed the car and pulled closer to the gate. With sullen efficiency the guard took his name and directed him toward visitor parking. He made it inside at least. Doubts pulled him toward the exit; stubbornness pushed him forward.

Before he stepped from his rental car, the security escort pulled up alongside. Clearly, the place was run like a top-secret facility and he didn't have a clearance. Two burly men motioned for him to climb into the back seat of their jeep. Not a word was offered. They walked him through the reception area, scanned him, handed him a badge with his name printed in bold black type, then guided him through a labyrinth of corridors to President Fereno's office. Security was so tight, Greg couldn't catch a glimpse of the manufacturing area. When George Fereno invited him in, the guards took up a military stance outside the door.

"It's good to see you. You've brought the contract?" Fereno asked, taking his seat behind the chrome desk.

Draperies covered the eastern wall of the expansive office. Greg stood holding his briefcase in both hands, the AMEURO contract inside. "Yes, Mr. Fereno. There are two sections which need updated figures. Anytime today would be fine. Bringing CAM and European Motorworks together is an unusually large merger, so I need to verify your manufacturing assets for our banker."

Fereno's smile faded and he picked up his phone. "I'll schedule your tour for this afternoon after lunch," he said.

"No, sir. I've already had lunch. I'm ready to tour now."

Foster's insistence dared to be stopped. Fereno raised his eyebrow with a bemused smirk and redialed the phone. "This is Fereno." During the pause he rubbed his chin with the end of the receiver, pondering the situation. This young fool played like one of the big boys, staring with unblinking hazel eyes into the face of his own mortality. Fereno didn't believe the gibberish about new-men or god-men. Men were men. The weak ones died. Only the strong ones survived. He was a survivor and this kid could only hope to pressure him. The smirk twisted into a smile as he spoke. "Yes, it was. We have a guest who wishes to tour the facility." He nodded. "Yes, the main assembly line first." Again he nodded, then frowned. "Yes."

Greg rested his briefcase on the edge of the desk, noting that whoever was on the other end of the line was over Fereno. That wasn't his business anyway; hidden ownership was no problem for the law firm or the banker. Solid assets were the main thing— solid assets and the reputation of the company. The labor issue that prompted his visit was important only to him. The room held no visible clues. So far, he was safely relegated to hallways and these silent walls. He heard a muffled whistle and checked his watch, 12:13 p.m. It could be a lunch signal, except he heard the same sound when he first walked in the room. George followed his look to the draped wall and hung up the phone.

"Our tour guide will be here any minute. I'm sure you will find everything to your satisfaction. Yes, you're right," he added, pressing a button on his desk monitor, "the office does overlook the assembly line."

The drapes opened and light burst into the room from the narrow skylight that extended the length of the building. Greg inspected the plant below. Men and women worked at their stations with a series of steps ordered to complete their section before the slow-moving conveyer belt moved it beyond their reach. These steps were repeated every three minutes. *Trib*, he thought, *how maddening, no talk , no view, nothing but this wire here, that one there all day, every day. This monotony continued to the noisy drum of automated machines assembling frames along another slow-moving belt.*

"Ever been inside a plant?" Fereno asked.

"Excuse me?"

"Have you ever toured an auto manufacturing plant?"

"No, I haven't." So how should he know what to look for? He knew why George smiled benevolently over that disclosure. What could a lawyer expect to recognize in a field so far removed from his own? But the level of security was proof enough that something was different about the place. Manufacturing plants usually had moderate security. That, he did know. He had made the trip; all he could do now was look around and make some calls. Pretense wasn't one of his talents; befriending Fereno wouldn't be easy.

Greg set his briefcase on the floor and stepped closer to confide, "You know, that's one of the reasons I came here, George. Cars are sort of a hobby for me. My dad owned a repair shop when I was a kid." There was some truth to it. He had watched his dad fix the family car and as a teenager helped with an oil change and other minor repairs. "I really appreciate your setting this up for me." Again Fereno's left eyebrow shot up, accenting the angular jawline that dominated his slender face.

Maybe he had assumed the worst about his visitor. Still, meticulous attention to security was why he was alive. He studied the young man. Being a good judge of people had saved his hide countless times. Maybe the kid was naive. Maybe not. "Well, Foster, you can see the whole works today. You'll start at the main assembly area and end up in the design department. We have some prototypes you can see. Of course we expect you to hold what you learn in strict confidence."

"Certainly. As your legal counsel, I'm bound by the ethics of my profession."

Ethics, bound by ethics. Fereno repressed a sneer.

STEADY snoring filtered from the adjoining room; the guests had exhausted their welcome and left. His boss was sound asleep. Server slipped from under the covers and followed the narrow ray of light toward the window. He pushed the heavy tapestry aside and peered down twelve stories to the ancient Roman streets. Vatican City illuminated the skyline; the Festival of Nation's was well underway. Elitists from around the globe were there networking and securing their positions. But it was Malchor's visit to the papal hierarchy that stirred Server's memory. Decades earlier, eager idealism drove the young Mal to embrace the Church, and the same idealism later set him searching for deeper mysteries. What was the benefit?

Malchor knew the hidden mysteries.

The knowledge fed his pride.

What was the point?

Power?

Yes, that was it. Not some idyllic utopia, conceived in the minds of gods. Power, conceived in the heart of man.

"The heart of man is . . ."

His eyes followed the lone truck snaking along the street. The road he traveled serving Malchor troubled him. What was the point if mankind couldn't become better. What was it about the heart of man? James released the drape. The weariness in his soul matched his hope for the future.

STEVE Winston pulled the copy from the wire service. It was no surprise. If California wanted it, either Oregon or Washington would be next, and from there the rest of the nation would follow. Autonomous Voting for all. The bellwether states lead again. The castrated ram would lead the flock to another level of semiconsciousness. He was another castrated ram—Jenna saw to that. Teeth clenched, he typed feverishly, preparing the big scoop for evening newscasters. They would play this one big on all the stations, with a little twist for *Channel One:* an in-depth review of the political scandals of those beacons of morality, the legislature. The public believed a candidate's private life didn't matter, until his private fingers reached into their pocketbooks. Meanwhile, lawmakers were sucking the system, like swamp leeches. Empire building was the political creed and greed. He knew the voters would love Autonomy. They wouldn't miss representation. Steve stifled the thought that he would. He stared at the monitor screen, ignoring the hectic media-center scene around him. He would very much miss representative government, the way it was supposed to be, anyway. He dared the thought—*What price, peace?*

FACILITATOR David Winston moved covertly past the multicolored primroses that lined the walk at the superintendent's private residence. He circled to the back. Outdoor lights cast eerie figures across his path as he groped his way around the patio chairs. He had expected to watch from a distance, checking out Werling's habits until he was satisfied there was no problem. His morning call to the dorm matron changed that plan. She reported that Pamela Bardon was summoned to Werling's office, then sent home for a family emergency. A quick check of her file showed Winston nothing. Her diversity readout confirmed his growing fear. Her appointment with Werling was the last entry, and they were seen walking to Werling's house. No one saw her leave. Shaking with fatigue and anger, Winston checked his watch. The guards were in place.

FRANK Higgs watched the clock. The message was ready to go. He relished thoughts of revenge and fumed over his loss of sleep. David Winston played Zorro and earned kudos, while he played messenger. He was up half the night, and Malchor wouldn't give it a thought. It wouldn't hurt for the Facilitator to lose more sleep. He punched line two.

The professional dissident, startled awake, caught it at the end of the first ring. "Yes?"

"Be ready by 8:00 a.m., Friday, code four."

"And it couldn't wait," Raven growled.

"Who are you to challenge . . ." Frank shut his mouth. This one needed a lesson, too. "Just do it," he snapped, slamming the receiver.

AT WERLING'S house, two phones rang, one in the study downstairs and one in the upstairs master bedroom. It seemed an eternity. On the fourth ring a lamp lit the bedroom and Milt answered, his voice gravelly. "Trib, it's not five o'clock yet! Who is this?"

"Werling, this is Facilitator Winston. I know it's early but Malchor has an urgent message for all Academies. You need to turn on your fax. He'll be transmitting in about one minute." From the yard below, Winston watched the shadowy figure pulling himself together. "I'll call back after you get the message."

"Yeah, sure," Milt grumbled and slammed down the phone,

sending a jolt through Winston's ear.

The phone secured in his jacket pocket, Winston waited. The hall light flashed on, then the study light. It was time to move. Stan was waiting below the deck. The guard quickly hefted him up and Winston climbed over the railing. Through the sheer drapery he saw her sitting in the superintendent's bed, staring straight at the lamp. He raised diversity to his lips and commanded, "Take him. Now!" When Winston opened the sliding door, she didn't move.

Downstairs, the fax purred to life and Milt stood transfixed, reading the personal message from Malchor. The last line spawned a string of oaths that turned to shouts when the guards burst into the room. He recognized Stan and flung his phone in a rage. When he ran toward the hall, Lance tackled him and four guards trussed him like a wild bull.

Winston heard Werling bellowing obscenities and struggling with the men. Knowing Milt's fate gave him little solace that he hadn't checked it out sooner, that he hadn't stopped the creep in time. Cautiously, he moved around the bed toward her. She rocked back and forth, moaning; her blond hair hung twisted over her delicate shoulders. He didn't want to frighten her so he hesitated. "Pamela," he whispered, "it's all right. No one's going to hurt you." She slumped, crossing her frail arms in front of her flat chest.

David Winston took the blanket, draping it over her shoulders. With a shudder, she drew the blanket protectively around herself and he carefully lifted her off the bed. She was barely ninety pounds, feather light in his arms. At the head of the stairs, he stood waiting until Milt was hauled thrashing into his office and the door closed. Then he descended, cradling her, desperate for the right words, whispering comfort and healing. "What he did was wrong," David soothed, "it wasn't your fault. He will never—ever be back. Malchor has issued the Transformation order and by this time tomorrow, Milton Werling won't exist in this realm." At this, she rested her head against his shoulder, quiet tears spilling onto the blanket. By 7:00 a.m., the victim was under medical care and the predator was on Malchor's plane headed for D.C.

Drained, David retreated to a guest room and had barely stretched out on the bed when Stan walked in and told him the latest.

"No, Stan, you did the right thing," he said, yawning. "I'll sleep tonight. I need to see this." David pulled on his wrinkled khaki slacks and shirt, snatched his jacket off the chair and hurried toward the student center. "How many are there?"

"About twenty."

"Who's the leader?" In the distance, picketers waved hand-lettered signs and chanted.

"The one with the blue ski mask."

"What's that they're saying?"

"Werling's a predator."

"Trib! What's with security here? Who leaked that?"

"None of my men, and campus security wasn't in on it. They think he had a stroke."

"When you carried him out on the stretcher, did anyone see him?"

"No, sir. He was sedated and covered with a sheet."

"Well, dig around and find out how these fools found out," David said, close enough to hear the chanting for himself. "Did the news release hit the papers?"

"Yes, and the media. Flags are half-mast over the tragedy. Did you want the memorial service for tomorrow?"

"That's fine."

"Campus security is waiting for orders. What do you want us to do about this?" Students were crowding around the dissidents, fascinated by the show. Signs bobbed up and down; WERLING HURTS KIDS, DOWN WITH SYNTHESIS, ACADEMY STIFLES FREEDOM.

"Stan, you stick with the leader," Winston directed. Then he grabbed the bull horn from Ric Hoyt, the Campus Security Chief. "I'll talk to the kids," he told Ric, "you get those dissidents."

Winston circled around the gathering crowd and ascended

the temple stairs.

"Students, cancel thoughts!" he ordered. Students turned in unison to face Youth Facilitator Winston and the skirmish in their midst faded from their collective mind. "What is Harmonious?" he shouted, kicking aside a STOP SYNTHESIS sign.

"All is harmonious in the Synthesis of life!" they answered.

"Go to class immediately," Winston commanded, manning his position on the steps until the student center was vacant. Weary, he turned and entered the temple.

IX DISSIDENTS

THE dissident leader stuffed the mask under his shirt and merged with students, attentive, obeying the Facilitator's command to leave the area. Stan Jonez followed, out of uniform, making his way toward the Grad building entrance. The dissident's goal was obvious, with a gate only thirty yards beyond the building.

Closing the gap, Stan hurried up the steps and shoved himself through the double doors, quietly excusing his roughness. Compliant students moved aside. Broad shoulders, crew cut, military bearing, he wasn't one of them. He surveyed the passages and caught a fleeting glimpse of the leader's beige shirt. Determined, Stan dodged past the stragglers and rounded the corner. The man walked briskly toward the back exit. With no students in the narrow hall to hide behind, Stan ducked into an office doorway and spoke quietly into Diversity, ordering an unmarked car. Within seconds the muted slam signaled his prey's exit. He tore from hiding, footsteps reverberating on the tile floor. At the door, he waited for the nondescript dissident to flash his ID pass at the gatekeeper, then saunter toward the car lot.

Frustration was building; he couldn't get a clear look at the guy's face. Medium build, regular features, brown hair, Trib knows what color eyes; from a distance he looked like half the young men in Boston.

At the curb, Stan flagged his assistant, Ben Harris, and threw himself into the still moving blue Ford. A tan sedan pulled from the far end of the lot. Stan and Ben wound through the city in silent pursuit.

"WHAT have you done with my children?" Paul Williams asked, turning to search the dark eyes of his amateur interrogator.

"They are well cared for."

"There's valid concern for what the state calls care. My sons were dragged, screaming, from my arms."

Facilitator David Winston broke from the man's scrutiny, shaking his head. "I'll look into the matter." He pointed to the documents spread out in front of his suspect. "You've had time to read the charges," he glanced toward the mirrored window across from the dissident, "and have been apprized of your right to remain silent." The sterile four by eight foot room echoed his harshness and proved Winston's inexperience. He stood leaning over the end of the battered metal desk. "Well?"

Paul shuffled through the pages, reviewing each of the charges. "Yes, I've read them," he answered, turning the sheets toward the Facilitator. "First, this was not a false report. My car was taken from the driveway around six o'clock this morning. I was having devotions with my wife and children when we heard the engine start. I reported it to the police by six-thirty."

"Why did you wait so long?"

"The line was busy."

"911 is never busy."

"It wasn't an emergency. I didn't use 911."

"Why did you take thirty minutes?"

"Sir, I explained that to Chief Andrews. We finished praying."

"Who finished praying?"

"My family."

"Sounds like you didn't want your car found." Winston's blunt words signaled agreement with Stan's earlier conclusion. It was a weak defense. "The second charge is trespassing to disrupt the goals of Synthesis," he snapped.

"I did not trespass," Paul responded calmly. "I was home all morning."

"Why didn't you report for work?"

"I was told to wait for an officer, so I could report the theft of my car."

"The department has no record of that order."

"But, they do have my call about the car."

"Where is your wife?"

"She went to a friend's house to borrow books."

"I listened to the police recording."

"Then you heard what the woman told me to do?"

"Negative." The man had reported a theft, but no instructions were recorded. It would have been a convincing alibi if he hadn't been seen. "You know my men followed you home. They saw you park in the driveway and hop the fence. They found the mask in your trash can. The same mask I saw you wearing while you blasphemed the state." Winston's frown deepened. "The third charge says you refused to enter your children in approved schools. Therefore, you prevented your children from developing appropriate attitudes and skills."

"We educate our children at home, in appropriate traditional academic subjects." The man sighed, lines of concern creasing his forehead. "They are advanced for their ages in the five basic areas."

"Appropriate subjects!" Winston struggled to suppress the rage that pulsated in his temples. The man was either a fool or demented. His accusation ripped through the room. "They are not prepared for Synthesis!" he yelled. Startled by his own outburst, he felt desperate to be out of the shrinking room. He reached for the knob, shouting orders toward the mirror. "I want this man in court immediately and sent to reorientation by tonight. And round up his wife Beth, or whatever her name is."

"Please, Sir. How will it benefit the state to destroy my family?" He whispered, tears streaking his ashen face. "We are innocent of wrongdoing. Do what you will with me, but please return my children to their mother."

Winston gripped the knob, unmoved by the dissident's plea, disgusted to see an adult cry.

"We've taught our children to respect the state's authority," Williams declared.

The Youth Facilitator's lips formed a thin tight line of disapproval. He gave one backward glance toward the pitiful dissident before slamming the door.

Winston waited for the psychologist to finish assessing the children. No sleep for forty-five hours. No. It was longer than that with the time change. He hadn't slept since the North-central tour. The nightmare of the flight to Boston and the apprehension of the superintendent was bad enough without this dissident problem. Pity was what he felt for Paul, once the rage subsided. If he wasn't so tired . . .

The drab room was small and dimly lit. He touched the top button on the panel. While the drapes opened, David slumped into the metal chair facing the observation room window. At least the adjoining room was suitable for children. Pictures of kittens and puppies in whimsical poses brightened the walls and in the far corner multi-sized teddy bears filled a large straw basket. A crammed bookshelf stood in the center of the wall with inviting, soft, throw pillows stacked alongside.

The children obediently completed the last of the aptitude tests. The doctor then rose from the table, gathered the papers, patted the seven-year-old on the head and left the room without a word. Once the door closed, the ten-year-old left his seat and knelt beside his little brother, stroking his hair, whispering.

David leaned forward and turned up the speaker volume.

"You'll be fine. No one's going to hurt you, Jamie. No matter what happens, you know that I love you. Mom and Dad love you, too." Tears trickled from the corners of Jamie's eyes and he nestled into Richard's arms.

Both boys looked like their dad, brown hair, just a shade lighter, brown soulful eyes, average build for their ages, straightforward genetic coding. Probably could have qualified with proper training. David checked Diversity. The dad told the truth about one thing: the boys' SAT scores were high. It was a tragic waste of resources. David checked with the Academy

116

Research Department to see if the reorientation program for young, gifted children was operational.

The older boy, Richard, sang a rhyming tune, something about family being brought together by a Father God. David bent closer to the speaker trying to grasp the words, but gave up and relaxed into the chair. There was no rush; no one was going anywhere. Richard tenderly wiped away Jamie's tears and kissed his cheek, then solemnly folded his hands and bowed his head.

HIS red trike bumped along the narrow walkway. Attached to the back, a rusting red wagon hauled two battered yellow dumptrucks and a flawless new road grader. Green shoots glistened with dew on each side of the boy. The child kept his eyes to the ground, careful to keep his rig on the gravel, away from the rich brown soil. A feeble movement caught his attention and he stopped pedaling so abruptly that his cargo of trucks clanked into the grader. Curious, he reached down and rescued a grey night crawler from the path of his back right wheel. The cylindrical shape had little sections. Lifting it closer, he looked for eyes. He prodded it with his finger until it wiggled, sending a cold sensation across the palm of his hand. Satisfied, he set it down next to the closest zucchini plant and pedaled toward the tree line.

By the time he felt his stomach rumble, the young David Winston had built a stick fort, excavated two truck loads of rocks from his dig and unloaded them in Fran's rock garden. On the trip back from the second dumptruck run, he parked it by the back porch and went in to wash for supper. The smell of baked chicken drew him to the silver roaster on the table. Places were set. Davy climbed onto his chair and peered over the silver rim. A row of chicken thighs stretched between buttered red potatoes. He sat and waited. Three small pans were still on the stove, steam bubbling from under their lids. No one came to serve him.

Tension aggravated the pain in his stomach, finally forcing him to look for his parents. The house had never seemed empty before. He was alone. The kitchen carpet shifted under him as he walked toward the living room, then it moved backward, taking him back toward the table. Scared, he ran to keep ahead of the pull, past his parent's empty office. The hall stretched before him, yet the faster he ran the further he had to go. He could hear his father's voice just out of reach. Lunging forward, he grabbed the doorknob and turned it.

Inside, his father turned, saw him and frowned, then brushed past him. Davy froze, holding his breath. Mother stood by the window clutching his Pooh Bear, tears streaming down her soft cheeks. "Mommy, what's wrong?" Davy sobbed, running, grabbing her around the waist. His eyes squeezed tight; he felt her hands stroking his hair, her words soothing him.

"AUGH! What's that?" a woman shrieked, sending a new terror pounding through David's chest. Jolted to his feet, his eyes wide open, his pen and notebook clattered to the floor. The surrounding observation room imploded in his mind. And the children . . . He stepped toward the window. What was that woman doing to the children?

The Sergeant charged across the small room, slamming two food trays onto the table. She then yanked the thin black book from Jamie's hands. "This is public property!" She screamed, her hand poised to come down on the child's head. "You'll pay for this!" As David flipped on the intercom to intervene, Richard leaned sideways, blocked Jamie and pleaded. "It's my fault ma'am. It's my book; I gave it to him."

Her hand stood ready to strike. David stood braced to yell. Pacified, she lowered her hand and shoved Richard back to his seat. The uniformed, middle-aged woman bent the book's binding, then ripped the pages in handfuls. Repulsed, she tossed it into the trash, took the older boy's food tray and dumped the contents. Chicken strips, potatoes and green beans slithered from the plate, splattering on the remains of the book. She hissed at the boys and slammed the door behind her.

Shaking with fury, Facilitator David Winston stepped into the hallway in time to block her exit. Cold hatred still radiated from her deep-set eyes. He had noticed her earlier. She was strikingly attractive. But not now. The sight of her perfectly groomed hair revolted him. "What did you do to those boys?" he demanded.

"Well, I . . ." She stammered, regaining her authority. "I did my job," she said, her chin set in defiance.

"Your job is to traumatize my wards?"

"They're dissident brats."

"You will never, I repeat, never abuse children again. Do you understand?"

Ms. Evans took two steps back, unsure of her ground. This man was too young to be ordering her around. She weighed the risk of brushing him off. The Facilitator bit didn't impress her. But then her job could be in jeopardy. She shifted uncomfortably. "Well, I . . ."

"Never!"

"But they're just . . ."

"Never avenge the father's crime on the children," he said evenly. "Reorientation is a delicate process."

Evans fluttered her eyes. "I'm sorry sir. I didn't realize." She did realize. Reorientation for her would not be as pleasant as for the children. "Of course you are correct and I was out of order."

"What I just saw," he questioned, "is that common practice for this department?"

Cooperating at this point couldn't make things worse, so she decided to take her comrades with her. She took a penitent stance. Grave concern registered on her face. "Yes, sir. I'm sorry to say, we follow strict guidelines."

"Zealously, no doubt," he muttered, vibrating with exhaustion. "You now have new orders then, don't you? No one is to frighten the children. All the children are mine. Is that clear?"

Relieved, she nodded, "Yes, sir. All the children are yours."

"Tell your boss I'll see him later this week with new guidelines for juvenile detention."

After her dismissal he slipped into the men's room. He cupped his hands under the faucet and splashed cold water on his weary face. No wonder she was reluctant to hear him. Bloodshot eyes stared from the mirror; his hair stood up at a right angle above his eyebrow, sparse stubble dotted his chin and the wrinkled blue shirt hung over his belt. He looked worse than the dissidents.

Back in the observation room David picked up the pad and pen and settled into the chair, his mother's tear-stained face again vivid in his mind. He had seen her cry that one time.

Paul's sons stood over Jamie's food tray debating what to do. The little one insisted he wouldn't eat anything unless Richard joined him. Taking the fork, he speared a strip of cold chicken and offered it to his brother. The older boy conceded, pushing the two chairs together. They sat down, folded their hands and closed their eyes.

David watched in disbelief. The older boy talked to their God as if he were in the room, asking him to bless the food and help their parents. Then the boy took Jamie's hands in his and continued. "Father, please keep a hedge of protection around my dear brother. Guard him from any plan of the enemy. In the name of Yeshua." Content, the boys took turns with the fork.

Academy children never shared food. And they certainly never defended another classmate. At least, as a child he had never felt a need to defend anyone and risk disfavor. *Unique sibling behavior*, David thought. All Academy children were called siblings of each other. Which really meant no one was a sibling. The conclusion was upsetting; David dismissed it as evidence of exhaustion. He retrieved Diversity, checked on Stan and arranged to transfer the boys to the research department.

"FOR Trib sake what happened?" Kendra gasped. "Your clothes are hanging off of you."

"Thanks! That makes me feel better."

"No, really, I want to know," she said, pulling David into her Spokane, apartment. "You look like a refugee."

"Thanks again. Does this refugee get a small hug for surviving?" he said, stopping in front of the couch. "It's been a very long three months."

She snuggled into his arms and confessed, "I did miss you. When you didn't make it last weekend I was so disappointed that I meditated for half the night before falling asleep."

David closed his eyes and held her, wanting to hold her forever. She owned his heart, where his deepest passions joined his noblest thought. "I love you, Kendra," he whispered.

"And I love you, too," she admitted. "But where are you staying? Or maybe I should ask how long can you stay?"

"Not long enough." He released his hold and they sat together. "The guys and I will be staying at the Ramada tonight. I leave tomorrow afternoon for San Juan."

"Oh David, such a short time."

"I know. I'm going to talk to Hegie about us. I think I would do a better job as Facilitator if you traveled with me."

Her face brightened with a grin. "Yes, I could help you. And you wouldn't come back to me with your ribs sticking out."

"Yeah. I went a couple days without sleep and got run-down. Then, I caught some kind of virus. The Midwest weather didn't help. Anyway, I couldn't shake it till I was in Hawaii."

"Why didn't you tell me you were sick?"

"Now that sounds like something Jenna would say."

She swatted his arm. "I could have sent you some herbs and glyconutrients."

"Sure," he laughed. "Sounds good to me. Next time, I promise."

"What happened with the Boston dissidents?" she asked, changing the subject, annoyed he was placating her; he was the sick one, not her.

"The leader never confessed, but was convicted on solid evidence. Those Believers are an interesting group. We could probably ignore them if they didn't cause trouble. Unfortunately, the local police messed up and we never found the wife." Watching Kendra nod her head in response moved him to consider Paul's lot. Due to his one radical act, he lost Beth and his children in one afternoon. What a fool. Yet, his children were wise.

Kendra tilted her head, curious that he stopped speaking. He shrugged and continued. "Twelve families just vanished with her; left everything behind. No one noticed. Whole neighborhoods were questioned; but they didn't see a thing. We turned it over to the Feds. They'll find them soon."

"You left the boys at the Harvard Academy?"

"Yes. They're developing a reorientation program designed to slowly wean dissident children from their past. The doctor will observe their habits for several months; do a baseline study so he can personalize the therapy." David paused, staring at the tapered beauty of her hand resting on his.

She never knew David to show this much feeling. He was troubled. She waited.

"I never saw children act the way they did."

"Were they violent?"

"No, not at all. They were devoted to each other."

"You mean like best friends or roommates?"

"No, more than that. Remember when we learned about the pathogenic nature of families, and how they use each other, feeding off each other's weaknesses?"

"Yes. Sociology 201."

"I didn't see anything pathogenic. These boys were protective and giving."

"Fascinating."

"Watching their behavior made me think about you."

She laughed, incredulous. "How's that?"

"Because that's how I feel toward you."

Time was the enemy when he was with Kendra. The day

sped past. His security guards rotated shifts around the building until he forced himself to say goodbye. Then, alone in his room, the night crept along, reluctantly giving way to the dawn. As planned, she met him for an early morning swim at the hotel pool where again time accelerated. They splashed and played like five-year-old kids, until their rumbling stomachs forced them to order brunch. Wrapped in beach towels, seated next to the pool fountain, they bit into Monte Cristo sandwiches and devoured them. Laughing, she brushed powdered-sugar from his lips with a light kiss. For dessert, David insisted she share his Casaba melon slices. He'd never shared his food before. It pleased him. Everything pleased him. He didn't want to leave.

"THOSE are the kinds of things we have to watch for constantly, David. I'm proud of your quick action," Facilitator Hegelthor commended. His face had hardened when he heard the details of Werling's arrest at the Harvard residence. Few things disturbed him and he quickly calculated the risk. The Plan was running too smoothly to let some little thing get out of control and alarm the people. "How's the new superintendent working out?" he questioned. "Was the transition smooth?"

"No one on campus knows what happened, only my men. Even the campus police think he had a stroke." David pulled an envelope from his inside pocket and offered it to Hegie, who opened it, read it and gave it back for delivery to Malchor. "As you see from the report, Dr. Blanche Halmon is doing a fine job." The director was thrilled with the promotion. Since the campus was completed, Werling had spent the last month slacking off, and she was running things anyway.

"And the child?"

"Therapy was successful. She has no recall of the incident. There was no physical damage. Apparently he was grooming her. Thank Trib, he hadn't raped her. She had put up a fight so he sedated her and backed off. We confiscated and destroyed boxes of old pornographic comic books and videos."

"Who treated her?"

"Dr. J. D. Cannon from Florida. He thinks she was molested by a stranger when she was visiting her secondary caregiver."

Hegie smiled, nodding his satisfaction. "Sounds like you took care of everything."

He was more than satisfied with the job David was doing. Later, they did rounds together. Hegelthor believed students needed to see him several times a week, so he spent two hours every afternoon interacting with pupils, rotating visits to classrooms and dorms. Megan Kassan, the cherubic little girl rescued from Spokane Protective Services, ran up to them in the primary building and hugged them both. David was gratified to learn she excelled in her studies.

It took David two days to find the right time to bring up his request. They were finishing a private lunch in the Dome, and Hegie had opened the way by asking about Kendra. After a brief update he disclosed the most important issue on his mind. "Sir, I need your advice."

Hegie set his dessert fork down and gave his full attention for two reasons. Lately, David rarely referred to him as "Sir," and he rarely needed personal advice. "Yes, David?"

"During this past year, we have made tremendous progress in furthering the goals of Synthesis. The Academies are rapidly nearing completion and expanding their influence into the community. Impartationist International is nearing a merger take-over of the National Teachers' Union. The few vocal dissidents in NTU should be neutralized by this time next month. When that is accomplished, I hope to approach Malchor regarding my Union with Kendra. I believe she would be of assistance in working toward Universal Synthesis."

David gaped at the Facilitator's mobile face. Movement was discernable, first in the large man's diaphragm, then in his upper chest. Then peals of laughter poured forth and his dignified persona melted into near hysterics. David shifted uncomfortably, heat rising in his face. He didn't find anything humorous about his urgent need for Kendra.

"Yes, yes!" Hegelthor chuckled, regaining his composure.

"Mother Nature's fertility cycle returns. Spring approaches. Now, there, just relax. I, too, was young once. As for advice, double your meditation time. I'm sure Malchor will consider your request based on the furtherance of Synthesis." At this, he again broke into laughter.

Mortified, David flushed crimson.

IT WAS the only place of refuge. No prodding eyes stared, finding humor at his expense. Familiar engravings covered the walls of the San Juan Academy temple; David's mind floated toward detachment, beyond the reach of humiliation. His heart pulsed slowly to a new mantra. "I am" echoed through his body. Candles flickered as they had throughout his life, drawing him from the outer to the inner world, into himself. He was content with this, yet allowed his mind to focus as Hegie's words resurfaced. "The deeper you go the less your flesh will influence you. Buddha teaches that desire causes suffering, so we release all desire. You must master flesh even as you must master power. Knowledge is the beginning of power. You must control all power. Keep your will and use the power for Synthesis. Never let power control you. Remember, never, ever let power control you. It could destroy you, sending you to a lower incarnation." Master power; the words sent another mantra pulsing through his body. Refreshed, he rose from his knees. "I am power," he repeated.

STAN and the men were already on the plane waiting while David dialed home and asked Fran to call Jenna to the phone.

"Hello, Davy. Why aren't you here yet?" she asked.

"Malchor returned from Europe and wants me back by tonight. I'm sorry Mom. I'll be back out in April."

He could hear sadness in her voice. "Well, I'll look forward to seeing you next month. Guess I'll have to eat these muffins myself."

"Is Dad there?"

"No, he's coming in tomorrow. I'll let him know you can't make it."

"Coming in from where?"

Jenna explained that Steve was delayed at a media strategy session, so was staying in Bellingham. David wasn't satisfied, but decided not to press the issue since he wasn't there either. Stirring up demands for Autonomy was probably keeping his dad and the media extra busy.

ONE new, ornately framed picture graced the Public Relations Office wall. There was Frank, looking on as Malchor spoke with the Pope in Rome. "Very nice," Winston said. "You must be really proud of this one." Hearing no response, he glanced over his shoulder and caught the pasty scowl on Frank's face. Pleased, he continued to study the pictures with feigned interest. "I haven't received the final report on the Harvard dissident protest. I don't suppose any of your people were there, were they?"

"Absurd suggestion!" Frank scoffed, his neck puffing out like a toad. "I only set up public demonstrations."

"So what happened to the rest of the people besides Paul Williams?"

Frank pulled a folder from his file. "Here's a copy of the report. All of them were convicted and sent to the Liberation Dome."

Winston took the file and opened it. "Why weren't they sent for reorientation?" he asked, numbed by the harsh judgment. Liberation, without penance, could mean reincarnation to the lowest of planes for a dissident. He noted that Paul was serving time in a work detention center. *Perhaps in his next life . . .*

"Except for the leader, they all had records of repeated offenses," Frank blurted. "The state did everything it could to help them accept enlightenment." He busied himself, shuffling through the side drawer. Winston's miserable time in Boston suited him fine. And the extended illness was an added bonus that, he noticed, still showed on the Facilitator's weakened body. The nineteen protesters had been of use and were no longer needed—and at this point their silence was more important to

126

Frank than their future. Raven would be eliminated, later.

"It does seem the transformation was carried out ahead of time," Winston said, scrutinizing Higgs. "I expected to interrogate them myself."

Frank slammed the drawer shut with a bang, and sprang to his feet with surprising energy, shouting, "I have work to do and you have no authority to question me about my . . ." Words stuck in his throat when Malchor stepped through the door.

Malchor Inyesco's rare look of amusement turned into a piercing glare that set David two steps backward and forced Frank back into his chair, petrified. "What seems to be the problem?" he asked firmly, first looking at the sniveling figure of his long-time P.R. Director, who sat voiceless, then at David.

"Sir, my apology that we interrupted your day. I was trying to understand the disposal of the dissidents," David said, barely recovering from the shock of Malchor's presence himself. He offered Mal the file, hoping the mockery in his voice hadn't been heard. "I assure you, we will not have this problem again."

'Yes, I'm sure you won't," Mal said, scanning the report. "Justice was swift, wasn't it?" he added, looking with curiosity at Frank. "I expect your report on my desk by five o'clock. I do hope your behavior won't require reorientation."

Frank nodded weakly as Malchor and David left his office. Eliminating David would not be as easy as writing the report.

ORDERLY procedures gave way to the bizarre as he wound his way to the center of the maze. The cold semi-darkness pierced his flesh and settled a clammy grip on his heart. So this was what Malchor meant. Overcoming the unknown was only a small step: defying his dependence on reality and order would bring freedom. The crystal star was positioned high enough to catch the subtle hue of the lesser light. David laid his hands on the cool symbol, chanting his mantra. His surroundings faded, externals bending to the internal. He accepted the thought that reality began with him; he was the center. He whispered, "One with Earth my Body, one with Creatures my Soul, one with Cosmos my Spirit." Clouds drifted, finally blocking the light. David waited patiently until the clouds passed and crystal facets reflected tiny moon shapes. Weariness had settled in his bones, weakening his resolve to meditate all night. Chilled, he turned from the star.

Leaves brushed his body from head to foot as he followed the prescribed path and emerged from the maze, wondering what awaited him on his spiritual ascent. Malchor had honored him, entering the temple with him, allowing him to watch as the candles were lit and the ritual circling was performed. Soon he would know all mystery and create his own reality, his own truth. Kendra would be part of that reality. Resolve deepened; he would not remain like Malchor, but ascend even further.

At the back entrance, the guard saluted, opening the door, and David took the stairs to the second floor. On the landing, movement in the darkened hall caught his attention and brought him to an alarmed halt. "Who's there?" he demanded.

Server stepped from the shadows, a finger to his lips. He motioned for David to follow him to the library. Again, they stood before the window facing the moonlit temple. Again, Server pointed toward the place of worship, shaking his head. Then he drew his thumb from his right shoulder across his own neck in warning. His wiry fingers wrapped around David's forearm. The eerie whisper grated from his throat. "There is no freedom without reality."

Transfixed, the young adept stared while James released his grip, moved away and melted into darkness.

SHE stood in their office doorway observing his rapid data entries, waiting for a good time to interrupt. Greg worked all Saturday morning on the CAM records, matching labor hours with payroll records. The graveyard shift outproduced the others, greater output with fewer workers. Reana stepped closer, looking over his shoulder. She could see where his efforts were leading. His questions were valid; the place was clearly hiding something, yet Hegie had assured him there was nothing to the slave labor charge and nothing to the political prisoner theory. Greg was commended for his work in the merger of the new AMEURO Motorworks Corporation, given a raise and promoted to full partner. His continued obsession with the matter frightened her, it was no longer their business. She began rubbing his tight shoulder muscles at his first pause in typing. "It's been the best year, even with the outside pressures," she said tenderly. "Can you take a week off in May? My schedule's clear."

Greg glanced up from his research. "I'm sorry, Rea. What did you say about pressure?"

"I said, the pressures are worth it."

"How's that?"

"Well, a year ago next month, we didn't have any pressures."

Greg nodded absently, her hands bringing relief to the muscle knots at the base of his neck. *Next month*, he wondered, *what was she saying about next month?*

"But we didn't have each other, either."

That was it, he remembered, mentally scolding his lapse. It would be their first anniversary. He swivelled his chair around and pulled her onto his lap. Off balance, the chair slammed against the desk in a precarious backward tilt and they were seconds from crashing to the floor. Playfully, they regained their balance, clinging to each other.

The feel of her pressed against him made everything worth it. "Yes, Rea, the pressures are worth it. For me, life began when I first held you."

Her lips brushed lightly across his forehead and down his cheek. "Can you take a week off in May? My schedule's clear."

"Where would you like to go?" he asked, guilty about ignoring her. "You name the place and I'll make the request."

"Cancun. I hear the beach is perfect."

"Then Cancun it is."

"How about if we start celebrating early? Like this afternoon?"

Without a word, Greg kicked the door shut, balancing, swivelled their chair around and shut down his computer, then drew her closer.

THE next week, a birthday card arrived a month late, delivered to Greg's desk with the usual stack of opened and prioritized business mail. He puzzled over the unfamiliar name and the simple personal message, then checked the client file. No Jules Lazzari was listed. What did the man mean about waiting for his next call and looking forward to their next visit? Without going through the secretary, Greg dialed the number scrawled below the signature.

The receiver was lifted before the end of the first ring and a man answered expectantly. "Yes, Lazzari here. Is this Greg?"

"Yes."

"Thought I recognized your voice. Thanks for calling. When can we get together again for lunch?"

"Well, uh, Jules," Greg sputtered trying to place the man's voice or his name or anything about him. "What would be convenient for you?"

"Today, for lunch, would be perfect," Jules said, adding, "Santo's Deli, twelve o'clock sharp."

Click! Greg held the receiver out, staring open mouthed at the speaker holes. The guy must be local. Maybe they exchanged business cards at the Deli, when he first hit town. But how did that warrant a birthday card? Greg checked the time; it was already eleven thirty-five. With the slow elevators it would take ten minutes to get to the first floor Deli. Hoping to cancel lunch, he hit redial and waited. After the sixth ring, he hung up then set aside the Maryland Savings and Loan contract. On his way down to the first floor, he determined to simply take charge, excuse himself to this Jules person, and take a sandwich back to his office.

At the deli, Jules grabbed hold of his hand and shook it like a best friend, directing him toward a corner table, ignoring Greg's awkward protest. "I knew you wouldn't mind if I picked up a turkey and havarti on rye for you," he said. "Unless you'd rather have pastrami. I'll trade if you want."

Greg studied the strong Latin features: dark brown hair, black piercing eyes, neatly trimmed beard and mustache, stocky build. He knew he had never seen the man in his life, so why

130

was he mute, sitting at the same table? "Say, I don't know what or who you think I am Jules," Greg blurted, "but you know and I know that we have never met or talked before today."

Jules smiled and shook his head enthusiastically. "Yes. Yes. Of course you're right." Still smiling, he continued, "Does CAM mean anything to you?"

Greg examined the man's expression, the wall behind him, then his sandwich.

"I know what you're doing," Jules confided. "I used to work for CAM. You're right about the, uh, labor situation. I used to work the graveyard shift as a supervisor."

"How do you know about me?"

"The dissident underground; we've been watching you since that first confrontation, when you began working with CAM."

"If you know, then CAM knows."

"No, if CAM knew, you would not be sitting here. Please, Greg. It's important you eat your sandwich."

Ice water helped him choke it down, but he refused to say anything further throughout the meal. Meanwhile, Lazzari chatted conversationally, wolfing down his sandwich and a thick slice of cheese cake.

"You have my number. Please don't call from your home; the housekeeper works for Fereno."

"What? Norma works for Fereno!" Efficient, considerate, she was all the things they wanted in a housekeeper. Every afternoon, from Monday through Friday, she simplified their domestic lives, freed them from cooking and cleaning. "That's not possible."

"That's why I had to contact you. She's a private detective, a former IRS agent. Who would suspect her? Does she have access to your data?"

"No. I keep it protected. The only one who knows is Hegie."

"Hegelthor doesn't know what's really going on at CAM, or rather AMEURO. He'll think you're disturbed if you keep pressing him."

"Then what can be done?"

"Will you meet with us?"

"With who?"

"With the people working to expose Fereno."

"If you know everything, why do you need me?"

"Because you know the banker." At that Lazzari stood up, clapped him on the back and left him gawking at the abstract design splattered across the wallpaper.

X   INITIATION

BALTIMORE Convention Center bustled with workmen. Security monitors dotted the walls and metal detectors stood sentry at every entrance. The race with time was feverish. Delays threatened to force a twenty-four-hour work crew. David Winston insisted the area be ready seven days before the Impartation International Conference opened. With three days to go, he watched the foreman push for efficiency and push for completion. The area had to be secured.

In the past year, favored with a major media promotional, Impartation had attracted new members from all teaching levels. Political clout and low liability insurance enticed education unions and associations worldwide to vote and merge their membership. There remained one major hold out. Irritating, suspicious of Malchor, and headquarted in his neighborhood, the National Teacher Union must merge immediately. It was the last organized group with any clout and vocal opposition. Timing was key and the offer to negotiate a compromise had worked. NTU officers didn't want to give up any of their power, yet they had agreed to attend the conference. With that accomplished, Malchor was leaving nothing to chance. He would meet privately with the officers before addressing the entire assembly.

The schedule was complete and the packets printed, boxed and ready for distribution. At the registration table Facilitator Winston surveyed the cavernous convention center, then reviewed the order of events. After the opening ceremony, there would be five days of training and breakout sessions. Malchor, as keynote speaker, would end the conference at the Friday Banquet. Months of preparation were winding down to another major victory for Synthesis, for mankind.

Winston watched, empowered with their progress, while Frank made security checks with Stan. Franklin Higg's attitude had changed dramatically after the scene with Malchor. He worked twelve to fifteen hours daily, the first one to the project and the last one to leave. Winston suspected from the looks of Frank's wrinkled shirt that he hadn't made it to the Bay Hotel, but had slept in their convention office.

Again, Winston hit redial on his cellular; this time someone should be home. On the fourth ring he heard Greg's distinct hello.

"Greg, it's me, David."

"As if you need to tell me," Greg said with a chuckle. "What are you up to?"

"Literally, up the street from your office for the past week, but haven't had time to stop by or call."

"Conference time already?"

"It starts the first Monday in April."

"When can we get together?"

"Next week, probably by Wednesday," David answered.

"Good, I'll work this weekend so I can spend some time with you."

"Sounds great, I'm ready for more of that pizza."

"Me, too. Call me Wednesday morning."

"Will do. See you then." David turned back to his job, hoping to finish shuffling work orders by 10:00 p.m.

SUNSET had come and gone before Server made it back to his room. All afternoon the Tribunal had talked while he served them, working out their strategy for controlling the conference. For hours he had worked robot-like, distracted by the urge to leave the men, lock himself in his room and dig through his things until he found the book.

Boxes of mementos crowded the walk-in closet, stacked above and below his clothing. Unsure where to begin, he shoved aside the row of black slacks and pulled out the first box. He had never gotten around to labeling things. Opened, the contents stared up at him. Why on earth did he still have his baby shoes? He picked through faded pictures of his family. His parents with his three older sisters gazed lovingly down on him, the baby. He'd been a surprise for his middle-aged parents. Staring at the picture, he realized what a big surprise he was. His sisters were young adults.

His mother was forty-nine when he was born, yet she had never aged to him. She was love and warmth while his father was a rock of strength. But his father died by his fifteenth birthday. James was so busy with soccer practice he didn't notice the gaunt look of cancer that haunted the elder Lawrence face. The four-year battle ended one cold winter day. Two days later, sunlight glared from the snowy Brookline, Massachusetts, graveyard where the family gathered. Mother leaned on him, grasping her faithful black leather volume to her bosom. For James, school filled the vacuum and his mother's loss faded from his awareness. After that, holidays still brought the family together—until that last time, when his mother's death severed his ties. The old ache stirred in his heart, a reminder of his loss.

He hadn't seen his sisters since. Sobered, he dug to the bottom of the box with no results, except a passing curiosity about the whereabouts of his older sisters and their families. There was a strong possibility they weren't living meaningful lives. In that event, it occurred to him, he was better off not checking into it. He marked the box with bold letters. *Childhood.* Then shoved it aside and pulled out the next box. Where had he put her book?

Woodcarving magazines, a whole box full, why had he saved them? He hadn't carved anything since his mother's death. He pulled out the hand-carved fruit bowl, the eighty-third birthday gift, given just weeks before her death. She'd cherished it. With the bowl secure on his desk, he dragged the box of magazines to the door for disposal.

Back in the closet, he pulled out another box. He knew he

still had the book. She gave it to him the same day he gave her the bowl, said she couldn't read anymore and knew most of it with her mind anyway. She made him promise to open it and read it. He intended to, but his job demanded everything he had, and soon he forgot. Three decades later, he still hadn't cracked the book cover, so what was the sudden push for nostalgia? There was no spare time for wives tales and myths, but the promise stuck stubbornly in his mind. He had made it; he should keep it. Then it could rest in peace.

He pulled out a stack of college term papers, flipping through to check the titles. Half the subjects were woefully outdated, including the one about what his family heritage meant to him. Inside the yellowed packet was his lengthy argument for the importance of the traditional family. His views had been painfully idealistic. Right or wrong, the state had to intervene in the real world for the sake of the children. Remembering the scramble of mid-terms, he reread three of the papers, replaced them, labeled the box *College*, and then pushed it underneath the row of slacks. It was getting too late to dig through old boxes.

"HEY, what are you doing here?" Greg asked, startled; then ignoring the clamor of other professionals, he dropped the menu and welcomed David with a warm hug.

"Even Facilitators have to eat," David reciprocated, clapping his old roomie on the back.

"So how did you know I was here at Unos?"

"Your secretary. I called to see if we could get together for lunch. You'd just left the office. So, here I am."

"You're fast; I haven't ordered yet. Here's the menu." The young men ordered and caught up on surface news by the time the lunch salads arrived.

It was their first visit since Greg's reorientation, so David probed cautiously, asking questions to see if his friend remembered the Andel incident. He was relieved to hear a recital of the accepted version. A tragic accident sent the classmate to a higher plane, and left fleeting sorrow for them, but enlightenment

136

for Brockston Andel. David happily canceled the thought and finished his lasagna.

For the first time, the Youth Facilitator couldn't tell Greg about his business—too many classified areas where the dissident teachers were concerned. Fortunately, detailing his last visit with Kendra and sharing his hopes for unity took up the half-hour. Greg's enthusiasm over the prospect confirmed he should broach the subject with Malchor after the conference.

"Everything's ahead of schedule, so I can take some time tomorrow night if you want to go to the gym or do something else." It was a simple suggestion, yet Greg reacted, stumbling over his response.

"Well, I uh, I'd like to, but I . . . I have to finish up some business so we can have a clear Wednesday."

"What's so all important?"

The color in Greg's face deepened, and then faded, as he busied himself with the remains of his spaghetti. "It's just some contracts I need to review. Pretty boring stuff."

Troubled, David persisted. "So you'll be working late at the law firm?"

"Yes," he answered, then shifted uncomfortably, "but if I can get away by eight o'clock, I'll give you a call. What's your room number?"

The guy was a lousy liar. David considered pressing for the truth, curious that his friend could have anything to hide. He shrugged the urge aside and handed over his card with the room number scrawled on the back. Maybe on Wednesday he could get his buddy to open up.

RAVEN soaked up his new prosperity. He was on call. The penthouse was a big improvement over the dive he'd lived in for the past five years. One simple assignment for the Public Relations Director and he'd hit it big. He prided himself in his work. Always had.

The Marines had trained Henry Schlockman for a successful career at the Pentagon, where he supervised military appropriations and schmoozed with D.C. powerbrokers. When his appetite for women got him dishonorably discharged, his old friends kept him in bread, butter and women. They knew who to call when some flunky got out of line. Raven was good at intimidation and expert at covering his tracks. His military record read honorable discharge within minutes of his former commanding officer's untimely demise. His trade name, Raven, suited him. Just the threat of Raven's revenge kept the powerbrokers in control. Standing on the balcony overlooking Baltimore's Harbor, he laughed aloud. His reputation was starting to outrun him. With religious zeal he returned to his rigorous workout, first martial arts then weight repetitions, followed by jogging in place.

Loud ringing persisted until he finished his fifth mile and picked up the receiver, pacing the room, cooling down. "Yes?"

"Trib! What took you so long?" Frank hissed, "You're supposed to be on call."

Raven held the phone and waited. He never made excuses, never groveled.

"You know I can't talk if he's around. He should be back any time," Higgs whined.

"Yes."

"Well, did you get the permit?"

"Of course."

"Good. I have your security clearance. You need to report for duty this Friday at 8:00 a.m. with the rest of the security guards. You got the schedule?"

"Yes."

Frank watched the door. He ran his dry tongue over his lips. Months earlier, the Speaker of the House had recommended the man, but Frank knew that his other jobs were nothing compared to this. Fear slithered along his spine while visions of Malchor's angry rebuke festered in his mind. "You know if this gets botched, I never heard of you."

"So what's new? You big boys are all alike. I do the work and take the risks; you relax and build your little empires."

"How are you going to do it?"

"Do what?" He wanted to hear the weasel say it.

"You know," Frank fumed, "terminate Winston." When the words slipped out, he realized it was stupid. Raven could be recording him. *You will not be taken alive*, he thought, then sputtered, "So how will you do it, and when? I don't want any public scene." He knew it would work; Raven would fell David and he, Franklin Higgs, would gain hero status, shooting the assassin point blank in the face.

"You relax, enjoy the conference and leave the grimy details to me. I have five different scenarios and I'm flexible. When the right time comes, I'll take care of your little problem. Just remember, I'm the professional . . ."

The knob started to turn. Frank slammed down the receiver and bent over the security floor plan printout. When David walked in, he didn't look up from the desk until the Facilitator asked if he had eaten lunch.

"THINGS working out with you and Frank?" Malchor asked, showing David into the library later that evening.

"Yes," David answered, checking his boss's face for any portent of trouble, "he's been most cooperative. That's why we're ahead of schedule. Is there some problem?" he asked. "When I received your message, I left immediately."

"No. No problem. We simply felt we should brief you on the latest dissident strategy." Cyrus and Arion sat in their favorite chairs in front of the fireplace, the coffee table again laden with fruit and muffins. David declined the offer of grapes from Cyrus and sat down. The lunch lasagna sat in his stomach, defying digestion. He forced his pulse to slow, relaxed and waited for instructions.

"David," Malchor resumed, "there are times when we have to do things which would under ordinary circumstances be totally unnecessary—times when we have to take certain actions to secure the success of Synthesis. These actions may be uncomfortable for us and painful for others, for only a short time, of course." Mal reached over and gave his protégé several reassuring pats on the arm, then proceeded. "Like going to the dentist to have a cavity filled. First the dentist must dissolve the cavity, then he is able to fill the empty space with new material that protects the tooth from further decay. So it is with education. There are certain areas of decay, or people, that must be removed in order to preserve the goals of the Tribunal."

"Which, of course," Cyrus said, "will promise a world free from discord. One Body, one Soul and one Spirit united under Synthesis."

David looked from Malchor, seated beside him, to Cyrus. Harsh actions were sometimes necessary, as he had seen at the Boston Academy. As long as there were undisciplined people, someone had to keep them from wreaking havoc. The Tribunal sat, waiting for him to speak. He paused, unsure about what to add, then agreed. "Yes. I have found strong measures to be necessary at times." Remembering Frank's hasty termination of the Boston dissidents, he added, "I hope our goal would be to reorient as many people as are willing to learn from their mistakes."

"But, of course, if we ourselves don't insure justice how else could we continue our own upward evolution!" Arion reassured, cheerfully, "which leads us to the plans for bringing unruly teachers into compliance with our goals." At that, he smiled and nodded for Malchor to continue.

"The National Office of Instruction has begun weeding out unfit teachers with standardized testing for academics and attitudes. Attitudes are especially important! Certainly, the various associations and unions have done a splendid job of using closed shop to eliminate competition." Malchor proudly went on repeating examples of his handiwork. It was the fifth time in David's hearing, yet accepted as news each time. "The successful movement for vouchers and school choice was the biggest hurdle. Still, we attracted the best students to our private schools and managed to shut down unaccredited opponents by congressional means or otherwise."

"All of which brings us to the mother's milk of power.

Compulsory dues have long been the keys for getting our goals through the maze of government. Compulsory membership in Impartation International will bring in billions. Favors do cost money."

David grinned openly. The mechanics of how Mal secured his far-reaching position of influence was obvious. So obvious, he hadn't noticed. *Dues!* He thought. *News worth repeating.*

"Even though our people," Malchor continued, "have controlled the various teacher groups and suppliers since the beginning of public schools, we feel the time is right to bring everyone in the field together under one name. Today, even the most divergent groups agree with our basic goals."

"But the dissidents?"

"Some of them are ours. We've infiltrated all of the significant groups."

"What about the traditional home-schoolers?"

"Unfortunately, we haven't been as successful there, too many are refusing vouchers. However, our people control their state conventions through the Speakers Bureau. Also, we have a few key zealots that we—use. But there's no need to concern ourselves with them. First, we consolidate public and private education, then we'll bring in the independents."

"The conference will be monitored closely," David interjected, "so any sign of disruption will be dealt with quickly. I didn't realize you had the dissidents under such scrutiny. Perhaps some of my precautions will prove unnecessary."

"On the contrary," Mal said, "we leave nothing to chance. All your precautions are necessary. Oh, and one more important point, before we move on to targeting. Congress has just given us the power to revoke the certification of any educator who refuses to vow allegiance to Synthesis. It ties in with the international law. The seamless web is unstoppable."

"Excellent," Cyrus exclaimed.

Unnoticed, except when he poured drinks, Server stayed within hearing range. If he kept his head turned to the right, he could catch all but the lowest decibels. For years following the explosion, James Lawrence couldn't distinguish sounds; then things began to improve. Lip reading became unnecessary. It was more convenient for him, however, not to hear, and he easily tuned out, floating along with his orderly routines, removed from efforts to communicate. There was no reason to hear, no reason to speak. His purpose was only to serve. Still, it was beginning to bother him to hear the Tribunal's words and plans. Hearing brought with it accountability; but, accountability to whom or to what? . . . the Tribunal, Synthesis, himself, David, maybe to the truth, maybe to the memory of his parents, his mother? The dilemma agitated him, disrupting his tranquility. James wished he couldn't hear. People equated with tooth decay, needing to be dissolved, painted a graphic picture in his mind. *Trib!*

Dutifully, James rolled the large screen closer to the group and handed Mal the remote control. The laser video was ready to view.

Faces animated the screen. Facilitator Winston fixed the names and faces of the targeted people in his mind. These were the men and women who would either pass or fail. Malchor supplied personal data, weaknesses, then strengths that could be twisted into apparent weaknesses.

Cyrus watched David with increasing interest, sensing the young man's deepening spiritist perceptions. He would press Malchor for David's Initiation, preferably before the conference. It could only strengthen their cause.

When they finished, Mal graced his protégé with a fatherly gaze. "The information is entered into your Diversity unit; however, to further insure contact with us we have a special gift for you." At that, Malchor presented his Facilitator with a gold Piaget watch. "The button on the left side, if you pull that out, you will open communication with me. Try it." David slipped his nail under the tiny button and pulled up. Instantly, a barely audible sound vibrated from Mal's watch. "Whisper something, not so close, at a normal distance." Mal held his Piaget up to David's ear.

Pleased, Winston noted identical watches on the other

Tribunalists. He could hear distinctly his own words as well as Mal's pleasant chuckle and reminder that this was for emergencies only.

"Now, let's get on with it," Arion interjected. "I have a golf game this afternoon."

Cyrus nodded and set the pace. "By Wednesday we will know whether or not your target people are with us. If they aren't, our Special Forces will remove them from their hotel rooms early Thursday morning, around 1:00 a.m., and you will proceed without them."

"What about hotel security?"

"We've taken care of the details. There will be some scandal about moral indiscretion and the accused will be sent for reorientation. Press releases about the sting operation are ready to go. We'll fill in the names later. They won't know what . . ."

Concern flashed across David's face; a brief betrayal. Server caught it and slammed the coffee pot onto the tray, distracting everyone.

Malchor waved the pot away like a minor irritation. "Certainly this is one of those necessary unpleasantries," he said, looking at David's serene face. "We will all be grateful when the world will be as One and we won't have to deal with dissidents of any sort."

Winston joined the Tribunal in grave nods of agreement.

WITHIN four hours, Facilitator Winston was in Baltimore, standing across from the stately concrete and glass office building where Greg Foster worked. He had slipped from his hotel suite, leaving his guards to keep others from disturbing his meditations. He locked his bedroom from the inside, then tiptoed through Stan's adjoining room and into the hall. Getting back into his room would be the problem. Now, he stepped into the shadows, pretending to wait for a bus. The gray wig, horn-rimmed glasses and rumpled tan suit gave him a weary city employee look. He slouched to complete the effect. Busses pulled up, then moved along; finally David popped a coin in the newsstand. The paper was bulky, so he dumped all but the sports section.

After sunset, he saw Greg walk down the wide concrete stairs and head away from his townhouse, around the corner of the building. David was stuck at the light, anticipating Greg's next move toward the cabs, lined up on the other side of the street. He couldn't wait for two lights to get to the cabs, so when traffic thinned, he crossed on red, then barely made it through the next green light. Greg was pulling away from the curb in a blue City Cab. The next driver was haggling with a potential passenger about driving to Annapolis. David ran to the next one and stuffed a twenty in his hand. "That's just the bonus for staying with that cab," he shouted above the street noise and climbed into the back seat.

Commuters honked in protest when the cabby swerved into traffic and then at the light turned right, cutting off oncoming cars. When they were a comfortable distance behind the lead cab, he examined his passenger in the rear view mirror. "Hey man, you look like one of them TV detectives."

"Great, that's great," Winston mused. The point was to fit in, not stick out like a star. He ignored the man and watched the back of the blue cab.

"Well?" The cabby pressed, looking at him again. "Is that what you are, a detective? Don't want to be part of nothing bad."

"Yes, sure that's what I am," he reassured him, sensing the man's urge to pull over and dump him on the street. He needed the cabby's cooperation. "There's nothing bad going to happen. So don't lose the guy, O.K."

Gnarled work-worn hands gripped the wheel; he knew the fair-skinned young man wasn't the criminal sort—a novice detective, maybe. A real professional wouldn't need a cab. He was used to weird things happening; every day he had some new story to tell the kids.

Controlled breathing gave Winston a calm front but had no impact on his shaking inside. Fear washed over him. Narrow townhouses closed in, swallowing the thin lines of traffic. What was he doing following his best friend through the suburbs of

Baltimore? On the other hand, if Greg was up to something out of sync, who else could help him?

The lead cab double-parked barely long enough for Greg to step out. David held his breath, afraid of detection, until his quarry turned and headed toward the corner meeting hall. Unnoticed, they pulled through the intersection, then stopped.

"Good job," David muttered, pressing another twenty into the driver's hand, relieved to be on his own.

Two joined and converted town houses were the hub of the area. People walked in and out, alone or in small groups. Several older men were standing on the wide entrance steps complaining about the latest price increase for domestic cars. Grateful for the cover, David stepped in behind a group of couples in western dress on their way to the basement square dance. Fresh paint fumes from the spotless entrance hit his nostrils and he paused to read the bulletin board. Bright posters announced the week's activities.

The main floor held the popular bingo games. Noise and laughter seeped from under the double doors and a glance through their windows showed wall-to-wall tables lined with players. Nudged from behind, David excused himself and moved aside for two older women. The taller one asked if he didn't want to come play, then looked at him curiously from his gray hair to his smooth skin, then back to his gray hair. He shook his head no, and turned back to study the notices. Nothing to interest Greg in the basement, nothing on the main floor. The second floor hosted an array of classes and meetings. The third floor offered classes and activities for children, a neighborhood sitter service.

David joined the people going up the stairs to the second floor. Children scampered past on their way to their classes. Rooms 201 to 205 were filling up with their respective members. Ladies were pulling out their yarn and crochet needles in 202. Art supplies were spread out in 203, with multi-sized blank canvases ready for the artist's touch. Men and women were already in the lotus position in 204, serene music settling negative

145

energies. With an overwhelming urgency, David wanted to join them.

Room 206 wasn't scheduled, but light shone under the closed door. David touched the knob and listened as a murmur of voices rose and fell from within. *Now what,* he thought, *walk into the lion's den and say Hi?* Across the hall the chess tournaments were getting underway in 205, so David quickly found a chair that faced the door. He feigned interest as a teenage boy challenged a matronly woman.

Greg stood by the door in room 206, scrutinized by the eight men and three women crowded around two large tables. A creeping fear, crowded out his regret. Finally they turned and proceeded to play rounds of poker. Small stacks of coins accumulated for the winners while Greg waited awkwardly for Jules Lazzari to arrive and introduce him.

To anyone looking in, they were a group of friends playing penny ante. To Greg they were a bomb, timer set, ready to blow his world apart. The gaunt leader at his table looked familiar, avoiding eye contact as he deftly dealt the cards. Deep set, light brown eyes caught subtle cues for more cards with professional ease. By the third deal, Greg Foster knew where he had seen the man they called Taylor—at the first contract signing, when he was new in town. Taylor led the demonstration against Fereno. It had been hit and run. They showed up, raised a protest, then he disappeared before the police arrived to haul away the group. *Who did I expect to see at a dissident meeting?* Greg chided himself. *Malchor?*

David stared at the door to room 206 and almost bolted when a dark-featured, bearded man stopped in the hallway to argue with a willowy blond. He strained to catch their heated words, looking away when she glanced toward the chess players. She ordered the man to do something and he protested. Opening the door to 206, she stepped aside, leaving him alone in the doorway. Winston could see a few people playing poker, and as the door closed, he saw Greg greet the new arrival.

The sweet scent of *Unforgettable* lingered as the woman

walked into room 205. Sweeping past him she flitted from one set of players to another. David wanted to stare at her, captivated, but avoided her, following instead the youth's attempt to check his matronly opponent. Violet eyes shone from flawless features. Flirtatious laughter drew the attention of every able-bodied man in the room, including the youth who reaped a speedy checkmate.

Greg was relieved to see Jules Lazzari at the door. Immediately, the games stopped. Taylor directed Jules to pull up a chair next to Greg, then proceeded to ask what kept him.

For the next two hours Greg listened to their personal stories of tragedy. Every man and woman there had watched a loved one sink into the pit of slave labor at CAM. Jim Taylor's brother disappeared after challenging Fereno's unbridled authority over the private lives of his employees. The youngest member of the group, nineteen-year-old Margaret, lost her father because of his political views. He had never heard of Fereno. His mistake was to publicly oppose President Chamberlon's compromise with Congress on National Security. His White House staff position was filled with a more amiable team player.

Believing their loved ones were still alive and languishing at CAM drove the dissidents to risk their own safety. The new merger left them cold with fear that their people would be terminated at the Liberation Dome, or sent to European or Siberian AMEURO plants. They were desperate for hope and Greg's presence gave them a small glimmer to hang on to. So far, their efforts had failed to arouse the apathetic public, or Justice herself, to any action. Their stories began to blend and blur in Greg's mind. Who was he to make any difference? People with far more influence than his had been silenced.

The group stared, waiting for an answer, and Taylor repeated himself, more urgently, "Will you help us?"

Panic thrust her razor-edged fingers into Greg's mind and he opened his mouth to make an excuse, but said instead, "I'll need to see what I can do."

The group relaxed and Taylor reassured him, "I know this

is a big step for you. We understand and are grateful for any help."

Greg recovered his senses and added, "Now, I'm not making any promises. For Trib's sake, there may be nothing I can do. It doesn't seem logical to me to offer myself as some sacrifice to AMEURO for any cause. You've made it clear tonight that all previous efforts to change the practices of CAM have failed. Perhaps CAM is a necessary cog in the wheel of evolution."

The group turned to Jules and again Taylor spoke their hearts. "You said he was one of us. What have you done?"

Jules, chastised, motioned for Greg to follow him, heated anger rising to his face and settling in his brooding eyes. "I'm trying to help you people get rid of that vermin Fereno," he growled.

"No." Jim Taylor replied evenly. "Bitterness blinds you. You seek revenge; we seek justice."

"Fools!" Lazzari fumed, shoving Greg toward the door.

They left the startled dissidents, quietly closed the door and stepped across the hallway. "Marci," Lazzari commanded from 205's doorway. David caught the instant contempt on her face— contempt that settled into a plastic smile as she waved farewell to her new admirers and joined her seething escort.

Greg, from behind Jules, could see the chess players and their friends' startled faces, gawking, curious about the rude man. Marci glided toward them in her light-blue, skin-tight sheath, chattering cheerfully. "Jules, Sweetie darling, I'll make you some tasty cherry torte and you'll be all happy again." David was close enough to the door to hear Marci hiss before she planted a kiss on Jules' mustached face. And David was close enough to be seen by his friend. Confusion registered in Greg's eyes. David grimaced and struck up a familiar conversation with the woman chess champion at his table.

The hands on his Piaget crept along, five minutes, then ten. David watched as 206 revealed her guests; singly and in small groups the men and women bid their farewells. They were all strangers, probably dissidents, so he entered brief descriptions

148

in his Diversity unit. With the last of the group gone and the lights out, David left his post in 205. Other students were mingling in the halls, drifting toward the exit. David stopped in the foyer to call a cab, then strode into the night air. Damp with perspiration, a chill started at his neck and soon enveloped him. He didn't know what he should do first, call Greg or Hegie.

He stood on the corner waiting for the cab, unaware of the person behind him until the question registered. "Mind if we share a cab?"

The ride back to Baltimore harbor was awkward. Talking would have been dangerous and pointless. Still estranged, they paid the fare and stepped from the cab to the curb of the Stouffer hotel. David slipped off the wig and glasses and stuffed them into the first trash bin they passed. They were walking past the U.S. Constellation before Greg spoke again. "Why?"

"You were lying. I could tell."

"So, why follow me?"

"Why lie to me?" David countered. Light reflected from the pristine waters, in sharp contrast to the darkness of soul that threatened to extinguish their friendship.

"Why did you follow me?"

David shrugged and explained, "I was concerned for your safety. I guess it was stupid, but I thought you might get hurt or do something . . ."

It hadn't occurred to Greg that he was followed out of concern. Ashamed, he saw that his suspicions about his friend's loyalty were unfounded. "I'm sorry, David, I was out of order. This thing with the dissidents just came up. I never intended to meet with them. That Lazzari fellow sought me out. He asked me to hear their stories. I was going to back out, but Fereno is still a mystery. I thought they had something I could use to expose him—maybe get him replaced with an Academy graduate."

"After your meeting tonight, what do you think?"

"It's a mixed situation. Jules and his ditzy friend Marci aren't much, if any, better than Fereno, but the other people seem sincere and basically honest. They want to see their loved ones released from Fereno's grasp. However, I don't know the facts. I don't like the idea of slave labor, but, if those who are there have broken the law or are working out their karma... Well, who am I to interfere."

"Are you going to contact Hegie?"

"I don't . . . know."

Alarmed, Winston stopped to face his friend. "What do you mean? You must tell Hegie immediately!"

"But, what if the dissidents are telling the truth? What if Hegie doesn't want Fereno removed?"

"If he doesn't, there must be a good reason for it."

"I don't know."

"If you don't tell Hegie, then I have to."

"No you don't. You can give me a few weeks to look into the credibility of the dissidents."

"For Trib sake," David Winston snapped, barely controlling himself, "either you call him or I call him."

"For Trib's sake?" Greg questioned, searching his friend's eyes. "To us that means Tribunal, everything evolving toward the Tribunal's master plan of Synthesis."

"Of course it does," Winston responded, impatience straining his voice.

"To those people I met tonight, it has another meaning." Greg breathed in slowly, then released an audible groan. The strain of the past week shadowed his face. "Trib means Tribulation. Tribulation for them, at the hands of the Tribunal."

"Do you hear what you're repeating? That's blasphemy! The Tribunal reigns with justice, not tribulation! For everyone!" Exasperated, he turned abruptly and left Greg, knowing it would be a miserable night. It took Winston until 2:00 a.m., in the Bay Hotel coffee shop, to frame and transmit his new request, asking Hegie to help his friend.

JAMIE lay in the corner of the couch, his thumb pressed against his mouth, his arm wrapped around the worn teddy bear. The room was deadly still; the macaroni dinner, hardened, sat untouched on the table. He stared at the door. Waiting.

Still unrested from his Tuesday nightmare, David paced in front of the viewing window, waiting for the Boston Academy research department's team leader. After watching the child's vigil for another thirty minutes, he left the viewing room and slowly opened the door. The child sat up expectantly, but settled back when another stranger entered his room. He curled his legs up tighter, cast his eyes away from David's and put his head down on the teddy, his brown hair blending with the fur.

"What are you doing?" David whispered, kneeling in front of the small frightened figure.

"I'm waiting," he sighed.

"Who are you waiting for?"

"I'm waiting for my mommy to find me," the child whimpered, his eyes filling, a tear trickling down his cheek.

The Youth Facilitator choked back remorse and grief for Jamie's loss. His own vigil darted from the past to tempt him. In his first dorm, he had waited by the window after everyone was asleep, watching for his mother. "Your mommy is busy and she can't come right now," he lied, "so she would want you to have fun and learn new things while you're here."

"Mommy," he cried.

David stroked the child's fine hair until Jamie wiped his fists across his eyes, sighing deeply.

"The bad people," he continued, "won't let me see Richard."

"They won't? Why not?" David blurted.

Taking courage that he had a friend who would help him, the seven-year-old made his case. "They told me he's not really my brother, that everyone is my brother. So I can't see him till I know he's not my brother. But, he is my brother and they aren't telling the truth. Why don't they want Richard to be my brother anymore?"

A simple question, *why?* Now, it was David's turn to sigh. "Because they think you'll be happier with everyone as your brother." The idea sounded hollow, very hollow.

"But I want my real brother. Please, mister, may I have my

151

real brother? I promise I'll learn what you want and eat my food and clean my room. Please?" At this the boy was sitting up eager, hopeful.

"I'll see what I can do."

"Thank you, sir," he said, reaching out to shake hands. "My name is Jamie Williams. What's yours?"

IT WAS a short flight back to Baltimore. The Williams' boys were back together and on their way to the San Juan Academy, where they would receive gentle reorientation, personally supervised by Hegelthor. On impulse, David dialed Kendra at the Genetic Selectivity Center. He gave the controls over to Stan and moved to the back of the Aerojet, waiting on hold. Yes, he knew what it was like to wait for someone. Jamie had been so excited to see Richard that he had hugged David and twirled around the room. Richard, sensing the Facilitator's authority, had made an urgent appeal to stay with Jamie, promising they would both continue to excel. David was convinced and the reunion helped numb his disappointment about Greg. David plugged his other ear and held the phone closer, straining to hear her voice.

"David, I'm sorry to keep you waiting."

"I just had to call you to tell you I love you."

"And I love you, too. Where are you? I can hardly hear."

"Over New York, on the way back to Baltimore—I'm at the back of the plane."

"I thought you were getting ready for the conference. What are you doing in the air?"

"Everything's set for this coming Monday and I needed to follow up on Superintendent Halmon in Boston. She has Harvard running efficiently, except for the research department. The team leader was too rigid with the Williams' boys I told you about. Anyway, he forced separation too soon, so I sent the boys out to your area. Hopefully, after reorientation, they'll qualify for the Academy."

"But what about their mythological indoctrination?"

"I think, with careful handling, they'll accept Synthesis. We won't know what's possible if we don't try."

"That's a good point."

"I forgot to ask you about that child."

"What child?"

"With the depressed parent. What happened?" David made his way back toward the front of the plane and settled into a seat behind his security guards, where he could hear better.

"That was a hard case," she answered, "but the boy's in the program in Santa Barbara and is doing fine. He wasn't affected by his mother's prescription dependence and she's completely recovered now."

"Good. I'm still planning to see you in May."

"Well, I'm just sitting here waiting. Say, have you heard from Greg and Reana?"

"Yeah, everything's fine," he said, panic seizing his throat. He hadn't even thought about what he should tell Kendra. "Well, I need to get back up front. We're getting close to the airport. I'll call after the conference."

"Bye, and remember, I'm waiting."

"Trib," he muttered, heading back to his seat. He knew he should have told her.

THE closet door stood open as Server pulled out the three remaining boxes. Things were labeled and he felt better, knowing where his earthly treasures lay. His mother's worn leather book sat on his desk, still unopened, while he sorted and labeled the contents of two boxes and dragged another box of magazines to the door. Again, it was too late. Too late to open the book. He finished in the closet, shut the door, then reached to turn off the desk lamp. Curiosity made him linger; he touched the cover, opened it and read the faded inscription.

To my beloved Charlotte,
May God bless you in life, in love and in eternity.
Your faithful husband, Victor.

Below those words were carefully penned the following,

To James Victor Lawrence,
God blessed me with you.
I pray for His sovereign intervention in your life,
that He will draw you to Himself,
that you will know His truth and know His blessing.
Love, Mother

Scarred fingers traced the words, reaching toward his past, touching his mother's heart.

MOONLIGHT streamed from the circular skylight, emitting an erie halo over the altar. David, ceremonially bathed and gowned, followed Mal, Cyrus and Arion in the ritual circumambulation, three times around the altar, symbolizing the sun's rotation.

Flickering candles cast shadows on Malchor's face as he listened to David's confessions and further secured his allegiance. Weaknesses, doubts, anguish over Greg's actions, longing for Kendra, poured forth until he felt that his mind had been sucked from his own body into Malchor's unblinking eyes.

The incense-filled darkness welcomed David's memorized vows of allegiance: allegiance to the unity of Adviata; Gaia his mother earth consciousness; the coming christ, Maitreya, and the Vedantic truth of his soul's eternal divine godhood. He remained kneeling and concluded the blood vow after Cyrus. "I submit in obedience to the will of Tribunal to forgo all purpose and desire, including any union with woman, until so ordained, and by blood oath, on penalty of live evisceration, to preserve my vows eternally."

The words uttered, Cyrus touched David's forehead and he collapsed to the floor. The voltage left him limp and he was lifted onto the cleared altar. Cold marble sent icy chills along his spine as Cyrus' razor sharp dagger searched him for any thread of resistance. Instantly, he was out of his body, looking down, bemused by the solemn scene. Cyrus took the drugged male goat from the priest, slit its throat and drained its life blood into the silver bowl, held by Malchor over David's chest. The Tribunal drank, then poured the remainder of the thick red fluid over their initiate's body.

Again trapped in his body, David focused upward on Malchor's glazed eyes while the pronouncement of Cyrus echoed in the temple chamber. "David Alan Winston, your new name is Nimrod Dagon, god of purging fire and god of purifying water, incarnate, eternal refiner of children." Goat's blood oozed across his lips and down his neck. He pressed his lips together, revolted. The contents of his stomach surged toward his teeth forcing him to swallow hard. Cyrus, Arion and Malchor were circling, chanting incomprehensibly, swaying to the undulating rhythm of the flutist. David swallowed the burning bile again. Six temple women joined the three men in their ecstasy. Frozen in timeless horror, David lay drenched in blood, ignoring enticements, watching his masters at play, until a priest lifted him off the altar and led him, benumbed, to the bath.

XI DOUBLE JEOPARDY

FACILITATOR Winston never slept in—not even on Sunday. He stretched and opened his eyes, expecting to be in the Baltimore hotel room and expecting a full day ahead. Instead, he was at headquarters. The unsettling memory of his initiation hounded him out of bed and into his clothes. It would take at least an hour to get to the hotel if he didn't eat, and no matter what he did, he would be late for the 1:00 p.m. appointment with Frank. He reached for his cellular phone, dialed the convention center office and left an apologetic message that he wouldn't be in until 4:00 p.m. In an effort to be friendly, he invited Frank to dinner. They would finish reviewing the conference plans by 7:00 p.m., then eat.

STAN parked at the entrance and stepped to the curb while his men pulled up behind in their Ford Explorer.

Minutes later, David held the steering wheel of a sleek, black Lamborghini, cruising at eighty mph, bypassing D.C. He grinned at his passenger and sped around slower traffic while the guards trailed. "Did you know Malchor had this for me?" he asked, relieved he hadn't seen the boss.

"For about a week," Stan admitted.

"This is great!" David exclaimed, yet his problem remained;how could he expect to control all power when he couldn't control the contents of his own stomach? He hadn't joined the revelry after his initiation, but it appeared Mal either didn't notice or didn't care. Troubling thoughts haunted him. Reality was his paradigm, the grid through which he viewed life. That had to stop before this new paradigm could flourish. Challenged, he knew he had to master revulsion before he would be ready for the second and third initiations. Reality and order still had him hooked. He had to control reality—design reality—create reality at his own whim. Meanwhile, he would enjoy the gift and, after the conference, learn more about his namesake, Nimrod.

SHE sat in the Bay lobby, watching for him. It was inevitable. He knew he had to face her, but the timing was lousy. Stan caught on, motioned for his men to check the restaurant and stood guard at the front desk as David Winston walked Reana to a quiet corner table. Even in her anger, she radiated beauty. Her blond curls shimmered, framing her freckle-kissed face, black pupils contracted in a sea of blue. She sat with her back to the dining area and chatted aimlessly until the waiter had their order and left.

"Greg trusted you," she accused as soon as the waiter was out of hearing range.

"That's why I had to help him," he said, expecting her to understand and agree.

"Help him!"

"Yes, help him. He was going in the wrong direction."

Trembling, Reana stared at her husband's dearest friend. His handsome features, innocent dark eyes and openness invited instant trust, but didn't guarantee anything. "Didn't he tell you?"

"Tell me what?"

"The truth, that he's not a dissident. He was just trying to find out about CAM."

"Then he should have talked to Hegelthor, not his new friends," he insisted, absently drumming the tablecloth with his fingers. The restaurant was vacant except for the guards, a perfect time to eat. He wondered what was taking so long. No bread, just water and an angry woman. He needed a distraction and looked around for the waiter.

She paused until he returned her stare, then continued forcefully. "They're not his friends. Trib! He never saw them before, except when that Jules guy tricked him into meeting for lunch."

Facilitator Winston drew back and frowned at her. "He sounded like a dissident to me," he said firmly.

"How?" she demanded.

"He believed their lies."

"No, he didn't. Greg only wanted to verify . . ."

"Yes. At Facilitator Hegelthor's expense. Don't be a fool, Reana. He doubted Hegie's honor."

Flushed with frustration, she leaned forward, "No, you're wrong," she insisted. "He loves Hegie!"

"Well, he'll love him more after he gets the help he needs."

She stared open-mouthed, frantic for the right words.

"What about you, Reana?" Winston asked, sincere in his concern.

"What?" she gasped. "Now, you're going to report me if I disagree with you."

"I care enough about you to do that."

"David, what's happened to you? I can't even talk to you. I can't be open with you."

"Why not?" he demanded, glaring.

"That's why," she said, pointing at his face. "You're arrogant! Who are you anyway? Why are you angry with me? You took my husband away from me and you expect me to be happy about it?"

"He needs help."

"No! You need help," she flared. "Greg trusted you, and you betrayed him."

"I didn't betray anyone," he insisted, shifting uncomfortably. "You're talking foolishness. He'll be back home within the week. Healthy."

Shaking her head, she pleaded, hoping to jar him loose from his stubbornness. "Those men, who broke down our front door, knocked Greg to the floor, handcuffed him and dragged him out, aren't going to leave him healthy."

"He shouldn't have resisted."

"How was he to know who they were? They . . . " Desperate, she reached across the table and grabbed his arm. "Do you know what they've done to him?"

"The report said he's responding well."

"What do you expect them to tell you? You go see for yourself," she implored. "I saw him this morning. They're not letting him sleep, keeping him awake until he confesses. What's he supposed to confess? He didn't do anything."

"Wrong!" Winston corrected. "He doubted Hegelthor."

Exasperated, Reana stood to leave. "I can't eat with you, David, while Greg goes without food."

"Trust me, Reana. Greg's going to be fine," he said, making a small effort to alter his obviously condescending tone. "They'll do what's best for him."

"Trust you?" she asked, incredulous.

The waiter arrived with the tray and began placing the filet mignon lunch specials on the table. Reana addressed the man apologetically. "Excuse me," she moaned, "I'm feeling quite ill." Turning abruptly, she stalked toward the exit without looking back.

Undaunted, Facilitator David Winston ate his serving and half of hers.

AT THE conference on Tuesday, team building continued in earnest. Small groups discussed community partnerships, curriculum, tracking systems and assessments. Leaders gave presentations that guided each group toward prescribed goals. After lunch, they assembled in the auditorium. Gil Duskin, president of the National Teacher Union, sat in a section with his delegates and weighed his options while he listened to Malchor.

"Your membership in Impartation International is vital to Synthesis," Malchor proclaimed, holding a hefty, gold necklace chain over his head. "What link will you forge to secure our chain of unity? What does peace mean to you?" he asked. The chain dangled from one hand until he attached a thin silver link to both ends. Held aloft, the chain was the focus of intense interest. The cameraman zoomed in for a close-up highlighting the silver link's frail contrast. Malchor stretched his arms out and snapped the chain. Broken, the link clung to one end. He shook it toward his rapt audience. The weak link spun off, hit hard and skidded across the stage.

When it hit the stage floor, Gil flinched. He stared as Malchor kicked it off the stage and into the audience. Three of his close friends pushed and shoved for the privilege of stomping the weak link into dust.

The lights dimmed and Malchor continued. "Peace is our only option. And you are our strong link to your community, to your parent, student and business partnerships. Each diverse link in this room must be brought into unity." He held a matching gold link up for their approval and with a twist linked it to both ends. "Look closely for any weakness. Where you see weakness, you must overcome it." He took a soldering tool and dropped a pearl of molten gold on the link. Minutes passed while he held the chain necklace overhead, searched the audience for resistance and then locked eyes with Duskin. Turning, Malchor motioned for Winston to come forward. When he fastened the chain around Winston's neck, wild cheers again filled the silence.

Beaming, Facilitator David Winston stepped to the podium. "Thank you, Malchor. We honor you, and we embrace Synthesis. Stand with us!" he shouted. "Stand up for peace! Stand up and stand strong with Impartation International!"

Surrounded by the cheering crowd, Gil Duskin rose to his feet. No one dared otherwise. Focus-group leaders stood in front of the stage while people were ushered from their sections. Soon rivers of people were flowing up the aisles to the front then back to their seats. Gil followed his union members. He knew all about facilitation, and had used similar, less dramatic, methods to neuter his opponents. Resentment burned deep. Gil didn't want to be a link on Malchor's chain, yet if Malchor had shown respect for his position, he would have tolerated the arrogance and considered merging. Instead, he was being shut out of leadership and facilitated like some mindless moron. He hated the humiliation.

Pleasant anticipation masked his face as he walked forward, smiled at Malchor and accepted his gold necklace. His group leader, Daniel Peppin, fastened it and hugged him. Gil hugged him back, stifling the urge to slug him. He returned to his seat desperate for a way to stop the inevitable. The note in his pocket, rejected earlier, promised a dim hope. The Wednesday meeting would be late and the secrecy secured. There was a chance that if his people read a statement contrasting Malchor's plan with his, they could block a merger. They had the numbers—if they stood firm.

BY WEDNESDAY afternoon teachers questioned all traditional techniques and thought patterns that conflicted with Synthesis. Any patriarchal approach was fair game and great sport. Old paradigms crumbled under the weight of peer pressure and were recycled into energy, energy to leap further beyond the constraints of the cognitive domain. Participants shared in small groups, revealed inner secrets, reveled in their own creative genius and believed they created Synthesis. Sensing the receptive mood, Winston instructed his break-out session leaders to prepare the group for their pledge. They were ready.

Of the fifteen-thousand teachers, less than 1% showed any signs of resistance. Winston followed their progress personally. Their private meeting with Malchor was positive, and though they questioned the authority of the Tribunal, they accepted the need for change.

After lunch Winston again addressed the cheering crowd, noting the minor lapses of enthusiasm. "Thank you. Thank you. This is your conference, your Impartation International." The crowd settled into respectful silence. "You are the pioneers of the future. The creators of the new reality. You will help reach the

162

lost masses for Synthesis. What you are doing today will be remembered throughout recorded history. The honor is yours."

Facilitator David Winston applauded them, smiling. These people lacked the benefit of Academy attendance, yet were amazingly equipped, reflecting the views of loyal university professors. Respected teachers from all parts of the nation were ready to take the tenets of Synthesis back to their public and private schools, ready to devote their careers to building the new being—ready to impart Synthesis. They in turn, stood and applauded him.

Winston continued as the crowd sat down. "San Juan Academy graduates, who served as group leaders, have reported your outstanding progress and willingness to be Impartationists. Without your efforts, humanity would be doomed to repeat the errors of the past. With your efforts, we will instill the principles of Universal Peace in all students, both young and old. As you have broken with the old paradigms, so you will help others turn from childish and selfish myths to unity."

Old Glory hung faded and limp in the corner—a relic from the decadent past. Triumphal music burst from the speakers and Winston turned for the unveiling of the Synthesis hologram. Murmured awe spread through the crowd. The shimmering, blue earth sphere, the silver likeness of Tribunal, and the swirling galaxy background brought everyone to their feet. Winston raised his arm in salute, palm down, and led them in allegiance to Synthesis. Those who refused to join in were duly noted on the security monitor system. Seventy-two individuals failed to comply.

"I TOLD you not to come near me, Raven." Frank muttered.

"Director Higgs, you really should use my professional name." Captain Brooks whispered, smiling. "Stan asked me to go over this evening's—uh, 'special events' with you."

Perturbed, Frank led the way to his office, showed the uniformed guard in and locked the door. "You're not going to do it tonight, are you?"

"Just relax, you look awfully guilty of something," he snickered, enjoying the tension engraved across Higgs' face. "Not tonight. Too many Special Forces roaming around. Just so there's no foul up, you should know the identities of the fourteen agents Malchor has posing as teachers."

Frank studied their pictures on the screen, fuming; he hadn't been briefed. Here were the top agents, so well disguised he hadn't recognized any of them. None of the agents would have played the games he was suffering at the hands of Raven, but then he couldn't risk their loyalty to Malchor or the Youth Facilitator.

Civil, he handed the disk back to Raven. "O.K., Captain Brooks, as Stan directed, show these to the Youth Facilitator during the break this afternoon. You might as well get acquainted with your prey."

Brooks started to leave, then remembered, "Stan wanted me to remind you, our main job tonight is to keep out of the way of the agents."

"I know that!" Higgs snapped. He shut off the equipment, followed Brooks out and watched him join two other guards at the auditorium door. He fit in well—average build, black hair and eyes, nondescript face, the perfect killer.

THAT night, only one person escaped the snare set for the recalcitrant teachers. Eldon Bowlin sat alone and desolate in the ground floor cafe, pretending to read. He had tried vainly to warn his friends. They either laughed or branded him a coward.

Like sheep, they gathered with others in the Bay Hotel's spacious honeymoon suite to organize a protest against Impartation International. Disguised agents filtered through the room, shaking hands, planting packets of crack, stirring up dissension. Tension mounted. In the heated debate, men and women loosened their collars, removing their jackets and coats. Precisely at midnight the noose closed. Scantily clad special agents rushed in, ripping at the teachers' clothes, attacking savagely. Those in disguise joined the fray, knocking their assigned roommates to the floor. Margot Landis, from Special Forces, managed to rip open the shirts of fourteen men before the photographers stepped into the room.

Gil Duskin found himself on top of his Vice President, Jean Padovan. Bulbs flashed as he pulled himself up and helped her to the couch. Eldon's warning replayed in his mind. Even his wife had begged him not to come, but his pride had drowned them both out. Just minutes earlier, by habit, Gil had slipped his hand into his slack's pocket and was stunned to feel the packet of powder. Fear gripped his throat as he urged Jean to leave with him. Then he was hit in the kidney, and on his way to the floor, his shirt was ripped open, buttons flying. It was too late. A harsh revelation screamed through Gil Duskin's mind, *Scapegoat! Malchor's scapegoat!* He knew he was dead meat on the butcher's table. Malchor had won.

AT 12:35 a.m. Eldon dialed from a pay phone and watched the travesty unfold in the lobby. *World Press* arrived, snapped more pictures and scribbled the latest scandal for the morning paper. Malchor performed in their midst, issuing his press release regarding the cleansing of the teachers' ranks and the high calling of Impartation International. Blinking at flash bulbs, the partially clad, dishonored teachers shuffled past, trying to cover themselves. Reporters swarmed Gil Duskin. Shoulders squared, he pled his innocence into the hungry microphones, all the while staring at Malchor. A police officer shoved him toward the exit.

Eldon gripped the phone and waited.

Groggy, Winston answered. "Yes?"

Reporters lined up to use the phones. Shaken by fear and anger, Eldon whispered into the receiver, "You know what they've done, Winston. They just killed freedom while you slept."

"Who is this?" Winston yelled, throwing off his covers, hitting the lamp switch.

"The only one you didn't trap."

"I didn't trap anyone," Winston insisted, rubbing his eyes,

stepping aside as Stan rushed into the room and grabbed the cell phone to trace the call. "Who is this?" he asked again.

Eldon shrugged, replaced the receiver and joined reporters surging through the lobby and out the front door. The police were loading their catch into busses. Eldon Bowlin, history professor and President of the now defunct American Education Association, trembled, pulled his coat around himself, and disappeared into the night.

WINSTON and Stan debated their options. It was worthless to try to locate the lobby caller. They wouldn't know who it was until morning, when everyone was fingerprinted and booked. Against Stan's advice they dressed and took the elevator to the top floor Sky Lounge restaurant. Once there, Stan nodded at Captain Brooks, relieved to see the group of off-duty security guards. A dozen other guests lingered at the bar. The hostess greeted them, explained the restaurant would close in twenty-five minutes, seated them beside a view window and took their order. Couples finishing their desserts occupied two other tables. The place looked safe enough.

Winston sipped a Decaf Almond Latte and watched the sparse city traffic below. There wasn't anything to talk about. Malchor did the practical thing—the pragmatic thing—the very thing he would have done, if necessary, to further Synthesis. A tense weariness settled over him. Stan was on alert, his coffee untouched. Every movement in the room had his attention; he was like a cobra, coiled, waiting.

Too soon, the waitress brought the check and cleared their places. Winston glanced down; the Piaget minute hand signaled the half hour. She stood impatiently while he signed. Without a word they walked past the empty tables. Three couples whispered over their drinks in the bar.

Stan walked beside Winston protectively, disgusted with himself for not rousing the other guards. As they approached the elevator, Brooks pushed the down button. "What floor you on?" Stan asked, ready to commandeer the Captain to escort Winston safely back to the suite.

"Sixth floor," Brooks answered, moving aside for Winston to enter the elevator.

Stepping forward to follow, Stan was struck with a blinding blow to the back of his head. By reflex, his arm shot up and partially deflected the next lethal chop to his jugular. Limp, he sank to the floor, gasping. As the doors closed, the Captain shoved his way in, knocking Winston against the elevator wall. Instinctively, Winston flicked the Piaget lever and braced to defend himself. Two silent, deadly shots ripped through his chest, slamming him backward, piercing the compartment.

Brooks chuckled a low growl as Winston slipped down the textured wall, clutching his heart, falling forward at his assassin's feet. "The Youth Facilitator is no match for Raven," he boasted. The doors crept open, and for an added guarantee, Brooks pushed the lowest parking level button before stepping into the peaceful hallway.

David Winston struggled for consciousness, pressing his fist against the wound in his chest, blood oozing past his fingers. He whispered, choking on his blood, "Malchor. Brooks, he . . . No. Raven shot . . ." He coughed blood. ". . . out second floor." Survival, the reassuring rhythm of his heart . . . He focused, felt his left lung collapse, gasped for air, forced the words out, "hit in chest . . . level E garage. Please hel . . ." Blackness closed around him. He was a small child swinging, climbing, higher and higher into the cloudless sky.

GAGGING, Stan pressed the down button from his knees, lunged into the next elevator and clicked Diversity. Malchor, already startled from a deep sleep by David's garbled words, ordered Stan to the second floor. Leaning against the elevator panel, Stan hit the button, gasping and wheezing, rubbing his neck. The blow should have snapped it like a dry twig. Guilt wound its tentacles around his heart, accusing him of unredeemable error. He was alive for one reason—to terminate Brooks.

167

Above the door the numbers descended, ticking off slow seconds from the fortieth floor down. Finally, he staggered from the elevator and listened. The door at the far end of the hall closed with a thud. Adrenalin surged; Stan raced down the hall, a man possessed.

Bursting through the door, he saw Captain Brooks walking unruffled toward a blue van in the delivery parking lot. Yards away, an ambulance screeched to a halt at the front entrance and the rescue trauma team poured out and into the hotel lobby. Like a pit bull locked onto its enemy, Stanley Jonez hurdled the outside rail.

Ben swerved to the curb in David's Lamborghini, straining to be in pursuit, hardly stopping for Stan. The target steered onto the dark deserted street.

"Thanks for getting here," Stan croaked, settling into the passenger seat, checking Diversity. There it was, replete with current address and phone number. He read aloud, "Henry Schlochman, code name, Raven, alias Brooks. Mercenary." They would close in, just enough to see who pulled his strings.

DAVID was minutes from death when the trauma team scooped him from the elevator floor with Malchor screaming orders at them. The first bullet had deflected off his Diversity unit, pierced his left lung and exited just below his shoulder blade. The second one sliced between his diaphragm and pericardium, exiting a bare inch from his tenth thoracic vertebrae. Twenty-three hours later, post surgery complications threatened to succeed where the assassin failed, wracking his body with acute pericarditis.

All medical personnel allowed in the area had security clearance and worked under the surveillance of the Special Forces team. For David, the days blurred together, a cycle of pain and darkness. Ghostlike images robed in green and white probed him, prodded him, stuck him and triggered his fever-induced delirium. He was vulnerable. Torn between death and life, his mind relived the past and fabricated the future. Initiation brought revulsion;

168

embracing Kendra brought elation.

Kendra's name was on David's lips when Malchor Inyesco entered the sterile room five days after the assassination attempt. Mal hovered beside his bed, gripping his limp hand, gently urging him to fight death. Somberly, Server positioned himself by the door, his head bowed.

After the 3:00 p.m. shift change, Mal resumed his vigil, bending closer, meditating on his mantra. Concern marred his dignified face and reflected sleepless nights.

David stirred, focused on his mentor and groaned, "The conference?"

Mal smiled, relieved. "So you have decided to stick around and finish your job."

"What happened?" David rasped, warily exploring his sutured chest wound with both hands.

"You were shot twice in the chest—by a dissident, posing as a security guard. He cornered you in the elevator, leaving the restaur . . ."

"Stan," David interrupted, remembering his guard's stunned look and outstretched hand. "Where's Stan?"

Malchor leaned back in the recliner and answered, annoyed. "He's out in the field, working off his blunder."

"I . . . I ordered him to leave the others."

"Stan knew better. And now you know better," Mal said firmly. "You go no place without your bodyguards. And I've doubled the number for insurance."

"Yes, Sir," he agreed, ashamed. "But the conference? I'm missing the conference."

"Missed," Mal corrected. "No problem, I finished it. Actually, your injury served as a unifying factor. When the NTU members heard that their President, Gil Duskin, hired Raven to kill you, they became our strongest proponents. And of course, no one wanted to be affiliated with the teachers caught in the midnight drug-bust orgy."

Closing his eyes, David withdrew into peaceful slumber.

THE withered hag pushed her rickety cart along the littered sidewalk, past decaying tenement buildings. Pausing in front of 2630, her eyes scanned the route she had taken. It was a miserable area, filled with the refuse of broken people who had no vision, no will to change and no hope. In disgust, she moved past two derelicts sprawled on the basement steps sharing a near empty bottle of vodka.

Descending the steps with her cart was like entering a sewer. Urine stench stung her nostrils. She hated excuses and excesses, especially those costly to society that she had to clean up after. Knocking on the cold steel door at the bottom brought no response. She kicked it with her hard leather boot and screeched, "Sonny, you answer the door this minute. Yer ole' man tol' me ta bring ya sumpin' ta eat."

The derelicts stopped drinking long enough to watch the old biddy swear at the middle-aged slob who answered. He peered suspiciously out his door, past the woman, past them, up to the black storm clouds. At the first drop of rain, he pulled her inside, slamming the door. The sots gathered their junk and staggered toward the alley way to seek refuge in the nearest dumpster.

Inside, a razor thin blade touched the soft folds of her neck and he hissed, "It better be good. Who are you?"

Instantly, her elbow found its target; intense pressure hit his diaphragm, the knife clattered against the empty bookshelf and he slumped to his knees breathless. Disgusted, she slammed her right boot into his side, leaving him curled up like a baby, squirming.

"Does the Raven dare peck at Dove?" she murmured, lifting the cart over his legs, carrying her bounty to the bare wood table. "You failed! He should have left you to rot down in this hole." She added lightly, "It's tiresome to have to clean up after stupid men."

Her words pierced his pain. He glared, pushing himself up from the cold, filthy floor.

She took food from the cart: bread, bags of fruit, eggs, vegetables, then pulled out milk, crackers and a four-pound block of farmers cheese. "I'm not going out in this deluge for anyone," she said, slipping off her wig and face mask, shaking her jet-black hair loose. Like a butterfly unfolding her wings from the drab cocoon, Dove shed her garb and stood in front of Raven, a beige body suit clinging to her supple frame.

Raven stood slowly, cautiously. "I did deserve that. I left myself wide open," he moaned.

"You're lucky to be alive," she whispered. "If Frank wanted you dead, I would have complied and you would, no doubt, be on to another plane by now."

"I don't doubt the fact," he said, noting the sarcasm in her voice. Mercenaries didn't bother with "higher plane" stuff. That was for elitists. He pulled off his wig and mask, threw them into the corner and sat on the unmade bunk bed. "So you're the famous Dove, the scourge of mortals, the bane of gods," he ventured quietly. "I lost some big jobs to you last year."

"Well, I lost a few to you also, this last one included. Frank is very unhappy that his enemy lives." She turned the lone chair and straddled it, facing her competition. "The Youth Facilitator should not be recuperating. It was a mistake for the Public Relations Director to send a man to do a woman's job."

Raven roared a hearty, nervous laugh and ran both hands through his oily brown hair. "Guess so," he whispered, "but I assure you Winston's rest will be short lived. Did Frank make travel arrangements for me?"

"No. He wants you to wait until Winston's next campus tour, and he wants it to look like an accident. Meanwhile, your botched job is being credited to the dissident teachers. Even David Winston believes it. But Frank's coming undone. If he gets close to the edge, it may be necessary to do something about him."

"It wouldn't be a great loss. Hiring me wiped out his investment account. How could he afford you?"

"Money's not everything, my sweet. There's jewelry—and influence."

Perspiring, Raven stood and shed his coveralls and bulky flannel shirt down to his black cotton sweat suit, tossing them on the bed. The cracked concrete walls of the dingy apartment mocked him, suffocating him. It was his pit, and the pendulum had swung dangerously close.

Hidden, Raven's anger raged, demanding action. Dove sat unblinking, unmoved, unfeeling. He focused on the object of his pain: the woman who dared stir his feelings.

He hadn't loved anyone since he was eight and lunged at the throat of his alcoholic father, screaming his hatred. His mother cowered, covering her eyes to block the beating he got. No. What he felt now wasn't love. He used women, conquered them, demeaned them—then dumped them. Instinctively, he knew conquering her could be deadly and wouldn't satisfy the urgency that ripped through him. He wanted her soul. But she was right, money wasn't everything. Walking to the table, he whispered his response. "Yes, there's also passion and power."

Her eyes flashed a warning, while a slight smile played across her mouth. "Don't act the fool twice in one day, Raven. I'm no one's whore."

Undeterred, Henry Schlockman sorted through the groceries. "True," he said quietly. "You're Bernedette Von Himmler, alias Marci, alias Jackie, et cetera. Born twenty-eight years ago, daughter of Lance and Stacia Von Himmler, former East German Stazi agents, to date the best detective team in Europe." Raven dumped the ripe apples into a cracked bowl. "You are, I must agree, their masterpiece. Trained from infancy to be the mercenary that could capture the notorious Raven in her delicate talons." Pouring two glasses of white grape juice from his only bottle, he handed one across the table. "Congratulations!" he said, clinking his glass against hers, "Salute. Now, relax, dear Dove, while I make the best eggs Benedict that have ever touched your lips."

"I never relax, Henry Schlockman," she countered, unimpressed, "but cook, if you wish."

SPRING blossomed in Skagit County, Washington. The first weeks of April, the Tulip Festival attracted and accommodated

172

touring throngs. Busses and cars choked the narrow country roads, their passengers awed by fields of crimson and yellow on one side, pink and white on the other. Clear to the foothills, patches of color reached for the sun. The delays, the crowds— the lines were worth it, just to see the fertile fields crowned with multicolored tulips. Early on the twenty-third of April, the Facilitator's motorcade pulled into the near-empty Roozengaarde parking lot. Today the crowds would have to wait.

Owen Tyson, Stan's replacement, strode toward two guards sent ahead to coordinate securing the area. County Sheriff deputies had the roads blocked for two miles around. Finally alone, seated inside the black stretch limousine, David held Kendra's hand between his, watching the guards scatter to their assigned positions throughout the gardens. "So much for a simple drive to see the tulips," he offered cheerfully. "See across the road, those empty fields beyond the tulips? They were filled with daffodils a few weeks ago."

"While you were in the Baltimore hospital, fighting for . . ." she couldn't finish; fear again spread its menacing cloud through her mind.

Protective, he put his arm around her, drawing her close. She rested her head on his shoulder and wept unashamed, her hand gently touching his heart.

"I'm all right, Kendra," he whispered, "and you're with me now, for the next two weeks. That makes me a lucky man, to have so much."

"But, these past weeks were . . . nothing helped, David. I couldn't concentrate, meditate or get my work done." She looked up, his face blurred through her tears. "I only wanted to be with you," she moaned, "but they wouldn't let me, Davy. Sometimes," a deep sigh escaped her, "I miss how it used to be. Everything's so complicated."

"Yes, things were simple," he brushed her tears with his fingertips. "When I think about it, Kendra Marie, things weren't just simple, they were sterile. Institutional. Fine for children, yet," he saw Tyson's muscular hulk approaching to open their door and hastily planted a kiss on the tip of her nose, "as children, we didn't know what we meant to each other."

Tyson swung open the door and stepped aside, interrupting the declaration of affection that grew in her mind. She rubbed her sleeve across her eyes and stepped out into the fragrant cool air. "This is like our ninth-level field trip," she said for Owen Tyson's benefit, "only we had teachers watching us instead of a dozen security guards."

"This is better, much better," David said. Taking her hand, he walked her past the shop toward the windmill. "They have to stay out of hearing range. It's a good thing, because for every different flower we see, I'm going to tell you exactly what you are to me, and what I've wanted to say for these past weeks."

Walking along the narrow paths through the central hedged garden soothed her and strengthened David. Bright splashes of tulips, interlaced with lavender hyacinths and yellow daffodils surrounded them with a symphony of color. The attentive guards faded from their minds. They explored the flower-bordered grassy area, then the tulip field with neat rows of red stretching into the distance, merging into a solid carpet. Returning to the central garden, they retraced their steps past the gnarled trees and delicate blossoms. Later, they sat on a bench next to the windmill, sharing nature's beauty and a picnic brunch. A gently clouded, blue sky promised forever. He held her close and poured out his heart.

JAKE avoided him. Every time Steve Winston approached, the man had an urgent errand to run in the opposite direction. Finally, he had the ranch hand cornered in the garage. "All right, Jake, it's been months . . . Will you tell me?"

Uncomfortable, Jake's dark eyes darted the length of the room, looking for an out. Finding none, he shrugged and squared his shoulders, expecting to be fired for getting involved. "My woman will skin me alive if I meddle in this."

Sensing the tension, Steve assured him, "Look, I'm not going to fire you or repeat what you say to anyone. I just need to hear

174

what Jenna has told Fran about, you know, about me."

"Well sir, you've changed over the years, mellowed a lot. Mainly, it was your . . ." Jake paused, groping for the acceptable word.

"For Trib sake, man! My what?"

"Your stubbornness, sir."

"That's all?"

"Sir, that can be a mighty big thing to a woman who wants you to listen to her needs. And your stubbornness sometimes led to outright temper."

"Temper?"

"Yes, I remember seeing the fear in her eyes turn to . . . You can't love someone you fear. Your wife's love turned to fear, then to bitterness."

"Fear," he repeated, stunned. He never suspected that she feared him. Steve sighed, "Thank you, Jake." He pivoted and headed for the horse corral.

Relieved, Jake turned back to oiling the tools. Maybe there was some hope after all if his boss heard the truth and faced it.

THAT evening at the ranch, violet streaks spread through the cumulus clouds along the western horizon. Seated at the sundeck table, David and his parents soaked in the view and listened as Kendra shared the highlights of her morning arrival and the trip to the Skagit Valley. Fran quietly cleared the dishes, set her homemade German-chocolate cake before them, gave David an affectionate pat and left. Kendra and his parents weren't the only ones rattled by his near death. Both Fran and Jake had suffered the tragic drowning of their only son three decades earlier. Their pain stirred afresh as they offered support for Jenna and Steve.

Building the enclosed sun deck off the kitchen was what kept them focused on his recovery. Even Jenna found relief swinging the hammer and connecting two by fours, raising a structure for her son to enjoy. Her son lived. Fran loaded the dishwasher, comforted by their reunion, pleased they could savor the fleeting beauty of another sunset.

She flinched when Jake kissed the back of her neck, startled. "Sorry, didn't mean to stun you," he said, running his hands along the back of her cotton dress, pausing to knead her tense muscles.

"Yes, that's good," she breathed, "You're making up for it right now."

"I'll help you finish these," he offered, taking the scraped plate from her weary hands. "You remember what I told you a couple months back about Steve?"

"Yes." She turned her black eyes toward him. He still saw her as she was thirty years earlier, smooth bronzed skin, waist-length hair parted at the center, pulled loosely into a circle at the nape of her neck.

"He listened. He wouldn't have heard me back when he first asked, but today he listened." Jake shook his head. "He was shocked to think she feared him."

"I think almost losing his son was . . ."

Reading her thought, he nodded, sobered. "Some things are too hard learned."

Steve's exhilarated laugh caught their attention and they both looked up. Jenna motioned for them. Puzzled, they left the kitchen.

"David just made an announcement," Jenna said as they opened the sliding door. "Go ahead, say it again!" she added, tugging his sleeve, realizing she didn't need to prod him.

"Malchor has given permission for Kendra and me to hold our unity celebration this December," David repeated, lifting Kendra's left hand up for them to see. The flawless, two-carat oval solitaire shimmered.

"David proposed this morning at Roozengaarde. It was very special." Kendra gazed from his beaming face to theirs and added, "We were sitting by the windmill when he knelt down on one knee and pledged himself to me." A soft blush rose in her cheeks, and she got up to hug Fran and Jake. "Naturally, I said yes."

Later that evening, Steve knelt beside Jenna's twin bed in their moonlit room. Weighing the risk, he reached for her, touching her arm lightly. "Jenna," he whispered, "May I speak with you, please, about us?"

She reacted as if stung by an electric eel. "No," she blurted, turned her back and pretended sleep.

EACH steel-reinforced concrete cell held chilled dampness at night and suffocating humidity during the day. Deryle Otis, the facility warden, didn't even try to comply with federal regulations for prisoners. Men sent to North Carolina to the Spartus maximum security prison didn't deserve equal rights, or any rights, for that matter. Justice herself put these men in his grasp and karma demanded he fulfill his duty. He relished greeting every new inmate and dispensing cruel doses of vengeance.

After two weeks of intense abuse, semi-starvation and interrupted sleep, Greg Foster unwillingly settled into the grueling prison routine. No more interrogation, just mind numbing pointless hours; no activities, no work, bare survival. Solitary confinement and solitary meals were broken by two hours a day in the exercise yard. Armed guards stood sentry, ignoring all, but deadly quarrels. Convicted addicts, pushers, killers, pimps, and thieves roamed the yards, venting their fury on each other and on the hapless dissidents. Greg found himself gravitating toward the dissidents. It was dangerous to stand alone. Men died when they stood alone for too long.

Hearing word of the Youth Facilitator's near-fatal wounds struck Greg a greater blow than any his tormentors could devise. It was Foster's fourth day in the yard when Gil Duskin was paraded by the guards; he had been convicted of obstructing Synthesis and plotting the assassination attempt on Facilitator Winston. After reading the terms of his life sentence, guards shoved Duskin into a group of hardened felons. Greg cheered silently when they swarmed around the stately man, punching, shoving, spitting, clawing, then, as he stumbled and fell, kicking him. Satiated, they left him in a heap on the asphalt slab and returned to their game of basketball. Greg glared at the moaning mass. In spite of what David had done to him, Duskin's death would not be enough to pay for injuring the Youth Facilitator.

A tight band of dissidents closed around Duskin, lifted him carefully and carried him to their corner. Jeff Ashmon pulled off his shirt and placed it under the man's head. Two others shaded his face from the sun, handing dampened paper towels to those who were cleaning his wounds.

Paul Williams, in his early thirties, soft spoken, brown soulful eyes, dabbed at the blood trickling from Gil's mouth. Once the dirt was cleared from the gash above the man's swollen left eye, Paul began wiping away the clinging spittle. With Gil's immediate physical needs met as best he could, the young man placed both hands on the President of the National Teachers' Union, lifted his eyes to heaven and cried out in anguish. "Merciful Father, cover this fallen man with unmerited favor."

Amazed, Greg edged closer; the dissident was weeping over a total stranger. The crowd gave way until Greg was standing over the scene, unobstructed.

"Holy One, touch this man, bring him to repentance, to face the truth about himself, to turn from evil. Your Son died in his place for his sin, so he could live to know You. Draw him to Your throne of grace. Teach him Your will and Your way. Heal him in the name of our Paschal Lamb, Messiah."

It was easy for Greg to see who the Believers were; their lips were moving in agreement as Paul spoke. He looked down to watch Gil reach for Paul's hand, groaning, confessing his need for Maker.

First, Greg was curious, then amused, until the accusation of hypocrisy stabbed his conscience. So this was their world, their fantasy, so what? Wasn't their myth as harmless as his fantasy, his private world with Reana—the Caribbean beach, surf swirling around their feet, their bodies locked in an embrace? It was his escape from the abusive guards, the oppressive confinement. When reality threatened, he centered upon himself, repeated his mantra and withdrew into his inner world. When reality threatened, they centered on their God. But wasn't that the problem?

Prejudice surfaced from the past and was again questioned. The teacher's words had challenged the student to silence. Greg was that student in the tenth-track class. He never again entertained another question about tolerance until now. Ms. Lendel's words drilled into his mind; he could see and feel the classroom.

"Both the Chosen and the Believers are a danger to unity and future Synthesis. The cultists persist in refusing to accept their godhood, their responsibility on the evolutionary plane. No! We don't teach intolerance!"

Lendel strode up and down the aisles, emphasizing her words with a pointed finger and sporadic jabbing motions. "No! Our reaction to their venom isn't intolerance," she sneered. Greg gawked at her, then at David. They had never seen this kind of emotion from anyone. She slammed her Social Science textbook hard on her desk, drew a breath and continued, tight lipped. "Their false belief is poison." For emphasis, she lifted her coffee cup from the desk and stuck it under Greg's nose. "A drop of cyanide in this coffee could do what to you, Greg Foster?" Embarrassed, he answered it would terminate him and send him to a different plane. Smugly satisfied, she concluded, much to his relief, "Yes, dear. And while it could be a higher plane, if your karma is unfinished, it could send you to a lower plane. So you must all be protected from poison. Even one drop must be eradicated. It is our duty to expose and halt the spread of poison. Is it not?" she asked. The class, including Greg, eagerly mouthed agreement.

The entire student body was inoculated in similar fashion, given the official exposé. Mythical roots were shared by both the Chosen and the Believers. Their cruel

Maker forced man to obey harsh laws, forced allegiance, destroyed his own son, and threatened his own creation with punishment and extinction. Such myths must be eschewed by wise and noble scholars.

Greg felt disgust for Duskin and pity for the dissidents gathered around him. Their fantasy wasn't a pleasant one, and the price they paid was too high a price to pay for any fantasy, any myth, even his own.

THE exercise yard had served its purpose again. Deryle Otis sipped his lemonade from the balcony of his air-conditioned office, chuckling as he watched the dissidents' feeble attempts to doctor the fallen elitist. Otis delighted in watching the big boys fall. The ones who thought they were a class above him always bellowed their rights and demanded their privileges until they met his felons. He retired to his office, satisfied.

DISSIDENT Believers continued offering comfort. Behind him, Greg heard sullen words and turned to face Jim Reichlin, his muscular, stocky build barely restrained by the graying Floyd Warsol.

"Don't you know who he is?" Jim challenged.

"I know who he is. It doesn't matter."

"But it does. We're fools to help him. His union did everything they could to shut down our schools, turn our children against us, to hate us."

"The man has been blinded his whole life," Floyd agreed.

"And he should die blind for what he's done," Jim fumed, his fist wrapped around his hand-forged glinting blade. "Just let me at him! No one will know. They'll think a felon stuck him."

Greg was his only other barrier. Jim pressed his chest with his free hand and threatened, "Out of my way." Greg wasn't sure why he stood his ground. He had no desire to protect Duskin, and Jim meant nothing to him. Yet he stood, a wall, not responding, watching.

Floyd kept his hand firmly over the youth's fist. "I will not let you do this." Others stepped closer, faces tense. "Put it away now," he urged. "Your bitterness won't bring justice to victory. Only Messiah can do that."

The slight, bespectacled man at Jim's other side reinforced Floyd's hand with his own. "Maker permitted our enemy to fall into our hands," Terry affirmed. "It's our duty to love him."

Greg glanced at Terry, ready to defend himself if necessary, then back to Jim. The official exposé on Believers had said nothing about loving your enemies.

Pain mixed with the young dissident's anger and he blurted bitterly, "He can't expect me to love Duskin." Greg shifted, waiting for the answer, unconsciously holding his breath.

"But, Maker can and does," Floyd answered quietly. "You must resist bitterness before it grieves Him and destroys your soul."

Recovering, Jim argued, eyes dark with hatred. "How do you know Duskin's not in our hands just so we can stop him—permanently?"

"And I have a question for you," Terry enjoined. "What would you have done while Steven was being stoned? Would you have struck Saul?" Jim's eyes widened, knowing well what he would have done and Terry Murry drove his point home. "He was a leader, Saul of Tarsus, fervent enemy of the faith, hounding Believers to their death. He held the garments of the religious zealots who stoned Steven. Yet, Maker mercifully turned Saul's heart to the truth and renamed him Paul, the Apostle.

"Jim," Terry continued, "He has not called us to destroy the wicked. He has called us to have mercy on the lost and to love them." Downcast, Jim Richlin slowly returned the weapon to his inner pocket and melted to the fringe of the crowd.

When the signal blared, Paul and Floyd helped Gil walk to his cell, then obediently went to their own.

Back in his cell, Greg welcomed the solitude, succumbed to fatigue and sank onto his cot. Believers went beyond the official exposé of their mythology, far beyond. He wrestled with what his eyes had seen and his ears had heard. His years of learning failed the test of current reality.

That month, the exercise yard proved to be of greater benefit to the dissidents than it was to Warden Otis. Gil Duskin repented of harassing both the Chosen and Believers and convinced Greg of his innocence regarding the Youth Facilitator. One after another, most of the agnostic dissidents turned from faith in themselves to Maker. And Paul Williams taught the attorney what he had taught his two young sons. Greg Foster heard and believed. Before he was transferred to slave labor at CAM, he had transcribed Paul's copy of the book of Romans and concealed the tissue thin sheets beneath the lining of his shoes.

When confronted by the gloating Fereno in Chicago, Greg's feet were uniquely shod with the Gospel of peace.

XII   WATERSHED

IT WAS June 2, 2001, the opening day of The Council on Global Relations Summit in Aspen, Colorado. Irritated, Malchor had postponed his flight for 24 hours; his Youth Facilitator was still weeks away from complete recovery. With no better option, he arranged for Server to oversee David's care. Server spent the morning writing instructions for the two staff members replacing him. While the entourage lined up to board the supersonic Quasar, Frank attempted to impress them by giving David his latest autographed, framed picture of President Chamberlon. Malchor ignored him and reminded David to avoid excessive exercise, then boarded.

When the jet roared to life, David went to his office and tossed the photo into a drawer. He retreated to the library, content to have the place to himself. At the ranch he pushed the limits, added to his physical therapy routine and believed he was in good shape. When he returned to headquarters, exhaustion set in daily after three hours of work. He had to pace himself and let his body heal.

The reading area held the promise of comfort. David settled in front of the fireplace, propping his feet on the coffee table. Malchor's volumes lay beside him. He opened the fifth, *Chaldean Babylonian Mysteries*, flipped the pages to his marker, and reread the section aloud. "Nimrod, god of fire, father of the gods, perfecter, purifier of mankind; Kronos, Zoroaster, Tammuz, Baal, Adonis, Odin." He scanned the index for Dagon, turned to the first page listed, the chapter titled, *Dagon—Nimrod incarnate as*

Noah, god of water, regenerator of mankind. Mythology had never interested him before and the names weren't familiar. He read both chapters, disappointed with the farfetched legends of snake, sun, fire, and mother worship. For all of their power and supposed wisdom the fallible gods and goddesses had only complicated and mucked up the world for their followers. Hoping for enlightenment, he read the preface and the first and last chapters.

Server entered at noon and waited to be acknowledged. Winston pretended to be absorbed, looking up references, studying the incarnations and symbolism attached to his new name. Server set the lunch tray on the coffee table by David's feet and left.

David expected to feel better, less self-conscious, after Server left, but he didn't. His uneasiness grew as he read further. God of fire and god of water, it was an intriguing combination. Nimrod's role as god of fire, purifier of children disturbed him most. History told of generations of innocent children slain by the fiery arms of Moloch, purified by flames, sacrificed. Bizarre comfort came from visualizing those children reincarnated to higher levels, even perhaps to the student body of the Academy, to godhood and Synthesis. Suddenly his own face appeared in contorted agony, gaping mouth, terror-struck eyes, flesh seared by Moloch's fiery arms.

A heavy dank atmosphere settled over him, disrupting his thoughts. Words blurred together in meaningless verbiage. He reread the page aloud until the tightness in his neck ran its tentacles through his vocal chords, into his jaw. The metallic taste was real. Agitated, David left the books.

The door guard, Darin Fields, heard him coming, snapped to attention, saluted and moved aside as the Facilitator fled the building. Fields preferred the familiar routine, but chalked David's erratic behavior up to trauma. He stared long after the young man disappeared through the cavernous door of the temple.

DRIVEN, David was compelled to regain piety, the glow of holiness that came from sensing his own power and purpose.

He needed to feel pure. Once inside the door, he waited until his eyes adjusted to the filtered light. Purple ceremonial robes draped the slight frame of the ancient priest, Zoganes, as he stood before the altar, lighting six wax tapers, blessing the celestial Bee, Incarnate Wisdom. The Facilitator crept toward the pews, not wishing to interrupt the priest's oblations. Reverently, the man circled to the corner, motioning for David to approach the altar and the flutist to begin. Hypnotic music blending with flickering candlelight should have brought peace; instead, it brought revulsion. Horrified, he saw himself on the altar in his own blood, redeeming himself. Fighting nausea, David rose from the pew and knelt before the candles. His hands, clasped together, were wet with sweat. Meditation failed him. Slowly he rose, stepping back away from the altar.

Outside the temple, hidden from view by the dense birch grove, he clung to a slender tree. Time passed from day into evening while David resisted facing the abject revulsion the temple ceremony evoked in him. *Weak*, he thought. *You're too weak to master your fears.* Steadied by the solid reality of the tree; his forehead pressed against the cool, smooth bark, he concentrated on canceling the thought, the vision of his own bloody death. He shuddered, doubled over, retching, as deepening shadows closed around him.

Server hovered until the Youth Facilitator recovered enough to hear, then with strained effort he again forced words past his scarred vocal chords. "There is a better way, David." Coming alongside, he half-carried the Youth Facilitator through the grove, then along the back of the garage, out of sight of the guards, into his own quarters. Peace dispelled the darkness and David slept.

MORNING brought confusion and the memory of Server's selfless care mixed with his warnings of evil. Still troubled, David sat at his desk monitoring the activities of the nation's Academies; surreal images played with his mind. The wall beside his desk became alive with children's laughing faces, some recognizable by sight, others by name. Pamela Bardon, the girl he rescued;

185

Richard and Jamie, Paul Williams' boys; Megan Kassan, the child from Spokane. While David stared, each smile turned to alarm. Their shadows had twisted into wart-covered reptilian creatures which covered each child with darkness. The creatures were evil, if evil could exist.

The wall flashed back to normal, and he scanned his orderly office. It was odd that wives' tales persisted even at headquarters, even in his own imagination. He affirmed out loud, "Evil is mere illusion." The previous night's ills and Server's words flooded his mind. *The harmless words of an aging . . . But why?* he wondered. *Why? Even the thought of initiation . . .* It had to be weakness. He purposed to renew his efforts to overcome weakness.

STEVE finished the weekend job of resurfacing the runway with Jake. The place was empty with his family gone, increasingly lonely without Jenna. Even pretense was better than the place without her, and exhaustion was his only antidote.

A plan formed in his mind as he surveyed the leveled asphalt. Jenna was more concerned with maintaining their "happy family" facade since David's injury. She wouldn't just walk out and leave her son wondering what happened. It might work, with help, since there was more to gain for all of them than there was to lose.

"You're mighty sober for someone who just finished a job," Jake observed, coming up behind him. "Everything's put away. Is there anything else you'd like me to do?"

"Not tonight, Jake. You were a big help. Thanks."

An odd, expectant, questioning look on Steve's face kept Jake's attention. He waited.

Steve rubbed his arm across his grimy, sunburned face, exhausted. "Why don't you pull up a lawn chair: I want to ask you about something."

"Yes, sir," Jake said, remembering his questions, reluctant to get into the subject. He sat down, shoulders aching.

"I've thought a lot about what you said," Steve confessed. "You were right; I was stubborn." He had said the words before, from his head. This time he meant it from the heart. He meant it enough to change. "I was always forcing my way, ignoring what Jenna said. Self important, that's what I was."

"Yes, sir," Jake agreed, nodding thoughtfully.

"I guess it wasn't easy for any of you."

"No, sir."

"David's coming back Friday, June 29th," Steve continued. "He's doing the spring tour, then joining Kendra. They'll be here three days. Jenna always comes a day early to fix things up for him. I'd like to see her before that." Steve slid his chair closer. "I'm just asking for a chance to tell her I'm sorry, to make peace with her, call a truce or whatever. She won't talk to me."

"You know you can't force her to talk to you."

"I know, but maybe she'll be willing to talk if Fran is with her. If she knows I'm ready to listen, really listen to her."

SUMMIT week was over. Anticipating Malchor's return, David was up early, finishing his work. Both of Frank's Chamberlon photos hung on the wall behind him, out of sight. His monitor was showing the latest academic performance statistics, comparing the Academies by level. As expected, Student Learning Outcomes showed support for Synthesis nationwide.

When David's personal line rang, he grabbed it, eager to hear Kendra's voice, picturing her light brown eyes and petal-soft skin. Before he uttered a sound, frantic words hit like ice water on a griddle.

"David? David, is that you?"

He knew the voice; panicked, he took a slow, deep breath. Their last meeting leapt into the present. "Yes Reana," he said, "it's me."

"Thank Trib! David, they're going to . . ." her voice trembled. "They're going to terminate Greg."

"Terminate? Trib, Reana! You mean—transform." There was silence at the other end and David winced, disgusted he had made an issue of the proper term. "How can they do that?" he asked, turning to his computer, keying into Greg's file. It had been erased. "Who's they? On who's order?" he persisted. During his recovery he assumed Greg was back home, back with the program, back working for peace. "There has to be a mistake."

"I just got a notice," she said, recovering from his initial coldness. "I didn't even know where they were holding him. David, you were wrong; they never sent him home. I haven't seen him since the day before you were shot. This card just came from the Chicago Liberation Dome; he's scheduled to terminate next Monday. I knew it. I felt it. Fereno's got him at CAM in Chicago," she sobbed. "They want to know where to send his—his personal things."

"I only requested Level I Reorientation," David affirmed, continuing the search, trying to track Greg's file.

"I told you they would hurt him."

"Look, Reana, he got himself into this, listening to the wrong people."

"David, they're going to murder him!"

"Transformation isn't murder, and you know it," he insisted, battling guilt. "It's liberation to a higher plane."

"Is it? Well, whatever you want to call it, David, it's not justice. Greg didn't do anything to warrant termination and you know it!"

Dead silence.

Of course, he knew it. Transformation was for hard core and recalcitrant cases, like Werling. He held the phone, thinking she had hung up until he heard muffled weeping. "I'll see what I can do," he conceded. "Hegelthor's flying in with Malchor this afternoon; I'll ask him about it."

"Thank you, David. And thank Trib you survived."

"Yes, thank Trib." Images of the sterile hospital room and Malchor's worried face surfaced. He had almost experienced the higher plane. He had almost missed Unity with Kendra.

THAT afternoon, Hegie and the Tribunal arrived in separate planes, acknowledged David, and recessed to the library. David

188

paced the runway and filled the time gap talking with Don Samuels, showing him the new Astrojet III supplied for his biannual campus tours. In turn, the Colonel took him aboard Hegie's new Quasar. The Colonel was friendlier than David remembered, polite, at least treating him as an adult. They went past a lounge area in the middle compartment. An office held the updated, miniaturized replica of the brains of the Academy. Technology had exploded in the ten years since the landlocked model had been installed. The system had Greg's file and the files of everyone in the country, but getting into it with Don around was impossible. Don led him to the cockpit and was explaining the instrument panel when Frank paged him with orders from Malchor. Dinner would be served late. At 6:00 o'clock, Winston was to join them at the temple for mass. Hegie would see something was wrong. He knew it would be best if they talked before mass and he could explain the problem, seeking advice. Nagging him, fear grew by the minute. During his walk to the temple, winding his way through the maze offered an insignificant diversion.

Revulsion threatened to overwhelm the Youth Facilitator throughout the hour-long ceremony. He performed the expected ritual, circled the candle-lit altar, muttered ancient mysteries, knelt and opened his mouth to receive the unbloody sacrifice.

"Isis Horus Seb," Cyrus incanted, "the Mother, the Child and the Father of the gods, oh great trinity, we share in the transubstantiation of your flesh."

The rounded symbol of the sun stuck to his dry tongue. Like generations of adepts, David struggled along the path from reality to enlightenment. He knelt at the altar pretending worship of Mother Earth and various gods, waiting for the tasteless wafer to dissolve. Dusk devoured the light, birthing ghostly reptilian shapes which leapt and swayed to the flickering tapers. The Tribunal, gratified with their religious devotions, withdrew, removed their robes and dressed. Hegie's frigid steel-gray eyes noted David's mechanical obedience. He waited for David; together, they walked to the empty dressing room. For David, the silence was perilous.

"Thank you, sir," he offered, removing his robes, putting on his blue, cotton-knit shirt. "I needed to talk with you."

"Yes, David, I felt you did." Hegie remained robed and closed the door of the sterile white cubicle. "I have been monitoring your recovery. You seem to be doing well. What is it?"

Hands trembling, the young man slipped on his tan slacks and finished buttoning his shirt. "I need your help, sir, with something personal."

A bare hint of concern settled on Hegelthor's forehead. "Yes?"

"I have a weakness, sir, that interferes with my progress in Synthesis."

"Weakness?"

"The Initiation, sir."

Hegie waited, silent, unblinking.

"I threw up," he fidgeted, heat flushed his face, "and failed to cancel."

Facilitator Hegelthor allowed a faint smile. "Ah, yes, your first initiation. We still have no way to tell how a person will react." He patted David's shoulder. "You trouble yourself needlessly. I felt sick after my first time, even threw up."

"But how, how did you . . ."

"Overcome weakness?" Hegie finished. "Determination and repetition. I simply went to the temple more often, until gradually, nothing fazed me. You, too, will overcome."

Winston was encouraged by the admission from his paternal benefactor, his nagging fear absolved. "There is something else." He inhaled deeply, spoke cautiously, watching for any sign of rebuke. "From childhood, we were taught to control our bodily functions. As toddlers, we mastered our bowels; likewise, as adolescents, we mastered our reproductive drive. Therefore, our seed is preserved for communion and reproduction in unity."

"Yes, of course," Hegie approved.

"But, I was curious about the activities after my initiation."

190

"You question the indulgences of the Tribunal?"

"Sir, I don't mean to question. I only . . ."

Hegelthor interrupted, "Malchor didn't prepare you?"

David shook his head. "No, sir."

"The Tribunal is unique," he said, making a mental note to discuss the oversight. "They have completely mastered their bodily functions, minds and spirits; therefore, they are able to engage in physical union with a virgin priestess while still maintaining holiness. In essence, they merge with a representative of the goddess Diana, in likeness of Mother Earth herself." Hegie smiled benevolently in response to the young man's widening dark eyes. "Certainly, for the sake of Synthesis, you will save yourself for unity with Kendra."

At this, David was deeply relieved. He had no desire to merge with anyone other than Kendra, not even Mother Earth herself. Embarrassed, he added, "Of course, sir, I hadn't considered the possibility of indulging my urges before the proper time." He reasoned further that whatever the Tribunal did in their private rituals was their own business. Yet, the idea of indulging, beyond the grasp of immorality, gripped his imagination.

"Good," Hegie said, sensing David's acceptance of mastery over indulgence. "At the proper time Kendra will be instructed by the temple priestess, as you take instruction from the priest. She will, I am sure, do well as your personal goddess. Now, is there anything else you wish to discuss?"

David pictured Kendra's wholesome features, then remembered Greg. Time was scarce. He wouldn't have another chance to talk privately with Hegelthor once they rejoined the Tribunal, so he worded his best appeal and moved forward. "I understand Greg is at CAM, scheduled for transformation."

"Yes," Hegelthor answered simply, reaching for Diversity, coding into the confidential file.

"Would it be inappropriate for me to know the details?" he asked, risking disapproval.

Fortunately, for him, total success at the summit had left the August dignitary in a peak frame of mind. Glowing pride poured from his soul and passed as love for the entire human race, especially for the naive David.

"I will allow your question. The evidence against Greg Foster was more serious than you mentioned in your report. He was implicated by Jules Lazzari before the man was transformed." Hegie entertained a moment of suspicion, drew his large frame up, and peered down at David.

Realizing the futility of insisting on Greg's innocence, Winston sought a different resolution, remembered the dissident Rabbi and proceeded carefully. "How much time did Foster spend at Level I?"

"None."

"I know it's a Level II facility, sir, but the Haven has excellent results, even with hardened dissidents. Wouldn't it be pragmatic to utilize every effort available to protect your prior investment?" David reasoned distantly, avoiding any show of personal concern. "Greg Foster is, after all, a product of the Academy. Surely the Haven has a program to successfully reorient one of your own notable graduates."

"Very good, David," Hegie declared. "You're an excellent negotiator. If they don't have a useful program for my wayward children, then they had best develop one. Yes, Level II reorientation should be tried. Perhaps it is too soon to recycle Greg."

Recycle Greg? Trib! He hadn't thought of it that way, even though the liberation domes housed the nation's largest organ banks. "Thank you, sir, for your kindness," David said, elation bridled, reflecting on his insight. *Liberation helps useless eaters as well as those needing transplants. Recycling is part of humanity's duty,* he reasoned. *Evolution is only a form of recycling,* he concluded, hoping Greg would cooperate and prove himself too useful to recycle.

"Now, David, you look considerably better. Those negative thoughts that trouble you—cancel the thought. Remember to increase your visits to the temple for the sake of Synthesis."

Facilitator David Winston brightened and agreed, "Yes, for

the sake of Syn."

JUNE 15, 2001 dawned, taunting Steve Winston with the hope of renewal. Sunrise graced the balcony outside his Bellingham apartment, glistening from the petals of his single potted geranium. He lay in bed rehearsing what he hoped to say to Jenna. Jake had called to say she was willing to give him one hour, one hour to unlock the tangled bitterness of thirteen years, if he promised to continue the facade.

Anticipating his absence from work, Steve had prepared another news special on the progress of Autonomous voting. It was going well in California where citizens were enthralled with the idea of personal voting devices. Soon, anything the Governor wanted would be presented to the voters in outline form with the 6:00 o'clock news, and voters would respond yea or nay. It was as simple as that, no long costly debates, no pompous greedy legislators. The thought occurred to Steve that autonomy left legislation solely in the hands of the Governor, rubber stamped by masses of uninformed or purposely misinformed voters. It was what they wanted. He knew he wanted more.

The drive to the ranch was slowed by a traffic accident on southbound I-5; Steve exited as soon as he could and took side roads. Evergreens towered above him; intervals of open space blinded his eyes with the rising sun as he wound through the hills. Pulling onto their four hundred acres of pristine forested land, he realized the house was no longer visible from the road. The trees had grown, blocking most of the meadow and all of their lake from view. The ranch held promise of being a Shangri-la, if Jenna was willing.

They were waiting for him in the living room—Jenna's face hard, determined. Fran and Jake sat on the couch with her, visibly uncomfortable.

Jenna glanced at the clock, then glared at her husband. "You're prompt, as usual. You have one hour, as agreed."

Naked was how he felt, naked and vulnerable. Resentment bubbled below the surface, urging him to turn, slam the door and

193

be gone, slam the door on the past and on her. Instead, he chose to be naked. "Thank you, Jenna," he said, and as he said it, found he meant it. He pulled a dining chair into the room and settled in front of his wife. "I appreciate your willingness to arrange this meeting." He directed a frail, pained smile at Jake, then at Fran. "I owe you both an apology for the difficult times I put you through," he said, further stripping himself. "I was stubborn and unapproachable, arrogant. I'm deeply sorry."

Surprised, Fran clasped Jenna's hand tighter.

"Will you accept my apology?" he persisted.

Both Jake and Fran looked at Jenna, hesitated, then answered in unison. "Yes."

"Thank you," he said soberly. "But you, Jenna, you, I've hurt the most." The truth that he had hurt her was still fresh in his heart. His own denseness struck him again. "I didn't know how to love you the way you needed to be loved. I have only just realized that. I always thought it was you, that you were the cause of our separation. I was wrong, Jenna, wrong about so many things, and I know I still haven't seen everything I did to hurt you. I'm . . ." Steve fought to release his last vestige of pride, "I'm sorry Jenna for being self-serving. Please tell me what I've done to grieve you."

It was the lone tear from his troubled blue eyes that broke her hardness. She blinked back her own burning tears, searching his face. He had been unreachable, unteachable, and had taught her well.

"Will you accept my apo . . . ? No. Will you forgive me, Jenna, for failing, utterly failing, to listen to you and to love you?"

This wasn't the way she rehearsed it. She had formed the accusations, expecting to cut him down in his pompous arrogance. The three of them were looking at her, waiting for her answer. Bitterness screamed its vengeance, tearing, destroying. Jenna struggled for freedom. "I don't know, Steve. I don't know if I can."

"Are you willing to try?" he pleaded.

"Yes," she conceded by sheer will. Her body shuddered; she

covered her face and wept bitter tears, leaning against Fran for comfort.

ALMOST 3,000 miles away, Server continued kneeling beside his bed, his lips moving in fervent intercession. An unusual urgency had driven him from duty to Malchor into the privacy of his apartment. A few weeks had passed since he began to fulfill his promise to his mother, opened her book and discovered, to his amazement, that it was more than a compilation of myths. There was no division between the laws of physics and the recorded words. No ludicrous examples of false science common to legends. No flat-earth stories, just examples of human foolishness, rebellion, and reconciliation.

Truth, the objective reality of Maker, cut through the tangled self-serving philosophies of man and shed light on Server's sin-darkened soul. His simple childhood faith returned. He knew who he was, and who he was entreating on behalf of the strangers whose plight tore at his heart. Being burdened for David had become common practice. That he was burdened for the parents was curious to him, yet he prayed, chagrined he didn't remember their names.

FIVE minutes stretched into ten before Jenna regained self-control. Fran stroked her hair, whispering comfort that everything would be all right. Jake sat looking out the window, grateful things were calming down and that he still had a job. Steve was afraid to say anything.

Jenna sat up, accepting another tissue from Fran. She brushed her ebony hair from her tear streaked face and wiped her nose. "Trib, Steve, I'm not sure what to do. But we do need to talk and I'm willing to talk alone." She stood up with Fran and Jake, thanked them and assured them she wanted to be alone with her husband. They hesitated, then left at her insistence. They had done what they could, and weren't accountable for the outcome.

Steve stayed rooted to his chair. Jenna returned to the couch and faced him. It had been years since they looked, really looked into each other's eyes.

He broke the silence. "Jenna, I meant what I said. I want you to tell me how I hurt you. I need to know the truth."

"Where do I begin?" she sighed.

"Wherever you want, but I haven't seen you cry since David went to the Academy."

"Yes, that's where it started; I really didn't want him to go. I tried to tell you, but you wouldn't listen."

"It was wrong of me not to listen," he admitted.

"But, I guess you were right in sending him. Look where he is now."

"Yeah, getting shot at by dissidents," Steve muttered.

"Who knows, Steve. I wasn't comfortable with Malchor's agenda, but if Davy hadn't been at the Academy, he might have been exposed to worse, even to the plague."

"Not if you had home-schooled him."

"Well, it's too late to change that and too late to change the rest."

"What, Jenna?"

Pain registered on her face, then softened to a quiet grief. "You couldn't understand why I wanted more children."

He hadn't thought of children for years; once he had a son, it wasn't important. It was no small matter. He wanted her. She wanted children. In feeling his own need, he sensed a deeper loss. She had just cause for grief, and he had no excuse. "I'm sorry, Jenna. I was selfish, didn't want any inconvenience. I had my little routine and didn't want any surprises."

"That's been the problem with our whole generation. Children are an inconvenience. We're too self-serving to have time for little children. What kind of creature doesn't have time for it's young?"

Steve was struck with the truth of her words. He had barely made time for David, and that time was neatly scheduled and neatly executed, like some television documentary. "Not *we*, Jenna. You always had time. You were loving. That's it—you

196

were always willing to love generously. I wasn't; I measured love out like some kind of reward. I tried to make you hold back, deriding your love as weakness."

"I learned to do that with you," she admitted, "didn't I?"

"I'm sorry," he groaned.

"I'm sorry, too. Your error was no excuse for mine. I'm responsible . . ." She winced at the thought, then said, "I'm responsible for hating you."

"I gave you cause. I'm responsible for not caring about what you wanted and for not giving you more children." He cautiously reached for her. With equal caution, she allowed him to cradle her hand between his own. "Could you ever forgive me?"

"I don't know if I can. It's too late for so many things."

Things? he thought, knowing she meant lost sons and daughters. He hesitated to prod her, to push her too fast. At least she was talking, trusting him to listen. But when she said it was too late, he fought despair, wanting to grab her and pull her close. Holding her hand steadied him, giving him hope to continue. "Jenna, I didn't have anything going with Jessica. We were wrapping up an investigative report. She grabbed my arm, and you walked in. I never . . ."

"Steve," she interrupted, "I knew that."

"But you said . . ."

"That was just an excuse; I was already going to leave you. That's why I went to your office that day, to tell you not to come home."

"You did?"

Jenna saw his surprise and weighed her words carefully. If he was sincere, but weak, her words could cost her her future, her freedom. She clung to the thread of trust. "Yes, she saved me from having to tell the truth. I was afraid—afraid you would turn me in if I argued with you."

"You had reason to be afraid."

"What happened to you, anyway?" she asked. "Why all of a sudden do you want to know, or care to know, what was going on with me?"

Steve watched her face relax, fighting the desire to enfold her, cradle her, guard her from the haunting past. He held his place, the warmth of her delicate hand pressed between his. "When Jake told me you were afraid of me, it shocked me. I never saw it. Then I realized what I had done to you. I know what it is to be afraid. I have seen raw fear, and I remembered the same look in your eyes, back when I belittled you and shut you out of my life." Remorse welled up. He shook his head and whispered, "When we almost lost David, nothing else mattered, except that he live and that we live, you and I and our love for each other.

"But something happened before that, what I was just saying about fear . . ." As he spoke, the stark scene unfolded in his mind. "I saw you were right about Malchor."

Reacting, Jenna glanced around the room, expecting lightning to fall or the police to crash through the door.

"Caution is second nature, isn't it," he said. "Have you forgotten what it's like to speak freely?"

She nodded, her black eyes again searching the room, fearful.

"We're not being monitored; we never have been. That's the one perk we have, remember? We're so obedient, we silence ourselves."

"You never can know for sure," she cautioned. "Things change."

"The place is clean; I checked it before coming inside."

"It pays to be careful," she said.

"It's clear, trust me. I wouldn't risk Malchor's wrath for either of us. I covered Malchor in Rome, back in March. I saw his wrath first hand. Well, I don't want you to misunderstand. I still think Synthesis is our only hope. The Plan is all we have to insure self-preservation. But Malchor, he's changed. He's not the same person I vowed allegiance to."

"Trib! You could bring the wrath of the Tribunal down on us if you're not careful, Steve."

"I'm careful. I'll do what's necessary. There's no stopping

this new order, and I plan to be on top of things, not underneath. But I want you with me."

Years of bitter resolve trembled under his steady, searching probe. Her hand was still cradled between his, palm down. His fingertips moved up from her wrist, stroking her forearm. She wanted to believe him.

"I love you, Jenna."

FACILITATOR David Winston had one stop to make before leaving for a spring tour of the Academies, and that was to see Greg Foster at the Level II Reorientation Center in Baltimore. The Haven grounds sprawled majestically across ninety acres on the southern shores of the reclaimed Curtis Bay. The facility was a state-of-the-art research and training hospital for psychiatrists, as well as the most effective center for altering dissident behavior.

Casually dressed medical technicians followed individualized reorientation prescriptions for their 387 patients. Greg was midpoint between four weeks of observation and assessment when Winston obtained a special visitor's pass. The tranquil grounds promised a speedy recovery from disruptive thought patterns. A soft-spoken male-nurse showed the Youth Facilitator the official tour. Exercise and recreation rooms, dining area and meeting rooms were occupied by cheerful, outgoing people. Winston had difficulty separating the staff from the patients. The place looked like a cross between a school and a hotel complex. He followed the burly nurse the length of two long hallways before entering Greg's airy apartment. Large picture windows overlooked the wooded acreage that secured three sides of The Haven.

Greg reclined on the floral love seat, eyes closed. He didn't respond when the nurse called his name, then repeated it, louder. David held up his hand and shook his head. The nurse shrugged and withdrew.

He tiptoed toward the gaunt form. His frown deepened and he bent closer. Telltale bruises marred the peaceful face. A series of small scars marked his left cheek and a faint layer of brownish purple extended from his right jaw up to his brow. It was clear why they hadn't let him in sooner. The tousled red hair showed a sprinkle of stark silver.

Remorse mingled with anger. "Trib," he breathed, "what's wrong with the fool bureaucrat that let this happen?"

Greg blinked and focused.

David's face was strained with worry. "Greg," he whispered.

"Davy, I hoped you'd come." Greg's voice cracked. He clasped his friend's extended hand, grimaced and pulled himself upright. Peering from sunken, dark orbs, his clear blue eyes sparked with hope.

Termination almost claimed those eyes. David shuddered, Transformation was rescinded two days before scheduled.

Greg broke in on his reflection. "David, I know you meant it for my good."

"I never meant you to suffer."

"Without suffering," Greg put a warning finger to his lips and continued, "I might not have learned the truth about myself."

Troubled, David followed him to the door.

"When a man knows the truth about himself, about why he's here, about his purpose in life, it's less likely he will use power and position for self-gain."

"You sound like a philosopher," the Facilitator muttered, closing the door softly behind them. The hall stretched ahead; a corner video monitor picked up every move.

"There's nothing like an injustice to make you ponder the meaning of justice."

"Or a brush with death," David added, "to make you ponder the meaning of life." They stepped out into the sultry daylight and strolled toward the small duck pond. A gaggle of ducklings paddled after their mamas, raising a crescendo of quacks.

"And what does it all mean to you, David?"

"Synthesis." It was his honest answer, the center of all meaning for him.

"What about justice?"

"Justice will be served by the Tribunal."

"When?" Greg asked, his voice steady.

The Youth Facilitator winced as if struck; he had no answer, then remembered the strict instructions for this visit. He was not to challenge or discourage any comments from his traumatized friend. He plastered a smile on his face and changed the subject. "I understand your law firm position is remaining open. They expect you to be ready to return to work in a few months, depending on your physical progress, of course."

"Or more accurately, depending on my mental and spiritual progress."

"I know you'll do fine, Greg." David was shaken by the countenance of his friend; it was that of a man facing death, accepting death, undefiled by bitter accusations. An unexplainable peace shone from his battered face.

"You're a brother to me, David, a true brother. But it will never be the same," Greg entreated. "There can be no syncretism for me between the truth and the lie. All things are not equal; all roads don't lead to knowing God or godhood. There is a true way and a false way and it's the false way that perverts justice. And it is falsehood that pretends mortals are gods."

David knew where the talk was going and resisted the craving to argue. *Myths die hard*, he thought, forcing himself to be still and listen. Ducks were a nuisance clamoring for food, swimming closer; one large drake left the water and waddled noisily around their feet.

"Maker is real. He is not a myth. He cares about every detail of our lives and He does communicate with us." To hold his attention, Greg held his hand on David's shoulder, with precious few moments to plant seeds. "These birds do me a favor, keeping my words from the ears of the controllers, but they can't keep you from hearing the truth.

"Man has free will. He can choose to reject the truth and embrace the lie or embrace the truth and reject the lie. The truth and the lie can never be synthesized. If my faith is in a myth, then it could be chalked up to another fantasy fling. However, what if Maker exists, and does care about us? What if He sent His Son to tell us the truth and free us from ignorance, hatred and self destruction? What if—David—what if, Maker is real? Wouldn't it be wise to listen and at least check it out? But, no! Instead, it is the one possibility that we are not ever allowed to consider. We can accept and believe anything and everything except that Maker exists and told humans the truth about Himself.

"David," Greg implored, his voice straining. "The mysteries distort the truth, exalt the deceiver and the deceived. Listen to me and listen to Maker. Don't be deceived! Synthesis will never bring truth or justice! And Syn will never bring peace."

Two psychiatrists, their stark white lab jackets slapping at their knees, approached briskly from the administration building. The ducks fled. Rigid disapproval lined the men's faces. Controlled environments were their specialty and there was no excuse for unmonitored conversation. David stepped toward them, greeting them, his hand extended. Out of polite habit, they shook hands. The older man opened his mouth to speak, when David interrupted, expounding on the tranquil setting, his confidence in their professional abilities and Greg's imminent cure.

Expecting to be exposed, Greg stood watching his friend wrest control of the situation and shower the intruders with praise. The visit was over. Greg silently thanked Maker, then thanked the Youth Facilitator, by title, for his benevolent concern and assured him of a rapid physical recovery. He left the group.

Facilitator Winston dismissed the experts with a caustic warning. "Both Facilitator Hegelthor and I expect you will be extremely careful to avoid further trauma to Foster. Failure to rehabilitate him will be regarded as your failure, not his. Do you understand?" They nodded mutely and hastened back to their offices. David showed himself to the front gate, confident his friend would be cured, confident Synthesis would bring peace, and yet unsure that the Tribunal even cared about justice.

XIII   REALITY

"Look, you had every opportunity and failed," Dove sneered, sliding the dead bolt into place, "so loosen up!" The liaison weighed in at a loss, intolerable. Raven, perched in his humid cellar, was still puffed up about his own importance. She eyed his blackened inch-long beard until he tugged at it self-consciously.

"OK," she said, "we might as well make good use of our time." Abruptly, she unfolded the note for him, then grabbed the battered skillet, turning the burner on high. "I brought some fresh halibut. I'll toss it in the pan while you get the salad going."

"Yeah, sure," he agreed, reading her note silently.

No more names used. They're picking up our conversation. As suspected, Jonez and Harris have you staked out. I've shaken them every time I've left. They've been waiting for me to return and are expected to close in today. No problem. There's a surprise for them on your doorstep.

Henry Schlockman whistled strands of *America the Beautiful* while he scrawled his message below her neat print. The isolation plagued him. He had already determined that Dove wouldn't leave without him and was ready to cooperate even on her terms.

She bent over squinting, reading his scrawl.

Do they have your name?

She shook her head, and he continued writing.

Why did you come back?

Dove took the pen and added,

Job's not done until you're clear.
The boss doesn't want you squealing.

"Don't burn the fish," he chided, smoldering that Higgs would think he would squeal. He carried the table to the inside wall, placing the chair on top. "I've fixed the place up since you were here last," he said, too loud. "I needed some closet space."

"You're such a genius," she teased, folding the note; "maybe I'll keep you after all. Say, how about a little music with our wine?"

"Tired of my whistling already?" he asked, switching on the radio.

"To me you're still a liability," she whispered. "Your little tour plot won't work; we'll just have to wait and take Winston out next time he goes into D.C. A simple freeway accident will do."

"What do you mean, we? This is still my job."

"Look, they've doubled security, especially with the 'assassin' still at large. We can't even get an accurate schedule on Winston. We'll just have to wait until things settle back to normal."

"What's happened to that guy they framed?"

"Headed for CAM."

Wordlessly they slid from their bulky disguises into ordinary street clothes, two ordinary people. Dove tucked her black braid down the back of her shirt and checked her makeup. Raven sawed though the last inches of plywood ceiling section. He hoisted her up into the landlord's first floor apartment closet, then followed. Generic dinner music played while the empty frying pan glowed red hot on the burner.

STATE Departments of Education were coming under Malchor's authority like lemmings heading for water. Each of the twelve regional Academies sent daily updates into the main computer department underneath headquarters. Winston spent the afternoon monitoring their reports, trying to forget Greg's words. His terminal screen showed the spread of Synthesis. States in transition were coded yellow. The thirty-seven states locked into the program were coded pale green. The Academies were designated with blue dots and blue lines of influence radiated out to level-one Academies under their control. Level-two schools were coded with green dots and level-three training centers were coded purple. The screen pulsated with change. Phase three, rapid expansion, was exceeding Winston's timetable.

Absently, he ran his hand along his chest scars. In April, Malchor had sent the conference delegation back to their school districts and linked them with their regional Academy superintendents. In reality, it was the assassin's attempt that had given new members an evangelistic fervor to recruit and, with Academy videos, train their people. At their hands dissident outbursts resulted in extreme reprisals of blacklisting, assaults and picketing private homes. Local unions and associations had turned from their denounced leaders and merged with Impartation International. Their dues money continued to multiply in Malchor's account.

In the midst of success Winston noticed one slight snag. A pattern emerged showing a minor imbalance that begged repair. Both coastal areas had sparse purple dots, a shortage of level-three students. The virtue of labor definitely needed to be expounded. He sent a brief memo off to Frank to begin a promotional advertisement campaign. Then he checked the vital statistics. Charts showed that the birthrate of the level-three labor class had dropped sharply in nine regions during the past decade. Abortions outnumbered live births four to one. How could he pull in students who didn't exist?

Eugenicists tax-supported, free health clinics in all the cities were doing their job too well. Their profit margin was eroding labor replacement. That, combined with the spiraling immunodeficiency disorders, was affecting the infrastructure tax base of major cities on both the east and west coast. Winston typed a report on the situation and sent it to Malchor, then made a note to visit Dr. Lee Thomas that night at the Midwest Academy. Hopefully, it wasn't too late to stop weeding out necessary laborers.

He turned back and finished checking Academy graphs. Level-one professional and leadership schools generated from their parent Academies. Level-two schools were by far the most common, with green dots evenly dispersed across the map. There would be no shortage of technicians and clerks. He shut the system down and stuffed the chart printouts into his briefcase.

ASTROJET III, capable of hitting 2,000 kph, cut hours off Winston's travel time; landing took more time than flight. He boarded the plane with his personal staff and twelve bodyguards at 6:00 p.m. EST and landed at the Phoenix, Arizona, Academy forty minutes later by 4:40 p.m. MST. Still within the hour, he reviewed Dr. Thomas's data for one hundred and forty-six level-three facilities in his area.

Student charts showed an unusual resistance to loose social-sexual standards. Their labor-class secondary caregivers held high personal standards, were healthy and reproducing. When the Youth Facilitator asked why the students resisted the new curricula, Thomas pulled out a stack of student publications which flatly challenged the intent and intelligence of the new curriculum and the local expert eugenicists. The experts were charged with planned genocide. Winston was fascinated by the students' common sense arguments. They knew they weren't beyond suffering physical consequences for promiscuous behavior, and they knew their numbers were being manipulated. Level-three students were clearly capable of the same self-control expected in level-one. He recognized the point his dad had made about the sixties.

It was unpleasant to admit, but he had misread the data, failed to account for fluctuations across the country, and failed to balance the population between regions. His disapproval of Dr. Thomas at the Superintendent's Conference had been too hasty. He spent the next hour tracking factors that influenced positive student outcomes.

The largest single factor proved to be the curriculum change. If the curriculum content was fallacious, it didn't matter how it was taught or by whom, the results were the same: negative. The old phrase came to mind, *garbage in, garbage out.*

Of equal interest were the figures comparing Thomas' Character Curriculum with the Self-Awareness Program. The behavioral graph showed an increase in sociopathic symptoms in regions where the Self-Awareness Program was successful. The need for expert psychological intervention skyrocketed and students felt better about doing worse in all fields. It was puzzling; Winston decided to appoint a committee of psychologists to investigate the situation and offer remediation.

Convinced that an immediate reversal was needed, Winston reinstated the Thomas Curriculum for level-three students and dispatched an order for eugenicists to stay off school property. Sexually transmitted diseases and abortion were, in retrospect, not the best ways to control the population or insure stronger genetic codes. He expected to catch some flack, but the data was firm; the Thomas program showed positive outcomes in all three tracks. He made a note to check out the possibility of conflict of interest between the eugenicists and level-three sex education. What better way to perpetuate your profession than to weaken students and make them dependent on your services.

Dr. Lee Thomas was keenly aware of the sad state of the new curriculum. The changes had forced him into a stifling compromise; all he could do was encourage student resistance. It stunned him when Winston approached him about the matter, willing to listen, ready to see the problem. The facts justified his character program. He sequenced his data on the conference table in front of the Facilitator.

The victory was sweet, a radical policy reversal. Invigorated, he showered the young Facilitator with gratitude and took him to the dining room for a five-course dinner. Afterwards, he whisked Winston around the campus in his own homemade two-seater pedimobile. Students waved in greeting as they passed.

The graying elder statesman exuded the vital energy of an adolescent. Winston wasn't surprised that the campus hummed with precision from the groundskeepers to the professors.

At 9:00 p.m., Winston collapsed into bed, exhausted. The Academy tour would end tomorrow. What he needed was time at the ranch, time with Kendra.

AT THE ranch, Jenna opened her eyes to a new day. She wished the past decade could be blotted from her mind. For her, their reunion was a disconcerting round of intense pleasure and paralyzing pain. The decision to let herself care for Steve, even to love him, unlocked the closed recesses of her soul. She felt like a child, vulnerable; like a woman, empowered. He lay on his side, facing her, eyes closed while morning light spread through their room. She watched his bare chest expand, drawing breath, realizing he, too, was vulnerable. He was not the same self-serving man who left her cold. Tempting her, old habits of distrust whispered and promised sweet revenge. Willfully, Jenna resisted. No, the present was too sweet to relinquish to the bitter past. She preferred the present and resolved to stay.

When he opened his eyes to the light, her affectionate smile greeted him, sweeping over him. He reached toward her, drew his fingertips along her chin and touched her lips. "You, Jenna, are my life," he whispered.

"And that," she added, taking his hand in hers, "gives my life new meaning. I do love you."

Each word went far beyond what he had expected was possible. It was real, real change, beyond his ability to make it happen, beyond his control, and he knew it. It puzzled him, forcing an unaccustomed gratitude. "Well, my love, do we have time for the horses this morning?"

"Sure. Davy called while you were sleeping. He won't be in until afternoon. We have lots of time."

Time was what he lost track of whenever he felt himself drawn toward her. All it took was a moment, her dark eyes unveiled, open, tender. He hesitated. "Do you still feel I should tell David about Malchor?"

"Yes. He will find out anyway," she sighed, troubled. "And it could be dangerous if he finds out the hard way."

"It could be dangerous if he doesn't believe me."

"There are so many more risks when you tell the truth."

"Yes," he agreed, shutting out the unpredictable future, leaning closer. "So far the risks are worth it."

Yet, in spite of distractions, the certain risk hung in the air.

WINSTON stood outside the Williams boys' quarters at Orcas Island Academy. Not wanting to trigger unhappy memories, he watched through the observation window. Their routine still included homage to a mythical God; however, the report showed progress. The caregiver had won their trust and would patiently introduce correct attitudes. Winston studied the records. Personal involvement raised the stakes for him; reorientation had to work for the boys and for Greg's mindless ravings. Imprisonment and slave labor had severely damaged his friend's ability to reason, more than he had imagined possible. It was imperative. Synthesis had to bring mental stability.

A baby lop-eared bunny nibbled at the lettuce Jamie offered, while the mother hopped along the back wall of the holding pen. Caring for his pets took up most of his free time. At the other end of the room, Richard climbed a ladder, adding the final spheres to a mobile model of the solar system.

While he finished going through their reports, Hegelthor arrived and observed the boys with interest.

"You've probably noticed that our sociologists have taken these boys on as a special project."

"Their data's impressive, documenting everything."

Light from the boy's room formed a halo, reflecting from

Hegelthor's silver hair. "Yes," he agreed, resting his hand on the young man's muscular shoulder. "So, how is Foster doing with his reorientation?"

David met the steel gray eyes with steady resolve. He wanted to mention Greg's mistreatment at CAM; instead, he stayed away from specifics. "I have confidence in the abilities of the Haven staff." He chose not to mention Foster's wild statements about Maker, expecting the professionals to deal with it without his help. "Greg should be back working toward Synthesis as soon as his health returns."

"Good," Hegie said, satisfied. "Your suggestion about reorientation was solid." The morning report had described Foster as a model patient, cooperating with his doctors, actively involved in his own rehabilitation.

They walked the grounds, talking about the past and the future. But for David Winston, the Academy would never again be home.

THAT afternoon, when David saw his parents together, really together, it hit him that they hadn't been together, ever, in his memory. Kendra had been right about the wall. Clearly, it had come down. Open affection replaced cool reserve. From the time he landed, if they were in the same room, they were touching. David followed them around, oddly embarrassed.

Their togetherness, across the table from him, sharpened his need for Kendra. He fiddled with his Piaget; each sweep of the second hand brought arrival closer. Long after dinner they continued to sit by the view window, talking, but saying very little. David was working up courage when Fran came in and served three frosty mugs of root beer float. Seeing they didn't need further attention, she said goodnight and left to join Jake in their quarters. David noticed that even Jake and Fran were openly hugging. He left his float melting, folded his hands on the smooth wood surface and asked the simple question that nagged him throughout their idle conversations. "What happened?"

Steve and Jenna, their hands still entwined, studied him,

glancing at each other, then back to him. He sensed they were weighing what to say, how to say it, like he did with the Tribunal.

"Well?" he pressed.

"You can see that your mother and I have rediscovered each other," Steve offered.

"I hadn't realized that you needed to until today."

"And I didn't realize I needed my family until you were shot. It sobered me up. Actually, a series of things helped me see I was going in the wrong direction and, now, your mother has been kind enough to give me a chance to make up for our lost years."

"Sometimes things aren't what they seem," Jenna added, momentarily placing her free hand on her son's still clasped hands. "There's no need to go into details, but our lives haven't been as united as they could have been."

"David, I have something disturbing to say to you," Steve interjected, "and I can't think of any way to soften it. Sometimes people aren't at all what they seem, especially people in positions of leadership. There is a tendency to put leaders up on pedestals above humanity."

"But our leaders are more highly evolved," David protested.

"What if you found that one wasn't?" Steve asked.

"Then that person could need reorientation—or possibly even Transformation," he insisted, remembering his unpleasant tangle with the Harvard pedophile, Milton Werling.

"Would you feel confident enough in your own judgment to make that decision?"

"Yes. I've been permitted to make difficult decisions. Sometimes, for the sake of Synthesis, it's necessary to go against the common pattern of unity and tolerance."

That was it, the key Steve needed to continue on safe ground. He sipped his float, allowing the breach to settle, then asked, "Have you ever seen or had anyone transformed?"

"I've never seen it, but I've had to recommend it."

"Are you free to mention the need, without giving the details?"

"Yes. An evolved person in authority was molesting a minor."

"So, it was recommended under serious circumstances. Do

you feel transformation should be used for minor infractions, accidents or misunderstandings?"

"No, the preferred treatment would be reorientation. Sending a soul from this plane to another for minor cause would be unjust, although we have to trust that karma would balance things."

"Yes, but do you agree that those in authority have a responsibility to act justly?"

"Yes, with some exceptions for the sake of Synthesis."

"What if an exception damaged Synthesis?"

"That would be serious."

"Good," Steve said, "I'm glad we agree on that point. Do you agree that those in authority should have self-control?"

"Certainly."

Both Steve and Jenna were calculating the risk of continuing with the exposure. They nursed their root beer as if it were their last.

David was curious, his mind racing ahead, drawing conclusions. He pushed his float aside and probed his father's deep-set blue eyes. "For a man who wasn't going to soften things you've done quite well. Apparently, someone in an evolved state of leadership has acted out of control and brought about an unjust transformation." The Youth Facilitator crowded out the thought of Greg's fresh brush with injustice, then went on, "And you are hesitant to mention names, which indicates that the unnamed person is high up."

"You've concluded correctly, but the unnamed person is higher up than you would want exposed," Steve said, pleased with his son's perception. "We, your mother and I, feel you must know the hard truth for your own protection, so you tread softly when dealing with this person. Please bear with me, stay open, don't cancel and I'll tell the event from the beginning to the end. "Understand, we are both committed to the concept of Synthesis. We believe it is the only hope for our shrinking planet. Thus, we devote our energies to the success of Synthesis. That devotion does not, however, blind us to errors in leadership. And we hope,

David, that your devotion to Synthesis doesn't prevent you from taking certain precautions—to insure your own health and future."

David pondered the "health and future" phrase. He had been willing enough to lay down his life for the cause of unity, but his own deathwalk had sobered his fervor. Caution sounded very reasonable. A simple hint of humor altered his tone. "Synthesis is greater than the sum of its parts," he quoted his catechism, then added, "and now that you've clarified your motivation, I'm braced and even eager to hear the details."

Dusk softened the horizon while Steve was preparing both David and himself for his message. Light from the kitchen mixed with the descending darkness, throwing shadows throughout the enclosed deck. The family sat rooted at the table. "Well, stay braced," Steve suggested, finally ready to plunge ahead.

"Back in March, I covered the Festival of Nations in Rome and I've never seen so many evolved notables in one place. During the event, satellite communications were my major responsibility, but I tried to be useful wherever help was needed. The program was flowing smoothly. We were staying ahead of the inevitable glitches that crop up when man and machine try to stick to a schedule. Then, I heard that one of the speech writers was having trouble getting his computer to print out a speech. It was Joe. You remember Joe Quinlan?" Steve asked his son. "We took some fishing trips with him in Puget Sound when you were at the Academy."

David nodded. Certainly he remembered Joe and his two sons, Mitch and Toby. Joe, proud of his mother's Italian heritage, made David eager to walk the narrow village streets of the old world. Both father and sons were full of stories about the family's lineage and arrival in Washington. When fishing, they usually caught their allotment the first hour they were out; then they set anchor, swam and joked around until it was time to head back. The memories were good.

Anxious, David wanted to hear what happened in Rome.

"Well," Steve said, "it took about twenty minutes to get the printout. He grabbed it from me and ran to give it to the main speaker. A few minutes later, I followed Joe to the dressing rooms to see if the schedule needed to be changed. Halfway there I heard someone yelling, so I stopped and waited at the door. It was propped open. There was Joe, fifteen minutes late, pleading for forgiveness. The man who was yelling at him had his back to me. He grabbed the script from Joe and struck him, knocking him against the desk. The look on Joe's face was—well, he was shocked, grieved, like he couldn't accept what happened. Joe struggled to stay on his feet. I was just stepping in to stop the fray when the man turned enough for me to see his profile. I froze."

David tensed, picturing Cyrus, waiting to hear the man's name.

"The man said, 'Send him to Transformation,' with a cold evenness that chilled me, sending me a step back into the hallway. Joe fell to his knees and begged for his life. The guard jerked on his arm and anesthetized him. I don't know what it was—some kind of skin patch? Instantly, it knocked him out and they carried him out the other door." Telling it brought back the fear. Steve broke out in a sweat; Jenna could feel his palm, damp against hers. Reflexively, he scanned the room and lowered his voice, "I was terrified I would be seen by him. I still have trouble believing it happened. But it did, David, it did happen and the man was Malchor," Steve Winston whispered, "Malchor Inyesco." Prepared as he was, David blanched at the revelation. His throat constricted.

Jenna blotted her eyes with her shirt sleeve and looked from her son to her husband, in need of reassurance. "You never told me what happened next," she said. "What did you do?"

"I stood in the hallway for what seemed an hour—really only minutes, then walked into his dressing room." He answered, sensing it was best not to probe David's feelings. "I had to tell him he was on in five minutes unless he wanted a different time slot. I didn't know what to expect.

"Joe had insisted on taking the script to Malchor even though I offered to. I would have been the one . . . Tension hung in the air when I faced him, but instead of being angry, Mal smiled graciously and asked me to carry the show until 3:00 p.m. so he could review his speech. Relief overwhelmed me, almost blocking my memory of Joe. I got out of there fast and changed the schedule. The Universal Children's Choir sang their unity songs next. Then the world heard Malchor's speech—every station carried it. It was all about the evolving perfection of humankind. Love and virtue dripped from every word. But they were Joe Quinlan's words, words he truly believed, words he ascribed totally to Malchor, words which symbolized the heart and soul of Synthesis."

Thunderstruck, the Youth Facilitator stared at his dad's face. The convoluted events of the past year threatened everything he knew to be true, everything he trusted. In the temple he had pursued illusion, wishing to be free from reality, only to find that a great deal of what made up his reality was an illusion, a shifting parade of half-truths and outright lies. Hearing his mother's voice soothed him, helped him focus on the present, harsh reality.

"Steve," she asked, "what happened to Joe?"

"During Mal's speech, I tracked him down. The guards had him in his room. I opened the door as if I belonged there. They were busy scooping all his belongings into plastic garbage bags and ignored me. Joe was stretched out on the floor. It was pointless to try to talk to him; his eyes were glazed. Finally, one guard saluted me and announced cheerfully, 'Transformation will make him a new creation,' like some fool robot. I responded, 'All glory to Transformation and Perfect Unity.' The words just slid out. I slunk out of the room, feeling like a traitor."

"But, Steve," Jenna protested, "we've believed that all our adult lives."

"Yes, I did—until last March."

"You've seen people go to Transformation before; people you cared about, even your own parents, when their time came."

"That was supposedly voluntary, and that was before I saw our hope for peace, our great leader, Malchor, have a temper tantrum."

Jenna shuddered. She had never doubted the incarnation process; people lived and learned, then evolved. That was the way she was taught, and that was what she believed. Any other prospect was a forbidding unknown.

"My dad warned me," Steve said, putting his arm around his wife. "He seared the words into my mind that power corrupts. Lord Acton said it differently generations ago, but Dad preferred to say that 'Power corrupts even the well-intentioned.' That's what has happened. Power has corrupted Malchor."

"Yet, we help him gain more power daily," Jenna lamented.

"Yes, we do, and I don't know what's next. Hopefully, for all of us, the Tribunal will self-correct."

David agreed, "Yes, that would be best. They could work within the Tribunal and balance power with . . ."

He couldn't finish; he sifted through his past experience for the essence that would balance power. Fear was the best he could find and that was not acceptable. How could fear stop a god from doing anything?

His son's face was ashen, desperation marring his dark eyes. Steve, fearing he had said too much, moved around the table. "David," he said, resting his hand firmly on his son's arm. "I know this is difficult, and we must never discuss the subject again. But it's a lesson for us, for our protection."

Trembling, David rose, pushing his chair back, staring at his parents. "I need some time to sort through this whole . . ." but he couldn't say it. The pain refused to surface. They had no idea what he had seen, what he had done. Nobody did.

His parents stood, wanting to offer comfort as he left the room and headed for the barn.

"Carmel will get a workout tonight and so will the guards," Steve surmised, drawing Jenna closer, kissing her forehead, reassuring her. "David's just like me," he added.

"Hopefully it won't take him as . . . ," She stopped the hurtful trend. "At least you never died from your midnight rides."

"There's something about the mountains at night, all alone. Just you, the trees, the stars, your horse . . . "

". . . and all manner of wild animals," she interrupted.

"It's peaceful. Max will keep the animals away."

"I don't know. Does he still have the teeth for it?"

"Don't worry. David's going to be all right. It's more likely that one of the guards will step off a cliff. He will probably ride up to the cave, where we used to go when he was little."

Jenna resisted, unwilling to let herself be comforted.

DAVID picked his way through the tangled brush; he had doubled back three times and considered giving up before he found the opening. A young cedar had taken root, and now, almost thirty feet high, its broad branches camouflaged the narrow entrance and the familiar stone face. Excited, Max sniffed around underfoot, tangling with David who was stepping over an unyielding branch. Regaining his footing, he reached the entrance only to find it partially blocked with rocks and dirt. There was no way he could get into the cave without excavation. Disappointed, he retreated to where Carmel was tethered to an alder and spread a blanket over her back. The cave could wait until another time.

He and Max scaled the rocks and settled down on an extra horse blanket he had had the sense to grab from the barn. Max curled against his side, content. The ever-present guards stayed out of sight, secured the area, kept their vigil. He heard Owen station two guards and set up three-hour shifts. David lay awake, feeling the cold earth and a dozen rocks under his back, betrayal mocking his soul. Lecturing himself, he got up, foraged for a protective cushion of pine needles and cocooned himself in the blanket.

A faint glimmer of the North Star pierced the cloudy sky.

"HOW did you see it?" Ben asked. "I would have been blown into molecules. I didn't see anything."

"And I would have been with you since I was at street level with no protection." In their darkened hotel room, Stan Jonez surveyed the crumpled suit draping his partner's sturdy frame.

217

"You really need a good tailor," he mumbled.

"Come on, don't change the subject. How did you know to get behind that dumpster? How did you see that line?" Ben asked, peering through the night visor and into the Raven's new D.C. home. Confident of his escape, he had booked a suite in the Hilton and already ordered room service, charged to his new debit card.

"Well?" Ben persisted, "What do I have to do to get an answer? You saved my skin. You owe me something."

"Yeah, I guess I'll have to do penance for that . . ."

"Our man's out of the shower," Ben interrupted, "taking his dinner tray in his bath towel. This scope sure works good through drapes. I can make out the carrots on his plate," he said, focusing the lens. "You'd think he would come up with a new occupation for his new alias, Bruce Gibbs. Wasn't Henry Schlockman already an insurance salesman under a different alias?"

"No, that was for real, before he joined the Marines. Which brings me back to how I knew about the line. You remember when the hag went down the stairs and was kicking at the door?"

"Yes."

"Didn't you wonder why she leaned her cart against the opposite side? Usually she kept it to the right, like she's right-handed, but she had it on the left. Then she turned clear around to grab the cart and pull it inside."

Ben rubbed his chin; he hadn't noticed. It was a near-fatal oversight. He gaped at his comrade, sprawled on his queen-sized bed, shoes off, ready for deserved sleep.

"Well, I forgot about it. Then, when I was headed for the cellar window, I glanced back at you, starting down the stairs, and it clicked. She'd set a booby trap. So I grabbed you."

"Thanks."

"Anytime."

"Maybe we should grab the Raven next time he showers. If he gets away, we'd be tracking a naked jaybird."

"Sounds like we've been undercover too long," Stan said, smiling through a yawn.

218

"This Raven guy eats like a pig when he's alone," Ben observed. "Hey, what did Mal say about us losing the girl?"

"You don't really want to know," Stan said, pulling a pillow over his head.

"WE WERE shortchanged a whole day, David. If I didn't have to go to Chicago for that Genetic Engineering Conference, I could see you off on Monday," Kendra complained.

In the shadow of the Astrojet, David hugged Kendra, welcoming her, trying to focus on their reunion. That morning a hot shower had loosened the mountaintop chill from his muscles but his mind was still darting from excuses to accusations. Mal had to have an explanation. Joe Quinlan must have done something else, something his dad didn't know. He would find out and clear things up.

"Are you all right, David?" Kendra asked, pulling away, hefting her overnight bag strap onto her shoulder.

"Here, I'll take that." He lifted the burden from her and, clasping her hand, walked toward the ranchhouse. "I'm all right. Still don't have the usual stamina, though." He was grateful she hadn't arrived the day before; it would have been worse. "So you have to be in Chicago on Monday. What time?" he asked, already altering plans.

"The conference registration opens at noon—lasts until Friday. I'm booked on a nonstop from Spokane at 7:00 a.m., our time."

"I'll take you to Chicago," David said absently. "I was going straight to headquarters . . ." he was watching his parents come to the back door. Their faces were drawn, their arms around each other. "Do you need to stop in Spokane for . . . ?"

"Great Trib, David!" she whispered. "Your parents are holding each other. What happened . . . "

"I'm not sure," David said, amused that her question mimicked his, "something about a second chance." By this time they were in hearing range and Jenna flew down the steps to give Kendra a welcoming hug.

219

While Kendra was near, betrayal weakened, loosening its grip on his soul. As soon as they had some privacy, she bombarded him with questions. Should she order her dress? Would the December ceremony be on the east or west coast? Who should attend? It was a pleasant diversion until she asked who should be in the unity party and if he had told Greg and Reana. Against his own intentions, he lied, said they were fine but he had been too busy to call and tell them the latest. It was the truth that he hadn't told them; unity had been the last thing on his mind.

ALONE in her Chicago Ramada Inn room, Kendra hung up her clothes and set out her cosmetics, reflecting on the weekend visit. From the minute she stepped off the plane in Bellingham, she had felt a barrier between them. Something wasn't right. Later, when she asked if it bothered him that his parents were suddenly more interested in each other than in him, he laughed, recognizing the fact. It helped and the barrier faded as they spent more time together, but it didn't altogether disappear.

The conference packet lay sorted on the desk, organized so she would only carry what she needed for each day. On impulse, Kendra picked up the phone, dialing the familiar Baltimore number. It rang five times, then a recording came on. Kendra redialed, figuring she had made a mistake. It took a third repetition of the disconnect message for her to accept that the Foster number had indeed been disconnected. Determined, she dialed long distance information. There was no new listing. She then called their business numbers, only to be informed that they no longer worked at their respective positions. Alarm gripped her as she dialed David's personal number. The phone rang until his recorded message came on. She left her number, asking him to call. Frustrated, she redialed the law firm and asked for Greg Foster's new business number. The secretary said that no information was available.

Meetings dragged on all afternoon. Kendra had been excited about hearing the latest in bioengineering, but with Reana on her mind, she missed half of the main speaker's presentation. Back in her room she noticed that a message was waiting. She dialed the front desk; David had returned her call, and said he would call again. She dialed his number and hung up when his recorder came on; phone tag was pointless. She dug out her schedule—Tuesday, Thursday and Friday were booked solid, but Wednesday, the Fourth of July, was filled with Synthesis celebrations: a bus to the city parade, a mid-afternoon barbecue, an evening costume party and fireworks under the stars. The conference organizers had done it up big. Kendra went to the lobby, signed up for everything, then used the lobby phone to make round-trip flight reservations to Baltimore. She booked a morning flight.

XIV DRAGON OF DEATH

TEN minutes passed with David's feet planted on the hard marble floor of the headquarters foyer. Measuring moments in tidy increments of time, the grandfather clock towered over him, a giant of metal and mahogany. His first painful wait flickered through his mind. He had failed then, succumbing to negative mental accusations, and yet Malchor had received him, an unworthy devotee. Determined he would not fail again, David repeated his vow of allegiance to both Malchor and to Synthesis.

At 6:00 p.m., dinner was served in Malchor's private quarters, with the double doors opened to his fragrant garden. When David arrived to join the Tribunal at the small, round table, they were in a heated debate about dissident reorientation. Joining the inner circle, again filled him with a sense of power and purpose. He sat reverently across from Malchor with Cyrus to his right and Arion to his left, his back to the manicured floral display of perennials. Server attended, removing empty dishes, filling wine glasses. David avoided staring at the man, James Victor Lawrence, scarred in loyal service, believer in mythology. He tried unsuccessfully to remember what Server had said to him about a better way.

The three men were eying him, and Cyrus held his glass midair, waiting for an answer. David had been inattentive. He fumbled to respond to the unheard question and desperately settled for a slogan. "Blessed be Synthesis!" he exclaimed, lifting his glass in a toast. "All power to the Tribunal to insure truth and justice." The gesture was successful, distracting them, leading

223

to a string of affirmations.

Grinning at David, Cyrus intoned, "Ah, the wisdom of youth. Of course we will bring justice to the dissidents. Whether we have them reoriented or transformed post haste to another plane, justice will be served." His sweaty palm and cold fingers loitered on the Youth Facilitator's bare forearm. "I'm delighted you will be spending the July fourth celebration with us in D.C."

Under the leadership of Cyrus Nascent, the Cosmic Spirit Council had progressed past traditional barriers, encompassing and swallowing up denominations, sects and recognized religious affiliations worldwide. The man was loved and revered by the relevant world. Still, David had difficulty meeting his compelling hazel gaze. He conjured a perfunctory smile. Abhorrence traversed his spine, settling its claws on the back of his neck. Justice would not have been served by Greg's Transformation and was definitely not served by the spiritual head's not-so-subtle attraction to him. To David's relief, Malchor won his reprieve from Cyrus by asking him to report on the progress of the Academies. During his brief report, a subtle turf war continued between Malchor and Cyrus, ending amicably with Malchor's reminder of their separation of powers between Body, Soul, and Spirit.

After dinner, Winston heard the Tribunal allude to their mutual leadership over the Peacekeepers. Their power and influence extended further than he had thought. He knew that the National military branches, Malchor's Special Forces, their personal security guards, and even local sheriff and police departments were united as members of the Brotherhood of International Peacekeepers. But leadership of that union had shifted from the United Nations directly to the Tribunal. Impartation International was to education what the BIP was to law and order. They set the occupation standard worldwide. If someone failed to exhibit the proper attitude, they were easily replaced by someone more amenable. Winston figured correctly that the Peacekeepers' compulsory monthly dues were a sizable contribution to the furtherance of Synthesis.

Uncomfortable, David contended with his conscience; lofty idealism quaked in the face of turf, power and greed. An urge to get back to the ranch germinated and grew when the subject of private property rights erupted into an impassioned debate. Arion was the only member who still supported the concept.

"It has to go, totally!" Cyrus insisted for the fourth time. "We have no right to purchase little pieces of Mother Earth as if she were merchandise. She belongs to herself! It's our duty to protect her, care for her." Cyrus stopped and waited for Server to set the chocolate rum cake at his place, then went on to ask emphatically, "How do we dare presume to own her?"

David had always agreed with the concept of Communal Earthkeepers as it applied to people in general, but balked at the thought of the ranch—his ranch. He dug into his own piece of rum cake with possessive fervor. If Cyrus was right and all property should return to Mother, who should or would decide who could live on and work the Winston land?

"We're not really owning her," Arion rebutted, "We're only paying for the privilege of caring for her. People are better motivated to care for their own acre of Mother than for someone else's acre."

"We have regulated all we can, Arion, and still some people use the land to make a profit at Mother's expense. The abuse of our Mother must stop!" Malchor's fearsome dark eyes bore into Arion's cool blue ones. "The people are only beginning to give her the reverent worship she deserves."

"And worship is the pivotal issue here," Cyrus said, burying his dessert fork in the rich, chocolate frosting, rolling the utensil until both sides were thickly coated.

His own plate empty, David caught himself staring at Cy's loaded fork.

"Certainly, it is," Arion agreed, dissecting his cake into neat little cubes. "But, the average person needs to feel that he is a part of Mother, and people feel more strongly about what they call their own, their own part of Mother."

"Would you consider the merits of redeeming the land?" Mal

225

suggested, his cake still untouched. "It's working well in England. When the owner dies, the family has the first privilege to lease the space from Mother. If they don't have the funds to keep the land, they are allowed to rent it on a monthly basis, with contracted terms, of course."

"I think we're another decade away from that, but it will work here," Arion agreed.

David was on the edge of his seat, curiosity burning an imprint on his face. At the first pause he leaped into the fray. "Who will collect the money for Mother?"

The Tribunal looked from each other to Winston, whose face revealed it was an innocent question. Together they responded, "We will, of course."

"No one else could be trusted with such a solemn task," Cyrus added, licking his fork clean.

"How does one stay pure?" David asked. The words stupidly committed, he had to proceed. The three men gaped at him, expectant brows raised.

Standing vigil, James Lawrence sucked in a breath and feverishly prayed for mercy. There was no good reason for him to approach the table, no way he could bodily prevent disaster from falling on the young Facilitator.

"I mean sirs, in the light of unrestrained power." A dark look now blazed from Malchor, and Winston hastened on, wishing he hadn't opened his mouth. "I don't in any way presume that you would have any difficulty; rather, I ask for my own benefit. Malchor, how do I, uh, as I am graced with further authority, keep from misusing what you give me?"

Once the question was focused on the youth's potential weakness, the men were sympathetic and full of reassurances. David heard Server's faint sigh of relief. Cyrus mentioned something about the felicity of Mother Earth and the law of karma, while Arion interjected a word about self control. Malchor took the lead in explaining the process to his naive Facilitator.

"You have many steps to travel, as I replicate myself through you," he said gently. "Be assured, as you progress through the series of Temple Initiations, you will evolve beyond the grasp of temptation. Then, you will be ready to lead in your area of authority, with the purest of motives."

Almost to himself David said, "And my character would be perfected, but until then, where do I draw the line with telling the people what I know to be true? When I say something that isn't . . . "

"My dear David, "Mal interrupted, "character is bigger than that, bigger than truth, bigger than honesty, bigger than any of its minor parts. You must not let any of those minor things interfere with Synthesis. It's the outcome we look at."

Arion pulled an 1840 silver dollar from his shirt pocket and handed it to David, telling him to flip it in the air.

Surprised that he would want him to handle a rare coin, David hesitated, then took it and flicked it with his thumb. It spun upward, then landed heads up.

"Do it again," Arion said.

Again David flipped it, and it landed heads up.

"Do it again," Arion repeated.

Perplexed, David flipped the coin into the air; this time it landed, tails.

"I wanted you to see that it can land on either side. Can it land any other way?"

"The coin has two sides, heads or tails," David answered, noticing the men had settled back in their chairs, expectant.

"For you David, it's still either one way or the other, heads or tails, truth or lie, honesty or dishonesty. But reality, like character, is bigger than that for the Tribunal, and will be for you." Arion Tempera flipped the coin high. Spinning silver arched through the air and landed on its edge, rolling several inches to a stop, still upright on the polished ebony table. David gasped and sat rigidly at attention, his mouth open.

"As you can see, David," Arion explained, "for us it is the same. Not heads or tails, but both. Two sides of the same coin; good or evil, right or wrong, truth or lie, it's all quite relative. Whatever we do is pure, above any law."

"Then why do we teach ethics?" David blurted, still staring at the coin. He had heard the argument of relative ethics, but this was concrete. Arion plucked it from the table and returned it to his pocket.

Both Arion and Cyrus left the subject of teaching to their peer. Malchor slowly pulled his dessert closer and pressed his fork through the smooth, chocolate frosting, into the moist rum cake. "Don't conclude that we disregard the positive. Even though all things are relative where the progress of Synthesis is concerned, we endeavor to follow the path of ethics. As you were taught, ethics serve as a guideline for our interpersonal relations. Now you are mature enough to recognize it also, as a convenient restraint for the masses." Malchor savored his first bite, then lapsed into a history lesson. "Last century, when we removed morals and ethics from education, the goal was to break with the old paradigms, to set people free from past superstitions. It was amazing how quickly people dropped old standards and proved they needed us. Once chaos served its purpose, we stepped in and rescued the people from their own uncontrolled excesses and restored order. It was an important step for consolidating power. People now recognize they need us to lead them into this century."

"I see," David responded, and he did see more clearly than he had before.

Arion asked David directly, "Remember the first principles of change? Create or embellish the problem, excite opposition to the problem, then come forth with the solution. We, naturally, are the solution."

"Yes, of course," David recalled, "thesis, antithesis, then Synthesis; Hegel's brainchild."

"Yes! yes! yes!" Cyrus exclaimed. "And at last we have crossed the millennial threshold."

David felt out of his league, on the threshold of an abyss. Guilt crept into his mind for doubting the Tribunal, for wanting to keep the Winston land, selfishly, for his family. He excused himself and escaped to the bathroom. Cold water gushed from the tap over his hands; suspicions bubbled to the surface. Grandfather Winston's words nagged for a permanent foothold. He felt the heady pull within himself and knew that power could corrupt the well-intentioned. Power felt too good.

He pondered his reflection in the mirror, and what it would take to prevent corruption. *Fear isn't an effective barrier*, he thought, *except for deviates. And what could an embryonic god have to fear? Yet, corrupt is the flip side of pure, two sides of the same coin. Or is it? Corruption could be the absence of purity, not the opposite.* Willful, he throttled the thought. He had his duty.

Minutes later, when he returned to his seat, the debate had switched to Autonomous voting. Mal argued that the people would be ready for a special international election within a year, while Cyrus felt the stars weren't in proper alignment, and that the election should be national instead. Malchor conceded to keep it national. Arion, balancing on the back legs of his chair, insisted they would never get away with having an extra-constitutional election. "You can't ignore the Constitution," he repeated; "the next step is a Con Con."

Cyrus put David on the spot, asking him his opinion. He had never given a Constitutional Convention any thought and sided with Malchor out of loyalty, even though he had reservations about the nation being ready. Pleased, Malchor raised both hands into the air as if pronouncing a blessing. "For the first time in Mother Earth's history, man—excuse me—people, will choose Synthesis, peace in unity, sacrifice in unity, diversity in unity. The dream of oneness will be realized. The first Tuesday in November will only mark the beginning. Tribunal will rule the world!"

"Yes, we will. If you take the proper steps and have a successful Constitutional Convention. You two have out-voted me on this. Just remember, if this fails," Arion warned, "I'm in charge of the Con Con. Now's not the time for rushing, with twenty-five years already invested."

"Twenty-five years?" David questioned.

"Beware, young one," Cyrus chuckled, "lest you become curious or informed in areas beyond your ability to synthesize."

"Cyrus," Malchor reacted, jaws clenched, not open to humor, "you overstep your boundary when you take it upon yourself to caution my Facilitator." Currents of anger crackled between them but Mal measured his words. "Winston must be free to ask any question; how else will I be sure of his progress?" Cy's pale face reddened; his eyes narrowed to yellow slits. David pressed himself into the back of his chair, distancing himself from both of them.

Arion brought the front of his chair down with a jolt. "Is this the way for Harvard brothers to speak?" he commanded, then softened. "I'm sure, Mal, that our brother Cy was merely attempting humor. You know how difficult it is for him to loosen up. Remember, brothers, all thoughts and actions are best restrained by the diverse perimeter of unity; remember your vows to each other, to Synthesis." Malchor and Cyrus retreated, allowing their anger to dissipate.

In afterthought, Arion spoke to David, "It was twenty-five years ago that we vowed our own allegiance to Synthesis." The muscular, blond Viking mirrored the ageless stature and features of a Norse god. Time had only made him more resilient. He continued in a powerful, calibrated tone, "Certainly, the Plan has germinated from the beginning of time. We, the Tribunal, took up the torch from our forerunners and are lighting the world with our brilliance."

Mesmerized, David was absorbing the words when another word hit, as if someone had said it loud and clear. *Arrogance!* He shifted, expecting to see that Server had broken his silence and spoken. Their eyes met and an insight passed, undetected, between them. Arrogance, pure and simple; the Tribunal presumed to be wise enough to rule the world, yet they couldn't get along with each other. At this point the three had their glasses raised in another toast to their own profound godliness, wise governance and enduring compassion for the plight of mortals.

Facilitator Winston's wine glass touched his lips, while the contents remained untouched. He wondered how far loyalty could take him, and then, like some sidelight, he pondered where President Reginald Chamberlon fit into the picture. The Washington, D.C., Fourth of July celebration would, no doubt, be revealing.

HARBOR breezes blew across the pavement, pushing back Baltimore's sweltering summer heat. Kendra Addington, tired from a sleepless night, stood at the gate, scanning the directory for Foster. Encouraged to find them still listed, she buzzed their town house. No response. Undeterred, she followed a tenant when the gate opened, then made her way past the landscaped rows of homes. Heaviness settled over her when she walked toward their place. The units on each side were well kept. Their lawn begged for water. Sheer draperies covered the windows, blocking her view inside. Kendra pressed the white button and waited, then held her finger against it, persistent. She sensed someone was home ignoring her and knocked on the unyielding door until her knuckles ached. Distressed, she finally walked away from the place and turned at the curb, glimpsing a furtive silhouette at the upstairs window.

REANA stepped back, hurried to her bedroom and buried her face in her pillow, isolated, cut off from Greg, her family and closest friends. She sobbed until exhaustion lulled her into a fretful sleep and kept her from the tedious afternoon hours.

Dusk was spreading its haze across the city when Reana awoke and turned to see the time. It would be another fitful evening, alone with the television, making herself eat dinner, making herself finish the piecework report she was doing in her home office for the curriculum department. They didn't mind using her work as long as her name wasn't attached, and she didn't mind as long as their money covered her food and mortgage payment. Reana crawled out of bed, rummaged through her closet for a long jacket, paused long enough to pull her hair into a bun and put on sunglasses. Even though it was late, she felt safer wearing them. She rarely left the house and knew there was no delivery on the Fourth of July, but the mail was still in the box from Monday and Tuesday. The hope that Greg had finally written compelled her to lock up the place and head for the mailboxes. As she expected, no one was on the platform.

KENDRA stood apart from the three adults in the playground area. Their children, clamoring for parental attention, climbed on the fortress, slid down the slide and ran to the swings. Across the sand she saw a woman step up to a mail box, dismissed the idea that it could be Reana, then noticed the glasses. *Who would wear sunglasses at dusk?* Curious, she circled, placing herself between the row of houses and the figure that sorted through her mail. The closer she got, the more convinced she became that it wasn't Reana. The woman was sloppy fat with dull brown hair drawn back, twisted into a bun at the base of her neck. Above her head, a bright light attracted a large moth that flitted past her hair. Distracted, the woman raised her face, watching the insect slam against the glass bulb.

"Reana!" The name escaped and hung in the air.

Startled, the woman turned, clasping her mail to her breast.

"No wonder you didn't answer my calls," Kendra scolded. "What's the matter with you and Greg? You're not fat you're . . ." The word, pregnant, stuck in her throat like a fish bone. She shook her head and went on. "How could you do this?"

"Trib! Keep it down, would you? I have to live here," Reana whispered, brushing past Kendra, who followed close at her heels, not wanting her to get away.

"You know you're supposed to wait five years. What's Greg thinking of anyway?"

"He doesn't know."

"What do you mean he doesn't know you're pregnant? Is he blind or something?"

Reana stopped abruptly. "Don't you know?" she asked, removing her glasses.

232

Kendra sidestepped to keep from running into her. "Know what?"

"About Greg."

"What about him?"

"Has David said anything about him?"

"Just that he's fine."

"Does David know you're here?"

Kendra shook her head, frowning.

"Does anyone know you're here?"

"No."

Reana took her hand and headed up the walkway. "Better come on in, but don't talk until we're in the office. The place is wired."

Kendra followed mutely, ready to burst.

THE White House State Dining Room was a display of red, white and blue patriotism. It looked radically different from David's first state dinner. All traces of gold were gone. Queen Anne style chairs surrounded the mahogany table, reupholstered in shimmering blue to match the hologram symbol of Synthesis that hung above the fireplace. President Chamberlon and ten selected advisors listened to Malchor's carefully pruned outline for effecting international Autonomous voting. Cyrus and Arion, seated on each side of him, were ready with specific orders for each team member.

David sat across from Malchor, noting that the symbol of Synthesis made an impressive backdrop for the Tribunal. The President and his men were nodding, an awed audience. For the Youth Facilitator, reverence had crumbled into an amused detachment. A belief took root that he held power over the minds of children and he alone had the ability to bring true leadership and justice to all the people.

Unbeknown to each other, the men and women now accepting their proper roles had been private guests at headquarters, thoroughly indoctrinated into the tenets of the faith and initiated in solemn ceremony. Only the President, however, was allowed to take the blood oath.

President Reginald Chamberlon sat at the head of the table, a king holding court. Since his party lost control of Congress in the previous election, he faced a battle against the very heart of Synthesis. In his eyes the men and women representing their various states had no business writing laws if they weren't furthering international unity. They were cooperative enough where the unions were concerned, but showed a disrespect for the Tribunal that couldn't be tolerated. The press was cooperating. Congressional railings against the Tribunal and Autonomous voting were billed as convulsive elitism. The new Congress had swept into power on the wave of voter hostility toward incumbents. They would soon be ousted posthaste in the sweep of autonomy. Congress was a necessary sacrifice. Chamberlon, however, was not going to be found wanting. The Tribunal needed him, and he was confident he had made a good impression on the Youth Facilitator. Earlier that day, during the opening ceremony, his speech had brought the assembled guests to their feet three times in hearty applause.

Contrary to Chamberlon's opinion of himself, Facilitator Winston envisioned a chameleon every time the President spoke. The man changed colors and direction at will; his sterling gray eyes swept the dining room, perceiving the pulse of the people. He was a perfect politician, forty-five, impeccable silvered hair, full eyebrows and a respectable mustache, handsome features. It was clear why the Tribunal appreciated his talents of persuasion. He would say or do anything for them, for Syn and for his own future as figurehead of the major redistribution center of the new world order. David was sure the man's tongue was sticky enough to catch flies.

SEQUESTERED in Foster's office, with the laser disk playing the Grand Canyon Suite, Kendra hesitated to speak. She didn't want anyone to know she was in Baltimore in the home of an obvious dissident.

"The sound system hooks right into the tape; our voices really

234

cannot be heard," Reana insisted.

"How could you let this happen?" Kendra whispered, still cautious, her eyes darting along the edges of the ceiling.

"I didn't plan it. I had a problem. Somehow, my arm got infected, so they removed the implant. They scheduled to replace it the next week, but we had a blizzard."

"That's no excuse for this, Rea," Kendra blurted out, pointing at her friend's distended abdomen. "That was obviously months ago. Just how many months? You look at least 28 weeks."

"About twenty-four," Reana lied.

"Good, you can easily get rid of it."

"It?" Both her hands took a protective position, fingers spread, covering her belly. "This is a baby," she said firmly, "my baby, Greg's and my baby, not an 'it'."

"It's not a baby until we call it a baby. And you know full well, it's not a baby and we don't call it a baby until the neonate survives two weeks out of the womb," the geneticist insisted.

"Well, you're the expert, Kendra; if you say it's not a baby, it must not be a baby," she said, stroking her prenate.

"That's better," Kendra sighed, reclining against the sofa cushions, hungry and tired, not in any mood to haggle. Frustration marred her countenance. It was late; she had missed her return flight and still had to make it back to Chicago by the 9:00 a.m. Genetic Manipulation lecture. Worse yet, she hadn't meditated in two days. She closed her eyes, centered on her forehead, and slowed her breathing.

Reana knew she looked frumpy and released the tight bun so her mousy brown hair fell to her shoulders. The heat had caused her to retain more water and her appetite hadn't returned to normal. She had lost a sense of what normal was. Normal was life at the Academy; now nothing was normal, especially without Greg. She hesitated to be blunt about David's betrayal. Greg had been more understanding than she was. She had no heartfelt bond for the traitorous Youth Facilitator, but her heart went out to her exhausted, well-meaning friend, and she considered wording to try to soften the blow. Distracted by a series of hearty kicks from inside her body, she absently returned to stroking her abdomen, musing aloud. "Since this isn't a baby, there's no logical reason to get rid of it."

"You're out of compliance," Kendra said meditatively.

"I know the code says we are to wait five years to have a baby. But you said yourself this isn't a baby. If it isn't a baby, I'm not out of compliance."

Kendra opened her eyes and stared at the white ceiling. She knew the code by heart. It did say baby—obviously an oversight. "Don't be testy; you know what the code means. We are to eliminate unpermitted prenates and neonates."

"Do you suppose they evolve to a higher plane?"

"Trib, Rea, they're not human yet!" Travel weary, she shook her head, studying her friend. The face was all she recognized; sorrowful blue eyes pleaded with her.

"How could the little ones not be human? They grow from humans," she whimpered. Tears brimmed to the surface, ready to spill down her freckled cheeks. "They are humans, moving through different stages of development from conception to Transformation."

"Don't be a romantic," Kendra argued. "No one is human until the law says they are." She eagerly mistook her friend's nod as agreement and stood up, walking to the door. "It's a good thing I never reached David; he would be shocked at both you and Greg." Rea opened her mouth to talk, but Kendra interrupted, "I'd better hurry to get what you need before the store closes. Just stay here and I'll let myself back in the house."

Once the door was opened Rea didn't dare make a sound or move from the recliner.

A painful hour passed before Kendra returned, crept back into the study and closed the door. Reana dozed peacefully, so she set down their wrapped, deli turkey sandwiches and emptied the contents of the abortifacient kit on the desk. The black, zip-lock seal, freezer disposal bag was folded into a six by six-inch square. An illustrated booklet gave step-by-step instructions, which included emergency precautions and numbers for local tissue recycle centers. Six months was the accepted limit for home inducement and it annoyed her that they hadn't taken care of the inconvenience sooner. She expected Greg to arrive so she could have him administer the drug and perhaps drive her back to the airport for the midnight flight.

Halfway through her sandwich, Kendra remembered Rea's odd questions about David and wanted to waken her. Instead, she left her food on the sofa and went to the kitchen for something to drink. The refrigerator held a dismal assortment of vegetables and two half-gallons of milk. She poured milk for Rea and water for herself, then returned to the upstairs study.

Reana was awake, staring past her sandwich to the supplies laid out on the desk. A dreadful fear slithered around her neck and she instinctively crossed her arms over the innocent life thriving in the safety of her womb. She thought better of arguing the case any further. When Kendra appeared with their drinks, she sat up, smiled weakly and took her tall glass of milk.

Sobered, Kendra closed the door, took a long slow drink, set her glass down, and opened the plastic container labeled step one. Two speckled tablets dropped into her palm. She leaned toward her wide-eyed friend and ordered her to open her mouth. Obediently, Rea opened her mouth and the tablets found their mark on her tongue. "Now drink at least half this glass," she said. Kendra Addington watched Reana swallow large gulps, emptying the contents. Then she grabbed her own glass, plopped down on the sofa, and finished eating, exhilarated that she had been of service. The problem was finally on its way to resolution.

Constriction gripped Reana's throat, yet she compelled herself to eat half her turkey deli. While she wrapped the rest for later, Kendra handed her the thin instruction book and hovered as she read it from cover to cover. It was twenty minutes before Reana complained about poor bladder control and excused herself to go to the bathroom.

On her knees in front of the beige ceramic bowl, Reana rammed two fingers to the back of her throat, gagged, muting the sound with her hand, and spilled the contents of her stomach into the water. Two speckled tablets floated above shreds of turkey and bread; small flecks of lettuce and tomato clung to curdles of milk. The milk had, thankfully, diluted the acid just enough. She struggled to her feet and flushed the toilet, watching the death pills swirl from sight. David had taken her Greg; Kendra would not take her baby.

Seated at the desk, Kendra circled the closest recycle center with a pick-up service. A three-day supply of pain pills was stacked next to the booklet. When Reana returned, she reminded her to begin taking the pills with the first contraction. "Have Greg read the instructions so he can be of help," she added. Then with her head tilted, she looked at her friend who was nestling into the recliner and asked, "What was that you were saying about David—and Greg?"

Like a red flag, the blush rose, blending with her freckles. Her decision to avoid the subject faltered.

"What is wrong? What about David?" Kendra said, still in the office chair, rolling herself closer. "You look like you're terrified." Reana's body shook from the effort of silence and her tears welled up, overran their boundaries and flowed down her cheeks. "Trib, Rea," Kendra pleaded, watching, forgetting the disconnection, taking hold of the phone, "should I call the doctor or something?"

"No!" Reana yelped, clasping her hand over her own mouth.

Reana's raw emotion sent an unnamed fear charging through Kendra and she dropped the phone to its cradle. Intensely, she reached for Rea's hand and pulled it, uncovering Reana's mouth. "Whatever has happened? You have to tell me. If it concerns David, I have a right to know."

An eerie calm settled over Reana Foster; she had more than her own future to guard. She paced herself with deep, even breathing. "Remember when David was shot?"

"Of course."

"Well, just before that, David was with Greg and something happened; they had a disagreement about one of Greg's clients."

"Yes, go on."

"Greg told me he thought he was set up by a dissident. Anyway, he went to meet with some people who were complaining about this client's company using slave labor. I guess they were dissidents." She pressed the flat button on the side of the recliner and sat upright, face to face, wondering if she could trust anyone with what she knew.

"So he went to a dissident meeting?"

"Yes, but he wasn't one of them; he was just . . . listening."

"What did that have to do with David?"

"David followed him; Greg recognized him and confronted him. Then, David turned him in to the authorities as a dissident."

"No! I don't believe it. He didn't say anything to me." In disbelief, Kendra pushed away, rolling the chair back. "This happened in March?"

"Yes."

"We've spent weeks . . . Why didn't he ever tell me? I asked how you both were."

Shaking her head, Reana mumbled, "I don't know. Maybe he felt . . . I don't know. I only know what happened to my Greg."

Kendra was so upset with David she hadn't considered Greg's plight. Embarrassed she asked, "What happened to Greg?"

Again, tears flowed unchecked, but her voice was controlled. "We were asleep when men crashed through our door—around midnight. Greg shouted, 'Hide, it's Fereno's men,' grabbed a chair and headed for the hall. The light was dim; they knocked him down, handcuffed him and kept hitting him. I screamed at them to stop and flipped on the light. There were three Peacekeepers in dress-blue uniform, and our housekeeper, Norma. She went to the office and pilfered Greg's papers. When she pushed past me in the hall I begged her to help my husband. They—they laughed at me and shoved him down the stairs and out to their Jeep. When I told David, he said, 'Greg shouldn't have resisted arrest.' I told him they were starving a confession out of him, but David insisted Greg would be home within a week." Reana's tears were dry and her face hardened with anger. "Instead they sent him to Maximum Security, then to slave labor at CAM; then he was scheduled for Transformation."

"No! They didn't!" Kendra blanched at the thought, then argued internally for the merits of a higher plane.

"They didn't. I pleaded with David for justice; he argued, then promised to appeal to Hegie."

"Oh, thank Trib!" Kendra blurted, relieved, higher plane or no higher plane.

"Greg is here, in town at the Haven, but they won't let me see him—say it would interfere with his rehabilitation. Anyway, I couldn't dare go see him like this."

"Well, you'll be able to see him soon," Kendra reassured, then added, "But, why didn't David Winston tell me?"

"I'm so sorry."

"You know we're supposed to take our unity vows in December?"

Reana lowered her eyes, resisting the urge to stroke her wiggling prenate.

THAT same evening, David was seated with the President and other guests on the second-floor White House balcony of the South Portico. Franklin Raynard Higgs IV waited until the night sky erupted with fireworks to lean toward the Facilitator and cheerfully share his news. "I suppose you've heard the latest about the dissidents?" he asked.

"No," David said, pulling away from the Public Relation Director's puffy, anemic face. It amazed him that Malchor tolerated the weasel's choleric effrontery. Yet he did serve a useful, necessary purpose, distancing his boss from the seamy side of things, tying up loose knots, be they friend or foe.

From loudspeakers, Unity Broadcasters blared a symphonic rendition orchestrated in time with the Laser Light fireworks display. David recognized refrains from *The Star Spangled Banner* and avoided eye contact with Higgs. Brilliant explosions of crimson, fanned outward, turning blue with a white perimeter.

"Excellent!" he exclaimed.

"Surely you haven't forgotten your Harvard fiasco?" Frank persisted, breathing too close to David's ear, pleased to finally catch his attention. "Ah, yes, I see you do remember Williams, Paul Williams."

"What about him?" David asked, expecting to hear he had confessed or embraced Synthesis. He feigned disinterest, turning back to the performance.

"The poor fool got himself in trouble for preaching at CAM. He's been Transformed, sent to a lower plane, I expect. Some people just refuse to learn from a lifetime."

David looked at the Public Relations Director. "So?" he asked, pointedly.

"Just thought you would want to know," Frank said, glowering, settling into his chair and immediately refocusing on the show.

Transformed! Trib, not transformed, David's mind screamed, *terminated!* Williams was terminated and he should have been reoriented. There was no good reason why he wasn't. The Youth Facilitator sat through the rest of the evening pretending enjoyment and civility.

It was past midnight when David Winston shed suit and pretense and lay across his bed, thinking about Richard and Jamie Williams, fatherless boys, motherless boys, parented by the state, really, parented by no one.

GRAY-BROWN scales rippled on the creature's massive back, while webbed wings undulated, carrying them miles above Mother's diverse surface. The Mid-East came under their shadow and stayed veiled in darkness, then Asia, then the African Continent, then Europe and South America. The western coast of North America loomed on the horizon. Winston leaned forward, eager to cover the continent. Next to him a dormant figure rose to his feet and seized him by the arm. Unleashed, rage boiled through David Winston and he struck blindly, severing the hold, knocking the stranger against the creature's wing. With both hands he lunged forward and grasped the man's neck, pressing his thumbs deeper, deeper, cutting off the airway, staring into the face. The face, it was the face, a familiar face—A scream tore from David's throat.

His own hands were over his mouth, his body trembling, his eyes open, staring at his bedroom ceiling. The face of Paul Williams lingered, grieving eyes, pleading eyes.

"HEY, Stan, our back-up's here. Wake up!" Ben urged, unlocking the door for four Security guards.

His hair askew, Stan was on his feet, spreading the floor plan across the desk before the guards made it into the room. "Everything's go," Stan said as soon as the door clicked shut. "We have the pass key. Here's the set up. You, Gary, keep your eye on Raven, using the visor. Joe, take the Lobby. Owen, stay here in the hall outside his room. Al, you watch the back of the building. Our prey drank his coke, so he'll be out for another two hours. Anyway, we're taking no chances; Gary, as soon as you see Ben and me in the room, have the ambulance pull up and our guys come up with the gurney. I want him on his way to headquarters by 4:00 a.m. That gives us just thirty minutes, any questions?"

"I thought you were going to wait until you could get the woman, too," Gary said, peering into the mercenaries' room, seeing one lone figure.

"Mal said to bring him in, so we're bringing him in," Ben said. He tossed his comb to Stan and motioned toward the mirror.

AGAIN, Winston soared, this time above the Northwest, circling Orcas Island. Power pulsated up from the creature's body and charged through him as if their bodies were one. He knelt down on both knees, stroking the cool, smooth scales; the massive wings slowed their rhythm. Together they arched high over the top of Mount Constitution and continued gliding above the trees toward the Academy.

Ahead, children poured from the buildings to greet them, their arms open, eyes bright with wonder. When the creature landed beside the Apex pillars, from his back David could see over the top of the dome. He slid over thirty feet down the front leg, then dropped to the ground from its webbed feet. Fascinated, he faced the creature. Ugly jagged flames spewed from its mouth, unnoticed. Fierce, blazing eyes compelled Winston's obedience. He turned, gathered children, pressed them toward the scaly reptilian face, and motioned for others to draw nearer. Each smiling face faded into a stony stupor as children were drawn closer, entranced. Winston forced them closer to the blistering flames until those closest fell whimpering toward the fire and vanished into ashes; puffs of steam rose skyward. Obediently, the Youth Facilitator continued gathering children while the image of Molech, purifier of children, loomed over him. Duty bound him to serve the insatiable appetite of the creature. He continued gathering the children. Innocence was devoured.

"No, Jamie, we cannot do this!"

Winston spun around, furious to see Richard shoving his little brother away from the others.

"But, he's so beautiful," Jamie lamented.

"The dragon's evil! Stay behind me!" Richard commanded.

"You will obey me, both of you," Winston hissed. "Evil is only an illusion."

"Then, how is it, sir," Richard Williams asked, "that this illusion is devouring the children and wants to destroy us?"

"The creature isn't destroying, he's purifying them."

"Then sir, where are they? What has happened to the children?"

The Facilitator stared back at the reptile. Flames leapt hungrily from its mouth, commanding more fuel. Blindly, Winston rushed at Richard and knocked the youth to the ground unconscious. He lay hold of Jamie, lifted the terror-stricken child into the air and strode toward the flames.

"No, David! Stop!"

A deep voice crashed through Facilitator Winston's defenses, halting him mid-step. Slowly, he turned.

Holding his hands out in an open appeal, Greg approached from the side. "Let the boy live, David. Evil wouldn't be satisfied with the world of children. It wants us all. You. Me. Kendra."

"You lie," Winston roared. "It wants us pure!" That instant his hold relaxed; Jamie slid to the ground, ran and threw himself on his brother's limp body.

"If the truth and the lie are the same, it wouldn't matter. But they aren't the same. Evil wants you dead. It hates you. After you help destroy the children?"

"No! Liar," David Winston screamed, lunging at Greg. His clenched right fist connected, knuckle on jaw, snapping his head back. His left fist sank into Greg's diaphragm, knocking him gasping at the creature's feet. Hysterical peals of laughter bubbled from Evil's slimy, scaly throat. It raised its webbed foot, razor sharp talons extended. Greg struggled to his knees and cried out, barely escaping.

Terror gripped David as blood-red eyes sought his, connected, infusing him with vile hatred, then looked past him and froze. With hell's king bound in place, Greg scrambled to safety and urged David to follow. Instead, David turned to see what held the creature in check. A winged being clothed with the brightness of truth knelt and lifted the Williams boys to their feet and *entrusted them to Greg. Serenely, the being stepped toward David.*

Recoiling, Evil shrieked in fury, "He's mine! He took the vow; he belongs to me."

David Winston shuddered under the compulsion to grasp vile power. Truth seared into his soul; he was weighed and found wanting.

Drenched in sweat, he lay face down on his bed, wet sheets clinging to his skin. Like old film clips, two decades of canceled thoughts crashed through tidy compartments of spoon-fed knowledge. The Academy had never prepared him for this. Computer parentage held a strange fascination; yet, Evil's parentage and claim on him brought bile to his throat.

David allowed himself to ponder, to sort through the forbidden. Brockston Andel had perhaps seen the same reptilian demons that had earlier shadowed his own office wall, or even the winged dragon. Fear had driven him to insanity. Greg had been unable to cancel demon images scrawled on paper by Andel's own hand. Fear slithered into David's mind. He stood on the precipice, urged by wicked forces to leap to his own destruction, and was pressed to do it now. Reality struck a sound blow. Evil was no illusion. Evil did exist and very much wanted him dead. But why? The simple question grew louder and more persistent, driving him from his bed into the shower. Warm cleansing water washed over his body. Truth washed over his mind.

XV GUILT

OVERCAST, the morning slipped into early afternoon, offering no chance for David to talk with Server. Mechanically, he went through the usual ritual and settled in front of his monitor, insuring the progress of Synthesis in each of the Academies. Time crept along until he finished typing his message for the superintendents. He was shutting down the computer when laughter disrupted the sterile silence. Frank's hollow noises interspersed with the rich throaty peals of a woman. As far as he knew, no woman had ever set foot in the weasel's room. Curious, Winston left his desk and peered into the office of the Public Relations Director.

Higgs, beaming, showed off his wall of fame, autographed photos of a dozen notables and a smattering of wannabes. The woman humored him with compliments about his collection, moving gracefully from picture to picture. Her brown hair was swept up into a soft swirl at the crown; a gray suit accented her tall supple body. Intrigued, Winston wanted to see her face but didn't care to give Higgs any satisfaction, so he turned to leave.

Frank saw him and called him back to meet his guest, "And this is our Youth Facilitator, David Winston. I'm sure you've heard him speak about the Academies," he said, standing too close to the willowy brunette, touching her shoulder possessively. "This is Synthia Rojan."

"Yes," she said, stepping forward, offering her hand, "I'm honored to make your acquaintance, Facilitator Winston." Her lavender eyes blinked slowly, appraising him from head to foot.

A rare blush of color rose in Winston's cheeks. "No," he countered, while flattery slipped a rope around his feet. "The honor is mine, Ms. Rojan." Her voice haunted him with honey smoothness, while her hand held his. A hint of mystery tempted him to linger. She was leagues ahead of Frank. "What brings you to Malchor's estate?" he asked. It was her eyes, cat-like, ready to pounce, that cautioned him. He had seen the look before. Disciplined enigma, much like the woman waiting for Greg's dissident, the one who had prowled the Chess room, captivating the men and annoying the women.

Higgs fluttered next to her, answering for her. "Your appointment is in five minutes, Synthia. We can't be late."

"That explains why I'm here," she cooed. "I certainly hope to see you again—when we have more time."

David nodded assent and watched them walk down the hall, then followed, even more curious about her audience with Malchor. Minutes later, he was at Malchor's door when Frank made a hasty retreat, mumbling something about her indebtedness. David was sure the woman wasn't the type to be indebted to any man, least of all Higgs. Later, when Server stepped into the hallway, David was still there. They nodded cordially; he continued and David followed him into the Library. It wasn't unusual for both of them to be bent over books in the expansive room. It was unusual for them to be together.

Caution was automatic, even though the library was safe. It was checked routinely for electronic devices to guarantee that the Tribunal's words were confidential and never monitored. Server broke the silence; facing the shelves, book in hand, he whispered, "It was arrogance; I know you saw it."

"Yes," David admitted. "I saw greed too."

"Yes. Good and evil are *not* two sides of the same coin," Server declared, "any more than love and hate are the same."

David stood silent, flipping the pages of *The World Almanac.*

"Is love the same as hate?" Server asked.

"I—I don't know."

"Do you hate Kendra?"

"No!"

"Ahhh, then you do know the difference." Server kept his book and went to the garden doors, opening them wide. He entered the sunlit floral haven, expecting David to follow at a discreet pace. "Do you wish to be holy or just to feel holy?" he asked as soon as the Facilitator was in hearing range.

"I expect if a person was holy, he would feel holy," David answered quietly.

"On the contrary, if one feels holy, one isn't."

The fleshy feeling of purity and holiness held a solid corner on Winston's pride so the elder's words cut deeply, but it was a clean cut, like a scalpel excising a malignant growth. The truth hit him with relief; no pretense was needed. Feeling holiness was a fantasy.

"Now then, do you want to be holy or to feel holy?"

"I want to be holy," David said, "but, how is it possible?"

"Good; then you see it isn't possible for an unholy being to make himself holy."

"I'm beginning to."

Server lowered his book and smiled in gratitude. They had a rare, providential opportunity for freedom. Cyrus and Arion were off controlling the world and Malchor was occupied in weaving a fantasy with Synthia Rojan. And the perceptible haze over David's eyes was beginning to fade.

James Victor Lawrence's voice had taken on strength and clarity in the few months since David heard his first rasping words. But the jagged scars snaking around his neck and the discolored pink scar tissue following his gaunt jaw-line were still graphic proof of his service to Malchor. Aside from his strong words, the greatest difference was in his once lifeless hazel eyes. Life and charity now shone from them. David's closest thought to describe the man's demeanor was that of opposites. He was the opposite of Malchor. He was humility. At Server's smile, unexplainable tears surfaced and stung David's eyes.

"Is Malchor holy?" Server asked.

"I believed he was."

"And so did I; but now?"

"No, Mal isn't holy."

"Are you a god?" James persisted, sensing David's openness.

"No!"

"How do you know you're not?"

"Because I'm not, I . . ." David shrugged, unable to find the words.

"What's the difference between mortals and so-called gods?"

"Mortals aren't omnipotent. Mortals make mistakes."

"Well said, and perhaps the most mortal mistake is declaring self-godhood."

Mutual silence gave David the time needed to reflect. He found the truth to be pleasant, where grasping at godhood had always been oddly unpleasant. After the seeds settled in his mind, he hesitatingly, then boldly described his dream in detail.

When David finished, James Lawrence set his unread book on the garden table, took a seat and motioned for Winston to sit down. "What do you think of the personage that helped the boys?" he asked.

"I could feel his concern for me. Without his speaking I knew he wanted me to stop, to turn away from—from feeding the dragon. I knew the dragon was evil."

"And the winged Being?"

"He was either holy or represented holiness. Which leaves me with my previous question. How is it possible for me to ever be holy?"

"When you learn to love Truth more than you love yourself, you'll have no need to ask." Again Server waited for the words to penetrate the layers of knowledge that sheltered Winston's mind from his present, sorry state of reality. "But, for now, while you ponder what truth is, keep your peace around Malchor. There's much to learn, much to be done."

"Will you teach me?"

"Yes, as I'm able." Server was awed; he had asked Maker

for an opening and was given not only the time but a willing student. A weight of responsibility for the young man's life settled in his heart. He knew if he stepped out rashly, the seeds germinating in David's soul could be crushed in Malchor's hand. For them both, he needed to listen carefully and walk wisely.

The afternoon sun warmed their backs and nurtured stalks of crimson and canary irises growing in the garden soil next to them. Server's lips moved in a silent prayer to Maker and he continued soberly, "We must use what little time we have—cautiously. For your safety, it is imperative you not allow yourself to sink into any hypnotic trance. That's what your meditation does. It opens your mind to manipulation by others. Don't cancel thoughts or allow anyone else that kind of control over you. It is true, you're responsible for your thoughts and must exert control over them or they'll run every which way, wasting your time. But we mustn't attempt to control our thoughts through eastern meditation. Instead, we are charged by Maker to dwell on truth and purity and whatever is good and beneficial. You'll lose what truth you have if you don't realize that it is perversion to allow any man to control your mind, and Malchor has controlled your mind."

The Youth Facilitator frowned. Admittedly, he had been a willing adept. It hadn't occurred to him that his thoughts were any other than his own, chosen by him.

James Lawrence stood, walked back into the library and Winston followed suit. "Wait until I'm gone before you head back to your office," Lawrence said. "No sense arousing curiosity. If Malchor is occupied, we'll meet here in the library Monday afternoon. Until then, I want you to ponder six questions. I know you've heard them before, but you were given false answers before the questions were asked. They are: Where are you from and where are you going? Why are you here and what is your purpose? Most importantly, who has sent you and whom do you serve?"

SYNTHIA made regular pilgrimages to visit Malchor. By the

251

end of the week she had shared his dinner table five times. David found his own access restricted, with the office door closed. He finally called Saturday and made an afternoon appointment with his boss. Promptly at 4:30 p.m., Server ushered him into Malchor's office, then Mal strode in from his private quarters wearing a light-weave, black silk suit. A garish two carat diamond tie tack held the maroon tie to his pale gray shirt. His heavy musk scent filled the room and made it clear their meeting would be brief. Mal neither sat nor offered David a seat.

David stood aloof, then launched into his mundane preliminary report which Mal interrupted. "I trust things are running well at the Academies. Is there any problem?"

"No."

"Good; dispense with the details. I want you to do a profile on Synthia Rojan. You did meet her, didn't you?"

"Yes sir, Higgs . . ."

"An interesting woman, isn't she?"

"I wouldn't know, sir."

Malchor chuckled and said, "That's just as well. As I was saying, I'd like to see a profile on her; might want to hire her as a personal secretary."

"I'll have it for you immediately."

"No, that's not necessary. I'll be busy the rest of the weekend. Monday afternoon will be soon enough."

Malchor motioned to dismiss him, but David pressed ahead. "There is one more thing."

"Yes?"

"I'd like permission to work on a special project."

"And what's that?"

"In all the library, sir, there's not one book or booklet about the history of Synthesis."

"Hmmm, you're right," Mal said indifferently, adjusting his tie, glancing toward the door.

"I'd like to remedy that problem and write your biography. The world should know the truth about your efforts to secure world unity through Synthesis."

"The rest of the Tribunal might feel left out."

"Their own personnel could compile their biographies—it could be a sort of a factual trilogy."

"Certainly."

"May I have permission, sir?"

"Yes, of course," Malchor agreed, "a solid idea. The people should know."

"I hope to do it in two phases. The first would be an overview, more like a time line, for use at the Academies this fall. The second phase would be a full length book, an in-depth analysis of your life of service to Synthesis due out by winter solstice."

"Excellent, and use my personal journal. If you have questions, just ask. I'll check the drafts when I'm in town."

"If it wouldn't be an inconvenience, sir." David stopped. The man was not paying attention; rather, he was humoring him as Scrooge would humor a child excited about a crayon drawing. "Server could proofread and help with the text when you're away. It would speed things up and spare you the time and trouble of working on the initial drafts."

"Yes, that would work. He knows . . ." A light knock on the door brought Malchor to attention. Eagerly he escorted David to the door, giving him full authority to write his biography.

The door opened and Synthia swept past them in a floor-length clinging beige gown, five feet, eight inches of Vogue elegance. Three strands of pearls were French braided with her hair, from her crown down her bare back almost to her waist. She was ready for dinner, the theater and Malchor. David expected she would write herself an intriguing chapter in Mal's memoirs.

STAN and Ben took turns grilling Henry Schlockman. For a week and a half they slept, ate and drank in the headquarters cellar, as much prisoners as the Raven. Orders were to stay out of sight and contact Malchor only when the mercenary cracked. But, even while Ben clipped his wings shorter, the Raven entertained an escape plan. He guessed correctly that he was held at Malchor's estate and figured Higgs would help if forced.

"Look," he growled at Jonez during the shift change. "You can drug me, beat me and starve me until I'm dead. By then, your Youth Facilitator will be as dead as I am. You better know— I do what I'm paid to do. There's another hundred out there ready and willing to take the buck and do the job. And one of them has already pocketed the silver. From here on, I'm not talking to anyone but Malchor himself."

"Well, you better sing fast and enjoy every breath," Stan whispered, glaring into his face, murder pumping through his own veins, "Winston's harm will guarantee your own slow, painful death." For good measure, he jabbed his thumb into Raven's jugular.

Spasms of choked coughing broke from his lungs and Raven went limp. His hands and feet in chains, he had no hope unless the guard cared more about Winston's life than sweet vengeance.

Raven's limp act alarmed both guards. Cursing, Stan grabbed his glass and threw water over the prisoner, thinking he had crushed the fool's windpipe.

With a handful of hair in his fist, Ben jerked Ravens's head upright, slapping him. His face was slack, eyes rolled back, convincing. Worried, Stan touched his carotid artery and relaxed. "He's all right; let him be."

They debated what to do while Raven listened, slumped in his chair. The decision weighed in his favor—to break silence and contact Malchor. Frank would have to free him to save his own neck.

It worked. Malchor had already left with Synthia and Frank took the house-phone call from Stan in his office. Quietly, Server listened in on Mal's private line in the library and scribbled the message. David, reading the words, paled and sat down clutching his chest. Higgs was silent when he heard that Raven had blabbed about another assassin stalking the Facilitator. Recovering, he assured Stan he would page Malchor, and notify him that the mercenary was ready to talk.

Hanging up the phone, Higgs panicked. Short of breath and sweating, he darted from his office, checking every unoccupied room in the building, working his way toward the cellar. When he saw the guarded door in the southwest corner, he knew they were in the wine cellar. Without returning to his office, Franklin Higgs ran to his car.

From the library garden, Server and David watched Higgs drive through the security gate in his tan Mercedes. Seconds later, Owen Tyson pulled into the sparse flow of traffic and followed him.

David turned, bolted through the library, down the stairs to the first floor, then to the wine cellar where he went head to head with a new guard.

"Step aside," David repeated.

"My orders are no one enters, no one leaves."

"Well, I'm giving you fresh orders," David said, flashing his ID badge. "Tell Jonez I'm here and I want to see Raven."

"Yes, sir." The guard pressed the second button on his cellular. "Captain, Facilitator Winston wishes to gain entrance." The guard listened, then stiffened, "Yes, sir, I'll let him in immediately." To Winston, he apologized. "I'm sorry sir, I should have known you; just trying to do my job."

"No problem, keep it up. No one else, except Malchor, enters this area, not under any circumstances."

The guard fumbled with the lock, opening the door to a second locked door. "Yes, sir," he said, unlocking it with a key chained to his belt. David passed through both doors and walked ten feet along a wide sloping corridor to the next guard station. That guard opened the wrought iron gate and pointed to a solid metal door at the far end of the darkened room. David descended six steps into the underground wine storage cellar. Dated rows of wine lined both sides from ceiling to floor; at the back a false wall was pulled forward, full shelves attached, revealing the concrete wall and steel door. David surmised it was a bomb shelter; he tried the latch, then waited.

The thick heavy door moved on its hinge, with Jonez pressing his weight against the cold steel. "Trib," he groaned, "I let you down again; four months and I delivered only half the payload."

"You never let me down," David protested, reaching for Stan's hand, gripping it. Gratitude constricted his throat, "I was responsible."

"It was my job, sir," Stan struggled with his professional role, choking down his emotion, "and I did fail, but take a look; then I need to debrief."

Raven stared at them both, a faint smile fading as David Winston locked eyes, walking closer.

The face of murder was average, plain average. A youthful clean-shaven face with friendly brown eyes stared back at David. Without the uniform, without the firm-set jaw, without the gun, there was nothing sinister about him. Light brown hair grew from his scalp and turned to a bottled black. David made no effort to mask his anger. Fury mixed with remorse—remorse that a man could be paid to kill, fury that this man was paid by someone to kill him.

"So you failed to do the job, Schlockman." Winston said evenly. "Bet your boss is disappointed with you." He stopped behind Raven's straight backed chair, flashing back to the elevator scene—the first bullet ripping into him, the second one knocking him against the compartment wall. He shoved both hands into his change pockets to brace himself, walked around to face his assassin head on and mused aloud. "The notorious Raven not only bungles the job, but gets caught. You lose. There's no market for used mercenaries." He bent closer and whispered, "*Nevermore.*"

At that David Winston turned and left, motioning Ben and Stan to follow. Stan flipped off the light, pulled the door shut and sealed it.

Deep darkness and dead silence penetrated Raven.

"TRIB," David breathed, stopping in the middle of the row of shelves, wine bottles packed securely. "I want to rip the weasel apart."

"What you said did," Ben offered.

256

"Good!" David said. "Thanks both of you for sticking with this guy and bringing him home." The guards acknowledged the thanks, but David sensed their sting of failure and continued. "Stan, Higgs went ballistic over your message to Malchor. He took off in his car with Owen tailing him. I wouldn't put anything past him."

"Sounds like we need to compare notes," Stan said, probing David's features in the dim light, unable to place what it was that made the Youth Facilitator seem a decade older. "Something's been bothering me about this, Raven. You remember that Harvard demonstration; that dissident I followed?"

"Williams?" David asked quietly. Remember was an understatement; haunted was more like it. "Frank told me the man was Transformed."

"That's too bad." Stan paused, looked at the steel door, then back at the Facilitator. "I think it was Raven."

"How . . ." David shuddered, waiting.

"When Raven got away with the woman, we lost them both. Then I saw this guy walking through a crowded mall. I knew the walk; when I got closer I saw it was Raven. I'm sure of it. Williams was set up. Who knows why? But the man I followed off the Harvard campus was the same man I followed through the mall, and that was Raven."

"Why?" David argued. "Why would anyone go to the trouble to set up some innocent . . . But you know what we had just been through, up all night. Then a dissident rally, out of the blue, on the campus grounds, and they knew about Werling. How did they know about Werling when even campus security didn't know he was a pedophile?"

"Insider," Stan agreed.

"Yes, and Frank was the only one besides Malchor who knew about Werling, and he just proved his link with Henry Schlockman. Why did Malchor tell me Raven was a dissident teacher? He said, Raven was hired by that union president, Gil Duskin."

257

"I never heard that one."

"It was all over the news. I don't know, something's not right. Except it unified Impartation International, against all the unions. They crumbled real fast. No one wanted to be associated with my near assassination. Let me give Owen a call." David reached for Stan's phone and pressed security line five. Owen Tyson answered and reported Frank's safety deposit withdrawals from two banks, one under the alias Daniel C. Denning. While they talked, Higgs was shoving cash toward a Unity Air agent, buying one airline ticket to Mexico City for D.C. Denning.

When Winston hung up, Ben voiced what he had already figured out. "Higgs hates you with a vengeance, Facilitator. Everyone who works here knows that. You upset his little fiefdom and took his place in Malchor's eyes. I'm not surprised."

"I think it's time to check his baggage," Winston agreed.

BY MIDDAY, gossamer clouds joined forces with gentle breezes to tame the August heat. Riding horseback, Steve and Jenna Winston circled the spring-fed lake, surveying their land.

"Steven, I'm not used to all these feelings; they're interfering with my job," Jenna lamented, reining Carmel in alongside Lanny, slowing to a smooth rolling gait. Her categorized and packaged life had unraveled on the inside. On the outside she was the picture of composure, even in jeans and tee-shirt.

"Positive or negative feelings?" he asked, taking a closer look. Her shoulder length black hair was clasped into a silver barrette at the base of her neck. Deep-set dark eyes and high cheek bones gave a regal appeal. Without her, beauty didn't exist.

"Both," she said, after a painful pause.

"I hope the positive ones are associated with me."

"Yes and no," she confessed. "The past creeps in, especially when I think of David. A heaviness comes over me, like when I first heard he was shot. It's as if something even worse is going to happen. If he does accept what you said about Malchor Inyesco, how will he manage?"

"He's no fool, Jenna. He'll manage like we do. He'll do his

job, what he has to do to survive and to come out on top of the heap. He'll do fine," Steve reassured. A protective surge of affection welled from his heart.

Still, worry creased her forehead. "I don't know."

"Sounds like you need to concentrate on canceling the negatives."

"But sometimes you can't just wish the negatives away. If someone is stepping on your foot, or your face, for that matter, steps need to be taken to stop them."

"You know this can't be stopped. We have no other viable choice. Synthesis has to work. We have to make it work, and we will, Jenna. We will."

Jenna knew she could trust him with herself, but tomorrow loomed untamed and Synthesis rang hollow. She clung to the flimsy hope that her son was, no matter what, a survivor. Evergreens spired heavenward from the surrounding mountains, soothing her, a legion guarding her future.

IT WAS a dangerous impulse that urged David to demand a visitor's permit. Determined, he framed a careful appeal, pulling rank as the Youth Facilitator to check the progress of reorientation on an Academy graduate, and it was granted— no questions. Within minutes, David's motorcade lumbered up Interstate 295 toward the Haven, slowed by the departure of late afternoon D.C. tourist traffic. In the passenger's seat, with Stan driving, he had time to think. His own gullibility bothered him. He had fallen for Frank's set up, ordered Paul's reorientation, and destroyed the Williams family. David knew his brash actions had doomed the innocent man. His own two hands on the man's throat would have been more merciful. Guilt pressed in, wrapping condemnation around his soul. Silently, he walked from the cars through the checkpoint, leaving his guards following the efficient staff nurse. She strode ahead and held Greg's apartment door open for the Facilitator, then disappeared back down the hall.

Inside, at the narrow desk, Greg set down his volume of the

Encyclopedia Britannica and motioned his guest over as if he expected him. "The library was discarding this old set; they were happy to give it to me," Greg said, waving his hand over the leather bound row of reference books. "What a wealth of knowledge. I never had time for this kind of thing at school. Just today, I read from Chinese Art to Civil Rights. You might try it sometime." For David's benefit he flipped through the pages slowing at Church History, then returned the volume to its empty space.

They bantered about Chinese Art, the looming football season and the weather, then headed outside toward the small lake. Greg's bruises had faded, the small scars on his left cheek were barely visible and a good twenty pounds filled in the hollows, but the growing burden of guilt prevented the Youth Facilitator from being elated over his friend's healing. The quiet gardens offered no cover, so they continued their banal talk and gravitated toward the recreation center.

AT THE D.C. airport, Tyson didn't need any backup help in securing Higgs. The mere thought of physical restraint had reduced Franklin Raynard Higgs to a blob of jelly in his captor's hand, needing help to the car. Malchor had been notified and his Special Forces team was already combing through the ex-P.R. Director's files and belongings.

SOUNDS bounced off the walls in the Haven gymnasium while Greg led David halfway up the risers. "You heard about Williams?" David asked quietly, pointing at the volleyball team member who had just served and scored.

"Yes," Greg answered, carrying on the facade.

"Malchor's public relations director, Higgs, set him up. I think it was to get to me. Trib!"

"Yes, he scored one. Trib it is," Greg said loudly for the orderly passing underneath them. The room echoed with the scorer's victory shouts, then receded to the game's typical grunts and rubber sole screeches.

260

"Higgs hired the same guy to kill me."

"What was his name?"

"Henry Schlockman alias . . ."

"Raven," Greg interrupted. "I've heard of him. At CAM he's sort of a folk hero."

"Well, I expect he'll be meeting his fans soon."

"Werling can put him in charge of CAM training for new mercenaries."

"Werling?" David gasped, unnerved.

"Hey, good play," Greg shouted at the heavy set server who lobbed another over for a point. "Yeah, Milton Werling. Fereno has him practically running the place. You know him?"

"I caught him messing with a minor, a student. He was supposed to be Transformed!"

"Guess they figured he wasn't ready for a higher plane. He was the one who messed up my face and . . ." Greg noticed the intern getting closer and repeated the score. When it was safe he went on. "He's the one who had Paul Williams terminated."

A long groan rose from David's midsection. "Fereno will probably put Higgs in charge of public relations."

"Bet on it. They use everyone's talents." Foster smiled, animated, a picture of his former carefree self, diametrically opposed to the seriousness of their subject. "You know they don't let Reana visit me," he continued, "and I've heard she's barely making it on piece work. As for my treatment, whatever you said to the doctors worked wonders; they are making it impossible for me not to succeed. They want me out of here, but I probably won't be released until October. Could you stop by and see Rea and help her with whatever she needs?"

"I doubt she would want to see me," David mumbled.

"Just let her know I'll be home. Hey, I never thanked you for not turning me in last time you were here," Greg said, his smile genuine.

"You were right about—justice."

Where David's not turning him in was a crack in his allegiance to Synthesis, this admission was a break. Greg risked direct eye contact. The trust was there between them, earned the hard way. Thankfully, the intern assigned to watch them was distracted by a minor skirmish on the court. Greg took full advantage. "Justice has stumbled under the burden of Syn and won't be brought to victory by any man or group of men. David, Williams knew he would never make it out of CAM, but when he found out I was being transferred, he gave me a letter for you. Right now it's in the beginning of 'w' in the Britannica." While he spoke, Greg again pretended to be absorbed in the game. "When we get back to my room, I'll go into the bathroom and you get it yourself. Watch out for the monitor."

Winston nodded, feeling sick to his stomach. He lowered his voice and asked, "Who do you serve?"

"Maker."

"Why?"

THAT night, Special Agents were finishing their task and carting out boxes of evidence when Winston's motorcade arrived. Both the P.R. Director's office and his suite were barren except for the furniture. Even the walls were picked clean of photographs. Depressed, Winston went from Higgs' office to his, straightened the papers on his desk, took down the obnoxious photos of Higgs and tossed them in the trash with a stack of curriculum junk mail. He had failed to contact Reana. Her phone was disconnected and she didn't answer the buzzer. When his guards followed him to her door, it didn't surprise him that she wouldn't answer. It did surprise him that he was unable to contact Kendra. The weeknight phone messages to her Chicago hotel room hadn't been returned. For the second time that day, he dialed her home number. The first time he had left a message. This time there was no answer and her recorder wasn't working.

Server entered Winston's office carrying Malchor's five journals and set them on the desk. Each journal held five separate yearly planners bound together. Malchor Inyesco wrote his first entry January 1, 1976 AD, a student of Harvard's freshman class. On the first page he listed his goals for the year. Each following page opened to a new week; the days were filled with brief notations. Methodically printed, his challenges and achievements were listed along with significant events. David scanned the first planner. A few confidential entries showed Malchor's youthful opinions and reflections. He easily accomplished his first goal and was elected Freshman class president.

Server didn't dare risk being monitored, so he typed a message on David's computer keyboard setting a Monday afternoon appointment to work on Mal's history, then withdrew.

David skipped his late night dinner, went to his room, took out his dictionary and opened it. By talking to Server and Greg, he had stood at the edge of the cliff, plunging forward away from Synthesis and two decades of spoon-fed knowledge; he was in a free-fall, headed for sure termination—and then what? What was there after life ended, if he wasn't evolving to godhood?

Carefully he unfolded Paul Williams' letter secreted behind his I.D. badge and spread it out between the pages. It was unaddressed and unsigned, a necessary precaution, written with a disciplined hand.

Dear Brother,

Be comforted; my job is finished and I'm prepared to meet death, confident the seeds I've planted will, by Maker's grace, produce life in others.

These past months, Maker often reminded me to pray for your blessing. In obedience, I have interceded for you, and have been assured of your future. I am compelled to write and tell you what I know to be true about Maker and Humanity.

In the beginning, Maker formed the Cosmos, a multidimensional burst of designed energy was shaped over eons to sustain life on our Earth home. Each purposed molecule vibrated in obedience, each constellation, by name, declared His plan. Humanity was formed to tend earth, be fruitful and multiply. Yet, humanity's primal purpose was loving communion with Maker.

Love requires free will, free choice of the beloved. Man chose Evil. Fallen, he embraced lawlessness and sought godhood. To cover his guilt he accused Maker. Eschewing Truth, he invented vain philosophies, hollow myths and a priesthood of fleshly greed and power. With self-righteous pretense, this tower of Babel putrefies earth, rots Body, Soul and Spirit.

The goal of Evil was, and is, to destroy humanity and rule above Maker. And Man, scorning Truth, falls into the deception of the Evil One. Thus each generation chooses who to serve, Maker or Evil.

Maker selected the Chosen Ones to keep His Law and tell the world that He is Holy and we are not.

David stopped. His eyes drifted over the page. . . . *reminded me to pray for you . . . hollow myths . . .* Myths were tiresome, a diversion for children, at best. Distracted, David forced himself to continue reading.

Maker's love is demonstrated throughout Creation. Maker loves you and me. His Word, His only begotten Son, became our flesh and blood Messiah. Two thousand years ago, Messiah left Sovereignty to become man and dwell with the Chosen Ones. He lived and taught love, resisting the temptation of Evil. Sinless, He took our lawlessness upon Himself and died for us, in our place, crucified by wicked men, rejected by the Chosen, then abandoned at death by most Believers.

Evil reviled Maker's love for man as weakness. Arrogant, he believed he could keep Messiah in the grave. But, three days after the crucifixion, Messiah conquered death. Love prevailed. Sinless, He broke the chains of death. Messiah rose from the dead and walked the earth, taught Believers, then returned to Maker in heaven to prepare a place for us.

Today, Messiah is our High Priest, interceding on our behalf before Maker. He will return. Today, Evil prowls earth, promising power, deceiving nations. Evil will be exposed and cast into utter darkness.

Until then Maker's Spirit draws us, teaches and comforts us. Both The Chosen and Believers await Messiah's coming, eager for Him to bring justice to victory. I pray that you will embrace Maker through Messiah.

Maker impressed upon me to ask you to look after my little ones and return them to my family. This possibility is beyond my understanding, but not beyond His Providence.

I'm grateful I was deemed worthy to meet you and pray for you. Be comforted.

Your brother in Messiah

Comfort was not what David felt when he finished Paul's letter. Blood Guilt screeched and howled in his mind, making it difficult for him to follow the message, demanding he rip the letter to shreds and throw himself from his bedroom window. The shrill voice sent shudders of fear along David's spine and confirmed that Evil did indeed want him dead. In his dream, when confronted by the being, the dragon sounded the same, claiming David's soul. Despair shoved its demon claws into his heart, telling him he was lost, without hope, a murderer of innocents. A desperate, wordless cry for help exploded in his mind. If Maker didn't exist, what mattered?

Trembling, David read the letter again, forming the words into their intended meaning. Greg had said about the same thing—the opposite of what Malchor's books described. If Greg and Server and Paul Williams were right and Maker was more than a myth, then Mal was wrong. With Malchor—Good was Evil; Evil was Good.

David bent over the dictionary re-reading the letter a third time, then carefully closed the book, his head pounding with Greg's answer to his final question. When he had asked Greg why he served Maker, Greg answered simply, "Because He exists. He created me. He knows me and wants me to know Him." While David prepared for needed sleep, he pondered who he served. By the time he flipped off the lights and stretched his six-foot, one-inch frame on the fresh sheets of his king-size bed, he knew who he served. He served himself. Even his years of service to Synthesis had always been service to no one but himself. Another thought nagged him into a restless sleep. In serving himself, had he in reality served Evil?

THE apartment was lifeless. Kendra had disconnected her answer machine when she heard David's concerned voice, asking her to call. She threw her energies into her job, distributed the latest scientific data on genetic engineering to her staff and processed a record number of students for the Orcas Island Academy. Her office was now the terminal for all students feeding into the Northwest Region's Education system. Her evaluation of a student's profile set the course for which track the student would follow. Kendra enjoyed investigating the rare exceptions, those children who, by some quirk of fate, jumped track and excelled beyond their abilities. She worked overtime on Saturday to test a ten-year-old female student, slated for level-two technical training, who was gifted in astronomy. The drone bureaucrats kept botching the transfer to level-one until, out of necessity, she called Hegelthor. He agreed to review the girl's case.

Aside from the relief of work, Kendra's every spare minute was filled with either Reana's grieving face or with David's words of longing. There was no good reason for his deception. In lying to her, David Winston had soiled their past and their future. She deliberated the possible reasons. None could be excused. Her white satin unity dress and headpiece hung in the closet taking up a third of the space, mocking her plans. It was late. Exhaustion settled in and, again, David's voice begged her to call. She slid into bed and forced herself to focus on her forehead. Eyes closed, she patterned her breathing and drifted into mindless space.

SUNDAY, a cool morning breeze rustled the pages of Malchor Inyesco's second journal. Winston was so engrossed, he didn't hear Server enter the library with a breakfast tray. When he set it on the coffee table, David looked up, surprised. A victory smile was spread across James Lawrence's angular face. The man looked years younger and David realized he was younger than Steve, his father. James was lean and sinewy, not the frail old man Winston had perceived the year before, bent over, defeated by life's weight.

He stood erect and spoke clearly, "Good news, David, Mal is on holiday and won't return until tomorrow afternoon."

The Facilitator closed the journal and set it on top of the others. During the dark pre-dawn hours, he had made the decision to study the issue systematically, hopefully, not emotionally, and either set aside the claims of Maker or embrace them. The fact that Synthesis was lacking was not proof that what the Believers claimed, wasn't. He had believed a lie his entire life and didn't plan to waste any more time on Evil, myths or fantasies.

Without ceremony, David plunged into the subject. "I was taught relativity, that good and bad serve the same purpose: self perfection; that reincarnation would bring personal godhood and cosmic unity, that all paths lead to the same god."

"True," Server acknowledged, "I believed that way for a quarter of a century. It's disturbing to reflect on past errors in judgment, isn't it?" David nodded, intense, leaning on his elbow with his fist partially covering his chin. "Gullibility," Server continued, "isn't something to brag about, but you have a better reason than I. You were raised in the fog. I was raised in the truth and turned my back, once I tasted the promise of godhood." A dark brooding shadow fell over his features, remorse for the wasted years. He sat down in the upholstered chair across from the Youth Facilitator, his back to the door, in case a stray security guard entered the library without knocking.

"I clamored after every exotic myth that promised purity," Server elaborated, "and moved further and further from the truth. What amazes me is the Tribunal takes their religion so seriously. It is, after all, a designer religion, tailored for each new day, not grounded in reality or any truth. Each adept has his own little fantasy, as if truth can be manipulated and altered by the whim of mortals. I certainly had my own fantasy world. Empty, mindless . . ." James' voice faded and he shook his head.

"What about the claim that all paths lead to god?" David asked, not wanting to dwell on fantasy.

"Do all roads lead to Dulles airport?" Server questioned.

"No, many, but certainly not all."

"If you had to catch a plane there, which road would you take?"

"The fastest and most direct road. So what do you believe is the fastest and most direct road to god, whomever or whatever you believe him to be?"

Server smiled at the familiar disclaimer and explained gently, "What I believe would be foolish if what I believed were not true reality. I could believe that this book is God, but it isn't. How could a true God be made with human hands or human minds? God is not whomever or whatever we believe He is. He is not a being of our own making. Rather, He is who He says He is and He says He is Elohim. The Chosen know Him as YHWH, and revere His name so highly, they won't say it. The Believers know Him as Abba, a child's term for father.

"Don't take my word for it. The decision is too important. You would be wise to read the words of His prophets and His Son, Yeshua. But remember, in all the heavens there are only two beings who claim sovereignty, the Serpent Deceiver, called Lucifer, and the Holy God, Elohim. You've read the words of the Deceiver and his minions since childhood. To sum it up, the bad news is—man messed up and can't fix the mess in himself or the world. The good news is—Maker sent His Son, Messiah, to fix the mess in man and the world."

James went to the computer terminal and accessed the

library index, scanning through the list of volumes until he found what he wanted. He turned, slid the ladder along the north wall, climbed four rungs and retrieved a brown volume. He shifted several other books into the narrow space until it was swallowed up, then climbed down and handed the prize to David. "Now you will be blessed with the words of Maker. You'll want to use one of your book jackets to cover this. Chamberlon's latest book on World Peace has the perfect size." Pleased, James sat down and pushed the food tray closer to David. Absently, the Youth Facilitator lifted a slice of orange and took a bite.

"You asked about all paths or roads leading to a god," James continued. "There is a tragic truth to the claim that all roads lead to God. When the time of judgment comes, no matter what path is taken, all mankind will stand before the One True God. Those who rejected Him and chose the path of evil, hating justice and truth, will face their Judge. Those who believed Him and chose the path of righteousness, loving justice and truth, will face their Father, redeemed by Messiah.

"David, when you stand before Maker, will He be your Judge or your Father?"

"If He is who you say He is, I need to know Him. What's the most direct road, then?"

Pointing to the closed book in Winston's hand, he said, "Read it. Let His Word speak to you." Server moved quietly toward the door while David scanned the title page of the *Holy Bible*.

"Wait," he blurted. "You said Malchor controlled my mind. How is that?"

"Guilt," Server said from across the room.

"Guilt over what?" David asked.

"Your first day, you remember what happened as you stood in the foyer?"

"I—I waited."

"What happened inside, after the second hour?"

"Anger," David whispered. "I failed."

"Yes, and you were supposed to. Malchor would have left

you waiting until you broke."

"But why?"

"To secure guilt allegiance. It's an ancient guru method. The eager adept is left waiting until frustration gives way to anger, then the benevolent master appears to forgive the unworthy follower. It's very effective, isn't it? You still feel innately unworthy in his presence, as if he were a god. Still, he is mortal, a manipulative mortal, but nevertheless, a mortal."

"Trib," David muttered as the library door closed securely behind Server. Left alone he sorted out his thoughts and sifted through the pages of the book, searching for answers.

XVI UNITY VOWS

REANA gasped for air, grabbing the edge of the kitchen counter. Her mug of raspberry tea balanced on the edge, then clattered into the sink. She watched it gurgle into the open drain, trying to do what the midwife on the birthing video said about breathing. *Concentrate on letting it happen, block the urge to tense up; let the pain flow through you, release it, don't fight.* She whimpered. A shudder forced her mouth shut, fearful the audio monitor would alert some nameless technician to investigate the unusual sound.

The gentle twinges of Braxton Hicks contractions had changed noticeably the previous day, sending Rea into a frenzy of activity. The office was ready, but she wasn't. Her blanketed mat was spread on the floor in front of the vinyl couch, waiting. A layette was folded and stacked neatly beside the small wood cradle she salvaged from a yard sale. Fresh white paint covered scratch marks from previous owners and a new mattress replaced the mildew-soiled original. Sterile water filled the crock pot and sterile cloths were stuffed into plastic bags on the right end of a large, stainless-steel serving tray. Clamps, scissors, two pans and a water bottle shared the tray with twelve folded, disposable bed pads. Next to the tray, the picnic cooler sat empty, with the lid off, propped against the side.

She planned to cook up some meals for herself. Instead, here she was gripping the counter, now with both hands, the baby's head pressing against her cervix, forcing it to yield. Minutes passed, and the pain lessened, then ceased. Rea reached over the groceries and turned on the radio.

The silver-tongued talk-show host invited callers to give their opinions about a new Congressional scandal. Senator Clyde Murphy from Massachusetts was caught in bed with the female Ambassador from Cuba. The first caller, a teacher from California, argued against the dark age notion that what a person did in the privacy of the bedroom would influence their professional abilities. Her voice got a bit shrill when the host asked if there were any exceptions. "Absolutely not!" she insisted. When the host suggested plotting treason, she hung up. Rea could think of a list of exceptions from adultery to murder that would seriously impair a lawmaker's willingness or ability to write just laws. The media theme quickly settled on the solution, Autonomous voting.

Grappling with the concept helped distract Rea from her immediate problems: food spread across her counter—and real labor. The failings of representative government had taken up the entire year of upper division studies in political science. By the end of the year, she and the whole class agreed that money saved by ending legislative elections would be better spent on education. Rea was relieved the electorate was moving toward a change from the archaic representative system. Hurriedly, she tossed lettuce and tomatoes into the fridge. Her shopping expedition had ended just in time, but soup would have to do for meal planning. Within minutes water sizzled around the bottom of the pan. Quickly, she dumped the whole bag, three pounds of frozen skinless chicken breasts, into the simmering water, and followed with two bags of frozen mixed vegetables.

The next contraction, five minutes after the first one, confirmed that reading about labor was one thing and doing it was another. Rea slapped peanut butter and honey on two slices of bread, ignoring the subtle tightening of her abdomen until it demanded her attention. Again, she gripped the counter. When the pressure lessened, she put the sandwich together and into a bag, pondering the sisterhood of women who had birthed their babies alone.

272

Alone. The thought shadowed her while she poured seasoning and brown rice into the soup pot. It was seven minutes until the next contraction bore down, sending her to her knees for relief. The talk-radio host droned on, a safe covering for Reana's soft moans. Struggling back to her feet, she grasped the ladle, gave the soup mixture a last stir and put the lid on, turning the knob to simmer. She made three trips, between pains, to the office to fill her cooler with food and drink. Finally satisfied with her readiness, she filled the bathtub with soothing warm water, still trying to convince herself there were worse things than birthing alone.

"THIS is it," David whispered, shuffling through the investigative report. "I felt it. I knew it in my gut. She came here after me."

"But she found bigger game," Stan added.

"Temporarily, at any rate," David said, sinking into his chair, spreading Stan's report next to the terminal. "I was working up her profile, running into brick walls. The national files say Synthia Rojan is Miss Perfect from Denver, Colorado. She's good, too good." David set the I.D. photo for Bernedette Von Himmler up next to the screen I.D for Synthia. "Look at that." Deftly, David merged the Rojan file with the Himmler file; the genome code map was a clear match.

"There's more, David," Stan said, looking over the Facilitator's shoulder. "Frank kept a diary. You remember some time ago when that dissident Lazzari was transformed?"

"Jules Lazarri. Yeah, I remember," he said, still punching keys.

"Well. Frank had Bernedette Himmler on the payroll. She used Lazarri . . ."

"To get to Greg!" David interrupted, his eyes narrowing. "Frank had Greg set up, too."

"Through Himmler, and she didn't even have to pay Lazarri. He was a zealot. She had him thinking he was helping the cause. From Frank's personal notes it sounds like Lazarri was trying to get CAM exposed, some nonsense about slave labor. He tricked Greg Foster into meeting with him, then with the dissidents."

"That's what Greg said."

"But when Lazarri was caught, Frank made him feel he was too important to lose; like the dissidents couldn't win without him. Promised him probation if he'd implicate Greg."

"Yeah, I know the rest of the story." David frowned, squelching a correction about CAM. "When Synthia was in Frank's office, I saw the resemblance to Marci, but didn't check it out. Trib, no wonder they threw the book at Greg. Hindsight! What was that alias Frank used for her? Some kind of trade name, wasn't it?"

"Dove. Frank called her Dove, one time."

David typed in Dove. It was a match and he merged the mercenary file with the others. He did one more search then reviewed the pages coming off the printer. "What happened to the rest of these people, the dissidents that met with Greg? I sent descriptions in on them."

". . . dropped out of sight."

"All of them?"

"Yes. Peacekeepers didn't find a trace."

"Good!" Winston blurted, not thinking. Stan's puzzled look brought a quick, added explanation. "I bet that made Frank mad." Then to change the subject, he asked brusquely, "Is your report ready for Malchor?"

"Yes."

"This could get ugly with . . ." David began, then clammed up, shrugging off the opinion. Stan's questioning look begged for clarification, but the Facilitator held his peace. Malchor's preoccupation with the mercenary wasn't staff business.

DAVID was careful to draw no undocumented conclusions about Synthia Rojan. The profile outlined her true identity and her strengths and weaknesses in the four categories. She was well suited for her profession. His objective report lay on the desk with Stan's. A wordless half hour passed with David sitting erect in the private office facing Malchor Inyesco. The ebony desk surface stretched between them, contrasting with the sheets of white paper. Mal gave no response, not a flicker of reaction as he read each page, reread and compared the two reports, then checked his own data files.

Finally, he broke the silence, examining his Youth Facilitator. "And what is your personal opinion?"

"I . . ." Caught off guard, David fumbled for words, "My—My opinion is subject to yours, sir."

"Hmmm—and it is my opinion that Syn is very good at what she does, a charming chameleon. It was in your present interest that Higgs didn't hire her first, to speed your incarnation to another plane."

"Apparently, sir," Winston agreed soberly, "my work is not yet finished."

"True, it would have been a pity to have to train another . . ." Malchor studied the strain still stamped on his Youth Facilitator's face. It was a minor mortal failing, a limitation on physical endurance. "Well," Malchor added, "on to the failings of Higgs; he won't trouble you any further."

David sensed Mal was ready to end the meeting and the time wouldn't resurface for clearing up Higgs' web. "Sir," he said, "Stan's report records evidence that Greg Foster was set up by Higgs, apparently to harass me."

"Foster?"

"A former student at the Academy, and my roommate, he was an attorney in Baltimore until Frank had him set up on false charges."

"And where is this friend of yours now?" Mal asked, shuffling through the report, spotting Foster's name.

"At The Haven."

"I'll look into the situation."

"Thank you, sir. He's a gifted attorney."

"And, no doubt, a gifted friend?" Mal asked, looking up, not expecting an answer. He checked his watch and stood up, signaling an end to the briefing. "Friends are a pleasant diversion from duty, so long as one doesn't forget one's duty."

"That would be unthinkable," David said, excusing himself from the room.

Malchor's door was still open when Synthia arrived. She waited to be invited into the room, admiring the man's form while he studied the file on his desk.

On seeing her, he smiled his approval. She was a model professional in her tailored, dark blue suit and white silk blouse, her hair clipped back securely. He went to her, drew her into his office and closed the door.

Without a word, he seated her and handed her the Dove file, then returned to his chair. As she read, he watched her closely. Her performance was flawless. The pleasant, expectant expression stayed secure, page after page.

"I do prefer this name," Synthia Rojan laughed, closing the folder. Handing him the file, she leaned close, pressing her flawless cheek against Malchor's. "School friends called me Bern. But the sound of Synthia, when you say it, is perfect," she whispered.

"Your profile indicates you're more than qualified," Mal said, again shuffling through her file. He indulged Syn's diversions, fully enjoying the game. He was the lion king. She was the pubescent lioness, playful in the face of power. "You've read the job description for Public Relations Director?"

"Yes, and I would be pleased to serve you."

"Business will be business, and pleasure will be pleasure."

"At your bidding, Malchor."

"I expect unfailing loyalty."

"And you deserve unfailing loyalty."

Malchor flashed an uncharacteristic grin, feasting on Synthia's strengths. He had set his goals and achieved them, all of them, thinking there was nothing else to conquer. But Syn was a surprise, his first real surprise, unplanned, unanticipated, alive. She was a boundless improvement over the dour, methodical Higgs. "Frank left several jobs unfinished," he said, speaking professionally, grinning foolishly, escorting her to the door. "You can tackle them tomorrow. Take the rest of the day to settle into your office. My staff will help if you like. Tonight," he added, touching her cheek, "dinner's at seven."

"What about Winston?" she asked, pausing at the door.

"He's weary, showing the strain of Frank's revenge."

"How long has he waited for unity?"

"You've done your homework," Mal chuckled. "Spring was here and gone and December is many cold nights away."

"Perhaps spring could blossom in September?" Synthia cooed.

"So it has, Synthia, and so it will."

DAVID Winston glanced up at the volume-lined library shelves. Timeless words shared equal space with the ravings of fools and madmen. He sat at a table and reread the last entry in Malchor's fifth journal, dated December 31, 1999. The Tribunal had celebrated their internationally accepted date correction while skiing the Aspen slopes. They sped down the snow crowned Colorado Rockies as Father Time erased 1999 AD and instituted 2000 MS. All the arguments for waiting a year until the actual millennial change were ignored. Millennial Synthesis was official, a line in the sand between the old and the new, embraced by all leaders and followers of the World Order. David reread Malchor's last sentence, *Anno Domini is over, replaced by humanity's holiness.* He dared to consider, if there were any truth to the ancient holy writings, then Tribunal triflings were presumption at best. Was man usurping Maker and His timetable, to usher in a synthetic millennial peace? Whether Maker existed or not was still questionable. Yet one thing was unquestionable. Millennial Synthesis had not brought Winston or the world, lasting peace.

Server had alluded to the incomplete sixth journal and expected to have the 2000 MS year planner by the afternoon. Since Malchor was unwilling to let his current journal out of his sight for more than two hours, Server agreed to scan it directly onto David's computer. David, eager to get his hands on both, waited impatiently for their scheduled appointment.

When Server walked into the library empty-handed, Winston shook his head. "Where is it?" he blurted, before the door closed.

"Easy does it," Server warned softly, pulling a chair up, sitting opposite him with his back to the door. "Malchor feels you're overwrought with all that's happened. He wants you to take a break and just work on what you already have. I agree you've had enough to digest this weekend."

"So what's happening with Synthia?" David asked, disappointed, but accepting Server's point.

"You're surprised that she's replacing Higgs?"

Color drained from the Facilitator's face. "What!" he exclaimed. "But the report—she came here to kill me."

"True, and she changed her mind. That's why you're still around," Server said, convinced of Maker's mercy. "And she's still around because she told Malchor the whole sordid tale this last weekend, just before Higgs bolted. She has impeccable timing, doesn't she?"

"Impeccable," David muttered, rage building.

"Anger will not serve you well, David. You've seen that evil exists, yet it still surprises you. Stay focused," Server touched his arm. "What is the purpose of Impartation International?"

Looking at the broader picture, David's own insult shriveled in significance. Here was the world embracing a lie; in comparison, his complaint was trivial. He answered stoically, "To teach the tenets of Synthesis to the children, the youth and all mankind."

"And what does Synthesis promise?"

"Universal Peace."

"What if Synthesis is evil?" Server challenged.

"How can knowledge be evil?" David asked.

"Synthesis goes beyond knowledge. It is a belief system." Server pressed on, compelled to shake the Facilitator's mind set. "Can something be good and evil at the same time?"

"I . . . No. I assume that Evil is the opposite of good."

"Is Evil the opposite of good—or the absence of good, like

darkness is the absence of light?"

"Opposite implies equal value or strength."

"In some areas that could be acceptable," Server persisted. "But is it, in life and death issues? If the thesis is true and the antithesis is false, then what is the synthesis?"

David stared at the fireplace, silent as cold charred bricks.

WHENEVER the water cooled, Reana struggled to reach the faucet, finally leaving it to trickle. Water was almost to the rim, draining out through the overflow. Several towels behind her supported her back, another draped her shoulders. Wrinkled fingers drizzled warm water over her contracting belly while sixty seconds crawled an eternity around the bathroom clock.

Meditation offered relief, tempting her to trance out to escape the recurring pain. She closed her eyes, focused on her forehead—let her arms go slack, relaxing, sinking back against the towels, slipping lower in the water, knees bent. Water lapped at her chin, peaceful rest, sweet escape. A green forest, waterfall, Reana was in the lake swimming under the waterfall, holding her breath.

"LISTEN," Server urged, seated across from Winston in the library, "if the water is frozen solid, then it is not liquid. It is not both solid and liquid at the same time. It is one or the other."

"That doesn't apply."

"It is Synthesis that doesn't always apply. A thesis is an assumed premise. Synthesis isn't absolute truth. If the thesis is true and the antithesis is false, what is the synthesis?"

"False," David answered, perplexed.

"If the thesis is true and the antithesis is true, what is the synthesis?"

"Antithesis is an opposite," Winston repeated in textbook form. "Synthesis is the merger of opposites into a new thesis, an Hegelian whole in which opposites have been reconciled. However," he added, thoughtful, "if all things aren't relative, the new thesis would be measured against some standard."

279

"I agree." Server marveled at Winston's rapid progress. "And I accept the existence of a standard outside of and wholly independent from man's opinions, a standard of right and wrong. The Tribunal insists all is relative except their own opinions. And their opinions, no matter how mundane, deserve world reverence. Tribunal insists that all Synthesis is good. With no true standard, they choose to believe, or pretend to believe, that the process itself is holy, also. The process of arriving at Synthesis is for them, and for their followers, the convergence of the knowledge of good and evil."

David considered the possibility and concluded, "Then the convergence point would be the acceptance of opposites as reconciled into a unified whole; good and evil as one, all as one, all as god."

"There are opposites which cannot be reconciled. It's fantasy to presume that the truth and the lie are one. Good is mixed with its opposite, evil, and stirred in the caldron of Synthesis. But, what happens when you mix the truth and the lie?

"I read Genesis, Matthew and Revelation," David offered almost inaudibly, not ready to say what his mind recognized.

"And what did you learn?" Server asked, his heart filled with joy.

Facilitator Winston shifted in the straight-backed chair, uncomfortable with the knowledge that clashed against his paradigm, his world-view threatened. "That there's more, a different kind of knowledge to learn."

"Good," Server said. "When all else fails, there's always wisdom." The Youth Facilitator sat forward, concentrating, measuring every word, testing it. James took a full breath and continued. "Religion has long been man's attempt to remove his own guilt and make himself clean. The goal is either to reach God or become a god. But Maker doesn't offer us a man-made religion. He is not an ethereal Universal Spirit approachable through some discipline like Aikido. He is not made in man's image. He is a personal, caring Father; He offers Himself, His love. He made us for fellowship, and He wants our fellowship."

WATER, warm flowing water, offered comfort and sleep. A voice called to Reana, urging her to breathe, to breathe and sleep. But reality screamed; pressure built in Reana's head and lungs, threatening to explode, and her muscles contracted. Sputtering, gasping for air, she straightened her legs, pushing up out of the water. "My baby!" she cried. "What am I doing!" The contraction deepened; she leaned back against the towels, determined to do what was best for her baby, nothing less.

"WHAT kind of love is . . ." David stopped, the accuser stirring his memory. Grief and Guilt clawed at his mind, uprooting seedlings of hope. Server sensed the dilemma, prayed for wisdom and waited awkward minutes for David to continue. "How could a loving, just God let Paul die like that?"

James Lawrence understood the cry for justice that forced the question, an outrage against injustice, an underlying fear of culpability. "And how," he asked, his voice soft, "could a loving, just God allow His only begotten Son to die for the likes of us?"

Winston slouched, in no position to pass judgment on anyone, least of all Maker—if He did exist.

"Love like that is beyond my own ability," James acknowledged, "a self sacrifice. The Father and Son both knew there was no other way to rescue fallen man from the grasp of Evil. The Son accepted the price of His own death, to purchase us from our deserved fate." The Facilitator had dropped his carefully practiced front and his face registered need, his need to know the truth. Server continued, "In Eden, Evil promised man godhood through the knowledge of good and evil. And he promised immortality. Believing his lies separated us from fellowship with Maker, set us on the futile path of trying to earn holiness and self-godhood. Reincarnation is the best facsimile Evil could come up with—perpetual dying and perpetual striving.

"When man chose to follow Evil, Evil had a claim on man, a right, if you will, to destroy him. But when Evil killed Messiah and attempted to hold the holy and innocent Son of God in the grave, he had no just claim, no right and power to keep Him."

"But, Paul?"

"Death had no victory over Paul, because Evil had no claim. Paul's with Maker. You'll see him again, next time, as a brother."

The term, brother, was beyond David's understanding until he had watched the boys, Paul's boys. He groaned. *How could Paul accept my brotherhood?* Pain shaded his face. "His children, his wife . . . " he began, then pressed his fist to his mouth, silenced.

"Maker is a Father to the fatherless, a husband to the widow," Server said, his heart aching for them, with an understanding born from his own personal loss.

Willfully, David choked back shamed sadness. "How could a God allow this kind of abuse?" he demanded, desperate for solid answers. "Where is Justice?"

"Justice demands our death. Are you sure you want justice? James asked evenly, his eyes riveted on David's. "The earth's in travail and will be until the final harvest of those who have chosen and those who have yet to choose to love Maker. Can't you see?" he implored, reaching across the table, resting his hand on David's arm. "In the end, it's mercy that will triumph over justice. For now, thankfully, mercy is extended. There are still people who haven't made their decision, people like you."

Self-conscious, David looked at his whitened knuckles, unclenching his fists. Malchor was right; he was overwrought.

"Maker gave you free will; he didn't make you a mindless robot," Server continued gently, carefully. "You have free will. God risked giving you free will, knowing you might use your free will to kill Messiah, to kill innocence. You can choose to see the truth about your own nature. You can choose to turn from Evil. You can choose to protect innocence. You can choose to love Maker with all your heart and soul." Looking at David's face, he could see the struggle. Bitterness and Guilt were entrenched, visible in the proud set of the young man's jaw, while warfare raged for his soul's allegiance. "Paul knew and accepted the price of tribulation, the price he would pay for loving truth."

Cynicism managed to plant itself smugly, comfortably in the

Youth Facilitator's mind. David closed his eyes against the simplicity of Server's words. Without comment he rose, gathered Malchor's five bound volumes and left the library, retreating to the barren reality of his office.

COLD and long abandoned, the water lay motionless in the tub. Reana had retreated to the office hours earlier; the clock read 7:38 p.m., September 3, 2001. Sweating, she sat on the padded office floor, propped against the couch, two pillows stuffed behind her. Strands of hair fell from a loose pony tail and clung to her face and neck.

Intently, she studied the muted video; birthing looked so serene, almost effortless. The midwife coached and paced the mother through transition. Reana pressed fast forward and the delivery blurred past—baby's head face down, delivered, then turning face to the side, mouth syringed, shoulders and body delivered. The squirming, crying infant, placed in its mother's arms.

Irritated, Rea stopped the video. This was no time to be alone; no one should ever have to go through this kind of . . . She groaned, unsure she had the strength to go on, and dropped the remote control onto the tray. "Don't push," she said aloud, panting, her hands gripping her knees, knees drawn up close to her chest. She fought the compulsion to hold her breath and push, just to get it over with, just to stop the relentless pain.

"THERE you are, David. I was hoping to see you," Synthia cooed, lingering at his office door, expecting an invitation to enter.

Jerked out of his concentration, David didn't allow a flinch. Instead, he finished scanning page 472 from the 1999 Journal into his computer before turning to face Malchor's new Public Relations Director. "Congratulations, Ms. Himmler," he said dryly.

"Please, do call me Synthia," she said. "It's my favorite name." Her full lips broke into a playful grin, then formed a sultry pout. "I truly am looking forward to working with you," she insisted, "and I do understand your reticence."

"Really?" he said with forced levity, unblinking, staring into her lavender eyes.

"Yes, I do, and whereas business is business, I never eliminate anyone of value."

"Value? And by whose standard did you judge me?"

"My own, of course. Because you have value, you exist."

"Well then, I should be pleased that you value me above Higgs."

"Higgs?" The name rolled from her mouth buried in a hearty laugh. "You know as well as I that Higgs is, or should I say was a pawn, a boring pawn."

"And Raven?"

"An egomaniac. Incompetent, thank Trib! I could have missed this opportunity to . . . Well, enough of that," she said, smiling coyly. "May I come in?"

She was deadly—a poised cobra. With no option, he welcomed her into his office. For a long quarter-hour he parlayed and answered her banter with equal charm. When she prepared to leave, mentioning her evening interlude, he offered to help her retrieve Frank's business files from Security. She declined, pleased with her imagined success, but not as pleased as he was to have her out of his office.

Winston returned to scanning the journal, then worked through dinner compiling a time-line on the history of education. With fingertip ease, he sifted through The Library of Congress archive data retrieval system, copying pertinent data. It was rich with information. Beginning with the 17th century, David tracked the successful efforts of visionaries to mold and shape future leaders. History was a fascinating playground, totally absorbing, wiping out his life-draining anger toward Higgs. He needed years to compile an in-depth history of the revolution that had lead to Synthesis. A new search offered a list of books; two looked promising, one written decades earlier and another recently submitted.

Four minutes before 8:00 p.m., beeping pulled him from his

terminal screen. Reluctant, he picked up Diversity. At Malchor's firm command, David's spine stiffened and his interest in the Age of Enlightenment crashed. He was ordered to the temple immediately. Nausea swept across his stomach and dissipated. Fear tightened in around his chest, pressing up his neck. In haste, he left his screen on, his desk cluttered, crammed Mal's journals into the safe, slammed it shut and sprinted toward the temple.

Obedience had its limit. Persistent pounding built in his head. He played through escape routes all the way to the temple doors. If necessary, to avoid a surprise initiation, he would throw up at the altar. Self-control and sensibilities aside, it would buy him the time he needed to finish writing. Ever efficient, the priest greeted him, bathed him, helped him into a suit and shoved him into the darkened room, positioning him by the altar.

A delicate melody floated from the flute. Winston squinted, trying to distinguish Malchor from the ever-present priests. When the hazy forms came into focus, panic hit, weakening his knees. "Kendra," he whispered in disbelief, steadying himself, grateful the darkness wouldn't betray his shock.

Malchor officiated on the other side of the altar, facing them, and the head priest, Zoganes, stood beside the flutist. Kendra was next to David, a vision of beauty. Gossamer veiling from her pearl headpiece blended into the train that lay in graceful folds at her feet. Her satin unity gown glistened in the soft hue of candlelight. Desperate to protect her, he stared at her profile, calling her name again.

Breaking from Malchor's benevolent smile, she glanced at her groom, then back, watching for her cue. Malchor's arms rose toward them in blessing. She took David's hand and knelt with him before the altar, her eyes still fixed on the dramatic figure now towering over them. His priestly robe, his deep resonant voice were ornate additions compared to his eyes. With magnetic force, his dark, deep-set eyes drew her, probing her allegiance. She submitted.

"Nurtured by Mother Earth," Malchor intoned, "empowered by Knowledge, inspired by The Force, you have come together to be united in matrimonial Synthesis." Pleased, he knew the woman was well-suited for David. She would soothe the Facilitator, keep him happy, keep him focused on his duty. Together, they would triple impartation outcomes, and, with their genetic combination, Malchor expected an added benefit. He looked forward to direct influence on their children; their future progeny were his own.

It was wrong. Horribly wrong. Winston hadn't considered this could happen. After the long, difficult wait for unity, this untimely fulfillment robbed him. Fear for her safety overshadowed every desire, every future hope, draining him. He gripped her hand in his—too hard. Minutes crept by and Malchor's instructions in nuptial bliss poured forth. *Pompous, arrogant, hypocrite!* Verdicts screeched through David's mind, crowding out Mal's admonition to bear many children for Synthesis. A cold, deadly rage fomented beneath the Facilitator's calm mask. With his mouth, he joined Kendra in a pledge of allegiance to Synthesis. With his mind, he renounced each word.

Malchor motioned for them to rise, then spoke directly to his Facilitator. "David Alan Winston, will you take Kendra Marie Addington as your lawful mate, according to the rite of holy Mother Earth?"

"I will," Winston said, trembling, looking at his bride.

Her eyes were fixed on Malchor.

"Kendra Marie Addington," Mal said, "will you take David Alan Winston as your lawful mate according to the rite of the holy Mother Earth?"

"I will," she said firmly.

"I, Malchor, with all power vested in Tribunal, do hereby pronounce you United. You are one with Earth, your Body; one with Creatures, your Soul; one with Cosmos, your Spirit; one with each other, indivisible."

At Mal's nod, Kendra handed her husband the wedding rings. Repeating his pledge of fidelity, he slipped them onto her finger. In turn, Kendra slipped a gold band on David's finger, finally looking directly into his eyes, repeating her pledge. David lingered in one brief moment of joy, enfolded her in his arms, and touched her moist lips with his.

CONVULSIVELY, Reana took another deep breath, holding it, bearing down steadily, mentally counting to ten, pacing herself, then falling limp against the couch, eyes closed. The exhausting cycle repeated again and again for fifty minutes; intense searing pain forced her to stop pushing and lean back. The baby's head pressed against the birth canal, stretching the tissue thin; nerve endings pulsed a screaming protest to their limit. Reana cried out for Greg as the solitude closed in with another strong contraction. With two more contractions, her baby boy lay kicking, fully delivered.

Still shaking, Reana gathered the boy gently in a clean towel, wiped his face, and syringed his mouth and nose. He responded with a squeaky howl, scrunched face and blinking eyes. Overwhelmed, she lifted Jonathan Gregory Foster to her breast. His tiny fingers wrapped tightly around hers.

XVII   TRUTH

AT THE Omni Cancun Hotel, Kendra Addington-Winston opened the drapes of the honeymoon suite and peered outside. Exhaustion had brought a restless sleep, sparing her from David's touch. Now, the sunrise promised an end to her forty-eight-hour marathon. Shielding her eyes, she slipped onto the balcony. Eight floors below, a lone figure dove into the pool, disrupting the crystal surface. By noon the pool would be crowded. Already, she felt crowded, trapped. The bodyguards added an unexpected tension. They were there, protective, watching for anything suspicious, separated by thin walls, dutiful and loyal to Malchor and loyal to David.

Caribbean breezes carried hypnotic sounds of sand and surf and tousled her shoulder-length brown hair. Kendra eased into the padded deck chair and turned inward, drifting until her eyes closed. A private meadow beckoned. She was barefoot, dancing among translucent violets in an eternal spring. Meditation brought escape and relief.

David, asleep on the king-size bed, blinked at the sudden light, disoriented. He squinted and scanned the cluttered room for something familiar. Alone. No guards. His clothes were in a heap on the floor. He rolled over and saw a motionless silhouette on the balcony. "Kendra," he whispered. Shaken, he got up and fumbled into his khakis, remembering. The wedding party celebrated until midnight, when Malchor and Synthia walked them to the Astrojet. It was David's idea to leave headquarters that night, compelled to get his bride out of the place. Tired, they boarded and slept through the flight, awakened when they touched down at the desolate Cancun airport. The hotel limo was waiting and they were settling into their room by 3:00 a.m. While the guards carried in their luggage, Kendra kicked off her shoes and fell asleep on the couch. After a feeble attempt to waken her, David carried her to the bed and covered her, kissing her tenderly.

Their first hours of unity were anything but. He figured it was due to his nagging fear. His risk was now her risk, even as Greg's risk was Reana's. Risking himself to question Synthesis was one thing. This was different. He surveyed the room for the usual state-issue ceiling-mounted microphones. The place was clean.

Kendra didn't turn around while he dug through his luggage for his toothbrush and comb, retrieving them from the zipped side compartment. She was still in the same position when he finished dressing. Ready. He stepped onto the patio. Small talk and cheerful plans about some idyllic future loomed hollow and futile. "Kendra, I . . . " He began, and his voice faded; she didn't turn to greet him. He touched her shoulder. "I'm sorry. I've been distracted. So much has happened, and I know all this change, so fast, is . . ." No response. He shook her shoulder. Still, no response. Winston braced himself. His bride was still as death, deep into a meditative trance. He shook her again, rejecting the suspicion that, since their vows, she intentionally avoided looking at him. Unless there was an audience, she looked past him, through him, around him, any place except into his eyes.

David knelt facing her and gently took her hands into his. Flawless milky skin drew him. He kissed her forehead and each cheek in turn, closing his eyes, savoring her floral scent. Enfolding her with his arms until her heartbeat joined his, he waited for her to respond. Inner tension built, burned within. He shuddered, pulled away, begrudging reality. She was not his.

"Kendra," he said, voice firm, fighting her detachment. "Kendra, stop!"

"All is harmonious," she whispered, lids opening, revealing

vacuous black pupils.

"Yeah, right," he muttered, repeating her name louder. "Kendra."

"I am," she intoned. "I am. I am god. I a . . ."

"No, Kendra. No!" he interrupted. "You're Kendra Marie Addington-Winston." He repeated her full name a second time.

Snapping to attention, she recoiled. "What do you want?" she demanded.

"You," he said, surprised at his blunt answer.

"Who do you think . . . ?"

"Your husband," he said, resisting the urge to shake her again.

"You've no right to interrupt me," she hissed. "Why did you?" Distrust tightened its foothold on her mind.

"Because, Kendra, I want to know what's going on with you," David pressed. This was not the woman he vowed to love, her face hardened, her voice a clear warning. "What happened? Just months ago we . . ."

"A lot has happened," she said.

"What?"

"I can't talk about it."

"For Trib's sa . . ." David stopped. Who was he to make demands? There were things he couldn't talk about, especially Trib. It was graphic proof Greg was right about tribulation and the Tribunal; either way, it meant the same thing to him. Trouble. And it meant trouble for her. The point muted his tone. "What can't you talk to me about?" he asked.

Dead silence; he waited. Neither of them moved. Neither of them spoke. Her rigid, unblinking glare, chilled him. "We have no other agenda," he said quietly. "It's just you and me, and I'm perfectly willing to stay right here until you decide to talk to me and tell me what it is that's changed between us."

Pretending was pointless. Dark thoughts crushed in, demanding she cut loose and vent fury. Instead, she deliberated, shrugging her shoulders. "All right," she said. "Why not?" She drew herself up, erect, stern, like a supervisor correcting an inferior. "You've changed, David. This past year you've changed into . . . I don't know. That's it. That's the problem. I just don't know you."

The words hit the mark. David flinched. This was his bride, delicate wisps of brown hair touching her forehead. He wanted to love her, caress her. Confusion drained him. "But, you came to headquarters," he said, "and married me. Why? Why on earth?"

"I thought I could follow through and do it."

"Do what?"

"Do what Malchor said."

"And what did Malchor say?"

"That I was to marry you, love you."

"July 2nd, on the way to Chicago, that was all we talked about: love and unity. Now, just over two months later, you say you don't know me." His calls hadn't been missed. They were ignored and erased. "So why did you take the vows?"

"What was I supposed to do when Malchor called me at work? My secretary put him straight through. I just picked up the phone, and it was him, his voice. I knew his voice, but could hardly believe he would call me in person," her voice softened to a whisper. "It was really him."

"Duty!" David exclaimed. "You actually married me out of duty to—him."

"Malchor," she corrected.

"This is sick! Really sick," he blurted.

"Sick? What's more important than duty to Malchor?"

"Loving me!" He slammed his fist against his chest and added, "That's what!"

"Facilitator Winston," she snapped, "you surprise me. Perhaps meditation will resolve your tension."

He begrudged it, but knew she was right. He was the one who had changed. Duty was always more important. Love was secondary, at least it was when her love secured his heart. "You're right," he admitted, "duty to Malchor was my job, primary to everything. But you loved me and I still love you. What changed that?"

"I really don't want to talk about it," she insisted. "What do you mean—was? Why did you . . . ?"

"If it's your duty to Malchor to love me," he interrupted, "wouldn't that include telling me the truth?"

The frown marring her face deepened into a scowl. "You, Facilitator, didn't tell me the truth. You lied to me!"

"What do you mean?"

"I saw Reana."

David's mouth went dry. "When?"

"In July," Kendra said in a crisp, edged voice. Anger surfaced and blazed from her eyes.

Numb, David retreated to the writing table and sank heavily into the corner chair.

Kendra pursued him. "Rea told me about Greg, about your turning him in," she accused, sitting across from him, teeth clenched. After a painful silence, she continued in a low staccato tone. "You said they were fine. They were fine, all right. Greg was imprisoned, beaten, almost terminated. And Reana was fired from her job, ostracized for being married to a felon. To further complicate her life, she was pregnant."

David was mute, nodding until the revelation about Rea's pregnancy; at that he sat upright.

Kendra continued. "You should have seen her. She was a wreck."

"Pregnant?" He shook his head in disbelief. "What do you mean she's pregnant?"

"Was. Was pregnant."

"What do you mean, was?" David asked, his mind reeling at the worst conclusion.

"It's all right, no untidy little problems for Synthesis. She was resistant at first, then did what she had to do to be in compliance."

"Aborted?" Winston's hands opened; he felt blood on them. Another innocent, fed to Evil. He clapped them together, rubbed them, reopened them. Nothing, just plain hands, hands that were

293

a party to murder. "God," he groaned. "Were You with her?"

Kendra eyed him curiously but dismissed his odd reaction. "Only to give her the abortifacient. I had to get back to the conference."

"Did you talk to her afterwards? Is she . . . ?"

"Her phone's disconnected," Kendra interrupted. "She sent a letter. She's all right, in spite of you."

"Greg didn't know, did he?" David moaned, picturing Reana alone, delivering a dead baby.

"No, how could he? You had him hauled off in the middle of the night."

"There's more to it, Kendra. I . . ."

"Look, Facilitator, just so you understand. I did love you when I could trust you. I don't trust you and, Malchor forgive me, I don't love you. What feelings I had for you died. They died when I left Reana alone in Baltimore. Duty can only go so far."

Duty! The word grated across his mind. Duty, above all. Yes, he knew about duty. "Greg's being released," David said, hoping to placate her and absolve himself. Instead, guilt grew stronger, squeezing his throat. "Frank had Greg set up, to get to me."

"Interesting. But, that doesn't change the facts. You turned Greg over to the authorities and then lied to me about it. So you were duped by someone like Franklin Higgs. And what does that say about you, Facilitator, sir. Even your ignorance doesn't excuse your lying to me."

"I'm sorry, Kendra, so very sorry."

"I bet you are," she said, rising, freer than she had felt in months. She could handle a business arrangement—for a while anyway. "We're scheduled to tour Chichen-Itza before it gets too hot. Are you ready?"

THAT morning in Baltimore, Greg Foster returned from breakfast to find two orderlies in his room. He watched from the couch while they dumped his belongings into five boxes. He knew the routine. Other patients had disappeared. In fourteen minutes they removed all traces of Greg's existence from his quarters and escorted him to the main office. *Except in Reana's mind, my existence will be erased as easily*, Greg thought. His stomach walls tightened around undigested oatmeal. *Just more inert material headed for recycling.*

The orderlies stood guard while a receptionist handed him an envelope and a packet of street clothes. She ordered him to change, without explanation. It wasn't until he climbed into the front seat of an ordinary cab that he realized he was free. *Free.*

"What day is it?" Greg asked the congenial cab driver.

"September fourth," the driver said. "Guess it don't much matter, where you come from."

"What's the day?"

"Monday. No. It's Tuesday. Yup," the man grunted a laugh, "Tuesday all day."

"Thanks," Greg said. They pulled away from the front gate of The Haven and he opened the envelope. He was to report to the law firm the following Monday.

"So where am I supposed to take you?"

"Home, best to take me home. My wife will be at work, but . . ."

"Hey," the cabby interrupted. "So where's home, guy. I don't read minds for a living."

Greg blurted out his address, excusing himself. The driver took Ordnance Road to Ritchie Highway and stayed on it, taking his time, clocking easy miles. Greg anticipated each landmark that brought him closer, closer to home, closer to Reana. Harbor Hospital loomed ahead; as the cab crept past, Greg was distracted by two columns of uniformed children waiting for their school buses. They stood at attention. The transformed children of the inner city project. Children in the longest column wore green; the others wore purple. "Color coded children" he muttered as they faded from view. He expected that few, if any of them had been selected for level-one. It was to their advantage if they weren't. Synthesis extracted the high price of mindless obedience. Sadly, there was more hope for a normal life, for seeing the truth, the further you were from any level-one

Academy. They drove across the Hanover Street Bridge and jogged toward Key Highway.

Minutes later the cab pulled up to the townhouse and Greg was out the door, hauling boxes. The driver dumped the rest of them on the sidewalk and left.

The place needed attention. He stacked the boxes in the hallway and picked up a handful of political flyers from under the doormat. Shutting the door he tossed them, unread, into the recycle bin.

Once the living room drapes were opened, cheerful sun rays played across the orderly space. Not a thing was out of place. His unfinished novel lay open on top of the *Newsweek* magazines right where he left it. A background symphony faded into the raucous talk-show introduction, and Greg headed to the kitchen, curious about the radio. Thick soup simmered on the stove. Dirty dishes filled the sink and dried food stuck to the counter. Greg turned and bounded up the stairs, alarmed. Their bed was unmade; clothes were strewn about. Gray water stood in the guest bathtub, stiff towels on the rack. Greg raced down to the basement laundry room; still no sign of Reana, more mess, dirty dresses piled up, waiting to be washed. The car was in the garage. Her name screamed through his mind. He prowled through the basement, opening the storage room, closing the door quietly, making no unusual sound for the state to investigate. Despair made a full-scale attack, urging him to scream, when a quiet thought brought hope. *The office. Of course, she's in the office, away from the cursed sensors.* He should have looked. Again he bounded up the stairs, then turned the knob.

"Reana," Greg moaned, shutting the door behind him. The air was heavy, dense and muggy. She lay at his feet, eyes closed, peaceful, covered up to her chin with a sheet. Greg knelt down, watched for movement, relieved when a breath proved his worst fear unfounded. "Dearest Reana," he whispered. "Merciful Creator, please let her be well."

Frail squeaks answered Foster's plea and his eyes settled on the wooden cradle inches away from his wife's pillow. Still on his knees he stretched, curious, looking at the infant. Tenderly, he lifted the baby from the cradle, examining the delicate features, touching the strands of downy red hair. With apparent intent, the infant clasped his hand around Greg's little finger and studied his face.

For a time, Reana was convinced the image wasn't real. It was illusive, another dream. Her unquenched longing for Greg was stifled by harsh reality time and time again. Yet, here he knelt next to her, holding their baby, quiet tears flowing. She whispered, "Greg?"

"Oh, Reana," he responded, cradling the baby, leaning down, closer. "Dear, precious Reana, If I had known . . ."

"Scars," she said, caressing his cheek. "You have scars? What have they done?"

"No. Rea," he assured her. "It's all right. I'm OK. It's what they tried to do. But they couldn't do it. I'm with you now. They won't take me again, not away from you, not away from . . . " Greg looked down at the peaceful infant, then at his wife.

"Jonathan, your son," she said, laughing for the first time in months, "Jonathan Gregory Foster."

For two blissful days they held each other, comforted each other, and thought of nothing outside of their home, their family.

THE sacrificial altar at Chichen-Itza stuck in David's mind, a dark shadow over everything he saw and did. Unaffected, Kendra talked of returning for the celebrated sunset of the spring equinox, to stand at the base of the Pyramid of Kukulcan. On that day each year as the sun set, tourists could see the illusionary snake slither in a fertility ritual, descending the last seven steps of the Northern stairway to rejoin earth.

Kukulcan measured seventy-five feet high, an impressive and accurate celestial sundial that proved the Mayan reverence for nature's cycles. The astronomer's stone carved calendar had held people rigidly captive to the astrological and ceremonial dictates of generations of priests and rulers. Ruins evidenced the demise of a gentle people, overcome by Toltec warriors and a steady progression of demon-crazed power-mongers. Their power demanded subservience and subservience demanded sacrifice.

Now, tourists drawn by folklore came in droves to wander through the ruins. That day, a bus load of people from Japan filtered along the narrow stairway and into the pyramid. Inside, David and Kendra watched others chat casually at the sacrificial altar throne. Centuries earlier, the victims' life blood had drained under the macabre stare of this craven Chac Mool figure.

Fascinated, Kendra questioned their guide about the ancient ritual. Ordinary people had worshiped and paid homage to the rain god, Chac Mool. He lay belly up, an open bowl never satiated by the beating hearts of men, women and children. David had touched the cold rough-hewn stone, repulsed. Time had not changed the nature of power in the hands of fools.

After the last bus left, the newlyweds stayed until the sun faded into the horizon. Neither of them wanted to return to their hotel room. The long limo ride back to Cancun was unbelievably solemn.

Six months earlier, David would have taken Kendra as a reward for service to Malchor. Now, having her next to him, distrusting him, agonized his soul. The wall was solid. No amount of persuasion made her listen or trust him. David had spent the tense morning ride considering his options. Simply demanding his conjugal rights and dispensing with any effort to reason with the woman seemed reasonable. She had no trouble setting her boundaries for their marriage. In reaction, boundaries of his own sprang up, soothing his ego. When they pulled up to the archeological zone at Chichen, it occurred to him that a subtle allusion to her need for reorientation would make her more cooperative. With that thought came the memory of Greg at the hands of Werling, then an even worse picture of Kendra in his lustful clutches. That grim picture throttled his temptation to play the fool with his own limited powers.

LATER that night, while Kendra slept unmolested on her side of the bed, David slipped from the covers and crept onto the balcony. Alone, but not alone, David Winston sank to his knees and reached toward heaven, whispering, "Maker, I am a fool. No. I'm worse than a fool. But, You . . . You must be real. I see evidence of You everywhere in creation. And I see evidence of evil. Please, I don't want to be a part of evil. Please," David's voice wavered and broke. Tears of unashamed remorse ran down his uplifted face. "Please, please, show me the truth about myself and about who You are."

Pride, Vile Anger and Despair burrowed deeper, jealous for their turf. With surgical precision, the Sword of Truth removed the shroud of death from David's soul. Demons hissed, screeching in fury, forced to release their stranglehold on David's mind. Whimpering, they retreated to the ocean floor. His nature lay bare; not a god, a man thirsty for power and corrupted by greed, a betrayer of the innocent. Humbled to the depths, he poured the vermin that occupied his soul upon the altar of Grace. With a grateful heart, David believed the Word and met Messiah.

For the remainder of their honeymoon, his settled serenity had a double effect on Kendra. She was both curious and agitated, agitated that he was oddly happy, and curious as to why he should be, given her rejection of his every private kindness.

UNRECONCILED, they returned to headquarters. David was troubled to find Cyrus there, already making plans for Kendra's initiation. After a silent appeal to Maker, the new believer made an appeal to Malchor to withhold the initiation until the winter solstice. That battle was barely won when the next round loomed ahead. Seeds took root before his eyes of a growing bond between Cyrus and Kendra. Malchor had been the recipient of her adoration, but was busy with Synthia. With Mal occupied, it was Cyrus who stepped in to groom and cultivate her adoration. To David, her motives were simple and obvious. She believed Cyrus was holy. David knew he was in no position to convince her otherwise.

Reluctant to have her out of sight, but fearing what Cyrus

could do, David urged her to return to Spokane. Malchor approved, aware that her abrupt departure had left the Genetic Selectivity Center in a quandary. They had sent a string of messages begging her attention when she returned from Cancun. For Kendra, the suggestion promised a reprieve. Even though drawn to Cyrus, she leapt at the chance to get away from David and mentally planned to stretch the two weeks in Spokane into months. Early Saturday morning, only days after their Unity vows, he helped her pack. With a mixture of agony and relief, he walked her to the Astrojet. The guards were witness as he stole a final chance to hold her, kiss her tenderly and whisper his love. Then she was gone.

DAVID retreated to the library and stood a forlorn vigil staring into the western sky. Occupied with the memory of their brief, strained time together, he failed to hear Server enter, but he knew who put a comforting hand on his shoulder. Looking at the gathering clouds, he sighed. "It's terrible to know what's happening and be helpless to stop it."

"Don't be alarmed, Brother. Maker doesn't want us to be taken by surprise," Server said. "That's why He forewarned us. I know it's tempting to try. However, He doesn't expect us to stop all the forces of evil." Server paused, a smile of kinship lighting his face. "We're only to do our part and trust Him with the future."

Reassurance drained the tension from David's shoulders. "James," he said, emphasizing Server's given name, "how could you tell I chose Maker?"

"Easy, David. When you left here, you looked at Malchor with thinly veiled hatred. I prayed for your safety, and suspected you left just in time. Now, I see charity. It's not possible to love enemies without grace."

"But now—she hates me!"

"No, she only wants to," he said with a soothing tone. "Your wife's afraid. After you held her, she walked past me to the plane. She was fighting back tears."

David groaned, shutting his eyes for a moment. "That makes it harder," he said. "It would be better for her, easier, to hate me." The words were barely out when, with reflexive caution, he stepped back from the plate glass, and James followed. Cyrus and Malchor had appeared across the garden on the steps of the temple in animated debate. Without Arion acting as a buffer, the two argued. Winston suspected it was about Kendra's initiation. Malchor was more than irritated over Cyrus meddling with his newlyweds and appeared to be making that point clear.

"Malchor and Synthia are leaving tomorrow for Brussels, with Cyrus."

"Good, very good; then I can get the time-line finished."

"I scanned all the logs into your disk. It should go smoothly. Oh," James paused, remembering, "before you arrived with Kendra, Cy was after Synthia. The web's getting tangled with her around, and Malchor's not going to like that either. He just hasn't noticed yet."

". . . and I worshiped him?"

"Scary thought, huh," James Lawrence said, attempting levity.

"Yeah, it is now," David agreed, smiling at his newfound brother in tribulation. It was new, comforting, unlike ordinary friendship. *Brothers*, David thought. *Brothers in affection, not coercion.* "There's someone I need to check on."

"Greg Foster?"

"Yes."

"He's been released, home since Tuesday."

"I need to see him, without anyone suspecting."

"It can be arranged."

THE visit was arranged sooner than David expected. The weekend skeleton staff and guards believed the Youth Facilitator was sequestered in his office working on Malchor's Tribute. Staffers dutifully held all calls. Server made occasional trips with the food tray, wore the Piaget and carried David's Diversity unit. It was a simple thing for James to short-circuit the main office

301

lighting and no one noticed when a third electrician left with the repair crew. It would be a simple thing for him to leave the grounds that night by himself to attend a performance of "The King and I" at the Baltimore Playhouse. Spiriting David back into the building would be easy.

A messenger had prepared Greg, but Reana wasn't ready to trust David with anyone she loved, least of all her son. When the crew truck stopped, she peered from behind the office drapes, holding her baby protectively. Jacob and Joshua Morris, the two uniformed men from Sparrow Electric, secured clearance to add an air purifier to the forced air furnace and promptly closed the circuits to the entire basement.

On cue, David carried the new unit into the home and down the stairs. He barely released the box when Greg clenched him in a bear hug. Unashamed, the men wept on each other's shoulders. The Sparrow workmen began altering the furnace system. This wasn't the first reunion they had arranged between lost brothers and they expected it wouldn't be their last. It was their greatest satisfaction.

David glanced at the dead corner sensor, clapped Greg on the back and pulled away, reluctant. "How can you ever forgive me?" he said, his voice husky, choking back grief.

"I told you before, I know what you intended," Greg said, still holding onto David's forearm, beaming. The veil was gone. "You meant to help me. Don't ever forget, I wouldn't trade what I know and have now for all the promises of Synthesis."

"No, Greg. You don't know. Not the . . . I convinced myself it was for you, for your good. Oh God!" he moaned. "It wasn't for you, Greg. It was for me. Me! My fear that you'd do something . . . That what you might do would reflect on me. That if I didn't turn you in for the slightest infraction, I might be suspect. I wasn't loyal to you. I was trying to prove my loyalty to Malchor, to Synthesis. No. I don't deserve your trust or your friendship."

"David!" Greg urged, gripping his arm, hard. "You're mortal, same as I am. Let go of it! I understood and forgave you months ago. I'm not innocent either. I was going to make a hero of myself, exposing CAM. Besides, you never intended for me to get hurt."

"But Reana and your baby, there's no taking back what's happened to your baby. Kendra doesn't understand what . . ."

"Wait a minute, David. He's all right. Our baby, Jonathan, is fine."

"Baby? But Reana aborted."

"No, David, she didn't. She couldn't do it."

"Thank you," David said, eyes closed, the weight of murder lifting from his soul. "Thank you, thank you."

Greg waited for his friend to stop praying, "Rea knows everything about me," he said "and what happened to me. She believes. She's one of us."

"She is!" Winston marveled that it hadn't taken her months of studying, months of struggle. Celebrating the news, he realized Reana never was burdened with the layers of pride that stunted him. Eager for forgiveness he asked, "May I see her and . . ."

"I'm so sorry, David," Greg interrupted. "She's not ready. It's not just the baby. All this has been extremely hard on her." He wanted to relieve the added burden, but couldn't. "How did you know about the baby?" he asked. "Rea was sure Kendra wouldn't tell anyone."

"She didn't exactly tell me. It was more an accusation than a telling. We took our Unity vows last Monday and were on our supposed honeymo . . ."

"Kendra's here?" Greg interrupted.

"No. Not now. She was here. She's back in Spokane. It's not like you think, Greg. She . . ." Winston paused while Greg's concern grew. "I'm paying some consequences. I never told her about you, and what I did. I lied to her."

"Rea told me," he said slowly.

"Kendra doesn't trust me, won't even listen."

"Give her some time."

"There's not much time left, Greg," he whispered. "I've strengthened Malchor's hold on the minds of too many children, spread knowledge without wisdom, judgment without discernment. Given the chance, I would have killed Truth itself.

303

I have to do something about Malchor."

"Are you sure?"

"Yes. It has to be done, for me as much as anyone."

A solemn separation interrupted their heartfelt afternoon. When they parted, the fear of never seeing each other played like a dirge through their minds.

THE next two weeks flew past. Each morning, the Youth Facilitator rushed through his duties, sending minor memos to supervisors. Afternoons were consumed with compiling the Synthesis time-line and rewriting his tribute to Malchor. Finally, after copying both onto a disk, he erased his hard disk drive and back-up system. That last day at headquarters, he methodically sabotaged the smooth operation he built for Malchor. On the surface, the program hummed smoothly. Underneath, there was a fine web of mindless data, designed to burden the system and the technicians with problems.

It took him the remaining evening hours to write a program to disarm the Diversity units and purge the files of dissidents' names. Files would appear intact. But the names and genome data would be scrambled into meaningless gibberish. He estimated it would take months to scan dissident data from other sources and longer to stop his message once it hit Hegie's computer system. His self-propagating Trojan horse was encrypted and interwoven in the data stream between the CD Rom tracks. From San Juan it would spread through World Net to personal computers, reprinting his speech and the time-line at random intervals until purged. Wearily, he cleaned his desk.

He rehearsed the routine so many times that the last night at headquarters, he dreamed it. When he stood before the camera to give his speech over the air, demon Fear knocked him to his knees. From his knees he cried out to Maker and struggled to his feet, only to be knocked down again and again.

Sunday morning, the 23rd of September 2001 MS, dawned with an autumn chill. David packed a travel bag, taking only necessities, one change of clothes and his tuxedo. Folding Paul's letter, he placed it inside the cover of the small Bible from Malchor's library and slipped it into his chest pocket next to the disks. Kendra's picture, a warm smile beaming from the frame, was the last thing he saw while closing the door on his past. At the foot of the stairs he was surprised to see Server carting three large suitcases toward the door. He picked one up and fell into step, musing softly. "What do you have here, a ton of bricks?"

"Obviously you've taken no thought of tomorrow," James chided, whispering.

"There didn't seem to be any point."

"Great, a fatalist, looking for an early demise."

"Well?"

"Sorry, young man. This is not your last brave penance for a prideful life." To David's bewildered glance, James confided, "You do your job and let me do mine. Just be ready to move when I say."

UNLIKE his troubled dream, everything went smoothly and the flight to the San Juan Academy in Washington was uneventful. Following the landing ceremony, Hegie was preoccupied with a dozen visiting dignitaries from United World. Winston fulfilled his duties as Youth Facilitator, talking about the wonders of Synthesis with dour elders from Europe and Asia. After a noon reception, he was able to break away. It was acceptable for the Youth Facilitator to roam the campus of his childhood, reliving fond memories. Hegie and the elders gave approving nods as he left.

James Lawrence waited outside the dormitory while David completed his first mission. Inside, the Youth Facilitator checked the Williams boys' progress and complimented the reorientation team. Flattered, the Director helped the boys into their jackets and saw them to the door for their first outing since their arrival. Five months of gentle indoctrination was beginning to show on Jamie, who had begun to parrot children's songs about Mother Earth. Richard was another matter. Approaching his eleventh birthday, he was five feet tall and occupied with the care of his little brother. David had noticed the boy was evasive and avoided

305

any direct conflict with his instructors. He cooperated and gave the appearance of progress. Overall, the Sociology Department considered their project with the boys a success.

Jamie took to James Lawrence immediately. The foursome was approaching the trail when the child reached for his hand and fell in step beside him. James moved through the area as if he were born there, naming the vegetation, pointing out scurrying forest animals. Together, they stopped to watch a black-tailed deer amble unconcerned across the trail. Taking advantage, David continued walking until out of their hearing range. He probed Richard about his beliefs, concerned the boy had compromised the faith of his father and might balk at leaving the Academy.

"So Mother Earth has guided your steps?" Winston asked, studying the boy for his reaction.

"Mother has always guided me," Richard nodded.

"Which Mother?" David persisted.

"Surely, we have only one Mother," the youth said brightly, then added with a sweep of his hand, "and look at this fertile earth."

David smiled; he could hardly have been more evasive himself. "And what of Maker? Do you believe in Maker?

At this, the boy didn't answer, instead he asked, "Who is Maker?"

Silent, they left the trail and circled to the northeastern base of Mt. Constitution. "Maker is who He says He is," the Youth Facilitator answered firmly.

Richard tilted his head, not trusting what he heard. Facilitator Winston pointed toward the water. Barely visible against the skyline, a sleek blue-gray seaplane skimmed the choppy surface toward them. The conditions were ideal; a cloudy ceiling was closing fast and threatening a misty rain. At that hour, on campus, the guards were being briefed, along with reinforcements, in preparation for Malchor's arrival.

Richard stopped in his tracks just yards from the shoreline, looking back, anxious for Jamie to catch up, then gaping at

Winston. "You delivered us to this place," he said. "Now what will you do to us?"

"I have this for you," Winston said, taking the book from his jacket pocket. "There's no time now, but inside there's a letter to me, from your Father." Richard's eager hands closed around the book, and he secured it, zipping it into his jacket pocket. "When you have time to read the letter, please forgive me for what I've done to your family," he said, heartened when the youth nodded his head in bewildered agreement. "Go with this man today. He's taking you to friends of mine, who will see that you and your brother are reunited with your mother."

"Mommy?" Jamie cried, joining them. "Will I see Mommy?"

Richard stared hard at David, then answered, "Yes. Yes, Jamie. You will. We both will."

Within seconds the two men had stepped into the water and lifted the boys to the seaplane. Humming softly, the plane rose to meet the horizon, undetected by radar or the guards.

James Lawrence was the last from the water, his fist still closed tight, holding within, warmth from the child's trusting hand.

Winston stood on the shore stuffing their Diversity units into his back pockets. "Well," he sighed, "now for the hard part."

XVIII   THESIS ⋈ ANTITHESIS

MALCHOR Kneal Inyesco was on the San Juan Academy dias between Facilitator Hegelthor and Synthia Rojan. He cherished the place of honor, applauding the children's chorale rendition of the Synthesis Pledge. David, seated to the left of Synthia, soberly looked past her at his mentor's profile, then at the upraised faces of the student body audience. Trusting, believing faces, row upon row of human souls, young adults formed in the image of Maker, molded into the image of Malchor, stamped with his signet. Their illusional state pained him.

Select dignitaries paraded past and delivered tributes to Malchor. Ambassador Eckert took his turn and spoke at length on the progress of the European Academies, then settled in happily behind Synthia Rojan. She was the only low ranking personage on the stage. Her pervading scent was Jasmine, spicy floral, a silent calling card. Belying her professional appearance, David saw her knee pressed against Malchor's leg.

Server had promised a diversion, and none could be more effective. Protocol had been defiled and Hegelthor made little effort to hide annoyance. Synthia was out of place and Malchor's attention was divided.

Their otherwise amusing adolescent behavior was inexcusable excess when played out in front of the Academy and the Youth Facilitator. Hegelthor looked on with an air of offended dignity that went unnoticed by Malchor.

Earlier, during the 4:00 p.m. shift change, Facilitator Winston's second feat was accomplished when he slipped into

309

a basement cubical and programmed Hegelthor's computer system with his disk. Now, his third test loomed. Imagined scenes of discovery and defeat gave way to the quiet resolve that steeled mind and will. Speakers' tributes blurred past him with a redundant sameness, as if one writer had penned them. Three index cards were tucked into his jacket pocket, with a brief outline of his own speech, just the bare bones to keep him on track. The other speakers used the screen and read their words supplied on the Teleprompter as needed. His polite refusal of the service had caused a brief stir, threatening the technician's job security. No one ever refused the service during televised events. Annoyance deepened the technician's scowl while he spoon-fed the speech to Chairman Frederick Hodges.

STEVE and Jenna Winston snuggled together in their ranch family room enjoying the broadcast, anticipating their son's appearance. A brief letter from David telling of his early unity vows with Kendra lay open on the coffee table. Both were disappointed they weren't invited but were past belaboring lost moments, preferring to relish the present. And now, things were too good to believe. Their son was at the top of his field, and they were secure with each other and their jobs. In the letter, he mentioned his plans to bring Kendra for a visit during the winter break. Still, they hoped to see him sooner, after his speech, before his return to headquarters. Jenna watched her son on the screen, her head on Steve's shoulder, feet curled up comfortably under an afghan.

ON STAGE engaged in reviewing his own speech, David Winston barely caught Hodges' introduction. Applause erupted; he walked to the podium and forced a smile. The past, present and future converged in his mind. Memories whispered. . . . childhood innocence betrayed . . . thirst for knowledge . . . lust for power . . . blood guilt . . . Kendra's anger . . . Greg's forgiveness.

Jared McNeeme, graduating with a doctorate in

astrophysics, was considered average by Academy standards. Facilitator Winston was his hero, a role model to claim as a close relation. When the auditorium doors opened that evening, he was the first one inside and took a middle seat in the front row. Hegelthor's two sons, Thomas and Armond, were in their reserved seats beside him. For a year, he had watched Winston at a distance, unknown yet feeling known, trusting.

Life in the balance, Winston stepped forward, poised. Two television cameras were aimed at him, synchronized for direct shots, profiles and audience sweeps. He was on. Hegelthor and Malchor faded into his peripheral vision and the students captured his total attention. His words were for them, for Kendra, for his parents, for anyone willing to hear.

"Students of Academy and students of life, we are here, all of us on the premise of learning. Not just learning for its own sake, robots collecting data, but learning for a purpose. And our defined purpose is—we must learn to be a better human race, a better species, points of light in the cosmos.

"We journey together on this blue sphere; let us journey with our eyes and ears open to reality. Truth, objective reality, stands either in opposition to or in support of our perceptions. And our unified perception is that our Species, Homo Sapiens, is at the crossroad, even as we have crossed into this millennium. You are poised, ready to leap beyond the realm of four dimensions. Yours is the promise of godhood in the evolution of humanity, as beings of Synthesis, the Synthesis Species.

"You hold your future in your hands. Your past is filled with the precise steps needed to prepare you for your role in this evolutionary model. Here at the Academy, your role has been predetermined by mentors, based upon your genetic pattern, spiritual sensitivity, intelligence and emotional disposition. You are today the measure of precise input, with your future mapped in amazing detail."

In the audience, Jared blinked. He hadn't thought of himself as a product. The sterile idea of being the measurement of input hammered home.

311

"Yet to know where you are going," Facilitator Winston exhorted, "you should know where mankind has been, where the accumulated knowledge and wisdom of our species has etched its path. It is in grasping the what, when and where of life that we are drawn to investigate the how, question the why and seek the who of cosmos. The basics of investigative reporting and science were applied to academics by each of you for years. Your challenge now is to apply the quest for objective truth to your personal life and to settle for nothing less than this high calling. Demand honesty within yourself. Recognize practical proof within creation. Seek truth at any price."

Self-generated creation, Hegelthor corrected mentally. Annoyed over his own preoccupation with Malchor's liaison, he refocused on David.

"In the past, while there were many groups of people, fewer than two dozen complex societies were known as civilizations. Seven have existed in the past 10,000 years. These civilizations, formed by humans working together either for the common good or for enlightened self-interest, have left their imprint on our earth. Desiring to pass knowledge to their progeny, they lived the history of education. They passed knowledge and wisdom from the savage, to the peasant, to the priest, to the simple man, to the philosopher, to the intellectual, to you.

"Recorded history reveals certain principles. Human progress was realized when people took responsibility for personal choices. Human progress was strangled by authoritarian central planning. You purpose to do what has never been done: successful synthesis of these opposites. Today, sensitive centralized planning, adopted by personal choice, unites your spiritual energy in a new system that hopes to inspire creativity, resourcefulness and sustainable progress.

"At present, history is simplified for you. Memorization is discredited. Details are irrelevant and inhibitory to progress, stumbling blocks for minds that would question where you have come from, where you are going. Yet the questions persist, begging answers. What has filled the measurement of time and space, what design wrought, what purpose fulfilled brought us to today? In condensed history, you learned that three ages have passed, The Age of Origins, The Age of Exploration, and The Age of Development, and we have restructured and transitioned to the fourth age, the Age of Synthesis. It is Synthesis, which promises to satisfy all questions, balance each thesis with its antithesis and result in absolute unity."

Simply put. Jared agreed, thinking history an odd topic for the occasion, but accepting the benefit of a reminder. Students hadn't bothered with history for years.

Energized, Winston surveyed the youthful faces, noticing Hegelthor's sons and the intense young man in the first row. Hegie was staring at Synthia's knee, which was still pressed against Mal's leg. It was perfect—a carnal illustration of hypocrisy between words and actions. "Malchor," David said, hoping the cameras caught the scene. "Malchor," he repeated, sweeping his hand in Mal's direction "is duly honored as your model, your mentor and your goal—the evolved Being of Synthesis. He deserves your recognition for what he has done to draw you together, to disarm opposing philosophies and beliefs, to reach toward the future, to level the field so that each of you knows your place and your purpose under the Plan. With excitement, you anticipate your imminent leap into world harmony, when all questions and all struggles will be no more and humans will achieve unity.

"You are here tonight acknowledging the godhood of Malchor as your forerunner. Ask and seek the answers, that you might know your true nature. What is godhood? What are the qualities inherent in the title god? Is god truth, knowledge, wisdom, love, justice, mercy? Is god creative mind, omnipotent, omnipresent? What is it you aspire to become?"

Impropriety. Not Jealousy! Hegelthor argued internally, disputing the taunting, recurring accusation that he was jealous of Mal's liaison. He looked at his sons. Thomas, his name sake, was undisciplined, weak, distracted, looking around the auditorium, while Armond sat at attention. Hegie canceled the distractions, concentrating on Winston.

"You consider truth as relative," David boomed. "Yet knowledge is gathered, with the goal of gaining wisdom and insight into how you should best live. For centuries scientists and philosophers reduced man to mere mechanistic functions, a simplistic equation of electrical impulses in a field of matter. They deified formulas and factoids and ignored evidence of a realm beyond the five senses, knowledge without wisdom. Wisdom sacrificed on the altar of limited human knowledge? Never Again!"

Wisdom sacrificed? Hegelthor pondered, intently watching David's mouth, shrugging off a sense of impending disaster. Winston's words dripped with jargon and platitudes, but the direction was too open, too many questions for young minds. Half-listening to the Youth Facilitator, the unfortunate memory of Brockston Andel surfaced and Hegie shot a glance at Malchor. The Tribunal tended to move too fast, bypassing needed preparations. Adherents needed to be brought to the Mysteries slowly, if at all; given time to own the process as theirs, a part of their nature, unquestioned. . . . *if at all* echoed in his mind.

"We are spirit, soul and body." David continued. "Creative mind reaches beyond the laboratory petri dish, beyond linear measurement, beyond the limits of man-made rules and societal boundaries. This truth accepted, you leap to adopt the conclusion of your mentors that you are thus preexistent, self-determining, enlightened ones. You accept that your own mind brought you to this time and place, nurtured you to this point of self-fulfilling godhood. You, the creation, are the creator. Does unfolding reality prove your quest to be a leap of faith toward light or darkness, truth or lie, life or death? But your questions were answered in your catechism; light and darkness, truth and lie, life and death are one, mere sides of the same coin.

"Humanity's highest potential is unlimited by antiquated notions of reality. Through meditation, your highest self is realized and actualized. As self-actualized souls you clear your minds of negativity and embody the Greek ideal while merging with the now achievable Brahmin.

"For you Synthesis explains all the questions about history, truth, life and justice.

"What is justice if injustice is relative? Consider—a child robbed of his parents, an innocent man condemned for the act of another, a family dissolved by arbitrary civil laws. Justice imprinted in your soul enables you to recognize when you see injustice. Don't allow that imprint to be seared from your heart."

It was difficult to sort out. Jared McNeeme frowned; he had never thought about justice. That his Facilitator mentioned it suggested his failure, yet injustice was a negative—something to be canceled.

Hegelthor stirred, shifting forward in his chair, closing scenarios playing through his mind. The students, like dry sponges, were soaking up David's words and their interest was measurable. There were few blank faces; even Thomas was engaged and listening. Hegie's focus of irritation now bounced between David and Malchor. Malchor was without excuse, but it had to be simple immaturity that moved the Youth Facilitator to give the graduates too much. Too much information. Too many questions. The possibility for wrong conclusions was too real.

Philosophical absurdities. Synthia mused to herself, observing David's sincere oration and Hegelthor's growing discomfort. That humans took themselves and their ideas so seriously was particularly entertaining. She had pegged David as too soft from the beginning. *Too much conscience and too much heart to be of much use.*

Facilitator David Winston spoke louder, aware of the scowl on Hegelthor's face. "Failed societies of the past ignored justice. Those societies which persisted in cannibalistic destruction of others, or suicidal self-destruction, damned themselves. Their societies collapsed under the strain of injustice, leaving behind a legacy of over forty-one hundred bloody wars.

"For your future, you open yourselves to all spiritual realms," David continued, encouraged he had made it so far, expecting any minute to be silenced. "Toward the close of this past century, people searched for the spiritual food that was outlawed by secularism. Then the new age dawned and spiritual frontiers opened. Consider, will those who hunger and thirst after truth be satisfied with illusion and falsehood?

"Malchor is the living symbol of Synthesis. He is the living example of the convergence of the knowledge of good and evil; the example of autonomous evolutionary humanity; the example of your hope for yourselves; the example of your future godhood; the example of your moral code walked out in life."

David paused, again extending his hand toward the exuberant Malchor while students applauded and cheered. "The seed of Synthesis was planted in each of us," Winston said, his voice impassioned, evangelical. "From our earliest years we have been nurtured by machines. The Diversity unit is our umbilical cord. The computer our parent. We have been molded into the image of Malchor.

"You know of him, but you do not know him.

"I do.

"I stand here this evening, as your Youth Facilitator, bound by the higher law of truth, to tell you what my eyes have seen and what my ears have heard, what the light of reality has revealed. It is written that you will know a seed by its fruit. So it is reasonable that you may know a man by how he lives. The inner heart flows into audible words and visible actions.

"I know the heart and mind of Malchor, the god man, the sum of Synthesis. And I have walked the road to godhood. I followed in the footsteps of my mentor, Malchor. I embraced the knowledge of good and evil, that good and evil are opposites of the same thing.

"The path to godhood has certain demands, a sort of blind faith that pulls you to lay aside any activity or relationship that impedes your Synthesis journey."

Hegelthor's uneasiness had shifted to alarm, David was saying *you* instead of *we*, *your* instead of *our*. He studied Malchor for some sign of concern. Instead, the visible set of pride in

316

Malchor's jaw, head tilted up, a smile settled smugly, accepting the praises, warranted public exposure. Had they been alone, he would have slapped the arrogance from Malchor's face. Seething, Facilitator Hegelthor considered his options, anticipating David's next words.

"This past quarter, I rewalked the road to godhood, retraced my footsteps to Malchor, reviewed the knowledge of good and evil and reexamined my faith in Synthesis. I found and embraced practical truth—truth about myself, truth about mankind.

"This crossroad is between the truth and the lie, and I was taking the quantum leap toward the lie, not toward godhood. The truth is, I am not a god. Malchor is not a god. God is not whomever or whatever you will Him to be. Malchor has deceived you." David clutched the mike, aware that Malchor's face flushed crimson and Hegelthor was rising slowly to his feet, futilely motioning for the sound crew to cut the power.

Synthia subdued her intense pleasure at Malchor's embarrassment and settled back into her chair. For a price, she would throttle the boy's ramblings. Barring any call to duty, she waited to see how the big boys would handle the problem, confident their bungles would raise her ante.

Throughout the auditorium, students showed a mix of open-mouthed wonder, confusion and veiled anger. Jared McNeeme vacillated between confusion and a brooding sense of betrayal.

Thomas Evan Hegelthor II, laughed aloud and his younger brother, Armond, told him to shut-up. From his vantage point Thomas calculated how long it would take him to replace the Youth Facilitator and reap the recognition he deserved. He had noticed each detail, Malchor's wayward hand, Synthia's knee and her contempt for Winston's outrageous speech. His father's distraction had been most entertaining and he anticipated the impending cold, calculated wrath.

David charged, his voice firm and strong, "The union leaders were set up in Baltimore, falsely accused, falsely imprisoned. They are innocent! Gil Duskin is innocent! A mercenary shot me, not a dissident.

"Don't let anyone control your mind through lies and canceled thoughts. Good and evil are unreconcilable. Synthesis is physical, emotional, intellectual and spiritual slavery— Synthesis is Slavery." Hegie was looming on his right, halfway across the stage. Winston rushed to his point, "Never cancel truth. Man is not god. Earth and things are not god. Maker created the cosmos and breathed life into us. History was rewritten to hide what He did for us, for you. Maker loves you. Seek Him and you will find . . ."

Thunderous applause interrupted David. Facilitator Hegelthor was beside him, clapping, benevolence glowing from his smile. David was motionless in front of the camera and dead microphone. A flicker of confusion registered when the Facilitator put his arm around Winston's shoulders in a public display of affection.

Pupils retracted into icy gray orbs; Hegelthor's voice boomed across the revived airwaves. "Rise to honor our Youth Facilitator for all he has done in the name of Synthesis. We thank you, Facilitator Winston." In response the crowd stood and Hegie asked, "What is Harmonious?" Winston was released and stepped back only to be engulfed by the Committee of Ten who spirited him off the stage, with Malchor in pursuit.

In the front row, Jared's reaction was visceral, controlled rage, contained by practiced, exacting self-discipline. Hegelthor was lying.

Thomas Evan II, laughed and cheered for himself and for his father.

"All is harmonious," the crowd answered, "in the Synthesis of life." Their voices resounded to the height and breadth of the great assembly hall, and added confusion to the men swarming into the prop room with their captive.

On stage, as an impromptu finale, Hegelthor led the group into a round of the pledge. Once the international program switched off, he continued addressing those students present and those linked by satellite. "Students," he said simply, "cancel thoughts! You will return to your dorms, prepare for sleep, then

318

meditate on the merits of Synthesis. You are dismissed."

Impressed, Synthia bid a hasty farewell to Ambassador Eckert, Chairman Bakto Himoko of the Asiatic Assembly and the remaining dignitaries and retired to Malchor's suite. Her phone call to Arion Tempera produced the desired outcome. He accepted her pledge of allegiance to him and to Synthesis. She covered herself and slept soundly.

TENSION continued to build after the final applause. Both Steve and Jenna felt like witnesses to murder, denying the scene, hoping they had heard wrong. It was an illogical hope that their eyes and ears had deceived them, mistaking an illusion for the real thing. But it was no illusion. David had registered confusion, and they had both seen Hegie's controlled reaction, warm smile, cold eyes.

Steve's hand rested on the phone. He wanted to call, talk to Hegie or David and get some clarification. But it wouldn't help. His son had stood on live, international television and said what those who really knew Malchor didn't dare repeat. He had set his son up for this. Guilt gnawed at him like a rat gnawing the pendulum support rope. With each minute, the pendulum swung closer to his son's neck, and he had strapped him to the table himself.

Seeking distraction, Steve peered out the window into the moonless sky. It only served as a blank page for the script, David's script, David's open charge against the highest knowledge of the elite. It could have been his own, if he had found something, anything, better than Synthesis. But in all his life he hadn't. He mourned that his son had risked his future on a fantasy, a myth of some Maker.

STUDENTS took their time filing from the auditorium, seemingly content with canceled thoughts. Jared felt caged, waiting his turn, avoiding eye contact with others. Temptation offered relief; canceling the truth he had seen and heard promised peace.

319

Backstage, Hegelthor pushed his way past two Peacekeepers and into the prop room. All ten committee members were crowded into the space, lining the narrow walls. Server waited quietly just inside the door, patient for the right timing. David, ashen, silent, was seated on a lone chair in the center.

Frederick Hodges was screeching unintelligible syllables an inch from his face when Malchor shoved him aside and took his place. "He's mine, just stay out of the way.

"Judas," he growled. "How could you betray me, and everyone else who ever cared for your worthless life? Answer me! How do you dare . . . ?" His fist was pressed up under David's chin, forcing his head back. Server, seeing his opening, slipped behind the chair and pulled David's arms back into a hammer lock.

"You," the Youth Facilitator whispered, straining for composure, "aren't who you say you are."

"You mindless fool!"

"You know you aren't a god," David continued, the mob quieted trying to hear him, "Don't you?"

"Oh, I'm not?" Malchor mocked. "I say you're terminal and you are. And that goes for everyone else in this room. If I command it!"

"Well, not quite, Mal," Hegelthor confided, motioning the others out, speaking in a soothing flow. "Please return to your quarters immediately. Thank you for helping. Further instructions are in your Diversity units. Unfortunately, our Youth Facilitator, in his struggle to purify Synthesis, has had a mental breakdown. Only temporary, I hope."

An eerie hush settled over Hodges and the group, and they filed toward the door, already retreating into their own meditative worlds. Hegelthor called in Peacekeepers to relieve Server and motioned for him to follow the others. At the door, with his back to the four men surrounding David, Server turned the lock and flipped the light switch off in one gesture with his right hand. He dropped a small canister with the other, jerking a face mask from his hip bag. Pandemonium erupted when the glass shattered, releasing CMZ fumes into the inky blackness.

David held his breath and threw his weight against the back of his chair, slamming backwards to the floor. He scrambled on all fours toward the small window on the south wall. Choking on the noxious fumes, Malchor stumbled forward, his hands on the neck of a guard mistaken for David. Already gasping for oxygen, the man sank to the floor trying to loosen the life-draining, steel grip. Hegelthor, face down on the floor, his hands pulled behind him, a knee in his mid-back, struggled to break free. Yelling muffled his choked commands.

Server stuck close to the wall, circling toward the dim outside light at the window. Reaching David, he deposited a face mask into his desperate hands. Clamping it over his mouth David gasped, inhaling deep breaths. Fumbling, feeling the sill then the metal, James released the lock and forced the window. From behind them, Hegelthor was screaming for someone to get off of him. With unintended roughness, Server shoved David toward the opening. Groping for his balance, David climbed out the window, dropping to the ground, with Server close behind. The two men scurried along the shadows toward the guarded perimeter exit.

Three minutes passed before Malchor loosened his grip and felt his way to the light switch. Furious, his lungs burning, he fumbled with the lock, finally throwing the door open and taking in the rush of air. His own victim still lay sprawled on the floor, hovering near death, and Hegelthor was face down, restrained by a bewildered Peacekeeper. David and Server were gone, the open window pointing the way.

DON Samuels saw them from the other side of the gate and stepped back out of the glare of the hangar lights, pressing himself against the wall.

Security hadn't been alerted. Oblivious to David's speech and the resultant chaos, two guards talked at the open airport gate. Duty was boring. Gate two was rarely used, except for special events like the Malchor Tribute. Dignitaries had flown in earlier and some had already left in small groups to fly across the globe in their private planes.

David walked several paces ahead of Server, at his normal clip, and nodded a greeting to the guards. He had passed them often on his trips to and from the Academy. "Things getting back to normal for you?" he asked, passing between them and through the gate. "Yeah," the sergeant answered, stepping aside. "It's been an interesting day."

"Good," David offered, looking back as Server made it through. "Have a great evening."

The low-toned alarm sounded and the gate closed automatically, leaving both guards on the inside of the gate. Perplexed, they coded into their Diversity units for instructions, while David and James ducked into the hangar.

When asked if anyone had passed through the gate, the Sergeant clicked off the names of twelve dignitaries before getting to Facilitator Winston. Within minutes Peacekeepers swarmed toward the airport, while the regular security guards were simply ignored and left uninformed. They knew not to ask questions.

Like a panther its prey, Don Samuels stalked them through the hangar and out the opposite side just as the overhead lights blazed. Uniformed squads, heavily armed, swept into the place, checking each corner and every conceivable hiding place. Outside, the fugitives ran along the four outbuildings to the last one and dove inside.

Don slipped in after them, challenging them gruffly. "I know you're in here."

David froze, perspiration dripping, his heart pounding, pulsating in his ears.

KENDRA's mind floated, her body relaxed, retreating into the solace of meditation. Seated on the couch in her apartment, her television set off, she slipped into her own special world where morning-glories filled the tree lined meadow. She was barefoot, walking in the midst of a gently flowing stream. Her guide,

Ramda, took her hand.

WITHOUT a word Jenna had headed toward her son's room, joined by Steve. Together they had sifted through his desk and drawers, looking for evidence. There was nothing. Relieved, they returned to the family room, where Jenna picked up his letter, her hands trembling. Rereading it, she searched for some clue, some subtle warning about his change of heart, his plan to publicly expose Malchor. Again, there was nothing.

"I SAID I'll help you," Don repeated. "Look, both of you. I've been following you since you passed through the gate. If I wanted you caught, I wouldn't be standing here, Hegie would. Now, there's not much time. Peacekeepers will be all over you in minutes."

"Why?" David whispered from the far corner.

"Because you're not going to make it out of here."

"Yes, we will. Just let us pass," James insisted.

"I can fly out," Don offered, "right in front of them."

"You can't do that!" David said. "It would be suicide."

"No. What you're doing is suicide. You won't make it to the water. Don't be a fool. You know they'll hound you until they find you," Don Samuels urged. "Too many people would be endangered."

"But I can't let you do it," Winston argued.

"No! You don't understand. What you said about Synthesis is true, and I have to do something about it," he pressed. "You're not letting me do this."

"The plans are set," James insisted, swinging his pack onto his back. "We don't have time for this."

"I'm telling you, it won't work," Don repeated, stepping aside, following the two fugitives out of the airstrip storage building and into the adjoining, darkened forest.

WINSTON'S private security force was housed in five guest rooms on the top floor of the men's dorm. Stan pulled back the drape and examined the peaceful Apex. Not a soul was in the commons. They had been temporarily excused from duty by Malchor. Stan Jonez was annoyed that he had been shut out of the process, his loyalty to Synthesis questioned. "Guilt by association," he muttered, "that's what this is, guilt by association."

"It seems that way," Ben agreed, "but, we'll be cleared and back on the job by the end of the week."

From where they were stationed, off stage, neither of them had followed David Winston's speech closely. It had sounded like a glowing tribute, so the subsequent confusion had left them both appalled. It wasn't clear to them who had stepped over the boundary, David or Malchor. Stan kept it to himself, but he was sure it wasn't David.

HEGELTHOR'S security office looked like police headquarters, with Captain Mark Griffin directing his Peacekeepers. Security cameras flashed simultaneous sweeps from forty strategic locations.

"You'd better figure out real fast exactly where things went wrong, Mal. This sets us back at least a year."

"Hegie, it wasn't me. Cy kept pushing for the initiation. Anyway, I don't think it had anything to do with us. It was Higgs."

"Higgs?"

"Franklin Higgs, my departed Public Relations Director, the one who set Winston up and had him shot. You know the kid hasn't been right since then."

"Excuses don't make good memorials," Hegelthor blurted, turning to leave.

"Gods don't need memorials," Malchor challenged, following him out the auditorium stage door. Both men jogged toward the airport gate.

EXHILARATED, he had won the argument, Don Samuels checked the digital readings. Except for the fluorescent panel, the cabin was black and quiet as death. Deftly, he prepared for take off. The grounds were crawling with security forces. From his lofty seat, he watched their fanned effort. Uniformed men and women combed every inch of the airfield in systematic order, while SWAT teams rushed into the surrounding buildings. Already David's plane was secured and the team descended on Hegie's Quasar like locusts. Don pressed the ignition, like he had so many times before, and the jets roared to life. Startled at the telling roar, the forces dropped their patterned sweep and surged forward, determined to stop the plane. Two men, closer than the others, headed to cut him off. Samuels kept his bearing, amused that they thought they could stop him with mere pounds of flesh. Only one had the sense to dive to safety as the huge tires lifted inches above the runway.

David winced, shaken by the impact that crushed the Peacekeeper. He had prepared to accept arrest and the inevitable termination, but he hadn't wanted to involve others. Foreboding descended upon him. One man already lay dead on the concrete, while both James Lawrence and Don Samuels were uninvited, and now endangered, rescuers. Spread out below, the runway was ablaze with searchlights and gun fire. He spotted Hegie running down the runway, screaming after his airborne Quasar jet. David felt James crawl alongside him and motion him to keep low. Peace settled over him. The brink of death wasn't new or frightening; he had touched it before and lived. This time he was ready.

As if driven by the same voice, Malchor and Hegelthor sprinted toward Winston's plane, ready to fly in pursuit, then stopped and headed back to the security office. The Quasar was already out of sight. Two small jet fighters streaked upward; Hegelthor knew they could never catch his plane. Global Airspace had to be notified not to intercept, just to track the Quasar. He would reclaim it when it landed; eventually they would have to land for fuel and food. Hegie placed the call from the security gate cellular. The connection was bad, but he got through and made it clear he didn't want anyone risking his plane. It was the first time in a decade that he felt powerless to guarantee what needed to be done. Malchor shook his head, disgusted the Peacekeepers had failed to stop Winston.

DON leveled out, cruising above the Pacific Ocean at 60,000 feet, headed toward the Himalayas. He hadn't dared turn on the radio or the lights so he checked the Piaget on his wrist, flashing the time, 8:23 p.m. It felt right. David was safe, out of their reach. Nothing had felt this right for a long time. Memories stirred; it was decades since that hot summer day. Don's dad had refused to accept the new paradigm, and to his last breath he insisted it was a crock. In his own home, against the patriarch's will, the intern had administered the injection. And Don was there permitting it, believing it was the kind thing to do, to spare him further pain. The cancer had eaten his stomach, but had not touched his courage. "I didn't want to lose any time with you," he said, struggling against the invading chemical. "Know the truth, Donald, know who..." The words had hung unfinished, haunting Don Samuels in the quiet hours of night, until this day when he heard David. It was Light shining in the recess of his spirit, cleansing him. And the Light grew bright, surrounding him, indwelling him.

XIX MOURNING

FORTY-THREE minutes had passed since David's suicide speech. With both hands flattened against the cool window pane, Steve peered into the darkness. The television noise was a backdrop to his numbing fear. When a solitary voice boomed over the air waves, he recognized his friend and turned to watch. Hugh Bancroft from *Region 10 News* was on the air. "We interrupt this program to bring you an urgent announcement."

Steve winced, bracing himself. He knew the procedure. The news must be bad, very bad. And he knew, when the scene shifted and a special reporter came on, that it was bad for his son. "This is Randy Collins reporting live from the San Juan Academy in Washington State." Behind the reporter, Steve could see the auditorium stage podium where his son had declared the unspeakable. "We have just received word that at approximately 8:25 p.m., Pacific Time, the Quasar carrying Facilitator David Alan Winston exploded over Puget Sound. Authorities are investigating evidence of a plot by a militant dissident group. It is believed that an explosive device was planted in the main compartment and intended for Facilitator Thomas Evan Hegelthor. One moment please; we're just getting word here from rescuers on the scene. What was that? Please repeat . . .

Paralyzed, Steve stared at the screen. A frown spread across Bancroft's face. "I'm sorry to have to report . . ." Collins choked, shaken, "Rescuers have just recovered a body from the frigid waters. The body has been positively identified as our Youth Facilitator David Winston."

Shock reeled through Steve; his knees weakened. Relentless, the news continued. "Rescuers are searching for the pilot, Don Samuels and Malchor's valet, James Lawrence. The trio was on the return flight to . . ."

Jenna leapt from the couch, clasping both hands against her breasts. One primal scream of travail surged upward, tearing past her vocal cords, drowning out the announcer. Stifling his own cry of outrage, Steve rushed to her. He had heard the sound before, wild and earthy, during David's birth. And now, her scream echoed his despair as the news bulletin, stark, shocking, flashed David's death around the world and killed their own future hope. She collapsed sobbing into his arms while the newscaster droned on, promising more details at eleven o'clock.

AT THAT moment, in her Spokane apartment, Kendra was at her dressing room sink brushing her teeth. Thoughts of David interrupted her peace, tempting her to try to make sense of his odd speech. When the doorbell rang, she hurriedly rinsed her mouth, slipped her slacks on and headed for the door, her blouse half-buttoned. The ringing was persistent.

Buttoning the last button, she swung the door open, ready for her impatient landlord to demand an explanation of David's words. Instead of his wiry, hawkish face, she was face to face with two uniformed Peacekeepers, a backup of four more men just feet away.

"We wish to speak with Kendra Winston," the husky captain said, flashing his I.D. card. "Captain Joseph Bradley, here."

Puzzled, Kendra faced the Captain. He was somber, a benevolent tilt to his handsome face. "I'm Kendra Addington-Winston," she stated, looking past him to his men. "What do you want?"

"We're sorry to disturb the tranquility of your evening, Mrs. Winston," he said, a brief smile fading into concern, "but there has been an accident."

"An accident?" she asked, fear hovering.

"Facilitator Hegelthor asked us to escort you to the Winston

328

Ranch. We regret to inform you, Mrs. Winston, that your husband has been, uh, lost at sea," he said, stepping toward her, prepared to give her his arm if needed, offering comfort. "Divers are at the scene hoping to recover his bo . . . him, that is."

"David, gone?" she blurted, stunned. "But, I just heard him on television. He's at the Academy," she insisted, refusing his help, her brown eyes wide, disbelieving.

For a moment Captain Bradley looked at her, taking in her gently arched eyebrows and oval face. So much better than her I.D. photos or any of the media spreads. His fleeting twinge of sadness over the loss of the Youth Facilitator turned to an unprofessional interest in the vulnerable widow in his care. "If you will, please, ma'am. Hegelthor expects us to be there within the hour. Wouldn't you like to pack some things?"

Numb, she turned, reviewing in her mind the strange look she caught in David's eyes. During his speech, a boldness came over him; his words carried the impact of some profound truth. It was confusing, frightening to her. She heard him challenge Synthesis and call Malchor a fraud. And yet, Hegie applauded him. It was incongruent. The question repeated. *Why did Hegie applaud?*

While she packed, a grim, bitter cloud settled over her. Anger replaced the first jolt of fear. Whatever the Captain said, she did not believe David was gone. Her husband's words were treasonous and his behavior worse, but she felt a responsibility to confront him. Her mind was set; she would see him and demand answers, and before she was through with him, he would wish he was gone!

IT WAS an eternal hour before the Winstons heard the planes approach and land. They expected the onslaught sooner and tried to prepare for the search, a threatening probe into their personal lives. They simply told Fran and Jake, and left any warnings to their own common sense. It wasn't necessary. Few people were foolish enough to record or keep anything not stamped politically correct. They heard Max bark and the barn door squeak open. Uniformed Peacekeepers were already fanning out, examining their grounds with cold precision. When the first knock sounded, Steve opened the door to find Facilitator Hegelthor extending his hand in condolence.

"Mr. and Mrs. Winston," he said kindly, "this is our shared loss. May I come in?"

"Of course," Steve answered, unnerved, stepping aside, his arm still protectively around Jenna as a troop of men followed Hegie, spreading like a plague through their home.

"Perhaps we could sit here, together," Hegelthor said, striding across the room and taking a place on the couch. Obediently, the couple took the chairs opposite, with their backs to the main house. "Please excuse my security team," he quipped. "They have their job to do." While he spoke, Fran and Jake were hustled from their quarters and seated behind them in the dining area.

Jenna directed a worried smile to her husband, afraid the set look on his face would betray the anger smoldering inside. She could hear the security force down the hall rummaging through her dresser drawers, doing more than a routine securing of the premises. "We are honored you have come to pay your respects, Facilitator," Jenna forced pleasantly.

"I assure you," he replied, "the honor is mine."

She had never seen him this close, distinguished and commanding of respect, but simply aging flesh and blood. His gray eyes showed benevolent concern, really too much concern, as if he had birthed David himself. That he dared show up was a mockery of her agony. It was her loss, not his, not shared. But, no trace of feeling was revealed and her face radiated with the poise that had moved her quickly through the rank and file bureaucrats into competent leadership. She gained an odd sense of control in not opening her mind to this man who had manipulated so many others into mindless service. "I do hope that our son has served you well?" she added with feigned sincerity.

Steve saw the game and set aside his own urge to protest

330

this invasion of his private grief. "Perhaps, sir," he said with a detached tone, "you could tell us what happened? We only heard a news bulletin."

Hegie was disappointed; he hoped for proof of disloyalty. He laid out the carefully constructed story of the sudden explosion of his own Quasar that doomed David to the salty water. The loss of James Lawrence meant nothing and losing his personal pilot Don Samuels had no national significance, except for a search for another pilot. With the air of an impersonal newscaster, he added that David's body had been recovered and identified, but was not suitable for viewing, while the others were the object of an ongoing search.

"Sir," Steve broke in cautiously, "I would like to confirm the identification—of my son's remains."

Hegie nodded consent and continued with minute details of the crash, repeatedly lamenting the loss of his plane. Meanwhile, the security team combed through the place, even down to the letter from David, which a lieutenant took from the coffee table and slid into a folder. Following Jenna's look, Hegie asked for it, read it and ordered it returned to her. She clutched it with honest gratitude.

The Captain then gave Hegie a handful of questionable papers which he examined. Satisfied, he gave them back and faced the Winstons. "What did you think of your son's speech?" he asked.

Steve spoke first, repeating their planned response. "We were alarmed, sir. How do you account for his odd ramblings?"

"Well," Hegie said, "I had hoped you could shed further light on that. We know how easy it is to forget important details in times of stress, so I'm sure you'll be happy to answer the Captain's questions."

Promptly, Jenna was taken into the kitchen where sensors were attached to her arms and she was probed. Captain Chris Fendel courteously read his script and recorded her answers, observing the patterned readout. Hegelthor, hovering between the two, pulled his cellular from an inner jacket pocket on the first ring. Steve strained to separate Hegie's words from the captain's drone.

"Don't give me that!" Hegie shouted, turning, stalking toward the window. "I don't care whose region he's from, I want the man's head, as well as the flunky who pushed the button." Steve watched color rising and a deep brooding settle in Hegie's usually composed profile. When Hegie's eyes bored in on him, he looked down at his folded hands. "Idiot," Hegie growled, turning his back again, "it was my plane. They would have landed eventually." The caller's words sparked Hegie's staccato order, "Any trace of the plane or equipment and I want to know. Strain the ocean if you have to."

This was the scene that greeted Kendra when she walked into the house, flanked by two Peacekeepers.

Abruptly, Hegelthor hung up and went to meet her, extending his hand in condolence. "Mrs. Winston, we share a great lo . . ." Kendra buckled and fell against him, interrupting his line. Quickly, he handed her over to Captain Bradley, who explained, "She didn't believe our report sir, but hearing it from you . . ."

Hegie nodded. "Well, take her to the couch and let her compose herself," he said with irritation.

"If I may, sir, let me?" Steve said, on his feet, already taking Kendra by the arm. Too shocked to speak or cry, she let herself lean on him for comfort and support.

When Jenna joined them, holding Kendra's hands in hers, Steve took his turn in the kitchen, then Kendra. While Hegie went over their verbal and neurological responses the three sat together, stone faced, under the scrutiny of the Peacekeepers. Finally, they were herded into David's Astrojet III, leaving Fran and Jake to grieve and straighten the mess.

EARLY the next day, news cameras again recorded in the San Juan Academy auditorium, broadcasting Facilitator Hegelthor's message to an eager audience. "During his lifetime, David Winston earned a place in our hearts as the Youth Facilitator. With skill, he brought our fragmented educational system into compliance with the highest goals of the Academy. For this he deserves to be honored. And of more importance, he had the courage to point out and bring to correction a flaw that threatened the heart of Synthesis. It is this feat that will immortalize his name. Henceforth, Youth Facilitator David Winston will be remembered for purging and purifying Synthesis. We are all indebted. Because of his outstanding sacrifice for the cause of freedom, he will be interred at Arlington National Cemetery Wednesday, September twenty-sixth."

The Winstons shared the podium with Hegelthor and the camera showed a properly brave trio, grieving for their loss. To Jenna and Steve, it was a sham to be endured. It was an unspoken wonder to them that none of the probing had revealed their own doubts about Malchor or Synthesis. For Kendra, each new affront, from the news of David's death to the probing, sent her deeper into herself, searching for escape.

OBLIVIOUS to headlines, travelers surged through the Chicago terminal, intent on catching planes. No one noticed when a woman with her infant and young daughter glanced toward a father and son at the ticket counter. Reana had arrived from the East Coast on a separate flight and had been waiting for over an hour. Tension eased when she spotted Greg and Richard. It worked, and they had made it. The two looked related, dark skin, hair and eyes, standing close, reading their tickets, preparing to board the 10:45 a.m., flight to Winnipeg, Manitoba. Next to her, Jamie fussed over the dark-haired baby in the car seat, imitating cooing sounds. His head itched and wisps from the cascading black curls tickled his ears. It wasn't a game he ever wanted to play again. Next time, he figured, his brother could act like a girl.

Their jet was crossing into Canada when the steward lowered the screen and dimmed the lights. Passengers had been served honey roasted almonds, pastries and drinks and waited to see Good Morning World. Instead, the Special Report on Youth Facilitator David Winston unfolded, a recap of Hegelthor's San Juan tribute. Reana covered her mouth and heard Greg's gasp from three rows away. Throughout the cabin, casual conversation stalled and even the stewardess turned pale. Tears flooded Jamie's eyes, and Reana spent the rest of the flight comforting him, her heart breaking for both Kendra and Greg. Thankfully, Jonathan slept.

RELIEF came for the three Winstons on Thursday, September twenty-seventh, after the Arlington Cemetery burial. They had endured hours of public performances and thousands of gawking supporters. When the scene played out, and the public went on to another diversion, they were allowed to return to their respective homes and their private grief.

Friday evening, Steve and Jenna watched the televised World Court judgment against Malchor Inyesco with intense interest. Cyrus hosted the ceremony and a court clerk read the pronouncement. Malchor was relieved from his duties as head of Impartation International for six months, and ordered to serve without vote on the Tribunal for a full year. Immediately following the announcement, Malchor was interviewed. He stood in front of the camera, a noble picture of brokenness, apologizing for his foolish, selfish ambition, asking the people to find it in their hearts to forgive him.

Steve had seen spin work before, and this had the usual result. World Op Poll recorded, two to one, support for the penitent Malchor. Strangely, while support for Synthesis soared, in California support for Autonomous voting continued to nosedive. Whispering, he confided to Jenna that Autonomous voting would probably hit bottom and bounce back up on the charts with amazing speed.

"Why?" she pleaded, "Why on earth did Davy make it all so important? For what?"

"I don't know, Jen. I think Mal pushed him too far, too fast," he said, pressing the remote control, shutting off the television glare. "I just don't know how he could believe all that stuff about..." Blaming himself, he drew her close, burying his face in her silken black hair.

She had asked him repeatedly what he saw when he confirmed the identity of the charred remains of their son. But, he couldn't say it; that there was no feature to recognize and that their son's graduation ring was missing from his right hand. Disbelief was tempting, building hope that the darkened, bloated body wasn't David's. The Piaget was there on his left wrist, warped, blackened and dead and the DNA code confirmed what Steve fought against, proof that his son was gone. All the lofty platitudes about transformation to a higher realm struck him as mindless dribble. What could he tell her? For both of them, life had little comfort—and less purpose.

ON THE second Tuesday in October, at 12:00 noon Pacific Time, Kendra was sitting alone in her office, screening children's genetic profiles. The files were skeletal; data entry technicians tapped away, building a labyrinth of facts. The past weeks hadn't diluted the shock; each morning she had to remind herself that it was true—David was gone. Anger only made it worse. It was an unwinnable argument. Escape to the recesses of her mind and her private meadow was the only thing that kept her composed. It worked. She was ready for lunch with just one more report to finish when David's name flashed on her computer. Instantly, her suppressed emotions welled up, threatening to break loose. She caught herself with a reflexive hold on the edge of her chair. Along with screens and printers throughout the world, her computer system scrolled and spit out Facilitator David Winston's Synthesis time line, a skeleton of the history of knowledge, and then his uninterrupted speech. Her attention was riveted on the screen while the speech was being printed, his words, his voice saying them in her mind. She clung to them, rereading his closing argument and his last unheard words.

"You are not God. What has been made is not God.
You've heard about Maker yet confuse Him with idols.
You recognize no distinction between myth and reality—
no distinction between the profane and the holy. I know

335

about Maker, but more importantly, I know Him person-
ally. It is Maker who authored the Truth Paradigm, which
prideful mortals hope to overthrow with all their old and
new paradigms. Professing both knowledge and wis-
dom, they exchange the truth of Maker for their myths,
idols and philosophies.

"It is Maker who set time in motion and breathed
life into you. It is Maker who loves you and wants a
relationship with you. Seek Him and you will find Him
through His Son Yeshua Messiah. He is the Way, the
Truth and the Life. The sum of your duty as a human is
to love the one true God with all your being and to love
your neighbor as yourself. Walk in freedom."

His words blinked from the screen. She stared while
Confusion swooped in and scrambled her thoughts. Determined,
she fought to grasp the reasoning and make sense of what David
had risked and lost. By 12:10 p.m. her own program resumed.

Office managers, educators and conscientious parents were
notified to cleanse their areas. It was a simple routine. They
gathered the pages and deposited them in recycle bins. A
majority of the people took it as another message from the
Tribunal eulogizing Winston and the purification of Synthesis,
but a growing remnant of curious thinkers squirreled away
duplicated copies. It was Kendra who personally cleansed her
department, gathering fifty-five sets from staff desks. One copy
for herself, folded and stuffed inside her jacket, was easy to cover
and justify.

Following her usual practice, she ordered lunch brought in
and sat at her desk, shuffling file folders. She picked at the deli
turkey sandwich, reconstructing in her mind her last intimate talk
with David. While visiting the ranch she had dropped her
reserve, building a fantasy around her future with him, visualizing
their unity, their shared goals for world peace. Later, unexpected
tension shadowed their plane trip, dismissed and unrecognized
as the direct result of her inquiry about their friends. It was the

subsequent trip to Baltimore that shattered that fantasy and any hope for a future with him. It was seeing Reana. The changes in her childhood friend were so stark that she wanted to run, to wipe the memory away, to believe that the wretched creature was some imposter. She had forced herself to stay and help, sensing that her help wasn't appreciated.

Reana's letter lay in her briefcase. It had arrived at headquarters, written two days after Greg's release, congratulating the Winston unity and urging her to love David. Greg's postscript had thanked David for all his help. The letter remained an oddity, a puzzle, an exhortation to love a betrayer, a liar, and in death, a traitor. Kendra dialed the Foster home direct. The number was still disconnected. Calling the law firm where Greg had been reinstated posed another dead end. The secretary informed her, with crisp efficiency, that Foster was no longer employed with them. Throwing caution aside, Kendra ran a check on the Fosters for parenting suitability. The screen showed the dates of Greg's arrest, his time in prison, at CAM, at The Haven and his release. In bold print, the last line stopped her cold.

Reana and Greg Foster, unfit. FUGITIVE DISSIDENTS.

They were gone. The realization hit; to her they were as lost as David.

When the phone rang, Kendra jumped, petrified some sinister alien had reported her for calling the Fosters. Gingerly, she picked the receiver up, pressing it to her ear.

"Kendra, dear," Cyrus entreated, "You've taken all of this so bravely." He paused, waiting for her acknowledgment.

"How thoughtful of you to call, Cyrus," she said, grimacing, relieved he couldn't see her. Then the reality struck that her thoughts were her own—private. In that moment, Fear loosed its slimy grip and hope sent out fragile roots.

His voice rasped on, working to uproot them. "If my responsibilities weren't so demanding, I would have you fly out

337

today—for the rest you've earned."

"I appreciate your concern, Cyrus, but I'm doing fine."

"Of course, of course you are. All the same, I do expect to entertain you for the winter solstice. Who knows," he started, then changed track. "Well, that gives you a bit over two months to wait."

"I'm sure the time will pass quickly," she said, begrudging the passage of each second, dreading another encounter. Remembering his pale, clammy hands clasped over hers at David's funeral, Kendra trembled. She had sought refuge next to him and looked up to him, expecting solace. Instead, Lechery peered from his hazel eyes and examined her with studied intent. Repulsed, she averted the look and focused on Hegie's eulogy. Raw fear kept her hands in his. Weeks earlier, she had played up to him, cherishing his every move with naive reverence. She sensed that David had known and tried to protect her, to keep her away from Cyrus. Stubbornly, she had ignored her husband and sought the lech out. She held the phone away, sickened.

"Kendra, you sound sad. It will be best for you to come to Rome right after the election in November, or better yet I'll come for you myself."

"But, I have to work," she blurted.

Cyrus laughed, a thin grating sound. "Dear Kendra, you're so conscientious. The Center will do fine without you. After all, certain sacrifices must be made for the sake of Synthesis. Your initiation will be all that you have anticipated and more—with me officiating."

With me as your sacrifice, she thought, suddenly seeing what had been so disturbing to David at Chichen-Itza, inside the Pyramid of Kukulcan. The ugly Chac Mool idol had been the sacrificial altar, used by priests to control, use and devour others. Cyrus would use her.

Cyrus continued, prattling about his plans to have her tour Europe and stay at the Cosmic Spirit Council Headquarters in Rome. Weariness was audible in her voice as she thanked him again for his concern.

Hopelessness set in with a verdict that there was no real escape for her. Cyrus would be waiting and she had brought it on herself. That afternoon a mind numbing detachment took hold and made her job progressively more difficult. She plodded through four questionable student placements. It was 5:00 p.m. before she shook off despair and admitted to herself that Synthesis was flawed and that a parallel between Synthesis and Cyrus existed. Annoyed, she chose not to meditate.

XX   HOPE

"ROJAN'S report says Lawrence, your old bodyguard, was a dissident Believer. Didn't you always call him Server?" Cyrus asked, pressing his point. "Guess he had a name after all. So, have you read the report yet?"

"Yes," Malchor groaned.

"And we spoke freely around him, I recall."

"But he was deaf, a deaf mute."

"Well," Arion interjected, "he managed to communicate with Winston."

"Hegie's not happy about losing his Quasar and all that equipment in the South China Sea," Cyrus repeated for the third time. "It's going to take months to replicate it all, nothing to salvage."

"No. Much longer," Arion corrected. "The computer system itself won't be ready for six months. I noticed there was nothing in the report about that Chinese pilot who shot down the plane."

"That was his last bull's-eye. He expected a medal, but got a bullet between the eyes," Malchor grumbled. "Frankly, I don't think Winston was headed for Singapore, probably Switzerland."

"What about that pilot, Samuels?" Arion asked. "The report leaves it open."

"Hegie insists he was hijacked. Loyal." Malchor shoved the report back across the coffee table to Cyrus. ". . . probably as loyal as Server."

"So," Cyrus quipped, "what do you think of Synthia's promotion as the new Director of Peacekeepers?"

"She's good, Cy," Malchor said, irritated that he had left himself open to ridicule, "better than you've had." Cyrus hadn't stopped gloating since she moved out on him. Staring at the loose fleshy folds sagging under the Cosmic Spirit Council leader's chin he added, "I'm sure she'll check out your operation next."

"Well, that will have to wait until she puts a stop to those print-outs from your dead hero," he rebutted, tilting his chin up slightly, "won't it?"

"Hey! That's enough you two," Arion interceded. "We all have to be more careful. With elections so close we can't afford any more snags." This second meeting of the Tribunal was not off to a good start. He had insisted they avoid Impartation International Headquarters until the investigation was closed. Now, with the report completed, they were back at Malchor's place, back in the familiar library. "What's your forecast for next Tuesday?" Arion asked.

"World Op Poll shows Autonomous voting gaining in California," Malchor offered, "but our political action committee pumped another four million into the campaign. It looks good, but today Supreme Court Justice Brok went national saying we're circumventing the Constitution if Autonomy affects Congress."

"Trib!" Cyrus exclaimed, "There's a sound bite—I told you we should wait. Election's coming up too fast. Get the media on this and vilify Brok."

"They are on it," Arion said, his voice dry, fatigued. "I heard him too."

"Tighten the screws, d _ _ _ it!" Malchor blurted.

"Look. The screws are as tight as they'll go without stripping. We're still cleaning up after your mess with Winston, so back off. If this fails, we'll use a State Initiative again next year to take care of the legislature. Meanwhile the ground work is all set for the Con Con. Already, President Chamberlon's expecting support in Congress," Arion said quietly. "And he's prepared an Executive Order for the peoples' right to a national referendum on Autonomy."

"A national referendum?" Mal questioned. "Brok will howl about that one. And there's already outrage over Executive Orders."

"Eventually," Arion muttered, "people will vote for what's good for them."

AT HER apartment building, Kendra paused in front of the newsstand. *One World Today* devoted the front page to Initiative 1776 and Autonomous voting. She scanned the first column—same stuff. No more wasteful legislature. If 1776 passed, in January the first order of business for the California legislature would be to convene a state Constitutional Convention. All that effort just to vote on their political demise. Autonomy was equated with the right to vote and media stars urged voters to call their legislators and demand they adopt the Autonomy amendment. Dissidents protested that each Senator and Legislator would be shifted into permanent non-elected state executive-branch jobs. The ten most powerful members expected to be on the Governor's Board of Legislation. Mainstream voters, however, thought of it as a necessary buyout.

California was just the beginning. Some talk-show hosts regularly risked their jobs challenging the state constitutionality of the election. As elections neared, key stations had begun dropping those programs. This created an unexpected backlash of angry listeners. *World Broadcasting Network* had canceled a favorite, Freed Lindberg, and outraged supporters were picketing stations throughout the country. In self-defense they put Freed back on the air from midnight to 3:00 a.m. Media resources stifled all negative news reports. Unstoppable, e-mail, the Net and fax machines were alive with facts and opinions. Kendra figured that the only people oblivious to what was happening were the nation's Academy students and Synthesis devotees like her parents. Everyone knew Congress was the next target.

She had spent a frustrating Saturday morning at her childhood Spokane home, asking questions and hearing what her secondary caregivers thought about Autonomous voting. It was cut and dry. If the Tribunal supported it as best for the country and the world, then so did they. Three months ago she had agreed wholeheartedly herself. That was when all the pieces fit neatly together, before David's disturbing questions and declarations, before Cyrus and his leering interest in her. It was an interest she knew he would soon satisfy at her expense. The thought of his hands on her was repulsive, a nightmare threatening her body, soul and spirit.

Disgusted, she decided against returning to her apartment and instead walked out of the foyer into the sunlit autumn.

Walking was her one freedom. She passed the library, crossed the Monroe Street Bridge and paused to watch the Spokane Falls at the same place where she had stood with David. She circled around to the grassy area, retracing their steps.

Forlorn, Kendra collapsed on a bench at Riverside Park. Her heart replayed the bitterness she had sown toward David; it had sprouted into hatred. He had lied to her and had deserved every word she threw at him. Some honeymoon. She could have let it go, she could have accepted his obvious regret. He had deserved trouble but not what happened, not unrecognizable, cold, charred flesh. A couple ambled past, hand in hand, whispering heart secrets, laughing, contrasting her grief. At the tip of the small Island a class of purple-clad preschoolers were herded by a teacher and his assistant. Energy bubbled from the children, eager to move on to the carousel ride. They were passing in front of her on the walkway when an older man slipped onto the bench beside her.

His back to her, he watched the children weave through the park toward the amphitheater. She had seen him twice before, avoiding him during her lunch breaks. Now, here he was, a stranger, sitting too close and she was in no mood for small talk with some other lonely person. She grabbed her jacket and stood, putting it on.

"You're no longer satisfied with Synthesis?" the old man asked.

Alarm tightened its grip. It wasn't normal, such a question, such familiarity. "Why do you ask?" she demanded, staring down at the top of his head. White and gray strands mingled together. His sideburns, slightly overgrown, blended with a trimmed darker beard. Tweed slacks, mauve shirt with a wool pullover, a typical Gonzaga professor, but not a typical question.

"Ah, but you've answered already," he said, face downcast. "Has all this statist computer-parenting really been in the best interest of the children?"

The romantic couple ambled back into view, still preoccupied with each other. Kendra held her place, nodded pleasantly at them as they strolled past, then sank back onto the park bench, weakened, her left hand covering her Diversity unit. "What do you want?" she whispered, turning to face her accuser.

His dark eyes met hers with intimate urgency. "You," he responded.

"Trib!" she breathed, shocked.

"I hope not," he said somberly.

"But the pl...plane?" she stuttered. Confusion threatened.

"Not here, Kendra. Later. Later, we'll talk." Her name passed his lips again, "Kendra."

His voice offered a healing touch to her unspoken pain. Fearful, she considered his offering, tears trickling down her cheeks.

Carefully, he touched them with his fingertips, and pressed them to his lips. "Dearest Kendra," he asked, "Will you follow me?"

Inside, her wall of control shook and the agony of past months demanded release.

"I won't pressure you," he promised. "Please, allow me to earn your trust."

She trembled and fought to compose herself. Still, her attempted answer came out as a groan. Covering her mouth, she managed an affirmative nod. Finally, with restraint, she reached out, touched his face and whispered, fearful to say his name. "Yes, yes, I will."

"We must leave now," he whispered, helping her to her feet,

directing her toward the deserted foot bridge. "Everything is arranged."

ARION Tempera's jet had already disappeared into the brooding winter storm clouds. Malchor hadn't intended to see either of them off until he heard the news. He leaned into the chill, hoping to catch Cyrus before he got to his plane. The blizzard wasn't expected until nightfall. But the Monday sunrise had succumbed to stormy turbulence. Malchor pulled his overcoat closer, tempted to head south himself, and walked faster. "Cyrus!" he yelled.

The huddled, scurrying figure stopped and turned as Malchor approached.

"Cy—thought you might be interested. A report just came in this morning." Malchor paused for impact. "Your widow ended up in the Columbia River."

"What widow? What do I have to do with any widow?" The term conjured a frail, elderly image in his mind, someone overdue for recycling.

"Winston's. Kendra Winston."

"Kendra? What happened?" Cyrus choked, gawking at Malchor. Icy wind whipped around his legs and up the back of his wool coat, chilling him.

"According to Rojan, Mrs. Winston was on her way to ski at Snoqualmie. She never made it. Her car veered from I-90 on the bridge over the Columbia River, just east of Vantage, about 5:00 p.m. Saturday. Witnesses said some semi hit her from behind, forcing her over the rail. They hauled the car out, but they're still looking for the truck and driver. Anyway, some recluse found her mangled body washed up downstream."

"Such a waste," Cyrus lamented, feeling cheated. Turning, he sauntered toward his plane. "And I was going to do so much for her."

GOD

STANDETH IN THE CONGREGATION
OF THE MIGHTY;
HE JUDGETH AMONG THE GODS.
HOW LONG WILL YE JUDGE UNJUSTLY,
AND ACCEPT THE PERSONS OF THE WICKED?
SE'LAH.

DEFEND THE POOR AND FATHERLESS:
DO JUSTICE TO THE AFFLICTED AND NEEDY.
DELIVER THE POOR AND NEEDY:
RID *THEM* OUT OF THE HAND OF THE
WICKED.
PSALM 82: 1-4

FOR HE ESTABLISHED A TESTIMONY IN
JACOB, AND APPOINTED A LAW IN ISRAEL, WHICH
HE COMMANDED OUR FATHERS,
THAT THEY SHOULD MAKE THEM KNOWN
TO THEIR CHILDREN:

THAT THE GENERATION TO COME MIGHT KNOW
THEM, EVEN THE CHILDREN *WHICH* SHOULD BE
BORN; *WHO* SHOULD ARISE AND DECLARE *THEM*
TO THEIR CHILDREN:

THAT THEY MIGHT SET THEIR HOPE IN GOD, AND
NOT FORGET THE WORKS OF GOD, BUT KEEP HIS
COMMANDMENTS:

AND MIGHT NOT BE AS THEIR FATHERS, A
STUBBORN AND REBELLIOUS GENERATION; A
GENERATION *THAT* SET NOT THEIR HEART
ARIGHT, AND WHOSE SPIRIT WAS NOT
STEADFAST WITH GOD.
PSALM 78:5-8

ACKNOWLEDGMENTS

To my parents: my mother, who risked her life to birth me and nurtured me in the reverence and admonition of the Lord, and to my papa who protected me and insisted I go to college. Even in my rebellious youth, both surrounded me with a sacrificial and unconditional love that built a bedrock foundation for my future.

To my family: my husband, Bob, who encourages my writing adventures and prays for me daily and my children and grandchildren who make life a rich tapestry of joy. My siblings, aunts, uncles, cousins, nieces and nephews are the best in the cosmos!

To my students: transmitting knowledge and love of learning was my job, but I most appreciated getting to know you.

To my friends: Gladys Allen, Marilyn Burke, Susan and John Allen, Jean Lytle, Sharon Harms, Margot Sudall, Pauline Sheehan, Elizabeth Hawkins, Linda Heath, Dr. Richard Perkins, Kandis and Larry Brighton, Sheryl and Gary Brennan, Shauna Brennan, Sarah and Solon Scott, Jeanie and Elmer Sommer, Judith, Alisha and Paul Hendrix, Jack Gardner, David Cutbirth, Linda Heath, Terina Treloar and Stephenie Venturo. Writing was the fun and easy part. It was the endless cleanup and rewrite that required a work crew. I am also indebted to many other friends, unnamed herein, for their prayers, suggestions, editorial corrections and insistence that I get this book out of my closet and into your hands.

To prayer intercessors: John and Connie Giesler, Lyle and Delores King and Lou Brown.

To Ben Harms, Erik Scott and Al Griffin for helping preserve my sanity through three computers and a zillion glitches.

ABOUT THE AUTHOR

C.A.CURTIS lives with her husband in the Pacific Northwest. This decade, her role has evolved from parent and educator to grandparent, author, public speaker and community activist.

Her experience includes teaching children from grades one through twelve in public, private and home school. In seminars and forums she presents such topics as *Politics, Religion and the Culture War* and *Influences on Education in America: Historical Perspective.*

She is currently a Congressional staffer working with a team of dedicated people who do their best to restrain federal agencies and help people untangle red tape.

For additional copies check your local bookstore.

How to contact Reality Publishing:

REALITY Publishing
PO Box 13576
Mill Creek, Washington 98082-1576

http://www.regeneration-ink.com

E-mail:
cacurtis@regeneration.com
realitypublish@netscape.net

1-425-357-9299
Toll free: 1-877-639-3999